A SAFE AND HAPPY PLACE

A SAFE AND HAPPY PLACE

A novel

James Howard Kunstler

Highbrow Press

Published in the United States of America

ISBN: 0984625291

ISBN 13: 9780984625291
Library of Congress Control Number: 2017903950

Highbrow Productions, Incorporated,
Saratoga Springs, New York

Highbrow Press
PO Box 193
Saratoga Springs
New York, 12866

ALSO BY JAMES HOWARD KUNSTLER

Fiction

The World Made By Hand Series
The Harrows of Spring
A History of the Future
The Witch of Hebron
World Made By Hand

Maggie Darling, a Modern Romance
Thunder Island
The Halloween Ball
The Hunt
Blood Solstice
An Embarrassment of Riches
The Life of Byron Jaynes
A Clown in the Moonlight
The Wampanaki Tales.

Nonfiction

Too Much Magic
The Long Emergency
The City in Mind
Home From Nowhere
The Geography of Nowhere

This book is for Claire Greene

"I ain't gonna work on Maggie's Farm no more."

— Bob Dylan

CHAPTER ONE

In the fall of 1967, a schlemiel named Don Bessemer from Short Pump, Virginia, got me pregnant. Well, okay, I got myself pregnant with his assistance. I fell for this superficial clod one rainy October afternoon when we were the only two patrons in a hole-in-the-wall called Café Ludovico off Astor Place. The place was so narrow there was only one row of tiny square café tables against one wall. I sat facing the entrance. He stepped in out of the deluge with his umbrella dripping and slid into the next table facing the rear, toward the espresso machine and me.

After the initial eyeballing, we both pretended to read our books. I kept on copping glances at him over my *Fundamentals of Stage Lighting* (deadly boring). He was scoping me out, too, over *Been Down So Long It Looks Like Up to Me*. So when our gazes eventually locked and I was flustered, I tossed out a lame quip:

"Depressing, huh?" I said.

"Huh?" was all he said back, drilling those penetrating, dark, slightly hooded eyes into me.

"Your book," I explained. "Down so long...."

1

"No, it's funny," he said, deadpan. "You NYU?" he asked.

"Yeah."

"What?"

"What what?"

"Year? Major?"

"Oh…. Sophomore. Theater."

"They actually teach that?"

"They actually do." I held up my book. "You?"

"Second year MA, English lit."

"Hey, that's original. You've got the turtleneck sweater and everything."

He ignored the crack.

"What's your name?" he asked.

"Erica. They call me Pooh."

"Pooh? What kind of name is that?"

"Like in Winnie the."

"Winnie the what?"

"The Pooh."

"Yeah?" he said. "Remind me what that is."

"You're kidding."

"No."

"It's a children's book. About a teddy bear."

"Oh, okay. Yeah. Sure."

"And you're going for a masters in English?"

He paused to light a cigarette. On his first drag the smoke boiled out of his nostrils like he was a dragon in the Chinese New Year parade. It did something to me, sorry to say. But he ducked my snotty question.

"Pooh?" he asked. "Who calls you that?"

"My friends. Originally, my Dad."

"You a daddy's girl?"

I had to think about that a moment.

"I guess I am, kind of."

I'll spare you the details about how we went to a dive called Jade Dragon on West 4th Street, and drank scorpion cocktails with the Lo Mein, and then ended up at his crummy apartment, which happened to be three floors above, where the deed went down. He was a dreamboat with no passenger aboard, an empty vessel, but he pretended to want to be my boyfriend for two more nights, and me vice-versa his girlfriend, until I realized what a hopeless clod he really was. He was writing his thesis on the novels of an obscure Carolinian named Braxton Craven, author of the forgotten gem *Naomi Wise, or the Victim* (1865), and he drank his red wine on the rocks, and the only other time we went out for a meal together (Jade Dragon again, for convenience post-sex) he made me kick in for half the check. I missed my pill the day of our initial encounter, as I learned the next morning when I studied the little cardboard dispenser wheel with each pill keyed to the day of the month. It was a fairly new routine for me, taking the pill, and wouldn't you know I fucked it up right from the start.

1967 was a good year to not watch the news, if you could help it. There was war around the world: Israel against Egypt, the bloodbath in Biafra, Vietnam of course, race riots in Detroit, Cleveland, Buffalo, Newark, Milwaukee, Memphis. The Red Guards were going nuts in China. Maybe the only good thing was that the Beatles' *Sgt. Pepper's Lonely Hearts Club Band* had come out that summer and they were still playing it everywhere, even Muzak versions in the NYU elevators. As it happened, I was not watching much news because a few days after meeting Don "Dreamboat" Bessemer, I got cast in a small role, Mrs. Squeamish, in a Restoration comedy called *The Country Wife*, by William Wycherley, the big fall main stage production. Just getting onstage in a theater department as large as NYU's was considered a big deal for a sophomore. Only the director, a young hotshot professor named Arnie Dremling, decided to do the play as a hippie musical à la *Hair*, the hippie musical that had just opened a few blocks away at Joseph Papp's new Public Theater that same month. Arnie Dremling: another original mind.

I'm sorry to say our version of *The Country Wife* was a howling embarrassment. We knew it after the first week. The rock and roll band that Dremling recruited could barely play their instruments. The songs (also by Dremling) were asinine and tuneless. The hippie costumes were idiotic. The set, which was supposed to represent Greenwich Village, looked like the nightmare cityscape from *The Cabinet of Dr. Caligari.* And there was a nude scene where three of us had to be topless for about thirty seconds singing one of Dremling's stupid songs — because we were competing with *Hair* for audacity, you see. Uccchhh! Mortifying. During the month-long rehearsals, everybody in the cast was bummed, grouchy, desperate to not be seen in this fiasco. And it was against this backdrop that I learned I was pregnant.

As it happened, I had Don Bessemer's phone number, but he was never home — or if he was, he didn't answer — and this was years before the answering machine existed, so I couldn't leave him a message. I went to his crummy building three times and left notes taped next to his buzzer in the vestibule, with the fry-o-later fumes from the Jade Dragon gagging me, but he didn't call, or contact me, or come to look for me at the college theater where I told him we were rehearsing, so I had to give up on the fantasy that he would take any responsibility for the deed. Not that I would have asked him to be a father, because also frankly, I'm sorry to say, I considered carrying the baby to term for maybe two minutes. You don't make a choice like that without paying a price in your heart sooner or later. Let's just say I was old enough to know that I was too immature to take care of a baby on my own. But I didn't have the money for an abortion, either.

My room-mate in Sieff Hall, Carol Keating (Art History major), was a Catholic who actually went to mass every Sunday, so I couldn't talk to her about it. I discreetly asked around a few people in the theater department and one particular sympathetic young woman on the dance faculty — let's call her Lynn — who was choreographing our musical numbers for *The Country Wife*, gave me the name and address of a doctor who would do the procedure. She had gone to him the previous year. She warned me to "expect the unexpected,"and wouldn't elaborate, because, she said, she didn't want to discourage me, but said he was a good guy and capable. She instructed me to drop a coded message with the receptionist that I was there to inquire about "special services." So, one blustery November day, I went to the address uptown on East 60th Street that Lynn gave me to see Dr. Jonas Nitkin. The place, in the shadow of the Queensboro Bridge, turned out to be a cat hospital.

It was unexpected, all right, but still I went in and dropped the code words on the woman behind the front desk as I was told to. She nodded knowingly and asked me to take a seat. Four other people waited there with their poor, sick cats. One by one, when called, they took their animals through one particular door on the right side of the room. Then, when they were all done, I was escorted by the receptionist through another door on the left side. Dr. Nitkin was seated there behind his desk in a comfortable wood-paneled office with lots of books. He reminded me of my father, in his late forties, a mild, intelligent face, a full head of steel-gray hair, tortoiseshell glasses, white lab coat open at the throat with a flag of red paisley tie showing. He sat with his manicured fingertips pressed together. For a painfully long moment, it seemed, we just stared across the desk at each other.

"You understand this is a confidential service," he finally said.

"I do," I said and told him who sent me.

"Do you have a lab report or just miss your monthlies?"

I dug into my shoulder bag and gave the papers to him. He looked them over. This was back in the days before at-home pregnancy tests. Lynn the choreographer had also directed me to a clinic off Sheridan Square for the test. I wanted to avoid the university health service, in case they tattled on you to your parents.

"Well, it tells the story, doesn't it?" Nitkin remarked, scanning the pages over his glasses.

I made a dumb, helpless face. He seemed to collect his thoughts for a moment.

"I know this is a hard thing for any woman."

"Really?" I said. "How would you know?" I was a nervous wreck, of course. But he was remarkably patient.

"I see a lot of women in here," he said gently.

"Of course. I'm sorry."

"The question is: are you sure want to go through with this?"

"Yes."

"Because if you're not sure, I'm not comfortable with it."

"I'm sure."

He appeared to measure me visually. "All right," he finally said.

"Where do you actually do it?" I asked.

"Come," he said, and stood up. I followed. He opened another door between sets of bookshelves and threw the light switch. It was a small room with white tiled walls and an OB-GYN table at center, along with surgical lamps, sinks, and other equipment. It was immaculate and smelled of antiseptic cleaner.

"Does it hurt?" I asked. Just looking at all the stuff was frightening. For some reason, the Nazis came to mind: Dr. Mengale. My own morbid thought shocked me.

"We give you enough sedation to be comfortable and relaxed," he said. "And some numbing medication internally. You're not very far along. The placenta hasn't developed. There's not much… material… to get out. Afterwards you'll have cramps and some bleeding, like a heavy menstrual period. I'll give you something for that and a course of antibiotic. Also some heavy flow napkins to get you home, but you might lay in extra supplies."

"Are these human drugs or animal drugs?"

He switched off the lights and returned to his desk. I followed again.

"They're just chemicals that have certain properties," he said evenly. "Only the dosages are different."

I apologized for my snotty question.

"I understand that you're upset. But I must ask you again if you really want to do this."

"Yes," I said. "I do. Absolutely."

"Sit down," he said. I did. "You'll bring three hundred dollars to the appointment. No checks or money orders."

That took the starch out of me. I don't know why. I knew it was going to cost a lot. I guess just hearing the number got to me."

"Wow," I said. "I just paid thirty bucks for the test."

"You're paying for expertise, safety, and cleanliness."

"I understand. I'll bring the money."

"Maybe you should consider going on the new medication that prevents pregnancy."

"The pill? I'm on it."

"You have to take it every day, as directed."

"Yeah. I missed one."

"Unfortunately, that's all it takes."

"I could shoot myself."

"That won't be necessary. You make an appointment with Mrs. Finkel out there. Don't eat anything from midnight before the day of. Expect to be here about three hours in all."

"It takes three hours?"

"No, twenty minutes. But you'll have an oral sedative an hour before and you'll rest here for an hour afterward." He touched his fingertips together again. It prompted me to think I was in good hands. "Oh, one other thing: don't bring anyone with you, including your boyfriend."

"Don't worry about him," I said with a rueful laugh. "We never even got to that stage."

"Kids these days," Nitkin said and stood up and cracked a kind of weary half-smile. "Well, I have to get back to my... other patients."

CHAPTER TWO

I made the appointment for the following Tuesday. That Sunday I called in sick for rehearsal to the stage manager— there were no nights-off under Gruppenführer Arnie Dremling — and took the train out to Oyster Bay, on Long Island, to talk to my father. Notice that I did not include my mother. It's hard to say when things went wrong between us but by the time I was in high school we were in something like a low-grade war. My mom, Marilyn (Trachtman) Bollinger, was beyond the grievance stage of competing with me for the affection of her husband, Larry Bollinger. What I felt from her for years was something like really active dislike, which she tried to cover up with florid expressions of endearment for the first thirty seconds or so when I returned home from an absence.

"Darling! It's so wonderful to see you...blah blah." The give-away was that I never even got a hug from her. Just an air kiss. Like I had an infectious disease.

After she attempted to induce you to eat the obligatory welcome home snack — some leftover crap in the fridge like six-day-old kugel — her mask fell away and the little critical jabs started rolling out: "You're putting on weight… what's with that hair…? If you don't start wearing a bra, you're going to look like something out of *National Geographic* before you're thirty… You know it wouldn't kill you to sew a patch on those blue jeans… what is NYU, a hobo jungle…?" And so on. She couldn't help herself. Then she would start in on Dad. "You know, your father has this cockamamie idea about (A, B, C, etc.)." All of Dad's ideas were cockamamie, according to Marilyn. And by the way, that's what I called her since high school: Marilyn, not Mom. It allowed me to put some psychological distance between us, like she was just another adult in my life, no closer than the lady at the dry-cleaner's. I'm sure it annoyed her, and I suppose I wanted it to.

So, this Sunday when I landed back home, I received the usual air kiss and the *Darling.*

"Where's Dad?"

Instead of answering my question, she said, "You look like hell. What's with this outfit? You're dressing like a lumberjack now?"

I had on a flannel shirt and jeans. That made me a lumberjack.

"And please, button up a little more. I can see a nipple."

I got a glass from the kitchen cabinet and tossed a few ice cubes in it and went into the living room.

"Your father's working," Marilyn said just as I walked out of the room. "Big crash on the expressway."

"I can't hear you?" You could say that a million times and Marilyn would never learn that the best way to communicate was not right after somebody walked out of the room you were in.

"A truck," she hollered.

My little brother, Bobby, sixteen, was sprawled on the living room sofa with the Giants-Steelers game on the old black-and-white boob tube. He said, "Hey, Pooh, How's it going?" but made these hand gestures to signify that he had to give the game all his attention.

"Did Dad go into the office?"

"Huh? Yeah."

Larry, My dad, was a photographer at *Newsday*, the paper that covered all of Long Island. They had a lot of readers. The population not including Queens and Brooklyn was over two million — greater than many whole states.

"Is he coming back?"

"Of course he's coming back," Bobby said. "He lives here, doofus."

I loved my little brother with all my heart, but sometimes he acted like he was nine years old.

"Do you happen to know what time?"

"I have no idea — Jesus Christ," he yelled at the TV set. A Giants receiver just muffed catching a long bomb of a pass. "Crespino, you klutz!"

I went to the big stereo cabinet in the dining room where they kept their liquor collection on top.

"What do think you're doing?" Marilyn said.

"No thinking required," I said and poured myself some scotch.

"Who said you could drink?"

"The legal age in New York is eighteen. I'm nineteen."

"You know that's not what I mean."

"You want me to put it back in the bottle?"

"Are you crazy, it's all watery now. Next time, kindly ask permission."

"Roger."

"Don't get smart with me."

"Roger means 'okay, I hear you.'"

"You could say, 'okay I hear you,' then."

"Okay. Next time I'll do that."

She made her eyes all slitty. "Why do you always have to start?"

"I'm not starting anything."

She followed me into the living room where I plotzed down next to Bobby on the sofa.

"Can I have some of that?" Bobby reached for my glass.

"Bug off."

"Hey, you sat down here."

He reached for the drink again and I slapped his hand, pretty hard. He pretended to cry.

"Shut up."

"You see," Marilyn said, putting on her raincoat. "You're going to turn him into an alcoholic, the example you set."

"Nobody's turning," I said.

She marched over to the coat closet near the front door.

"I have to run over to Roosevelt Field," she said, meaning the giant shopping center. That's how she was: if I happened to come home, she couldn't stand being around me.

"Would you like me to make dinner?" I asked.

"How would you do that without going to the supermarket?"

"I can look and see what's on-hand."

"Don't bother. Your father's bringing home Chinese, or so he said. If he forgets, I'll make him go back out again and get it."

You might not know from her manner that Marilyn was actually a physically attractive woman. She was shorter than me, about five-four, nice legs, brunette with a Jackie Kennedy bob, small hips, very bosomy. That was one thing I could thank her for: I was well-developed on top, too, and slim below. I know my father still found her sexually attractive. You could tell, the way he tried to touch her, put an arm around her, hold her. Of course she discouraged that whenever he made a move. "Stop it!" she always said in a particularly harsh way, like the squawk of a sea-bird. I think she worked on that voice when he wasn't around. I felt sorry for my dad. Anyway, she left, just like that, about ten minutes after I came home, without even asking anything about what was happening in my life.

"Do they fight when I'm not here?" I asked Bobby when a commercial came on between possessions.

He made a flip-floppy hand gesture. "Dad wants to buy this house."

"Huh? This house? They already own it."

"No, this broken-down place in the village. He thinks he can fix it up."

The house we were in was a split-level on a hilltop in a subdivision called Sound View because from a few places you could catch a little glimpse of Long Island Sound. It was built in 1955 when we moved there from Forest Hills, Queens, one among thirty-eight other houses that looked just like it except for the color of the shingles. "I wish he'd wait at least until I graduate from high school," Bobby said.

The game came back on. I watched the whole third quarter with Bobby. My father came home around four-thirty. I flew across the room. He dropped his camera bag and gave me a big hug. "Hey, little Pooh bear," he whispered in my ear. "Say, have you been drinking?"

"A little."

"Make me one, will you."

I did. And another for me, my third.

He told us about the accident he got called in to cover. A truck on the LIE plowed into a church van which spun into a station wagon. Seven dead, three of them kids.

"The automobile is going to be the death of America," he said. "Just watch."

"Yeah, well Mom's going to kill you first," Bobby said.

"Right," Dad said. "What is it this time?"

"You forgot to bring home the Chinese,"

"Aw, shit. Where is your mother, by the way?"

"She went to Roosevelt Field."

"All right," Dad said. "I'll go get the Chinese. Come along for the ride, Pooh?"

"He's going to show you the house," Bobby said.

"Did you tell her about the house?" Dad said.

"He mentioned it is all," I said.

"All right. I'll show you the house, then."

Dad chugged his drink and we left.

CHAPTER THREE

First, we stopped at the local Chinese place at the strip mall on Northern Boulevard. Emperor's Palace was a whole lot nicer than Jade Dragon in the city, but the smell of egg rolls frying only reminded me of Dreamboat and my situation. We ordered the usual favorites. They said it would be twenty minutes. Since it was Sunday, half the population of the North Shore was ordering take-out Chinese. Instead of sitting there waiting, we got back in the car. Soon, we pulled up in front of a dilapidated cottage in the old part of Oyster Bay village two blocks off Main Street. Darkness was falling, being mid-November. A street light on a telephone pole helped us see the house through the gloom. It was hemmed in by trees and overgrown shrubs, but the leaves were all gone.

"Jeez, Dad. This is straight out of a horror movie."

He laughed. "Use your imagination, Pooh bear."

"I thought I was. Help me out."

"Okay. It was built by the guy who was head carpenter on Teddy Roosevelt's house." He meant Sagamore Hill, a couple of miles up

Cove Neck, which sticks out into the Sound. "The style is called Carpenter Gothic. See the vertical siding. That's called board-and-batten. And notice all the grace notes, the arched windows with the matching arched shutters—"

"They're falling off."

"They can be fixed or replaced. That wavy wood trim up in the gable, it's called a bargeboard. The spandrels under the porch roof—"

"Spandrels?"

"The curvy brackets between the columns. Aren't they lovely?"

"Where'd you learn all this?"

"I'm interested. You learn when you're interested."

"It looks like no one's living there."

"It's been tied up in a legal dispute for ages, but a little real estate birdy told me that it's coming on the market."

"It's quite small."

"Well, you're gone and in two years Bobby'll be gone, too. It'll just be the two of us."

That took me aback. I kind of stared at my Dad, who in turn was riveted gazing at the old house. I didn't say what I suspected: that Marilyn would probably divorce him if he went ahead with it.

"Your mother's down on the idea, naturally, but I think she'd come around. You can walk to all the stores and restaurants on Main Street in two minutes without having to get in the goddam car. And the train station is also a short walk. And the expressway is turning into a death-trap when it's not a parking lot. You know how she loves to go into the city."

That was funny, because the whole past year that I'd been at NYU, Marilyn had never once called me when she came into the city, not for lunch or anything. Not one time. Amazing, huh? But I didn't want to prick Dad's little bubble.

"Yeah," I said. "I guess it would be convenient."

"I can see it all fixed up, Pooh. It'll be wonderful."

We sat there saying nothing for a while longer. When he started up the engine and reached for the gear shift I blurted out, "Dad, I'm pregnant."

He didn't throw a shit-fit or anything. This was one of his great qualities: he reacted to problems in a very measured way. He'd been in so many really scary situations flying bombers over Germany in the war, that everything afterward seemed easy. It was probably the reason Marilyn couldn't goad him to turn their disagreements into screaming fights. He just switched the ignition back off and turned to face me.

"Since when?" he asked.

"A month or so only."

"Who's the father?"

"It doesn't matter."

"Of course it matters."

"A graduate student," I said but didn't give his name.

"Do you care about him?"

"No, and he doesn't care about me, either," I said, and started bawling. He took me in his arms and held me, and petted the side of head.

"Oh, poor Pooh bear."

He let me cry for a good ten minutes before saying anything else. When I started to pull myself together he just said very calmly, "What do you want to do?"

"I want to get an abortion."

He absorbed it and eventually nodded. "Okay. I can make some calls—"

"No, I already found a guy in the city."

"Is he a doctor?"

"Yes," I half-lied.

"How'd you find him?"

"Somebody in the dance department at school. She went to him last year."

"A fellow student."

"No, she's on the faculty."

"A teacher from NYU sent you to an abortionist?"

"She's a good person."

"I'm sure she is."

Dad rolled down the window and lit a cigarette. I asked him for one.

"You smoking now, too?" he said. He seemed slightly more annoyed about that than about me being knocked up.

"I guess."

"Aw, Pooh, you shouldn't start."

"Look, you're sitting around in these rehearsals all night week after week waiting to run through two measly scenes. Everybody smokes just to fight the boredom. Come on, let me have one. My nerves are shot from all this."

He shook a Winston out of the pack for me and held out his Zippo lighter.

"What are you rehearsing for?"

"Nothing. This stupid play."

"You're in a play?"

"Yeah."

"When is it? Why didn't you tell me?"

"I don't want you to come see it. It's terrible. Complete piece of crap. Everybody hates it."

"What's wrong with it?"

I explained.

We sat there silently smoking in the dim glow of the street light. It started to rain. The windshield got all wavy.

"The thing is, I need three hundred dollars," I finally said.

He nodded but didn't speak for a while. I felt like a perfect shitheel knowing that it might affect his plans to try and buy the old house.

"All right," he finally said. "But not a word of this to your mother."

"I'd never mention it to her in a million years."

"When do you need it?"

"I'm going back in to see the guy on Tuesday."

"You already met him and all?"

"Of course. I had to check him out, bring the lab report, set things up."

"You trust him?"

"Yes. I do. He's a nice man. He reminds me of you."

"Ha!" Dad chuckled mordantly. "That's rich."

"The thing is, he insists on getting paid in cash."

"Okay, you give me the address and I'll meet you there on Tuesday with the money."

"Absolutely not," I said.

"What?"

"He said I'm not allowed to bring anyone else. Not the guy, not anybody. He insisted it had to be completely confidential."

"Okay, I can meet you somewhere in the city after—"

"Daddy, please, no. Just let me go through this. I'll call you Tuesday night from school so you know it's over and done with and I'm okay."

"I worry about you, Pooh."

"I know, Daddy. I know."

We sat a little while longer listening to the rain pound on the car roof. It was coming down so hard the rest of the world disappeared and it was just us in this humid little capsule.

"I guess I can be a grandfather some other time," he finally said with a sigh.

"You will be, Daddy. I promise."

That was it.

Then we went and got the Chinese food.

CHAPTER FOUR

Like I said, after I made the fateful decision, I couldn't dwell on the fact that a new life was starting inside of me. I had to keep pushing it out of my mind. I'm sorry if you hate me for it. That's just how it was then, in the fall of 1967, whatever effect it might have on me later. I was too immature, too busy, and too determined to get beyond this great big problem.

I stayed over in my old room at home that Sunday night and on Monday morning Dad took me to the bank and withdrew three hundred dollars in fifties. I drove into Garden City with him where the newspaper office was and he dropped me at the Long Island Railroad station there to go the rest of the way into the city. Then, it was back to rehearsals Monday night. We were opening *The Country Wife* (*Laugh-In* edition) Wednesday at the college theater. Monday was the dreaded technical rehearsal where they set the light levels and the sound cues and the scenery changes and all. You stood around on stage in your stupid costume — or chain-smoked cigarettes out in the seats — while the mighty Dremling asked for endless calibrations of lighting adjustments, or the idiots in the booth blew the sound cue for the eleventh time, or the rock band played one of the pathetic songs. It took five times as long to run through the goddam thing than usual, pure torture. I didn't get back to the dorm until three o'clock in the morning and my appointment with Nitkin was at noon. I barely made it to his office with five minutes to spare.

I won't bore you with the gross clinical details, except to say that it wasn't a whole lot different than going to the regular doctor. Nitkin was competent and considerate and Mrs. Finkel played nurse, and I was sedated enough that I didn't suffer at all. I remember them helping adjust my position on the table, with my legs in the stirrups, and a distant sound of meowing sick cats, then the suction of the machinery and not much else. After the mandatory hour of rest, I left with a little envelope of some extremely potent painkillers. Tuesday night was the full-on dress rehearsal. I actually went and performed, stoned to the gills on what Nitkin gave me. I called Dad from the pay phone in the lobby of the theater before the run-through. I think he was very relieved, even though my speech was slurred. I didn't even speak to Marilyn. I went through half a bale of maxi-pads that night. Somehow, I managed to remember my few lines and the stupid lyrics to our musical numbers.

I woke up the next day and I was okay. No fever. The bleeding was way down and the cramps weren't even so bad. The worst part, looking back on it, was that my body had geared up all these motherhood hormones, which it stopped producing abruptly when the pregnancy was terminated. This dumped me into a mental state that was like clinical depression, which I didn't feel the full force of until the end of the week. Performing the play was actually worse than the abortion. We had to do it for four nights. Ironically, my fellow actors came to call it "The Abortion" — though nobody but Lynn knew I'd just had one. Nitkin's pain pills got me through the ordeal. Nobody even wanted to go to the cast party Saturday at

Dremling's apartment when the ordeal was finally over. Anyway, I didn't go. It was just a college play and we didn't have to read any reviews in the newspaper. Then, everybody left for the Thanksgiving vacation.

CHAPTER FIVE

I went home and mostly slept for two days, coming out of my room only for a few bowls of cereal. That hormone crash was fierce. If my mind wasn't consciously grieving over a lost child, I think my body was. Luckily Marilyn left me alone. She didn't have much preparation to do for Thanksgiving because we rotated the feast year-by-year between her brother, my Uncle Morris, and one of my Dad's sisters, Aunt Evelyn or Aunt Judy, and our own house, and this year everybody was going over to Aunt Evelyn's in Great Neck. So my mother only had to make one dish, her "famous cranberry sauce," which had three ingredients (cranberries, sugar, and orange peel) and took about eleven minutes to make. So, thank God, there was no pre-Thanksgiving cooking hysteria.

Late Tuesday morning, I felt good enough to put on regular clothes and leave the bedroom. Marilyn had left a note on the kitchen counter saying she was out having her hair done and then going shopping. My brother's holiday didn't start until after classes at the high school that day. I called the one friend I thought I might actually feel better hanging out with, Ricky Spillman, who went to Kenyon College in Ohio. Starting back in junior high, we used to sing folk songs together, harmonizing into the tape recorder he got for his bar mitzvah. Later on we played in some school talent shows. He was never a boyfriend in the romantic sense — and not just because he was a late developer, physically, and rather chubby — but we were still quite close. When I called just before noon, his mother had to wake him up. He had just driven home from Ohio the night before.

"Hey, Pooh, what's going on?" he said, making stretching noises.

"Too much and not enough."

"Want to meet up?"

"Yeah, I really do."

"You all right?

"Nah...."

"What's wrong?"

"Nothing. Everything."

"Hmmm. Okay.... Still got your banjo?"

"I hardly played it all year."

"I'll come pick you up in half an hour."

See, I assumed that he would whisk me away from my house because that's what he always did. He understood Marilyn. She referred to him as "your little *fagallah* friend." She never missed an opportunity to put somebody down. When he showed up, I was a little shocked to see him at the door. He was taller, his baby fat had melted away, his hair was down to his shoulders, and he was growing a full brownish-red beard. He looked like a man now.

"What happened to *you?*" I said.

"I'm a slave to fashion," he said. "Hey, looks like your boobs have grown."

"I was pregnant until a few days ago."

"What?

"Yeah, for real."

"And now you're not?"

"That's right."

He tried to absorb that.

"You sure you're okay?"

"I'm getting over it. I can give you the gory details later. Can we just get out of here for now?"

"Sure. Hey, go get your banjo."

"Do I have to?"

"Yeah. I insist."

It was abnormally warm for Thanksgiving week, nearly sixty degrees, like Indian Summer, and we decided to go out to Moses Point on the hook of land that surrounded the bay of Oyster Bay itself. There were the ruins of a mansion there built by the Broadway producer Clifford Warren in 1928. Legend had it that he burned the place down for the insurance in 1935 at the height of the Depression after the failure of his big musical, *Topsy* (a.k.a. *Flopsy*), loosely based on *Uncle Tom's Cabin*. Ricky knew most of the lyrics to every show-tune ever written and all the ancient Broadway lore. There was nothing left out there but the foundation of the house and a swimming pool filled with greenish rainwater. But it had a nice beach and it was on the east side of the hook, protected from the prevailing winds. A half a mile across the water, you could see the rooftop and chimneys of Teddy Roosevelt's house on top of Sagamore Hill.

We collected armfuls of driftwood and to light a fire Ricky used the cardboard from the six-pack of Ballantine Ale that he brought.

"So, you got knocked up," he said as the kindling crackled and we sipped the first brews and lit two of his Tarrytons.

"Yeah." I told him all about it. How I met Dreamboat. The cat hospital. When the alcohol got into my brain, though, I couldn't shut up about *The Country Wife* fiasco. He loved hearing about backstage melodrama. We were in the senior play in high school together, *The Time of Your Life*, by William Saroyan. I played Kitty Duval, the prostitute, and he played Harry, a striving young hoofer. After the second bottle we started singing our old folk tunes: "Shady Grove," "The Blackest Crow," "East Virginia," "Pretty Saro," "The Cuckoo," "Plastic Jesus." We fell right back into our old harmony groove, though my banjo-playing was pretty rusty and I no longer had calluses on my finger pads after laying off a year. Between the second and third beers, he pulled out a joint and after we smoked that, Ricky launched into his vast repertory of Broadway tunes, which had much more complicated chord changes and I had to fake it on the banjo.

The weather started to change. Big clotted gray clouds moved in over the Sound. We ran out of driftwood and beer and we decided to leave. Going back to town I showed Ricky the house that Dad wanted to buy. We parked out in front of it for a while. It started to rain and it was so much like the night that I went there with dad the week before that I felt overwhelmed and started to weep again. Ricky hugged me and let me cry on him and after a while I started to kiss his neck and the beard on the side of his face and pretty soon he took me by the shoulders and gently pushed me off of him.

"No, Pooh. Let's not do that."

"What's wrong with me?" I asked, blubbering. I was pathetic.

"There's nothing wrong with you."

"You said you liked my boobs."

"I said they were bigger than I remembered."

"Well, don't you like them?"

"Sure," he said.

Of course, I knew how he was even in high school but I wasn't sure he was truly that way or just temporarily confused about sex. We never talked about it and still didn't. You just didn't back then.

"I'm miserable," I said and blubbered some more. "I hate NYU. I hate the city. I hate my life."

"What do you want to do about it?"

"I don't know. Light out for the territories."

"You want to split?"

"Yeah, I want to split. The city disgusts me."

"There's a place."

"What place?"

"This place I heard about."

"What did you hear about."

"There's this place up in Vermont. It's, like, an experimental community. It's called the Sunrise Farm."

"Yeah? What do they do there?"

"You know: live."

"Oh, real hippie types."

"Well, *Time Magazine* might call them that."

"Hippies give me the creeps. There's a head shop on McDougal Street with all these posters from India of the various gods that have monkey heads and elephant heads and eight arms. I hate that shit. It gives me bad dreams."

"I don't think this place is like that."

"Well, you've never been there."

"True."

He gave me a napkin to blow my nose that had been wrapped around a donut fragment from his road trip. We smoked more cigarettes.

"My parents would kill me if I dropped out of NYU."

"See, you just informed me that you're already considering it."

"I don't know," I said. I gave him a noogie on the shoulder for being right. He was very intuitive.

"We could drive up there and you could check it out," he said.

"When? During Christmas vacation?"

"We could drive up there tomorrow."

"Tomorrow's the day before Thanksgiving."

"Exactly. We'd get there just in time for it. I think you'd learn a lot about what a place is like by how they celebrate Thanksgiving."

"I'd miss the big gala at Aunt Evelyn's."

We both cracked up over that, since we were still stoned and he really knew my family dynamics.

"Do you want to go up to Vermont or what?" he said when we'd settled down again.

I took a big drag on that cigarette.

"Why not?" I said. "We could always just turn around and come home."

CHAPTER SIX

S o, we made this secret plan to leave early the next morning, Wednesday, before the big holiday on Thursday. Ricky was the second-oldest of five children and his parents were hosting their own giant holiday gathering so he felt he wouldn't be badly missed. My dad generally left for work at six-thirty in the morning. Bobby would be off to school at seven, and then Marilyn would get up around nine to lead her life of housewifery and shopping. That was their pattern. So Ricky pulled up at seven-thirty as instructed, and I pussyfooted out the door with my rucksack. I'd left my banjo in his car the night before. I couldn't bear to tell my Dad and Marilyn that I was skipping out on Thanksgiving — just imagine the histrionics — so I left them a note on the kitchen counter saying I went to visit a college friend in Connecticut and please forgive me, blah blah. It was a lame gesture, of course.

You know how exhilarating it is to start out on a road trip when you're young and have hardly seen anything of the world, let alone your own country. I was sent to Camp Mohegan Trails in the backwoods of Stockbridge, Massachusetts, for seven straight summers.

Our family, otherwise, was not big on trips or togetherness. We didn't tour the National Parks like other suburban families or go down to Florida on vacations, thank God. When I was too old for camp, I traveled around England and Scotland on one of those teen travel odysseys. But I'd hardly been anywhere else. The two summers before college I did kitchen scut-work at the Harbor Club, making the salads and helping the chef.

Ricky brought a big thermos bottle of coffee and a bag of danishes from the Deli Stop over by the train station. After we battled rush hour traffic to the Throggs Neck Bridge and finally turned north toward New England, it really did feel like we were lighting out for the territories. After Norwalk, we left the big freeway behind and hopped on Route 7, a two-laner, all the way up through Connecticut and then Massachusetts. We bought sandwiches in Stockbridge and made a little side trip out to Camp Mohegan Trails which, to my shock, had a realtor's "for sale" sign on the front gate. Boy, was that depressing.

"I wonder how much they want for it," I said.

"Think you might buy it?"

"Yeah, sure," I said. "I had the same horse here for years, a big gray gelding named Smoke. I wonder what they did with all the horses."

"Cat food, maybe."

"Don't say that!"

"Sorry."

"He was the sweetest horse. I was happy here."

"Maybe you'll be happy where we're going. It sounds kind of like camp."

"If we can even find it."

All we knew, really, was the name and that it was in the vicinity of Bennington, Vermont. Ricky had heard about it from a friend at Kenyon whose brother was on the commune. The only other thing he knew was that the head guy or founder went by the name of Songbird. He was apparently famous among the hippie underground. We got to Bennington around three that afternoon. While Ricky gassed up the car, I used the pay phone to see if I could get a number for Sunrise Farm from Information, but no such luck. Then we parked downtown and walked up and down the Main Street, going into some shops to inquire if anybody knew the whereabouts of the place. They seemed sincerely stumped except for one older lady in a card and *tchotchke* shop who smirked when Ricky explained that the place we were looking for was a hippie commune.

"There's a war on, you know," the lady said.

"With the hippies?" Ricky said, obviously putting her on.

"Is there something else I can help you with?" she said, with a withering look.

We went over to the post office and asked the elderly clerk on duty if he knew of an establishment called Sunrise Farm in the vicinity.

"Lots of farms out there," he said. "Dairy operations, mainly."

"This one's just people," Ricky said.

"Used to be a county farm for the poor, but they shut her down."

"No, this isn't like that."

"I can't help you, sonny, ma'am."

We left. It was getting dark already. I was discouraged. Ricky suggested we get dinner and decide whether to find a motel room and search some more in the morning, or just split and drive home. We found an old-fashioned diner on the north side of town, one of those aluminum-paneled trolley-looking things. It was busy the night before Thanksgiving, truckers and some families with bawling children. The waitress was our age and she had a look about her. Maybe it was the peasant blouse and leather thong around her neck, and the frizzy blonde hair. We ordered cheeseburgers and fries and Ricky asked if by any chance she knew about a place called Sunrise Farm.

"It's Sunrise Village," she said. "Not farm."

"Oh?" Ricky said. "Somehow it stuck in my head as 'farm.'"

"The guy at the post office said he never heard of it," I said.

"Oh, they know of it," the waitress said. "They just don't approve of it."

"Can you tell us where it is?" I asked. "How to get to it?"

"I live there," she said with a smile that suggested a privileged knowledge of secret wonders. It was smiles all around by then. We were so relieved that the place actually existed.

"My friend from college, Kenny Provost," Ricky said. "His brother is supposedly there."

She cocked her head a little as if she was amused.

"What college is that?"

Ricky told her.

"Wow. You heard about us all the way out in Ohio?"

"Yeah," Ricky said. "Halfway across the whole country."

"Do you go there too?" she asked me.

"No, I'm at NYU in the city," I said. "But we grew up together on Long Island."

"Lawn Gyland," she said, twiddling her pen. More smiles all around.

"Are you from here?" I asked.

"God, no," she said. "Marblehead, Mass."

"Oh, Mobblehead," I said, putting on the accent.

She pointed her pen at me, still smiling.

"The thing is," Ricky said, "I forget the brother's name."

"Scott," the waitress said. "Yes, he's there. Scotty Provost."

"Wow. How do you like that?" Ricky said. "No kidding."

"No kidding."

"From the little we heard, Sunrise Village sounds like a really cool place." I said.

"Tomorrow's the big holiday," she informed us. "It won't be like everyday normal life there."

31

"Sure, I realize that. But we came all the way up to see it?"

Her smile faded and she gave us a real hard look, like she was sizing us up. A bell rang behind the counter.

"I've got an order up," she said and bustled off.

"Did I sound pushy, like we're barging in on them?" I asked Ricky.

"Well, it is why we're here," he said.

We were both so on edge that we hardly said another word waiting for our food, and it wasn't long before the waitress returned with our giant plates.

"I made them give you some onion rings along with the fries," she said. "You looked hungry."

"Gee, thank you," Ricky said.

"The thing is, we don't take in just anyone," she said. "Any old drop-ins, you know? There's a process."

"Like applying to college?" I said.

"We don't give a shit about your grades or your test scores. That was a joke," she added when we didn't laugh. "People have to contribute something. There's a lot of work involved. We look for skills."

"Of course," I said. She eyeballed us some more.

"Look," she said. "I usually get off here between nine-thirty and ten." The clock on the wall said ten after six. "You've got a car, right. I assume you drove here."

"Yeah, we did."

"If you come back later, you can follow me there. Oh, there's a movie theater on Main Street if you need somewhere to hang out between now and then."

"What's playing?" I asked. Ricky kicked me under the table.

"I have no idea," she said.

"Can we crash at the village?" Ricky asked. "It'll be late."

"Yeah, we get visitors. People like you. All kinds, really. I'm Robin, by the way."

We didn't shake hands because we were both holding our drippy, juicy cheeseburgers. I introduced us, though, as Erica and Richard and thanked her again for the extra onion rings to make up for my apparently snotty cracks.

"We'll be back here around nine-thirty or so," I said.

"Okay," she said. "See you later."

Ricky left her a giant tip: five bucks on a seven dollar tab.

So, after we ate we actually did go back to Main Street and find the movie theater. There was little else to do until later in small town Vermont on the holiday eve. The movie was *Cool Hand Luke* starring Paul Newman as a prisoner in a southern chain-gang prison who refuses to follow the rules, and it was quite good. It also made me wonder what I might be getting myself into, because, like Cool-Hand, I was apparently not the world's greatest rule follower, and I got the feeling that Sunrise Village required you to adhere to their ways. But the movie made the hours pass quickly. It let out a quarter after nine, in time for us to get back to the diner. We drank cokes at the counter while Robin bussed off her last few tables, cashed in her tip coins for folding money, and said, "follow me."

CHAPTER SEVEN

Snow flurries started coming down as we pulled out of the diner's parking lot. Robin's car was one of those funny little Nash Metropolitans, a tiny, bulbous two-tone, salmon and white thing, like a cartoon car, that was easy to follow. Once you left town, it was mostly uphill, going into the Green Mountains. We'd gone about two miles out of town when the pulsing blue light of a cop car appeared behind us.

"Aw, for chrissake," Ricky moaned. He carefully pulled over. Luckily, Robin the waitress also pulled over to the shoulder ahead of us.

We sat there for what seemed like a long time. Finally, the officer got out and came up to driver's window with his yard-long flashlight, which he made sure to point right in Ricky's face. The officer was wearing a county sheriff's badge on a bomber jacket with a fur collar and one of those winter hats with three flaps.

"I'm sure I was going under speed limit," Ricky said to him.

"You're sure?" the deputy said quite facetiously.

"Well, we're driving up a mountain here behind another car with the snow coming down," Ricky said. "Kind of hard to speed, even you wanted to."

"Let me see your license and registration," the deputy said, pure deadpan.

Ricky started digging his wallet out of his back pocket, under his heavy coat.

"Can you just say why you stopped us?" Ricky persisted.

"You were following that car mighty close."

"Yeah, that's exactly right." Ricky said. "We are following the car to a place we don't know how to get to."

"What place is that?"

"Just a place, where she lives."

I noticed that when Ricky finally got his wallet out, and fished the documents from it, he slipped a twenty-dollar bill out, too, and sandwiched it between the license and the registration. The deputy took it and sort of glanced at it in his hand.

"Stay put," he said, and tramped up ahead to Robin's car. I saw him stick a hand in his pocket — stashing the twenty, I assumed.

"Stay put," Ricky muttered. "He's got my goddam license, for chrissake."

The deputy had quite a long conversation with Robin. It looked from his body language that he was having fun with her, maybe flirting her up. He wasn't shining the flashlight in her face, either. Rather, he kind of squatted down to her level hanging on the Nash's open window and rocking on his boot-heels. You couldn't hear what they were saying with our motor running, of course. I was a nervous wreck. The whole incident worried the hell out of me because I figured we'd get blamed for attracting the attention of the cops, and even if I wanted to stick around this commune, they'd have some reason to reject me.

Finally the deputy returned to Ricky's window, flashlight and all, and handed back his license.

"So, you going up to Never-Never Land, are you?" he said with a big smarmy smile.

"We're going to Sunrise Farm," I said.

"Village," Ricky corrected me.

"There's drugs up there, you know," the deputy said.

"We don't know anything about that," Ricky said. "We've never been there before."

"We're monitoring the situation," the deputy said. "Trouble could find you up there. Hippies and all."

"We'll be extra careful," Ricky said. "Don't worry about us."

"Oh, I won't," the deputy finally said and slapped the roof. "Go on, now. And don't tailgate!"

He lumbered back to his patrol car.

"He's not giving us a ticket," I said.

"Apparently not," Ricky said as he pulled back onto the highway behind Robin's car. "Tell me: is this Vermont or Alabama? Oh, look it's snowing. I guess we're not in Dixieland."

"Cops are the same all over now, I guess," I said. "The way the country's going."

As we got up in elevation, the flurries turned to heavier snow. We hopped off the main east-west road, Route 9, and headed south on Route 100. There were a few scattered new houses along the way, but mostly it was forest. Then we took a left on an even lesser, rougher county road for a ways, going downhill again into what would prove to be a very secluded valley — though you couldn't see much beyond the road itself in the dark. We managed to calm down by then, even laugh about it a little.

"Drugs on a commune," Ricky cracked. "Who would have ever thought?"

Finally, we came around a bend in the road, the little Nash slowed down and we entered the classic New England scene: a weathered clapboard church and some nice old houses on one side of a modest village green that the snow had been sticking to. Ricky had clocked it on the odometer: thirteen miles from Bennington. On the other side of the green was a row of several commercial buildings. One looked like a 19th century inn, with a big front porch, still partly under construction with ladders and a scaffold against one end of it. Down from the inn were a couple of red brick, three story business buildings, shoulder to shoulder, with empty storefronts, and some freestanding cottages further up the street. Across from the inn and all that was a great wooden heap painted mustard yellow with an arched front entrance, shop-fronts on either side of that, a mansard roof, and a tower at center. Robin's Nash swung around and parked diagonally among eight other cars there. We did likewise and got out. Lights burned within the buildings here and there, and in some of the houses, too. There was wood smoke in the air. I felt the strange vivid sense of coming home to a place I'd never been to before. Robin came over.

"Sorry about that cop-stop," I said.

"Did you get a ticket?"

"No, he let us off," I said. "We slipped him a twenty."

Robin recoiled a little. "Oh boy," she said. Another strike against me, I feared.

"I'm sorry. We didn't know. Of course, we weren't doing anything."

"They're on our ass all the time," she said. "But so far we haven't had to grease their palms. They seemed happy just hassling us for the sheer pleasure of it."

"We'll never do that again, I swear."

"Okay, I'm glad you didn't get a ticket. Come with me."

We followed her inside the arched doorway entrance of the big yellow building. First you passed through a kind of lobby area and beyond that through another doorway, into a theater with a proscenium stage at one end and a high ceiling painted blue, sprinkled with constellations, the figures and animals they represented outlined in white lines connecting the stars — the Big Dipper, Pisces the fish, good old Orion. At the rear of the stage hung an old, faded, painted backdrop depicting a fanciful mountain landscape with a lake in the foreground. In the rear was a graceful, horse-shoe shaped balcony.

"Wow," Ricky murmured. "This stuff is all original. You couldn't build it like this today."

"It was an Odd Fellows hall," Robin said.

"What was odd about them?" I asked.

"I honestly don't know. Anyway, we're odder, I'm sure."

If there had ever been rows of fixed seats for the audience, they were gone. For now, several long tables were set up in a U-shape with extra long tables to the side of each leg of the U and one near the stage end, leaving room for people to get inside the arrange-ment. A dozen people milled around, setting the tables with stuff from baskets and cardboard boxes: flatware, plates, candlesticks, decorations made from pinecones, sumac flowers, and red-ber-ried bittersweet vine. The scene made the hair on my neck stand up, it was so marvelous, like watching servants prepare a banquet for a medieval court in a great hall. I assumed this was for their Thanksgiving feast tomorrow.

It was quite cold in there, like they weren't running any fur-nace. I touched a big silver-painted radiator by the window and it was not even warm. More than a trace of marijuana smoke wafted around in the cold air. You couldn't fail to notice that the people setting up the room were all remarkably good-looking despite be-ing all bundled up in sweaters, scarves, and wooly hats. I wondered if they judged newcomers on their looks — or maybe that was just my own insecurity. Some of the men had beards, one had a droopy cowboy moustache, very dashing. Some of the women wore skirts over blue jeans, to stay warm I supposed, but it emphasized their lovely youthful femininity, their difference from the men and gave the whole scene an exciting overtone of lush sexuality. It also made me worry, of course, how intense that scene was in the village, and whether I could hack it. I still had some lingering soreness in my abdomen from the abortion. It reminded me that sex could be hazardous to your body and mind.

The trippy guitar solo in the Doors' song "The End" jangled at very high volume from speakers stacked in the front corners of the stage. The Doors' debut album was one of the big rock and roll events of the year. I admired their originality and energy, but the music had a sinister edge that made me uneasy, as if it was describing the dark, downer side of adulthood that we were all moving into. Getting pregnant when you weren't ready was only one kind of danger you could get into, I thought. There were musical instruments on the stage: an upright piano, a couple of electric guitars on stands, several big amps, and a drum kit on a riser behind all that, with mic stands and all.

"Is there a band on the premises?" I asked Robin. We practically had to yell in each other's ears over the music.

"Yeah," Robin said. "We have our own band. A lot of people here are into making music."

Ricky gave me the thumbs up sign.

"Do you guys play?" Robin asked.

"Banjo," I said. Robin nodded as if she wasn't sure that was an instrument worth playing.

Some of the people bustling around noticed us without making a big deal about it or offering more than a little nod or a smile. Robin gestured with a jerk of her head to follow her. She brought us over to a woman with a very fine-featured face puzzling over a clipboard, wearing a pea-coat on top of a long skirt, jeans, and hiking boots, with a watch cap pulled over her raven-black hair, and fingerless wooly gloves. She seemed older, mid-twenties, looked at once glamorous, capable, and intimidating — like she knew what she was doing (and you didn't).

"This is Maya," Robin introduced us, shouting over the music. We gave our names. Robin told Maya how we showed up at the diner and asked about the village. Ricky explained about his friend's brother, Scott Provost. He was not among those setting up the hall, Maya said. The Doors' song ended and the record changer dropped the Jefferson Airplane's *Surrealistic Pillow* on with that raucous, echoey opening drum riff that seemed perfectly suited to the big room. The song was beautiful and spooky, like Maya.

"It's lovely here," I said. "So... New Englandy." I instantly felt like an idiot.

"Well, you picked a fine time to come," Maya said. I was used to people from New York speaking sarcastically, saying the opposite of what they meant for effect, so I assumed the worst.

"We don't mean to barge in—"

"People come when they come," Maya said, with the weary smile of someone burdened with responsibilities. "And now you're here." Her vibe of authority was intimidating. I wondered if it would turn out that she was the mythical Songbird who supposedly founded the Village.

"Can we help out?"

"We're almost done here tonight. Tomorrow you can help. There's plenty to do. Robin will settle you in for the night. Then we'll see where it goes from there?"

Meaning, I guess, whether we might be invited to join the group, though we actually hadn't stated any intention to do that. I supposed everyone who dropped in wanted to sign up because the place, and everyone in it, were so beautiful. Of course, I was already thinking that I'd made a less than great impression. Just then, someone dropped a plastic tub of flatware. It made a startling racket. The others stopped and applauded. It broke the tension I was building up in my overactive brain, worrying incessantly. Everybody laughed.

We thanked Maya. Robin took us back outside and over to the building that looked like an old inn. There was a big room on the first floor filled with old sofas and stuffed chairs, and a fireplace going, with oil painting portraits in distressed gold frames of men in black coats and women in bonnets from a hundred years ago hung on the walls, and a half dozen other Sunrise people hanging out there by the fireplace, some with acoustic guitars, jamming. We didn't stick around down there but followed Robin up to the second floor, to a tiny room toward the end of the hall that was mostly occupied by a mattress on the floor with a quilt over it and a couple of old pillows without cases.

"It isn't much, but it's clean and dry," Robin said. "Bathroom's down the hall. There are some sheets in a hall closet, too. The door's marked 'bedding.' Breakfast is eight to nine downstairs. Well, I'm beat."

"Do we have to pay anything?" I asked.

"You can make a donation in the morning. Whatever you can manage. Talk to Maya. See you tomorrow."

"Thanks for bringing us back here," I said.

"You seem like nice people. Night all."

She left, closing the door as she did, as if to say we should stay in our room now. There was just an overhead light with a switch on the wall. The light cast stark shadows like a 1940s Bogart movie.

"What do you want to do?" I asked Ricky.

"You mean, like, stay or leave?"

I guess he wasn't thrilled with the accommodations.

"Oh, we're staying, at least for their Thanksgiving," I said. "No, I meant what about here, in this room tonight. You and me? What do we do?"

Close as we were over the years, we'd we never slept in the same bed together. So much went unspoken.

"Right. Of course." He kneeled down on the mattress. It was rather stained. "I wonder how many people have had sex on this thing."

"We don't have to make it." Uccchhh, I actually said that.

He shot me a look that conveyed about six different messages ranging from amusement to annoyance that seemed to add up to I should know better by now.

"I'm such an idiot," I explained.

"Let's go see what they have for linens," he said.

So, we ventured down the hall to the closet marked bedding and found stuff, pretty clean, actually, including an old wool army blanket, and by the time we made up the mattress I felt better about it. I took my jeans and sweater off but kept everything else on, panties, tee shirt.

"Do you mind this?" I asked. "I just can't sleep with heavy clothes on."

"Don't be offended, but I'm going to keep my jeans on," he said.

"Sure. Okay," I said, though it did bother me, like I might try to force myself on him.

We turned out the obnoxious ceiling light and lay there side by side, feeling each other's warmth. The windows below us on the first floor cast enough ambient light outside that you could see the snowflakes fluttering down across our window.

"You've changed since high school," I said. "You're turning into a man."

"I'm still the same inside. An insecure fat kid who likes show tunes."

"You're not fat anymore."

"But I can still sing the entire original cast recording of *Camelot*."

"You don't like girls, do you?"

"I like you. I love you, Pooh."

"Are you going to be okay in your life?"

"What a question. Of course I will."

I reached for his hand and held it. That was as far as things went. We didn't yak anymore and in a little while I could tell from his breathing that he'd fallen asleep. My brain could not find the pathway to that peaceful place. I could hear the muffled sound of song and laughter and guitar chords far away downstairs. Before long, I slipped out of bed and back into my clothes and found my sneakers and stole out of the room.

There were six people still hanging out by the fireplace in the big room downstairs, four guys and two women. A candle burned on a crude plank coffee table that looked casually whacked together out of old barn wood. One guy and one chick played guitars. Another guy had a mandolin in his lap — he was rolling a joint just then — and the second girl played jazzy Renaissance figures on a silver flute. A third guy was popping corn at the hearth in a long-handled antique covered pan. The fourth guy got up from the sofa and stood when I came in. He was diminutive, maybe five-four, but clearly a grown-up. He wore a kind of homemade-looking Robin Hood hat with a long feather in it, a blousy shirt with big sleeves, and very colorful gold and red striped pants with elfish pointed moccasins. Altogether, with his sharp features and goatee he looked like a puppet from a fairy tale. He hoisted a big jug of cheap red wine my way and said, "Want some?" with a winning, toothy smile.

I took the jug and swigged down a mighty gulp of the red and nestled into a corner of the sofa there. A smoldering joint soon came my way and before long I was quite happy and comfortable sitting there watching. You could tell they loved making music from their body language, the way they swayed and half-closed their eyes at times, and I thought if this is what it's like here then this is really for me. The leading musician was Alan Kaplan on guitar — I learned all their names later, of course — a dropout from Bowdoin College in Maine where he'd been a math major. He was a very accomplished picker, both flat and finger styles, and he seemed to be the one setting the pace for the others. They had been playing that dreamy, improvised riff of the kind that is natural when you've got a buzz on, but then the guy at the fireplace, Danny Musser, finished making popcorn and emptied the pan into a big bowl on the table, and picked up his fiddle, and the figures he played started to magically resolve out of the jazzy cloud into an old-time Appalachian tune I recognized: "Say, Darling, Say." It's often played fast and frantically, but they did it in a lovely, relaxed, rolling cadence. And after a couple of turnarounds on the instruments I felt so into the spirit of the moment that I started singing the words to it right there on the sofa, really letting loose. The other players all kind of woke up from their stoned, eyes-half-closed trances and gawked at me in a way that seemed to express delight.

> *Say little darlin won't you marry me*
> *Live in a holler 'neath the old oak tree*
> *Say darlin say*

> *In the old oak tree we'll make our home*
> *Never more in this world to roam*
> *Say darlin say*

After two more verses I cried, "take it," and Danny Musser kicked in on his fiddle playing long, lovely double-stops, and then Alan flatpicked a solo, and I wailed again through more verses, and then more breaks by the mandolin and flute players, and when they parked it, we all kind of sat there stunned.

"Wow," said the little guy in the medieval outfit, who had been banging a tambourine. This was Mark Tanzio, who was called Tanzy by everybody.

"Hey, you're a good singer," said the mandolin-player, Dave Padget, slender and angelic-looking, wearing a green and white sports jersey with the number 13 on it.

"Where'd you come from?" Alan Kaplan asked.

"NYU," I said.

"Are you here?" he asked. The others swapped amused glances.

"Hey, of course she's here, man," Danny Musser said. " I mean look, there she is."

The others tittered at the stoned absurdity.

"When did you get here then?" Alan asked.

"Just tonight."

"Are you going to stay with us," said the flute player, Alison, with blonde hair that looked like she ironed it.

"I don't know yet," I said. "I think I'd like to."

"Oh, you should," Alison said.

"Did you ever go to the jams in the square?" Alan asked. He meant Washington Square in the other village, Greenwich Village, where NYU is. There was a big folk music scene every Sunday around the old fountain in the square.

"I played there a few times," I said. "Are you from the city?"

"I used to come over from Jersey back in high school," Alan said. "Do you play anything?"

"Yeah, banjo."

"Sweet," Danny Musser said. "We're painfully lacking a banjo."

"I'm not that good."

"You must not play much," Alan said.

"I haven't had time for it at school."

"If you play more, you'll get good, I promise," Alan said. "Where's your banjo at now?"

"I left it in the car."

"Don't leave an instrument out in the cold," Danny Musser said. "It's not good for it."

"Yeah, I know," I said.

"Well, go get it," he said.

"Oh, yeah. Okay...." I was pretty stoned. I hurried outside and retrieved it from Ricky's Dodge Dart. The village looked magical in the snow. Very few lights were on at this hour. The intense stillness of the Vermont mountains was such a relief from the suburban pandemonium of Long Island and the never-ending churn of the city. Back inside, I put the case up on the hearth so it would heat up fast, but Danny told me to let it come to room temperature naturally. The jug went around again and they asked me what old time songs I knew. I noticed that the other girl, Jan Heathcoate, with her twelve-string guitar, had been silent, giving off a vibe that she was not delirious about me entering their music circle.

But then we were jamming again. They asked me to name some songs I knew. Apparently, we'd all grown up listening to the same records back in the early sixties, the Hootnanny years, when folksingers like The Chad Mitchell Trio and the Kingston Trio and the Limelighters and Peter, Paul, and Mary, Dave Von Ronk, Pete Seeger, Baez, all the old bluesmen, and Dylan, of course, were hugely popular. Folk songs were the lingua franca of our teen years, so by this time we were all pretty tuned in to a long list of favorites. I sang the murder ballad "East Virginia," and the Mississippi John Hurt song, "Louis Collins." Jan came in on harmony on that, and our voices melded so well that I began to hope she didn't resent me for being there. The jug went around and around, and more weed, too. I finally got my banjo out and, yes, the cold had thrown the tuning way out. But I had good pitch and got it tuned quickly, and started picking the intro to "Lord Franklin," about the English sea captain who disappeared in the Arctic seas searching for the Northwest Passage. It wasn't a very difficult song chord-wise, so I could play it pretty well on the banjo. Danny Musser and Dave Padget joined Jan and me on a very complicated four-part harmony. Padget had a wonderful bass vocal range. The song concluded on a soaring duet of woven harmonies between Danny's violin and Alison's flute. When it was over, I shuddered as from a chill, though it was toasty by the fire. The others seemed strangely subdued, too.

"Did we do that?" Padget said.

"Yeah, we did," Danny said.

"That was on another level, man," Tanzy said.

"Yeah," Alan said.

"Yeah, that pretty damn good," Jan said.

"You better stick around?" Danny asked.

"I think I'd like to."

"Put another log on the fire, Danny-boy," Padget said. Tansy rolled another joint and fired it up. The wine jug went around, too.

We continued playing some more old chestnuts: "Banks of the Ohio," "The Three Ravens," "The Buffalo Skinners," "Twelve Gates to the City," "Pretty Saro." It must have been two o'clock in the morning by then. We were all wasted and exhausted, just sitting there totally depleted, staring into space.

"Big day tomorrow, everybody," Tanzy said.

"That was real nice," Jan said to me before she peeled off, and I was relieved that she was glad to have me around after all.

"Yeah," Alison said with a tired little quasi-smile. "You pulled us together there."

She went off with Padget, so I supposed that they were a couple.

"We'll play again," Alan said before leaving, typical of him stating the obvious.

"Sure, I'd like that."

By then, Tanzy and Danny were the only other ones left. Both of them sort of hovered around me.

"Did they give you a place to crash?" Danny asked.

"Yeah," I said.

"Don't you have something to do?" Danny said to Tanzy.

"Only go to sleep."

"Time to go do it then."

Tanzy cracked his lopsided smile and repeated, "Yeah, big day tomorrow, I guess." He left and it was just me and Danny. I climbed out of the big cushy chair and made to put my banjo back in its case.

"Want some company tonight?" Danny said.

"I'm, uh, here with a... friend."

"Male friend?"

"Yeah, sort of."

"Sort of…?"

"No, it's definitely a guy. He's not, you know…."

"Not what."

"My boyfriend."

"Where is he? Did he nod off on you?"

"It was a long day. We drove all the way up from Long Island. We have a room upstairs."

"Is he going to stick around, too?"

"Probably not. He's out at Kenyon in Ohio. He loves it there."

"Good," Danny said, sweeping his long hair out of his eyes and grinning. "You brought something special here tonight."

"I'm so out of practice."

"No, you really pulled us together. I'm not kidding."

"Well, I sure had a great time. I haven't gotten to play with other people much."

"Sure you don't want to want to hang out with me?"

"I really shouldn't tonight." I didn't want to explain that I just had an abortion and all.

"Are you going to sleep with this guy you came with?"

"Believe me," I said. "That's all we're going to do."

"Well okay then. Goodnight."

I watched him cross the big room gracefully to the front door. He was quite handsome with his droopy outlaw moustache and long brown hair. The truth is, I was already imagining what it would be like in his arms.

Back upstairs, I carefully opened the door to the little bedroom. There was a lamp at the end of the hall and in the wedge of light that entered the room, I saw somebody curl around blinking at me, only it wasn't Ricky. It was a boy with frizzy blonde hair with no shirt on.

"Oh! Excuse me…!" I muttered, embarrassed that I had intruded on the wrong room. But then another body stirred beside him and Ricky's face appeared above the covers blinking too.

"Who are you?" I asked the strange kid.

"I'm Scotty Provost," he said.

"Oh," I said, all flustered. "You're the reason we're here."

"I am?"

We were all so semi-conscious that nothing really made much sense, except our discomfort of the moment.

"We can probably all fit on this mattress," Ricky said. I could tell he said that to deflect his own embarrassment.

"That's okay," I said. "I have another place I can go. Mind if I just borrow this extra blanket." They both just watched as I drew the old army blanket off the bed, leaving them with the ratty quilt. "It's okay," I said. "Go back to sleep."

So, trailing the blanket behind me, with my backpack on, and my banjo in my other hand, I went right back to the big main room downstairs, tossed more logs on the fire, and collapsed on the sofa with the army blanket.

CHAPTER EIGHT

I woke up to a rising commotion as many of the villagers assembled around the adjoining bar area of the downstairs where the kitchen staff were setting out breakfast things.

"Hey, why no eggs today?" some guy complained.

"Sorry," a woman's husky voice replied. "We want you to have room for the big feast."

"Oh, man, I'm, like, still growing."

"Good. Maybe you'll grow up one of these days," she said. "And by the way, I'm not a man, man, so quit calling me that."

That's how I greeted Thanksgiving morning. My head throbbed and I was horribly dehydrated. But I didn't want to make a bad impression so I forced myself to get vertical and folded up the blanket. Twenty-odd Villagers milled around over there, including Alison, Jan, and Padget from the night before, some others I sort of recognized from the Odd Fellows hall when we first got there, and some entirely new faces. The commune's main kitchen was back behind the bar. A stocky red-haired woman wearing a tweed newsboy cap and a food-splashed white apron came through the swinging door there — Sophie, the kitchen boss — with a big basket of hot biscuits. She set them on the bar along with a big plastic tub marked "granola," two half-gallon glass milk bottles, a quart jar of honey, a one-pound brick of butter on a plate, and a tub of peanut butter.

"Granola and biscuits today, people," Sophie announced. "No special orders. Get 'em while they last or go without."

There was a big commercial-size coffee urn set up, too, with an array of mismatched mugs. The aroma of fresh-baked biscuits and coffee percolating nauseated me and I went searching for a bathroom down in the wing past the bar. I found one, an ordinary bathroom with just one toilet and a regular tub-shower combo. The hook-and-eye lock on the door was useless — the eye screw was missing. Luckily, nobody came in while I threw up. Not much came out, either. I hadn't eaten since the cheeseburger at the diner. Then I had to take care of the usual routine toilet business, worrying that someone would barge in on me. And after that, I was desperate to take a shower. There were a dozen towels hanging from a line of pegs above the wainscoting, so I just grabbed one, hung it over the shower curtain, and jumped in. I stood there letting the hot water soothe my aching brain. Then I heard somebody enter the room, followed by musical splashing that was definitely the sound of a male peeing. After the flush, a hand reached in and drew open the shower curtain at the back end of the tub. A guy who looked barely out of his teens with a mop of yellow hair parted in the middle leaned in the shower.

"Can I come in?" he asked. I didn't even attempt to cover myself up.

"I'll be done in a minute."

"You're new here."

"Yeah. Got here only last night."

He stepped right in, totally naked, too, of course.

"Want me to wash your back?" he asked.

"Thanks. Maybe some other time," I said, parting the shower curtain at my end and stepping back out with the towel. "What do you have to do get a little privacy around here?"

"Walk in the woods," he said. "What's your name?"

I told him Erica but really Pooh.

"What? Like Winnie-the-Pooh?"

"Exactly! I'm so glad I didn't have to explain it."

"God, who doesn't know Winnie the Pooh."

"You'd be surprised."

"Well, glad to make your acquaintance, Pooh. I'm Billy Herman from Satan's Kingdom."

"Now you're goofing on me, right?"

"No, it's a real place. Just south of here across the state line in Franklin County, Massachusetts."

"Satan's Kingdom? For real? Jesus."

"You can look it up on the map. The name came from back in the early settlement days when it was all dark and daunting forest, full of demonic savages, the Pocumtuc Indians, to be exact, an Algonquin sub-group. You see, they had a mighty protein supply from the Connecticut River, and they grew corn, beans, and squash in the valley. It was a great place to be an Indian, so naturally they freaked out when the English showed up. And of course the English colonists were obsessed with witches and devils and all. To them, the Indians were the spawn of Satan."

"How do you know all this?"

"I'm sort of the village historian."

"Is that your job here?"

"Officially I'm on the grounds crew. We fix stuff up. There's no end to it."

"Can you fix the lock on this door? The screw-eye is gone."

He ignored that.

"By the way, you're very attractive," he said.

"I'm old enough to be your big sister."

"Incest is best. Come on back in the shower with me."

I was done toweling off and I'd dug some clean clothes out of my backpack.

"I'm all dressed now. See ya."

"Let's get to know each other."

"Fix that lock."

Back in the bar and dining room of the inn, even more people had drifted in from elsewhere around the village. The big room was filled with happy chatter. That sojourn in the bathroom had prepared me better for breakfast. I got a big bowl of granola and a biscuit with butter and honey slathered on it, and a mug of coffee and took it all over to a rocking chair near the fire where I could watch people. Some of them milling around with their coffee acknowledged my presence with a nod and smile. The new girl! I imagined that they were all people raised by nice families with good manners. Then I remembered my own family: the almighty Marilyn. Uccchhh! I felt guilty about not calling my dad, letting him know where I was, and that I was okay. Just then Ricky Spillman came down the stairs and shambled across the big room toward me.

"We don't have to talk about last night, do we?" he said.

"No. It's okay."

"It just kind of happened."

"Don't worry about it," I said. "There's coffee and food over there." He headed off where I pointed. I dug the birth control pill dispenser out of my backpack and duly took the daily dose with my coffee. As Doctor Nitkin said, you have take them every day! I had to wonder how long it would be before I ended up having sex again. It seemed pretty inevitable, even if I wasn't ready yet. I was worried whether the abortion might permanently affect my psyche, turn me frigid, make me unable to get to orgasm, or distort my relations with others in ways yet unknown. I did not feel like I was exactly the same Pooh Bollinger as before. I wondered whether I was crazy for even coming to what was obviously a sexual hothouse at this very point in my life. I worried that it appealed to something twisted in me. The combination of a wicked hangover and a dose of caffeine made me so edgy that I rocked back and forth in the chair to relieve my nerves.

Meanwhile, the glamorous Maya, from the night before was calling, "People! People!" from the center of the room, until the buzz of conversation ceased. She didn't have her clipboard this morning, but you could sense her air of authority. "This is our first Thanksgiving in Sunrise Village" — cheering, applause — "and you know we've been talking about establishing some instant traditions, ha ha" — crowd laughter too — "and it's been proposed that we initiate the first annual Thanksgiving hike up to Owl's Head to get those appetites honed up. So, anybody who wants to come along, meet up at ten o'clock on the path behind the sauna. It was thirty-four degrees when I came over here. The radio says a high of forty-two today, but it could be windy up on top. So dress accordingly. Kitchen helpers, food transporters, servers: you're welcome to go, too. It's an hour and half round-trip and the holiday meal is at five. There'll be plenty of time to do your thing. Additional Sunrise notes, you all, listen up! One of the washers in the laundry is down so laundry Group B's day will be pushed up to Saturday, assuming we can get a drive-belt on Friday. We will keep you posted. You vegetarians" — raspberries, laughter — "please make sure your names are on the V-meal list over at the bar. Songbird called and said he'll be back later this afternoon" — cheers, rude noises, laughter — "and finally, we have two prospective new villagers with us here today. Erica and Rick, raise your hands and make them feel welcome. Happy Thanksgiving everybody!" Cheers, whoops, applause. At least I learned that Maya was not Songbird. The trouble was, she was Maya.

CHAPTER NINE

Around ten, Ricky and I followed a bunch of the others over to the sauna, which was behind the inn. Last night's snow only amounted to a couple of inches and was already melting. We peeked inside the sauna building, a fairy-tale shack built so recently that the exterior cedar shingles were still fresh and bright looking. The room inside was dominated by an enormous wooden plunge tub that six people could probably fit into. The rest of the room was all sauna, with three levels of built-in cedar benches, and a big woodstove. The place was still warm and fragrant from an earlier firing but nobody was in there now.

Danny Musser, the fiddle player, was among the thirty or so hikers assembling at the trailhead.

"Hey," he greeted me with a big smile, hands thrust into the pockets of his navy pea-jacket, dark hair jutting out of his Che Guevara style beret. Che had been bushwhacked and murdered by Bolivian fascists just a month earlier. It was in the news. "Is this your old man?" he nodded at Ricky.

"Just my old friend from back home."

"Oh?" Danny, said. I introduced them. "She's a damn decent musician, you know. She played with us last night."

"Yeah, we used to sing together in high school."

"I hear you might not stick around."

"Probably not," Ricky said. "Back to school for me."

"You're over at Kenyon in Ohio, I understand. I went to Oberlin for three semesters."

Ricky and Danny quickly bonded over the wonders and marvels of life in the Buckeye State as the group moved out for the hike. I assumed Danny wanted to pump Ricky for more info on me. The hike was led by a tall, reed-thin guy wrapped up in a gray Swedish army surplus greatcoat, with an Old Testament style beard. This forbidding figure was Oswald Strangefield, one of the first and elder villagers. He was twenty-eight, like Maya, full-fledged grown-ups, authority figures to be trusted and respected. Strangefield was called by his last name, sometimes shortened to just Strange, which he seemed to like and encourage, as if it validated his air of mystery. It had only been a few years since Lee Harvey Oswald shot President Kennedy, and nobody could hear the name Oswald without a wrenching emotional reaction. So Strange just ditched it.

The mob of hikers formed into a procession as we embarked across a field between the inn and the woods. There was an odd square stone foundation in the middle of it, about two feet high, big rocks embedded in concrete, with ornate white fencing on top of it and a graceful arched front gate.

"What's that?" I wondered out loud.

"It's the original garden wall we built last spring," a voice beside me said, belonging to Billy Herman from earlier in the shower. It took me a moment to recognize him with his rectangular wire-frame glasses and wool watch-cap covering his golden head.

"Oh, hi, you."

"It goes down four feet, below the frost-line. Nothing will ever burrow under it. Woodchuck-proof, rabbit-proof, probably bomb-proof. It's called slip-form construction, cement mixed with fieldstones in a plywood mold. Maybe we overdid it, but it's built to last. We're going to add more planting beds outside of it this coming year. Songbird wants to get into the herbal tea business. We plan to clear another five acres over yonder —" he pointed — "for soybeans for our tofu operation. You like tofu?"

"I'm neutral on it."

"Yeah, It's pretty neutral stuff. But real healthy. And the market's wide open. Do you know anything about the history of this place?"

"Actually no."

"Allow me to fill you in."

"Sure. Go ahead."

By this time we traversed the field and entered the woods and were climbing uphill on a well-worn hiking path. There was less snow on the trail there because of the tree cover, mixed conifers and hardwoods. Billy spun out his history as we marched to the top of the mini-mountain called Owl's Head (elevation 2,039 feet).

"The village was first settled in 1791 in a grant given to the Revolutionary War hero Sebastian Beaker, who established a flax mill on the Marble River, which runs through town and then another sixty miles down to the Connecticut River. It makes a vertical drop of over a thousand feet along the way and there were many opportunities to harness water power. This site was particularly good, though it was geographically remote. There are two falls on the river here, the upper one nine feet and the lower fourteen. Colonel Beaker erected his original mill on the upper one. It was a going concern until 1816, the so-called Year Without Summer. That was when Mount Tambora erupted in the Dutch East Indies. The fallout produced a haze that circled the globe. They say the sun was so dim, you could look at sunspots on the surface with the naked eye. The flax harvest failed that year with a lot of other crops. The workers had to abandon the village, Beaker's Mill, as it was called then, or starve. By the time the weather got back to normal, the whole venture had failed. That was this place's first turn as a ghost town.

"Is it haunted?"

"Well, actually, it may be. I'll get to that. Nobody lived here for over twenty years. Meanwhile, the Great Gale of November 1827 killed eighty-four people as it ripped through Vermont. The raging Marble River washed away the first Mill building. It wasn't until 1839 that people returned. The utopian religious visionary August Timlin bought the forty-three hundred acres of Beaker's grant from the Colonel's heirs, and spent years trying to build a short-line railroad down the Marble River valley to North Adams, Massachusetts. The railroad business was brand-new and they had to learn how do everything as they went along. It didn't get very far. Meanwhile, Timlin moved ninety-three of his followers here with plans to manufacture a self-sharpening plough. Naturally, he renamed the village Timlintown, which was later shortened to Timlinton. He put up a sawmill and built what his people called the Great Common House. There's a drawing of it at the Bennington Library, five stories with porticoes on three sides. The Inn back there now is built around a tiny remnant of it. The group called themselves the Edenists. They believed in equality of the sexes and multiple marriage twenty years before the Mormons got into it—"

"How do you know all this?"

"It's my thing, history." he said. "You've got your thing, right?"

"Yeah."

"What is it."

"Music, I guess. I'm supposedly a theater major at NYU just now."

"Theater, huh? How's that working out?"

I laughed. "I'm here, aren't I?"

"There you go."

"So, you said they practiced polygamy, these people?"

"Only their version differed from what the Mormons did later on. Instead of just men having multiple wives, both men and women Edenists could have multiple love interests. They called them their Adams and Eves and they numbered them. Like, if you and I got it on, I might be your Number Three Adam and you might be my Number Two Eve. They didn't have to marry."

"That's rather charming."

"Yeah, quaint, huh? The nineteenth century was real big on systematizing things. Everything was treated like some kind of industrial project that had to be rationalized, even free love. The spirit of the age and all. So, these Edenists built a new factory where Beaker's Mill had stood and started turning out ploughs. Settlers were opening up the Midwest, establishing farms where the buffalo had lately roamed, and you needed a sharp plough that could cut through tough prairie sod. In 1846 a series of disasters struck. First, Timlin was sued for patent infringement by Cyrus McCormick's company out there in Chicago, which also made ploughs, and was closer to the frontier settlement action. Timlin lost the court case. They had to stop making ploughs. Then the Great Common House caught fire, killing twenty-two of the Edenists, a calamity. And then it turned out that a member of the inner circle named Fergus Haltzwanger, who functioned as the group's book-keeper, embezzled what remained of the group's assets and ran off with Timlin's Number One Eve. Timlin committed suicide. The railroad was left only partially completed. And the surviving Edenists dispersed by wagon train to the Willamette Valley out in Oregon. The town was abandoned a second time."

"This place has seen some very bad luck."

"We're trying to turn that around now," Billy said. "In 1861, a profiteer from Holyoke named Simon Alvord took over the plough factory for making US Army uniforms out of re-used wool, a product that came to be known as *shoddy*. The thing was, it didn't last long in the rain. He made a fortune on it, though. During those years Timlin's railroad was completed as the Marble River Line of the Boston and Maine Railroad. When the war ended, Alvord got out of the military uniform business, expanded the factory again to include a lower works on the second waterfall, and started the Catamount Marble Company. The quarry itself is a quarter-mile north of the village. It's all filled up with water now, the most beautiful swimming hole you've ever seen. Hardly anybody on the outside knows about it, and the place is pretty remote, so we had it all to ourselves last summer. You'll see. It'll blow your mind. The marble was a variety known as Cream Olympian, very popular for fireplace mantels. They transported the cut blocks from the quarry to the carving works on a quarter-mile rack-and-pinion cog railway. It was all downhill from the quarry to the workshops with the load and only needed gravity to move the cut stone. No engine necessary. Ingenious. The empty flatcar was then easily drawn back up to the quarry by oxen. This was the most stable and prosperous period for Timlinton."

"Amazing how they came up with these inventions."

"Yeah, except just a few years later along came the steam drill, which seemed like a boon at first but was the beginning of the end for Catamount Marble. They couldn't compete with larger-scale operations that developed at Brandon and Dorset. Simon Alvord died in 1903. Central heating was coming on all over America and nobody wanted fireplace mantels anymore. They tried to branch out into cemetery stones and mausoleums, but the market wanted granite for that, not marble. Marble rots away much faster in the weather, especially with air pollution from growing industry. The company went down the tubes. A whole bunch of workers had to move elsewhere. There was no government unemployment check back then. By 1911, the town was dead again. Catamount Marble had built its own mausoleum. The works are still there along the river behind the church, by the way. You can go in there. It's eerie."

The trail had gotten steeper now. We were getting up there in altitude. You could begin to see a distant blue landscape through the bare trees.

"So, the town was abandoned three times?"

"Actually five," Billy said. "After Catamount went out of business, the Boston and Maine shut down the Timlinton spur. That left it really isolated and abandoned. But then, after the First World War, the automobile came along and changed everything fast. You could get to places now that were inaccessible before. Another thing happened: the summer vacation was becoming a standard feature of American life. In 1925, a high flyer named Martin Atterbury bought the Catamount property all of a piece, including the inn. He repaired the buildings that could be salvaged and opened a mountain vacation resort. Atterbury was also a bootlegger and he used the old Catamount works as a depot for Canadian whiskey. It was the Roaring Twenties and all. Prohibition. After the Wall Street crash of twenty-nine, with so many people out of work, he had to depend for business on a shady crowd of people who were still making money around bootlegging: gangsters. He had a modest gambling casino up here, far from the prying eyes of the local police. Mobsters from all over the northeast would flock there. One night in August 1933, a hot-head crony of Dutch Schultz from New York named Nathan "Jelly" Monk murdered Atterbury and two hotel guest bystanders at a blackjack table in the Odd Fellow's Hall. Monk had been winning big and Atterbury closed the table. Witnesses heard the word 'kike' flung around. Bang bang. When the authorities finally got here, they discovered the stash of booze and the gambling operation and they shut it all down. Atterbury's widow, a former showgirl named Nan Langfit, tried to keep the inn itself going another year, but the mob never returned after the bust and the depression was still on. You asked about ghosts. Over the past year since we got here, several people have reported seeing the figure of a strange woman down in the tavern room of the inn late at night. She supposedly wears a red dress and sits weeping at the bar. It happens that the ones who have seen her are all the biggest heads in the Village. Probably on acid or mushrooms at the time."

"Maybe psychedelics open a doorway in the mind that lets things in that our defenses usually keep out."

"That's an interesting theory," he said. "Are you a doper?"

"I smoke. Not all day every day. I wouldn't call myself a head."

"Ever drop acid?"

"Actually, no. Not yet, anyway."

"Hang around here long enough and you will for sure."

"I'm not in any rush."

"Good. It's a heavy experience. Be careful with it."

Billy extended his hand and helped me climb around a tricky outcrop as we neared the summit of Owl's Head. The footing was rocky scree up there and the few trees were tortured-looking from the constant wind.

"So, the Village was abandoned again after the gangsters and all that," I said. "Was that the end of the story? I've lost count."

"No. A couple named Artie and Doris Stamm tried to turn the place into a dude ranch in 1953, but they didn't last three years. People in the horsey groove like it better out in Wyoming, I guess. They did fix up the inn again, though and stabilized the other buildings. And they put up a nice barn. Artie was a war hero. Distinguished himself in Italy liberating a hundred US prisoners held captive by the Nazis in a monastery at Campobasso—"

"How do you know all this stuff?"

"It was on microfilm in the Bennington Library."

"Sheesh…."

"Anyway, they bailed out and the property was sitting here vacant for more than a decade until Songbird came along and bought it."

"With the idea of starting this?"

"I think he had a kind of full-blown vision of what could be done with it. He's a very purposeful guy."

"Where did he come from?"

"Boston area. He went to Harvard. I'm not sure if he actually graduated or not."

"Where did he get the money?"

"Wealthy family. Lookit, we're almost there. I'm not quite finished."

"Sorry. Go ahead."

"There's one other odd thing about this place. Over the years, people have disappeared around here."

"Like, who? Regular people?"

"Hikers, campers. Most recently two women from the college down in Bennington. Anyway, that was in 1957, before we got here. There were others before them. We're surrounded by the Green Mountain National Forest. The federal government bought it all up. People go in there and sometimes they don't come out. It's a pretty big empty place for the eastern US. They make some mistake and their bodies are never found. Some probably go in there to end their life and succeed at it. Wow, look, we're here!"

We climbed onto the rocky summit of Owl's Head. It was a sparkling day up there, clear and sunny. You could see all the way down the Marble River Valley across the Massachusetts state line to Mount Greylock, maybe thirty miles from us. It felt wonderfully safe on this perch, protected from the awful grinding machine that everyday America had become with its jammed expressways and advertising-saturated airwaves. You could see where the machine lurked out there in the blue gloaming, but it couldn't get you here. I liked the idea that we were surrounded by a cushion of vast trackless forest. That pretty much sealed my decision to move to the village. Canteens were passed around. Some had wine in them. Then some joints went around.

"Hey, thanks for the history lesson," I said to Billy. "You ought to write all this down, you know, for historians of the future."

"Oh, I have been doing that. If only the Edenists had somebody who wrote down all their crazy shit."

"This place seems the opposite of crazy to me."

"We're not religious nuts, anyway. These are wild times in the old USA. I wouldn't be here if I didn't think it was the right place." He reached for my gloved hand and gave it a squeeze. "Hey," he spoke close to my ear, "we really should try getting it on, you and me. I like you."

"I like you, too, but we'll have to see about that."

"I could be your number one Adam."

"Ha! You were born too late for that."

"You're telling me…."

"Anyway, I have to go back to the city and get my stuff," I said.

Some of the people gathered brush for a campfire, but Strangefield told them to forget it, they might start a forest fire. It was interesting to see him exercise authority. Nobody argued with him. I kind of liked that, too, not being a fan of anarchy and disorder. We stayed up at the top about twenty minutes.

CHAPTER TEN

I was reunited with Ricky Spillman on the trail back down. The whole time I'd been listening to Billy Herman's concise history of the place, I could see Ricky up ahead, gabbing with one person after another.

"You've been quite the social butterfly this morning," I said.

"Just scoping things out," Ricky said. "I kind of like these people."

"But not enough to stick around."

"I've got to go back to Kenyon. I've got a life out there."

"But, you'd give this place the Good Housekeeping seal of approval?"

"Yeah, I think you'll be okay here. Look, I'm heading back to the island tomorrow morning, check in with my folks before I drive back to Ohio on Sunday."

"Can you drop me off in the city? I have to clean my stuff out of the dorm, then see if I can catch a bus back to Bennington."

"You're not going to check in with Larry and Marilyn?"

"No. They'll go nuts when they hear that I'm dropping out."

He gave me a look. Then said, "Okay, sure, I can take you into the city."

"I'll call them at some point when I'm beyond their clutches. Marilyn probably won't even give a shit, she's so self-involved. My father, that's another story."

"He really does love you."

"I know. It's pathetic. I feel bad about the tuition money and all."

"Of course you do. Tell him you'll pay him back."

"Yeah, like in 1990."

"Maybe you'll land a rich husband."

"Ha!"

"By the way, that guy Danny really wants to get into your pants."

"Everybody wants to get in everybody's pants around here, it seems like."

"I think he really likes you."

"Okay, he's attractive."

"Yes he is," Ricky said.

Despite my recent distressing encounter with near-mother-hood, I would be lying if I said I wasn't interested in the air of romantic adventure about the place.

I did happen to notice that Danny Musser walked most of the way back down Owl's Head with a big strapping blonde, a Valkyrie right down to the long yellow braid coiled on top of her head and the hiking staff she'd picked up that was like a Teutonic spear. I couldn't help feeling a twinge of jealousy.

"Hey, I heard something real interesting about this guy Songbird," Ricky said. "His parents were eaten by cannibals in the South Sea Islands."

I stumbled on a clump of grass when he said that. By then, we were back in the big open field behind the inn.

"You're kidding," I said.

"Nope. For real, they say."

"Jesus…. How could that happen in this day and age with guys in space and all?"

"Maybe you could ask him about it sometime. I'd love to know the details."

As we entered the inn, Maya came over and took me aside.

"Erica…."

She guided me into a nook between the bar and the kitchen. I decided to tell her right then that I went by the name Pooh, as in Winnie, blah blah. So I did.

"I was born Georgina," she said, as if confiding in me. "Ooooff, I hated it!"

"It's a mouthful. I was never crazy about Erica."

"You can be who you want to be here, Pooh. Or who the universe means for you to become."

"I hope those two things line up."

"I guess we'll find out. Looks like you're going to be with us for a while. Welcome to Sunrise Village. Officially."

I explained about how I had to go back to New York and get my stuff. She informed me that there was indeed a regular bus that stopped in Bennington. If I would call the village with my time of arrival before-hand, they'd send someone in a car to pick me up.

"Elliot will want to meet with you one-on-one at some point," she said.

"Elliot…?"

"Songbird."

"Oh, yes, the guy who…uh…."

"Is making all this possible," She finished my sentence.

"Right. That'd be, like… an interview?"

"A casual chat. There's no casting couch," Maya said and laughed musically. "He wants to get acquainted with everybody who comes here to stay for a while."

"Is it true that his parents were killed in the South Sea Islands by cannibals?"

"New Guinea, actually."

"Sheesh. How does that happen in the modern world?"

"There's still plenty of real danger out there. You can find it if you make an effort."

"This seems like a safe place, though."

"Good. That's exactly what we want it to be. Safe and happy."

"He's a mysterious presence, this Elliot Songbird."

"There's nothing weird about him. But he has a lot of responsibility."

"He's not around, apparently."

"He had to go to Boston on family business. He'll be back this evening. Since it's a special day today around here and you're off to New York tomorrow, I'd like you to help out in the kitchen with Sophie and her crew for Thanksgiving. We'll figure out a more permanent work assignment for you when you come back for good."

"Okay," I said. "Thank you."

"That's all for now," Maya said, dismissing me, with a fluttery hand gesture.

So I reported to the kitchen. What a chaotic scene that was. It was an old-fashioned restaurant-type kitchen, spacious, with a lot of equipment, but it looked like a bunch of six-year-olds had been let loose in it. Sophie the head cook was the chunky redhead with the newsboy cap who had been serving up breakfast earlier. She had three other helpers in there, all women: Josie, Karen, and Weezil. Sophie didn't bother to introduce me, though. She put me right to work. There was stuff strewn on every surface: piles of vegetables and peelings, pots containing mysterious liquids, sheet-pans with rolls rising, baskets of yams, butternut squashes, eggplants, onions, flour dust everywhere, various incomplete projects underway, bowls of stuff, a tub of bread cubes. The linoleum floor was disgusting, strewn with food debris and spilled gunk. The big steel sinks were filled with dirty pots and pans. From my experience working in the Harbor Club kitchen back home, I got a bad feeling just surveying the room as to where things stood for the holiday feast. The Harbor Club was never this chaotic, even on the Fourth of July. A clock on the wall said it was already twelve-thirty. Five giant turkeys were sitting in bus-pans on two rolling carts.

Sophie teamed me up with Weezil, who was busy spooning the bready-cheesy filling into what was going to be stuffed mushrooms. I had a sense that prepping the appetizers before attending to the turkeys was not a great idea. Weezil was a petite brunette with a cute pageboy haircut, a pretty face, and dark nipply boobs showing through her white peasant blouse. The mushroom-stuffing operation was set up on a butcher-block counter so we faced each other. Sophie was yelling at the other two girls who were taking forever to peel and pare enough apples for several pies. I could tell that Sophie herself was in trouble making pie crust because she'd already rolled some out and the fillings weren't nearly ready, and the dough, just sitting there, would be too warm to work with when it was time to put it all together.

"Are we in the weeds here?" I whispered to Weezil.

"Totally," she said and tried to suppress cracking up.

I'd hardly gotten a rhythm going when Sophie yanked me off mushroom duty.

"Do you know how to make pumpkin pie filling?"

"Sort of… I guess."

"Well, you can you follow directions, can't you?"

"Sure."

She slammed a copy of *The Joy of Cooking* into my solar plexus, making me gasp.

"Get going, new girl," she said.

"Where do I look for stuff?"

"Bulk dry storage, canned stuff, in the rear pantry. Spices and herbs in those cabinets. That wooden door with the big steel handle is the walk-in fridge. Eggs and milk and stuff in there. Pumpkins over there."

"Something's burning!" Weezil cried from her station.

Sophie darted across the room and yanked a smoking sauté pan off the eight-burner gas range.

"Fuck...!" she shrieked.

It was one of those restaurant-grade pans without a heat-sleeve on the metal handle and she burned herself grabbing it without a pot-holder. The smoking pan went skittering across the floor. Sophie ran cold water over her palm at the sink. "Just what I fucking need now!" she moaned, and then she started to cry. I searched around and located a chest freezer in the rear pantry. There were no ice cubes in it, but I found a box of popsicles and I brought one back out to Sophie.

"Here, put this on your hand," I said.

"It's a fucking popsicle!"

"There's no ice, but this'll help."

She snatched it from me and wrapped her hand around it.

"Christ.... I don't have fucking time for this. Go back and do whatever you were doing."

They didn't have any canned pumpkin puree. But there were three large pumpkins on the floor near the sinks. I looked them over, then shuffled back across the room to Sophie, who was back at her counter with a wet rag wrapped around her injured hand chopping more onions and celery to replace the stuff that had burned.

"Those pumpkins over there," I said.

"Yes...?"

"They're Halloween pumpkins."

"So...?"

"They're not pie pumpkins."

"What's the difference?"

I guess I assumed that she knew a lot about cooking because she was the one in charge, but she wasn't that much older than me, really.

"These jack o'lantern pumpkins are all stringy, without much pumpkin stuff in them, even though they're big."

"Look — What's your name again?"

"Pooh."

"This is what we've got, Pooh, so work with it."

"Well, okay, but if we don't start roasting those turkeys over there real soon, they'll never get done in time for the dinner."

"Of course they will."

"Those turkeys will take at least four hours."

"How do you figure that?"

"Twenty minutes a pound."

"Who says?"

"It says right here in that *Joy of Cooking* you gave me."

That clearly annoyed her.

"So…?" she said, and thrust her chin at me.

"So it's going on one o'clock and we haven't even prepped them to go in."

"Are we talking about turkeys now, or pumpkins?" Sophie said, her eyes going all squinty.

"Well, we're talking about both."

"Look, for now just figure out how to deal with your pumpkins and leave the fucking turkeys to me. I don't give a fuck what *The Joy of* fucking *Cooking* says."

"All right," I said, and spun around and went back to where the pumpkins sat. It seemed like I was on my way to making my first real enemy at Sunrise Village. It made me nauseous to realize that.

So I hacked the pumpkins open and cleaned all the seeds and fibers and crap out and cut them up into manageable chunks and put them into four big roasting pans in both ovens at three-fifty.

"What are you doing?" Sophie said from her central counter.

"We have to roast off the pumpkin."

"They'll cook when we bake the shit into pies."

"No they won't," I said. "You have to precook them and mash up the cooked pumpkin stuff with the eggs and cream and all."

"Well, I'm going to need those ovens for the apple pies real soon."

"So, what do you suggest?"

"I dunno," Sophie said. "Boil the shit."

"Okay," I said, seeing how Sophie and I were on a collision course and wanting desperately to avoid it. I had gone to take the pumpkin pans out of the ovens and was trying to figure out how "boil the shit" would work with the rind still on when I heard a thud and a clatter and a shriek. I twisted around to see Sophie on the floor on her back, thrashing around while she clutched her right arm and pretty soon her shrieks turned to bawling.

"I'll get help," Weezil said and rushed out.

Josie, Karen, and I kneeled down on the floor and tried to see what we could do for Sophie, but she just hollered, "Keep the fuck away from me!" between bawling spasms. A minute later, Maya came in with two men: Albert Ozmer ("Oz") the landscape crew boss who was as strong as a draught horse, and Walter ("Teck") Hesslewhite who was putting together a hydroelectric system for the village and could fix any machine. They managed to get Sophie on her feet and trundled her out of the kitchen — eventually down to the hospital in Bennington where, it turned out, she had a broken collarbone.

"Well," Maya said, exhaling a deep yoga breath and surveying the room with all its projects and messes. She seemed supernaturally serene, under the circumstances. "How's it been going in here?"

"Pretty good… great," Josie and Karen said — why, I don't know, since it was obviously a disaster area. Maybe Maya couldn't see it.

"Is everything on track for the big feed?"

"Oh, yes. Sure. Don't worry, we've got it all under control," they said.

"Great," Maya said. "I'll scare up some more helpers for you."

Then she left. Weezil came back in. She was laughing. She came over to me and squeezed my forearm, almost croaking like a bullfrog she laughed so hard.

"Oh, I'm sorry," she said. "I shouldn't. This isn't funny." That only got her croaking again. Karen and Josie lost it too and joined in. We all had a good hard laugh for a few minutes.

"We're good and fucked here now, aren't we?" Weezil said.

"We'll be okay" I said. "We've got *The Joy of Cooking*."

That was good for one last hearty laugh.

"Okay," I said when that died down, "let's get ourselves together and make this meal happen."

The others looked at me for a moment as if I was crazy. Then, maybe because I was taller than the other women, or because they were petrified of what to do without Sophie to order them around, or perhaps because they sensed that I wasn't intimidated, I found myself in charge of a Thanksgiving banquet for sixty-seven people. The others just deferred to me without further discussion or negotiation. To clarify my understanding of the situation, I made a little speech:

"We were never properly introduced," I said. "I'm Pooh Bollinger, from Oyster Bay, Long Island. I just got here last night. I'm no professional cook, but I worked in the kitchen at the Harbor Club back home for two summers, and we prepped bigger banquets than this. So, let's just do the best we can and try to be polite and helpful to one another."

They nodded briskly, as though I had introduced a marvelous never-before-heard-of way of doing things there. I started organizing the tasks in my head and rattled off assignments to the others, starting with Weezil cleaning up all the melty pie crust dough and starting that project all over.

"Let's clean up this greasy floor before somebody else falls on her ass," I told Josie, who went and fetched the mop and pail. I chucked the useless pumpkin chunks in the garbage and decided to use the butternut squashes for the pies instead. Nobody would know the difference. When the floor was clean, I sprinkled salt all around for traction like I'd seen Harvey the chef at the club do back home. Karen finished peeling and paring the last of the apples. I put her and Josie on the turkeys, starting with getting the necks and giblets and other crap out of the cavities and separating out the livers and getting a stockpot going for gravy with onions, carrots, celery, and parsley. It was all there in *The Joy of Cooking*, thank you Irma S. Rombauer, goddess of the kitchen. Meanwhile, I got the sinks cleared of the skuzzy pots and pans and then we were able to wash off the turkeys. Weezil had gotten a new batch of pie crust going in the giant Hobart mixer machine and at one-thirty we got the apple pies in one oven and the butternut squashes roasting off in the second one.

Maya sent in Mark Tanzio, Tanzy, and a compliant creature named Poppy — eighteen, the youngest person in the Village — to help. Both were pretty capable and fast, and Tanzy especially was eager to please. By now I'd discovered what an unbelievable disaster the walk-in fridge was: new stuff just crammed in front of the older stuff so that if you dug back far enough, the old food was rotting and disgusting. I asked Tanzy to take out everything in there, and throw the rotten stuff in the garbage, and then clean out the box and put the stuff that was still good back in some kind of coherent way. I apologized for asking him to do such a revolting job, but he was a good sport about it, and he knew that we were operating under emergency conditions. One of the things I learned about myself from this episode was that I had a true aversion to chaos and liked things really organized. It was an interesting revelation for one who had come to view her life as an aimless mess.

At that point, things got a lot better. There was a radio on the windowsill behind the sink and we turned it way up. The FM station out of North Adams, Mass., played The Mamas and Papas

"Dedicated to the One I Love," Van Morrison's "Brown-Eyed Girl," and the Hollies' "Carrie Ann" all in a row, and that energized the room as we got down to business. Just not having the crabby presence of Sophie around was a lift for everybody. The apple pies came out of the oven and looked beautiful. Weezil had cut out little stars and moons from the leftover crust and decorated the tops, and brushed on an egg wash that turned them all golden.

"Great job!" I told her and we hugged and jumped up and down.

At quarter to two we got the squash pies in.

Meanwhile, we made a mountain of stuffing for the turkeys. Sophie's strong suit was baking and she'd collected a lot stale bread for this purpose the previous week. We were lucky that there was a huge supply of butter in the walk-in. As soon as we got the squash pies out, the turkeys went in. It was quarter to three. Simple math showed that we wouldn't get the main course on the tables until seven at the earliest. So we consulted good old Madame Irma again and figured out some additional really simple appetizers to go with the stuffed mushrooms to keep the villagers occupied while they waited: deviled eggs, celery stuffed with cream cheese, and corn fritters. It took Tanzy two hours to clean out the walk-in and then I switched him on sink duty so that the constant stream of dirty pots and mixing bowls wouldn't pile up there while we worked. He was a really good sport. We'd managed to cram four turkeys into the giant twin ovens of the Garland stove and I didn't know what to do with odd fifth bird, which was just sitting on the butcher block all dressed up with nowhere to go. I'd toyed with the idea of trying to roast it in the fireplace out in the Inn's big room, but couldn't figure out a way to make that happen.

"Is there another oven in any of the other buildings?" I asked Weezil.

"There's a kitchen in the Gemini House," she said. This was one of the cottages down the street where some of the people lived.

"Can you go check it out, please? See if it works?"

"Sure."

On the chance that it did, I put Karen on cornbread duty, two giant pans of it. The recipe was right on the cornmeal box, and it was pretty much the same as Irma S. Rombauer's. I told her multiply it times eight. I was mixing a tub of cream cheese in the Hobart with some dry onion soup mix for celery-stuffing when Weezil came back with a positive report on the oven down in Gemini. I sent her and Poppy right back over there to bake off the rolls Sophie had left rising on sheet pans. When they returned, I sent them back again with the big cornbread pans. At four-fifteen, they yanked the cornbread, and the stuffed mushrooms went in. At four-thirty, the mushrooms came out and the fifth turkey went in. It might be ready in time for second helpings.

We were all in a state of amazement that the meal was actually coming together, emerging from a prior state we came to call The Great Chaos. We were even able to take a break and smoke our first cigarettes of the afternoon (everyone smoked). There was a half-full jug of Gallo burgundy in the pantry and we liberated it to toast each other, and even lifted our jelly glasses to the erstwhile Sophie. By now purple dusk had gathered in the eaves outside the kitchen window. The time remaining to Thanksgiving zero hour was like coasting down a gentle hill on a bicycle. We peeled crates of potatoes and yams. I rounded up every conceivable remaining vegetable in the walk-in, plus boxes of frozen peas and carrots and string beans and broccoli for a mélange, and finally cooked up a giant batch of Marilyn's famous cranberry sauce —the kind that took about eleven minutes to make.

Maya strolled back in at quarter after six, along with Dave Padget, the mandolin player, Scott Provost, Krista Ragnarsdóttir, the Viking chick who was actually a Tufts medical school drop-out originally from Iceland, and Robin, the waitress from the Bennington diner who rescued us the night before, plus two other guys I hadn't met named Brad and Gary. These were the waiters for the holiday extravaganza.

"Wow," Maya said, calmly eyeing how things had changed since earlier in the afternoon when they had to trundle Sophie off. I think she was stoned. We had tons of stuff all prepped, ready, and waiting in an orderly array to be lugged over to the Odd Fellows hall: baskets of cornbread squares and dinner rolls, tubs of butter, sheet pans of the aforesaid various appetizers, mashed potatoes warming in a big water-bath on the Garland, yams braised in maple syrup ready for finishing under the broiler, a cauldron of gravy and a big pot of water simmering to receive the defrosted mixed vegetables for their final baptism. In the preceding hour, we'd mopped the floor again, cleared the sinks and the counters of extraneous objects. "Frankly, I'm amazed that you got this together?" Maya asked. "How'd it happen?" Weezil pointed at me. Then the others did, too. It actually made me quite uncomfortable, so I held up *The Joy of Cooking*, pointing at it.

"Thank Irma S. Rombauer."

"Right on, Irma," Maya said. Then, sort of to herself: "Dharma with sugar on top." Yeah, she was definitely stoned. "Say, where are the turkeys?"

I informed her that they needed another hour in the ovens but we were ready to send out a whole lot of other stuff to keep the multitudes occupied while they waited.

""Groovy," Maya said. "Well, here's your wait staff." She turned and floated back out of the kitchen as if she was on a flying carpet.

"Okay," Padget said, "let's head 'em up and move 'em out!" He made the sound of snapping a whip: "Ksssshhh!" We helped them wrangle stuff onto platters set up on trays, and they were out the door. Tanzy snuck out behind them and returned a few minutes later with a fresh jug of red and a couple of J's. He was an excellent scrounger. My own sense of time started to get a little squooshy after that, but soon enough we were ready to liberate the turkeys.

Padget fetched Strangefield to carve them up, which he did with remarkable speed and finesse, having grown up on an estate in the New Hampshire woods, and hunted wild game since he was a little boy.

CHAPTER ELEVEN

Once the main course and all the trimmings were out of the kitchen, we realized that we didn't have to stick around there anymore. The pies remained all nicely lined up on the butcher block counter for the waiters to deal with later. Though I was dead on my feet from the kitchen ordeal and the hike up Owl's Head, not to mention staying up until after two in the morning the night before, I was very eager to see how it was going over at the Odd Fellows hall. Weezil and I headed over together. Not only were we exhausted, but also pretty lit from drinking red wine and smoking weed the final hour. We had to practically prop each other up staggering over there. It was cold enough outside to see your breath but it felt so refreshing after all those hours in the hot kitchen, like a plunge in the lake on a summer's day. The inky sky overhead sparkled with stars that were never so bright or twinkly back home. I couldn't remember ever feeling so happy to be in a place, certainly not back home or at NYU.

"It was so much fun doing all that," Weezil said. "Wasn't it great?"

"Yeah, it was great."

"Sophie's such a tyrant. They could put you in her job. Oh I hope they do!"

"That's a really hard job. It could turn anyone into a monster."

Weezil rose on her tiptoes and kissed me on the cheek as we reached the front steps of the Odd Fellows hall. You could hear the commotion inside. Weezil was such happy little creature. Her name, it turned out, was an inversion of her given name, Louise. I could tell we were going to be friends.

The scene in the great hall was dazzling, merry, and raucous. The tables set up the night before blazed with candles and groaned with platters of our Thanksgiving goodies. The villagers wore their flashiest outfits: spangles, sequins, silks, satins, feathers, jeans with little mirrors sewn on, long trailing gowns, big poofy flamenco skirts, Fred Astaire tails, naval tunics, buckskin shirts, circus tights, top hats, bandanas, rhinestone tiaras. It was like a Fellini movie. My everyday clothes were all splattered with grease and gravy and other crap, but I didn't care. Lovely Renaissance dance music played on the giant speakers in the background. Folks were eating, everybody talking intensely, laughing. There was plenty of wine and a haze of weed smoke hung under the high ceiling with its painted zodiac signs as though the big room had its own weather with clouds and stars and everything. Nobody noticed us slip in, thank God. I'd flashed on the mortifying thought that Maya would make a big deal of me saving the day in the kitchen, and I absolutely didn't want to be shoved into any spotlight like that. Nobody likes a do-gooder, really, especially somebody who is new on the scene. To my relief, that didn't happen.

Once in the banquet hall, I realized that I was absolutely starving, having only tasted a little of this and that all day long while we worked. I could see Ricky Spillman across the room yukking it up with Scott Provost and a bunch of people I didn't know, and I was about to go over there and shoehorn myself into his table when

Danny Musser came out of nowhere, took my elbow, and steered me to his long table nearer the middle.

"I saved you a seat," he said.

"Why...?"

"Because I like you," he said as though it should have been obvious.

He actually held out a chair for me like a gentleman and then poured me a white wine in a mason jar glass, told me to sit tight, and then went around to all the semi-obliterated turkey platters and serving bowls and scrounged up a fully-loaded plate for me of all the dishes we'd put out, including plenty of mashed potatoes and stuffing with gravy. I liked that he knew I wanted a lot of those particular items. It felt so good to finally sit down. I chugged the wine and attacked the plate as if I had straggled in from a battlefield. He soon refilled my wine glass, then went and got me seconds. By this time, there was some activity on the stage. Guys were turning on amps, testing microphones, tuning guitars. After a while, somebody turned off the recorded music. A chubby, Buddha-like guy with long black hair and a headband came out, sat down behind the drums, and whacked them tentatively as if warming up. He was joined by a guitar player whose flashy electric noodlings fed back and crackled over the amp. He wore just a patchwork satin vest and no shirt so he could display his excellent torso. They played some spacey, quasi-oriental blues figures for a while, sort of Country Joe and the Fish style, music you could just relax and settle into like a warm bath if you were stoned. They were joined by a handsome blonde guy with long spanielly hair and blousy shirt of white stars on a blue background, like the flag, and a floppy hat sporting an ostrich feather. He plugged in a bass guitar and began laying down lines. Some of the people out at the tables clapped and whistled.

Just then the waiters paraded through the door with the pies loaded on trays. That actually got more applause than the music, and just behind the pies, two men I hadn't seen around the village the past two days entered the big room. One was a black guy dressed in a common green USA army winter fatigue jacket. He had sunglasses on, of course, despite the fact it was night outside and kind of romantically dim inside the great hall. The other was a white guy with one of those three-flap military hats made of shearling wool, like the leader of the Mamas and Papas wore, but then a herringbone suit jacket and an oxford shirt with a red paisley tie that was revealed when he unwound his gray wool muffler. He had on John Lennon style wire-rimmed glasses and no facial hair, though his sideburns ran down low down along his ears. As soon as these two had entered the big room, a tangible energy pulse ran through the place. Guys came up to them and gave them the hippie high five. Maya fairly flew across the room and flung herself into the white guy's arms and parked a big kiss on his mouth, a tableau that provoked a lot of stoned and drunken cheering. Other girls flocked around him. The black guy had his admirers too. They brought him a wine and lighted joints.

"Who're those guys?" I asked Danny, with my mouth full of stuffing and cranberry sauce.

"That's Songbird, our benefactor," he said.

"Jeez, that's Songbird? He's all… preppy."

"That's Songbird," Danny repeated. "The golden prepster."

"I expected someone more like Mick Jagger."

Danny cocked his head and gave me the squint-eye. "Not hardly."

"Who's that with him?"

"That's Mule."

"Mule? Like the animal?"

"Yeah. He's Songbird's aide-de-camp."

"Is he, like, a Black Panther or something?"

"Let's just say he's a complex cat."

"Does he have a regular name."

"I would think so, but I don't know what it is."

"Hmmmph. Is Maya Songbird's girlfriend?"

"Yeah. She's his old lady. Stay out of her way around him."

Songbird and Mule went to a table right at front-center where a couple of seats had been saved for them. Maya and others bustled around getting them plates of food and bottles of wine. It was like King Arthur and Sir Lancelot had returned to Camelot from the crusades.

"Who's the old guy at their table?" I was referring to this flinty character, very thin, with a scraggly gray beard and an old-fashioned checked lumberjack shirt held up by wide buff suspenders. He looked like one of those ancient, gnarled New Englanders out of O'Neill's *Desire Under the Elms.*

"That's Mr. Heathman," Danny said. "Sumner Heathman. He was the only person living up here when Songbird bought the property. He was squatting in the Pisces house. He supposedly worked here years ago when the place was a dude ranch. Everybody thinks he's a wizard or a warlock. He can heal people, they say. I'll get you some pie."

I appreciated Danny taking care of me as he did, but I was getting quite trashed on all that wine and dope. A few more musicians came onstage, including Maya herself at one of the microphones, in a lovely, flowery top that fluttered with her movements as if she were a butterfly. A bright lamp came on up in the balcony projecting psychedelic blobs of colored light on the backdrop above the musicians. Finally, the band quit noodling and launched into an actual song, not a cover version of some hit off the radio, an original I supposed. I remember being impressed by how good they sounded. Some of the people left their seats and started dancing and grooving in the wide aisle off to each side of the tables.

"I have to go to bed," I told Danny when he returned with a wedge of pumpkin pie.

"Are you okay?"

"I'm plastered."

"Want me to walk you back?"

"No place to go back to?"

"I thought they give you a room to crash in."

"The guy I came with. He's using it."

"You're not using it together?"

"No."

"How come?"

"I told you, he's not my boyfriend."

"Oh?" Danny said, brightening up. "Well, there's my place."

"I'll go any place where I can lie down."

"Come on, let's go."

He grabbed the nearest wine bottle off the table, and snatched a candle stub and stuffed it in his pocket, and helped me out of my chair. I needed help. My legs were all rubbery after standing up most of the day. I needed more help walking out of the hall. Outside the stars above appeared to spin. I had to stop looking up there. Instead of invigorating, now the cold air made me feel shivery and sick. We'd gotten about a hundred paces down street when I let go of Danny and lunged for the picket fence in front of the Gemini House, and barfed over it into the weeds there. Danny patted my back until I was done.

"All that lovely food," I muttered, spitting out the residue. "What a waste."

"It's all right," he said. "Are you done?"

"Not sure."

"Might as well let it all hang out."

"Yeah. You're right."

I stuck my finger down my throat and made rest of it come up.

"How can you stand me?" I asked afterward.

"You're quite standable."

"Jesus...."

I reached for wine bottle and rinsed my mouth out with a big glug, and spat it out onto the weeds.

Then we were in his room upstairs in the Leo House where he lived with Padget and one other guy, Jodie Palko, who happened to be playing drums onstage back at the great hall. Danny's mattress was on the floor. He was a neatnik, though. The covers were pulled up and clean looking. There was a lamp and an ashtray on the floor, and a small pile of books with the paperback of *Catch 22* on top. A big black and white poster of Dylan hung over the mattress. Old Bob was saluting the photographer out in the woods somewhere and his lips looked all chapped.

"I gotta brush my teeth," I said.

Danny showed me across the hall to the bathroom and lent me his toothbrush. I cleaned myself up as much as possible without climbing into the shower. Drunk as I was, I still felt nervous about what might happen next. When I returned to his room, he'd put a record on his portable hifi. It was Bob, of course, singing his magnum opus, "Sad-Eyed Lady of the Lowlands," the jingle-jangle guitars behind that heartbreaking harmonica, Bob moaning those astonishing lyrics. The candle stub flickered on the windowsill.

Before I could collapse, he joined his hands around my waist, pulled me toward him, and made to kiss me. I tried to avoid his mouth.

"Don't. I'm still all barfy."

"You're okay now. You brushed, right?"

"Can't we just lie down?"

"All right."

So we did. That was the last thing I remember until I opened my eyes the next morning, and saw cool winter light coming through the window. My head felt like it was filled with weevils gnawing through my brain cells. I didn't have a clue where I was for several moments. I felt warmth on one side and rolled over and saw Danny's dark brown curls on the pillow. I dimly remembered coming there with him the night before but the rest was kind of a blur. And then I realized that I had no clothes on, no underpants, nothing. Well, I did have my little Timex wristwatch on. It said five minutes to eleven.

When you're that hungover, every moment seems like a calamity. Just keeping your eyes open brings on intimations of doom. I could hear the needle of the record player skipping through the grooves at the end of the album we'd left spinning on the turntable. *Thwit thwit thwit.* That annoying sound made everything worse. It occurred to me that Ricky might be worriedly waiting for me back at the inn, wanting to get in the car and head back home, and that I really had to get out of there. But first I had to talk to Danny.

I rolled all the way over and pressed up against him. He squirmed as if coming out of his dream and I felt his hand reach behind and find my hip.

"Are you awake?" I whispered.

"Good morning, beautiful."

He started rolling over. As he did, I propped myself up and held the covers up over my front.

"Hey, where ya going?" he growled. "Come back here."

"I have to ask you: did we have sex last night?'

He just kind of blinked back at me.

"Please, tell me. It's important."

"You really don't know?"

I was so frustrated and my head hurt so much, I started to cry. He reached up and ran the back of his fingers down my cheek.

"No, please. Tell me?" I insisted.

"What's the matter?"

"I had an abortion the week before I drove up here."

"Aren't you on the pill? Everyone's on the pill."

"I fucked up and forgot to take it just that one time," I said and started outright blubbering.

"Okay," he said. "We didn't have sex."

"For real?"

"Yeah. For real."

"How'd I get naked?"

"I took your clothes off."

"Why'd you take my clothes off if you didn't intend to have sex with me."

"You kind of helped me take them off."

"I did?"

"Yeah. And then you passed out."

"And you didn't take advantage of me?"

"I'm not a necrophiliac."

"But why'd you take my clothes off."

He readjusted the pillow behind his head.

"I wanted to see how beautiful you are."

"You didn't fuck me?"

"I did not. But I definitely wanted to."

"You swear?"

"I swear we did not have sex."

I nodded and snorfled up all the teary snot in my throat.

"Sorry I don't have any Kleenex," he added.

"Thanks anyway," I said. "Please don't be offended, but I have to go."

"Aw...."

"No, really, that guy I came here with, he's driving back down and I need to catch a ride with him. He's probably wondering where the hell I am."

"You're coming back, right?"

"Yeah. As soon as I pack up the crap in my dorm room down in the city."

"That must be weird. Living in a dorm in New York City."

"Everything about living in the city is weird."

"Well, okay," Danny said. "Then you'll be back. And I'll be here."

"You promise we didn't do anything last night?"

"Yes. I promise. Nothing happened. You were unconscious."

"I can't go through another abortion. I'd have to kill myself."

"You will not get pregnant from sleeping here last night — unless you're the new Virgin Mary."

"Okay. I'm sorry I'm so neurotic, asking you over and over."

"I'm sorry you had to get an abortion. Did you love the guy?"

I almost started crying again but managed to stop myself.

"No," I said. "It was just a dumb mistake. The whole thing. Including him."

"Can I kiss you before you go?" he asked.

"Oh... okay."

He rose up and our lips met. I put my arms around his neck. The covers fell away from my breasts and he placed a hand on one, touched the nipple with his fingertips, and then slid his hand under, kind of hefting it as if enjoying its weight.

"You are beautiful," he said.

"You're sweet to say so," I told him and finally got up and looked around for my various articles of clothing. I was sorry to have to put my jeans and my jersey top back on because they were so crusted with yesterday's kitchen crud. Danny was lighting his first cigarette of the day when I gave him a spastic little wave from the doorway and left.

"Bye...."

Ricky Spillman was indeed waiting in one of the easy chairs in the big common room at the inn, where I'd played banjo with the others that first night. It made me feel better to remember how great it was to play music and sing with the others, and know I would come back and do more of it. Ricky was obviously upset, but the only way he let it show was nervously jiggling his leg.

"Have a good time last night?" he asked, smiling, shaking his lanky hair away from his eyes, dragging on a butt.

I didn't know how to answer him. It absolutely stumped me. I don't think he even knew that I'd spent the whole afternoon toiling in the kitchen. There were already about a dozen villagers over by the breakfast bar, but this morning nobody had bothered to put out any food or made any coffee, I guess because Sophie was out of commission.

"I got shitfaced and passed out," I told him.

"Is that all?"

"Apparently."

"No action?"

"No," I said. "How about you?"

He stood abruptly and zipped up his coat.

"Well, I don't have to come back here," he said with a crooked smile. "Let's split. We can grab some coffee and donuts in Bennington."

He had my backpack with him, since I'd left it up in his room. It took me a minute to remember where I'd left my coat. Then I had to find out the village phone number, and stash my banjo in the Village office for safekeeping, and make sure that I took that day's birth control pill. It was noon before we were on the road again heading back into the real world. I didn't want to stay in it long.

CHAPTER TWELVE

It was around seven o'clock at night when Ricky dropped me off in front of Sieff Hall, my dorm at NYU. The appalling noise and commotion of the city inflamed my nervous system like a reprise of that morning's hangover.

"I hope it works out for you up there," he said as we sat idling at the curb.

Of course, we'd verbally dissected all the minute details of our two days in Vermont and what we'd observed about the dynamics of Sunrise Village on the long ride back. There was no more to say about that now.

"Call your folks," he added.

"Uccchhh. Do I have to?"

"You better. If you don't, they'll call in a missing persons on you, and then surely the police will call me before anyone else, so—"

"Okay. Of course. You're right. This is so embarrassing."

"Just let them know that you're okay."

"No. Not that. Believe me, I'll call them. The thing is, I only have, like, four bucks left to my name and I have to get a bus ticket tomorrow."

"Poor Pooh," he said, but then he reached for his wallet. He took out all the folding money and leafed through it and forked over everything but a five dollar bill, which he held up. "For the tunnel," he said.

"You're like my dad."

"We both love you, you know."

It made me tear up again. The cash he gave me amounted to thirty-eight bucks. It seemed like enough.

"I'll pay you back, I swear."

"Sure. Like in 1990, maybe."

"You have a great time out in Ohio."

"Hey, write to me!"

"I will," I said. I gave him a final big hug and got out. He peeled off.

As it happened, my roommate Carol Keating was actually up in the room because she was from San Francisco and she couldn't fly all the way across the country for a mere four-day holiday. NYU kept the dorms open for people like her but there was no food service during the break. Not that it was hard to find a meal in Manhattan.

"What are you doing here?" Carol asked when I barged in. She had no reason to expect me back the Friday night after Thanksgiving. It wasn't even eight o'clock and she was already in bed, all flustered. I suspected she'd been having a solo make-out session with herself. I told her I was dropping out and came back to pack up my stuff, but I was vague about where I was going because she was sure to tell the RA, who would tell the dean, and I didn't want it getting back to Marilyn and my father before I managed to contact them. You could tell she thought I was nuts. I had one large soft suitcase in my half of the closet. I couldn't pack everything I'd accumulated. Carol didn't want any of my extra clothes because she was barely over five feet tall to my almost five-ten. I ignored the schoolbooks, stacked on my desk. My father had given me a powerful Zenith portable radio that I wanted to bring with me. I asked her if she wanted my tennis racket, which I hadn't used once since coming to NYU.

"Not really," she said. "Do your folks know you're leaving?"

"I'm going to call them when I get where I'm going," I said.

"You're not pregnant, are you?"

"If I was, I'd get an abortion," I said.

She stopped asking me questions after that, though I hadn't meant to insult her Catholic faith. When I was all packed, I went to the pay phone in the hall and got the number for Greyhound Bus information. The guy told me to call the Yankee Trails line. One dime down. Yankee Trails did have a bus going to Bennington, thank God, but with a lot of other stops in between, leaving at six-thirty in the morning — uccchhh! — and arriving at three-thirty in the afternoon. They said the ticket was twenty-three fifty. With that giant suitcase, I'd have to take a cab uptown to the Port Authority Bus Station, probably a buck and a half, and it left me some extra money for food and cigarettes. To be polite, I asked Carol if she wanted to get a bite with me, but she declined. I suppose she wanted to finish what she'd been doing before I barged in.

Believe it or not, I went over to the old Jade Dragon on West 4th Street, where Don Bessemer and I had romanced each other — not out of any masochistic sense of nostalgia but because they served a humungous combo platter for three ninety-five, complete with tea and fortune cookies, and I was starving. On the way back, I dropped another three-fifty on a carton of Winstons, my smoke of choice, not knowing when I'd be anywhere near a store again after I returned to Sunrise Village.

When I got back to the dorm a little before ten, Carol was asleep. She had one of those little folding travel alarm clocks next to her bed. I borrowed it and set it for five-thirty. I fell asleep immediately, considering how rough the previous two nights had been. It was still dark when the alarm went off. I felt bad about it, but I had to switch on the light. Of course, Carol had woken up, too. She twisted around in bed and squinted at me.

"Goshdarn it, Pooh!" she said. That was pretty strong language for her.

I said I was sorry about nine times.

You know what Carol said to me when I switched out the light and made to leave the room for good?

"Stay away from drugs, Pooh!"

"Don't worry, I will. Good luck with college and whatever happens after. Life and all."

It was easy to catch a cab at that hour on a Saturday morning. I got a nice window seat on the bus and was asleep again as we rolled out of the terminal. By the time I woke up, we were pulling into the Danbury, Connecticut, station. I was hugely relieved to be out of the city, but after that there was something dispiriting about the procession of small towns we stopped at along the way. They all looked played out, spent, seedy, as if the war in Vietnam was visibly draining them of their vitality. The man next to me left *The New York Times* on his seat when he got off in Waterbury. It said American troops were fighting for another meaningless toehold in the Dakto region of the Central Highlands, a bump in the jungle called Hill 875. The paper said that a hundred fifty-eight US troops had been killed and more than four hundred wounded in the battle for that hill. It depressed me to think how detached the humdrum daily life of these little towns we passed through was from the carnage we were inflicting halfway around the world, plus all those young men losing their lives, many of them just my age. I could barely stand to read about it. Instead, as the sepia November landscape rolled by, my mind turned to the village and the recent memory of Danny Musser kissing me, holding his hand under my breast, and I spun out this fantasy about how I was going to be his old lady, and we would play music every night, and make love afterward in his tidy room, with Bob Dylan saluting us up on the wall — and I couldn't carry this thought any further because I had no idea where the life I was barely starting up there might lead. But at least I took some solace in the fact that my interest in sex was coming back.

A half hour after I called the Sunrise Village office number, Weezil drove up to the bus station in a beat-up Rambler. I was so happy to see her. She said that Sophie was back in the kitchen, as mean as ever, but not able to do much physically because she had her arm in sling. I asked her about Danny Musser and learned more than I wanted to. He had a reputation, she said, for sleeping with every new female arrival — but that she, Weezil, had already been there when Danny arrived last June, and they had never done it. She wondered what it would be like. She'd heard that he had a big one, and she was quite petite and small down below, she said. Right now, she'd heard, he was making it with Krista — the Viking chick. That certainly pricked the bubble of my fantasy. I didn't tell her that I'd passed out in his bed naked Thanksgiving night, or that I would prefer she didn't try to make it with him just now, if she could hold off. Of course, it seemed like everybody was making it with whoever they could up there, so why wouldn't he get around to Weezil eventually? And then, I thought, maybe he'd stop compulsively screwing everyone when he found the right girl, someone he really liked a lot, like me, for instance. My mind was just spinning the whole way out of town, and Weezil kept chattering about the various guys she'd made it with, and I barely took in a word of what she said. Anyway, when we got to the Village, Weezil told me I was supposed to go see Maya in the office over at the Great Hall. She had to go back to Sophie's kitchen to help put dinner out.

I left my suitcase in the vestibule there and went upstairs. I was glad to see my banjo case where I'd left it in the office. Maya was on the phone with somebody haggling about the price of some piece of equipment that came in either one hundred twelve or two hundred fifty gallon sizes. She pointed to the empty chair beside the desk, one of those solid old oak swivel chairs. I sat down. She concluded her call, sighed, and turned the full force of her attention to me.

"There you are," she said with what looked like an effortful smile. "Back from the city already. I hear your friend decided not to stay."

"There was never any question," I said. "He likes it at college."

"Of course. Some people do."

"Did you go?" I asked.

"Yeah. Wellesley."

"That's a very good school," I said. "I never could have gotten in there with my grades. You must be smart. What was your major?"

"Poli-sci," Maya said. I sensed she was impatient with me, and indeed she changed the subject, right back to business. "We've got you in room thirteen at the inn—"

"Thirteen? That's kind of ominous."

"Are you superstitious?" she asked.

"I don't know. Not really. Sometimes I feel like I have to avoid the cracks in the sidewalk. Of course, back in New York you're on the sidewalks all the time, and life is so nerve-wracking there it probably makes you slightly nuts. But I'm not a kook about—"

Maya cut off my babbling. I was certainly strung out mentally after traveling from pillar to post so much in a few days and getting so little sleep.

"It's actually one of the nicer rooms," she said. "It's on the south side of the building, warms up nicely in the winter sun. There's a bay window with a window seat."

"Oh. Groovy. Well, sure. Thirteen's fine."

"Great," she said. "That settles that."

She looked up at me with that strained smile again.

"Do I get a key?" I asked.

"We don't have keys. Last summer, a guy OD'd in his room. It took us twenty minutes to get in there. He didn't die but it was a close call. If you want, we'll give you a hook-and-eye for the door.

We can break through those easily enough, but it will inform casual visitors that privacy is desired."

"I get it—"

"Oh, and we don't tolerate any hard drugs — needless to say, but I'll say it anyway — anything that involves needles. If we hear about that, you are gone, gone, gone."

"Understood. I have no interest in hard—"

"We're assigning you to the housekeeping crew to start."

"Housekeeping? Like, cleaning up?"

"That's right. Most new arrivals have at least some experience with that. And somebody's got to do it. The other tasks around here require actual skills."

"I have skills. That was me in the kitchen Thanksgiving day. Remember?"

"Yes, I remember. But that was an emergency. Sophie's back on the job."

"I could still help out there—"

"That's not possible right now."

"How come?"

Maya paused and kind of drilled her eyes into mine.

"Frankly, I suggested it. But if you really want to know, Sophie said the two of you had a personality conflict."

"Jeez, we were barely together for an hour before she slipped and hurt herself."

"I'm just telling you that's how she feels about it."

I was thinking: *that goddamn bitch*! But I kept my mouth shut.

"Obviously it's a crucial position here," Maya went on. "Getting all those meals out every day. It's a lot of responsibility. Sophie's been here from the start. I have to respect her feelings and her experience."

"Well, sure—"

"And you won't stay in housekeeping forever. As I said, we put the new people there, and there are always new people coming, so you'll rotate out after a while."

"How many do you expect to take in eventually?"

"We don't know yet. That's something we're trying to figure out."

"I'd say a hundred, maximum, just eyeballing stuff."

She obviously wasn't interested in my opinion.

"I have just a few other things here," Maya said, lighting a Kool cigarette from the pack on her desk.

"Say, can I have one of those."

"Help yourself."

"I don't smoke menthols generally but sometimes they're hard to resist. Like when someone else lights one. The first is so refreshing, but after that it's—"

"I have some more phone calls to make," Maya said. "Can we just finish up?"

"Oh, sure. Sorry. God, yes, of course." I had turned into a blithering blabbermouth. I wanted to shoot myself.

"Have you ever had a sexual disease?" Maya asked.

"I got pregnant and had an abortion not too long ago."

"Oh?" Maya said, still looking through me like I was an aquarium filled with curious little fishes. "Sorry to hear that. Of course that's not a disease. Anything like syphilis? Gonorrhea?"

"God no!"

"We have to ask. We have an arrangement with a doctor down in Bennington who sees our people. If you have any problem, you come tell us right away and we will take you to see him. Understand?"

"Yes."

"This is something we dare not fuck around with, considering how much fucking around there is here."

I smiled, thinking she was being witty, but Maya did not smile back.

"He'll also set up your birth control prescription. You're on it, I assume."

"Sure, of course...."

"The world has enough babies — don't you think?"

"Well, uh, I guess...."

"You bet it does. What else... let's see...." She rummaged through some papers on a clipboard. "There's a room on the first floor of the inn that's sort of a communal clothing closet. Men's stuff on one side, women on the other. If there's any clothing you don't want or have gotten bored with, bring it there. You'd be surprised how much somebody else might like it."

"Sure—"

"And one final thing. I shouldn't have to say this.... Well, there is a lot of loose sex around here, obviously, but Songbird is off limits."

"Oh, of course—"

"You know how men are. They sometimes think with the little head, not the big head."

"Uh, excuse me? Their what?"

"Their dicks," Maya said, with an squeak of tension in her voice. "They think with their dicks instead of their brains."

"I guess you're right about that."

"Of course I'm right. Because of his position here, Songbird has to show an extra degree of restraint. Believe me," she said, lowering her voice. "Every chick here wants to ball him. And when all is said and done, he's just a pathetic, morally weak male human being. You know what I'm saying?"

"That men are pathetic."

"I'm saying keep your paws off him, to put it bluntly."

"I wasn't even thinking of—"

"Obviously you understand. That's all I have to say about that, and I won't repeat it. Now, since you're new, he wants to meet you one-on-one tomorrow. Go over to the Aquarius House at three o'clock. It's Sunday and that's a mellow day around here. Unstructured. No work, unless there's some project going that you want to work on for the sheer enjoyment of it. And the kitchen, of course. All right, we're done." Maya extended her hand across the desk. "I formally welcome you to Sunrise Village, where the present looks both ways, toward the past and the future."

We shook.

"Hey, that's a groovy motto."

"Its literally the truth," Maya said, as she squashed her cigarette out in the ashtray.

CHAPTER THIRTEEN

Room Thirteen, on the second floor rear of the back wing of the inn was pretty nice, all right. The window-seat needed a cushion. By the time I got up there, lugging that big suitcase, my radio, and my banjo, night had fallen and you couldn't see what the bay window looked out on. Three of the walls had gotten a sloppy paint job, and the remaining wall still showed the remnants of yellowish flowery wallpaper. The wood floor was painted gray. There was an actual full-size bed, an old scratched-up mahogany thing, perhaps left over from the gangster hotel era. When I tested it out, the springs were as weak as mush and squeaky. It would have to go. A mattress on the floor was better for your back, anyway. On my way to that closet full of bedding that Ricky and I had discovered the first night, I was seized by an impulse to go drop in on Danny Musser. So I left the inn, and hurried down the street without my coat to the Leo house. The sun had already set. In the hallway outside his room, I thought I saw some lamplight leaking under the door, so I knocked. There was no response. After a moment's thought, I reached for the doorknob and tried to open it. It only opened a half-inch and stopped. Apparently, a hook-and-eye lock was engaged on the other side.

"Who's there?" I heard Danny say.

I didn't answer, but recoiled from the door, and then tip-toed away as fast as I could. I assumed he was in there with the Krista the Viking, or some other chickie, but on my way back to the inn I realized he might have just been in there by himself, resting or reading, not wanting to be disturbed. It's not good to always think the worst of every situation and everyone. But then I also realized that he only spoke up when I tried to open the door, so maybe he was with someone after all. I got all worked up about it. Anyway, I found sheets and blankets in the closet and arranged my stuff in the room, and by six o'clock I wandered downstairs in search of some food.

Saturday night Sophie had off and her helpers put out trays of cheese and cold-cuts and peanut butter and bread so people could make their own sandwiches, plus bags of potato chips and a big platter of brownies. At six o'clock, many of the other villagers had gathered there by the old bar. I found Jan Heathcoate, the dark-haired guitar player, and sat down with her and Billy Herman at one of the many round restaurant tables that remained from the earlier years. I felt rather blue and didn't say much. Having three not great nights' sleep in a row surely didn't help. Jan wasn't wearing a bra and you could see her nipples and the nearly perfect shape of her breasts very clearly protruding against the fabric of her T-shirt. No wonder the men in the village were perpetually horny, the way we women advertised our assets. I wasn't wearing a bra either, though I had a shaggy sweater on.

Billy said great job on pulling together Thanksgiving, and this time I actually appreciated a little acknowledgment, and I said that Maya had just stuck me on the cleaning crew and they said not to take it personally, it was the normal routine there. I started to feel a little better, especially as I crammed down a ham and cheese sandwich — and I had to admit, Sophie really did make great bread. Just then, somebody put their hands over my eyes and I lowered my sandwich and a familiar voice said, "Welcome back, Pooh."

I corkscrewed around in my chair. It was good old Danny Musser looking so handsome in a turquoise western shirt with pink cactus flowers embroidered on it, and his long hair all fluffed up like he just got out of the shower, and that magnetic toothy smile beaming down. He leaned over and kissed me on the forehead. "Want to jam later?" he asked.

I was flustered to see him.

"Yeah, I dunno, I guess...."

"Be right back," he said.

He went over to the bar where the buffet spread was laid out and made himself a sandwich. I wondered if he got all showered and clean because a half hour before he was rolling around in the sack with Krista the Viking getting drenched in lady-juices. My jealousy was so idiotic I wanted to divorce myself. But then Dave Padget came over with Alison Bartosz, the flute player, and everyone started talking about songs and instrumental arrangements, and I got the warm, comforting feeling that I had been adopted by a great little musical family within the greater Sunrise Village tribe.

We did jam after dinner. I postponed calling my Dad. I wanted to reach him at work, where there was no chance Marilyn might pick up the phone. It depressed me that I disliked my mother so much, and I wondered if there was something morally wrong with me not being able to tolerate her.

Playing music after dinner tuned out all that noise in my head. We worked on several of the songs and harmonies that we explored that first night, and some new ones, and it was magical again. We all sensed it. And when we were done, I just went with Danny to his room. We didn't even talk about it. I just took his hand and followed him. The moon was out and shining through the window of his room. I let him pull my sweater off, and I unbuttoned his flashy shirt, and soon we were naked together under the covers, all warm and shivery, and he was surprisingly slow and gentle with me, like a good country music ballad, asking me along the way, "is this all right? Is that all right?" And I said, "Yes, you're all right… every thing you do to me is all right… now come inside of me, please, I can't stand it anymore…."

CHAPTER FOURTEEN

It was quite a night. I couldn't say when we finally fell asleep, but it was past noon when we woke up for good the next day. Luckily, they had some granola and salami and Fritos stashed at the Leo house, though it didn't have an actual kitchen, just an old metal camping cooler in the parlor. Since it was Sunday, we lazed around naked in Danny's room, eating greedily, drinking ginger ale out of the bottle, and listening to Bob moan about his *warehouse eyes and Arabian drum* on the record player.

"I like you," I told him after we made love one more time.

"I never would have guessed," he said.

"No, you're supposed to say, *I like you too*,"

"Oh…?"

"Come on, say it!"

I shoved him against the pillows and climbed on him and dangled my breasts in his face.

"I like you, too," he said.

"You like these, don't you?" I bobbled them.

"Pretty much," he said. "You're… something."

I climbed back off and grabbed the Frito bag away from him. "Thank you for the compliment."

"I mean it."

"Of course you do."

I wanted to ask him if I was going to be his old lady now, but I just couldn't. It seemed ridiculous considering what I knew about him, and where we were, and how things worked there. I didn't even like the popular locution, *old lady.* It was like something a dock-worker would call his sweetheart. Even if I'd landed in a place that was an actual hippie commune, I did not conceive of myself as a hippie. And though I was sexually liberated (ha!), I still felt that making love with somebody was, in effect, a kind of promise. But a promise of what? Eternal devotion and fidelity, I guess, which is rather unrealistic at age nineteen. Anyway, you can't enforce another person's promise. I just wanted him to say that I could be his girlfriend, but he didn't, of course. He just let it lay, and I let it lay for now, too, and by then I had to get going.

So I went back to my new room at the inn and tested out the nearest shower down the hall. Nobody barged in me, at least. And then I went over to the Aquarius house at the appointed hour, as instructed, looking for Songbird. The smallish cottage at the end of the village's only side-street was an interesting old wreck, with a single dormer on the second floor. The porch roof, apparently under reconstruction, was propped up by paired-together two-by-four braces. Some clapboards on one side of the building tentatively painted around a first floor window, as though they were testing out the colors: buttery-yellow with white trim. A rubber runner mat was laid over the as-yet-unvarnished new mahogany porch decking from the steps to the front door. I knocked and the door opened almost instantly, like someone was waiting there. I practically jumped out of my skin. It was the fresh-faced preppy guy I had glimpsed across the Odd Fellows

Hall on Thanksgiving night: Songbird. He had on khakis, a crew-neck sweater over a button-down shirt, and worn penny loafers, an outfit so unhip it was maybe super-hip.

"Oh, Jeez, it's you," I said.

He glanced over his shoulder as if pretending to look and see if somebody else was there, an overtly comic gesture.

"Who else would it be?" he said. "We don't have servants."

"Right, of course...."

I thought he enjoyed seeing me off balance.

"You must be Pooh Bollinger."

"You know my name?"

"Maya filled me in a little." he said.

Uh-oh, I thought: Maya. I hope I'm not already on her bad side. I guess I was staring blankly back at him like a moron, not knowing what else to say. In fact I was struck by something else.

"You know, you're a dead-ringer for Stephen Stills of the Buffalo Springfield," I blurted out. He didn't seem to have any idea what I was referring to so I sang the lyrics from their hit song of the previous spring. "*There's something happenin' here... what it is ain't exactly clear...*"

"Oh sure, I've heard that. That's the Buffalo Springfield, huh?"

"Yeah. You have the same sideburns as the guitar player."

"Everybody has sideburns these days."

"Yeah, I guess." I was practically squirming, as though my awkwardness was a garment I might shuck off.

"Come on in," he said. "It's chilly out there."

I stepped inside. Considering where we were, I was surprised by what I saw. First of all, it looked bigger inside than from outside. I think that was because the front room was like you might see in *House Beautiful*: very sparely decorated, no clutter, as if a whole lot of thought went into each object on display. There were two beige love-seats flanking a fireplace — where a nice fire was burning — with an antiquey coffee table between them that had ball-and claw feet, and neat stacks of big art books on top and a lovely old copper lantern with a candle in it. A bullseye mirror in a round gilt frame hung over the mantelpiece, on which were some giant seed pods, a shelf fungus, a small animal skull and other natural objects you might find on a walk in the woods. On one side wall was a great big framed Audubon bird print (a pelican), and on another a print of Claude Monet's red poppy field.

"Wow," I said. "You live like regular grownups in here."

"You think?"

"Mind if I ask: how old are you anyway?"

"Twenty-four," he said.

"I'm nineteen. I haven't reached the décor-buying stage of life yet," I babbled.

"Décor..." the word seemed to really amuse him.

"But then, until a few days ago I was living in a college dorm."

"Maya's in charge of... the décor," he said.

"Looks like she's doing a fine job. Hey, I like that color you're testing on the outside wall. The yellow."

"Yeah? Thanks."

"I bet they call it Buttermilk."

"I think its official name is 'Golden Cream.'"

"It's quite creamy," I agreed. He must have thought I was a ninny, by now. "My dad is thinking of buying an old house back home and fixing it up."

"It's rewarding, bringing things back from wrack and ruin. Would you like some tea?"

"Sure."

I followed him into the kitchen. They had one at least. It was pretty basic but nice. Butcher block counters. Nice cabinets. Hanging lights with frosted glass conical shades. He put a red enamel kettle on the burner. I watched him fuss with the tea bags. He put honey in mine without even asking, not that I was anti-honey. I sat on a kitchen stool. For a while we just sipped our tea.

"Tell me about your hopes and dreams, Pooh Bollinger, age nineteen," he eventually said.

That threw me off. My mouth fell open again.

"I… uh… can't say I've actually thought them out. Gee. Now I'm embarrassed," I finally admitted, though I'd been in a state of embarrassment since he opened the front door.

"Well, what brought you here to us?" he asked.

"Oh boy…."I took a deep breath and told him the plain truth about my abortion and how college seemed pointless to me after that — before that even — and how much I hated New York City, and how I heard about Sunrise Village, blah blah. "…so I just took a shot and drove up here and checked it out. It's better than I imagined. I love this place. I love the music."

"Music is turning out to be the art-form of our generation."

Hmmm, I thought. That was actually pretty true.

"Yeah," I said. "There are way more musicians so far in our generation than painters or writers, it seems like. I've been playing some banjo with Danny Musser and the others."

"Dangerous Danny," he said, with a snorty little laugh.

"He's a sweet guy!"

"Yes he is," Songbird agreed. He put his mug down. "What do you say we walk a little. I'll show you around."

"Okay."

He put on that shearling three-flap hat and a quilty ski jacket. He saw that I didn't have a hat, so he bent down to a basket near the door and fished out a pretty knitted wool one. It smelled like Maya: patchouli. We left the house.

"We expect you to put in a minimum five hours of work a day," he said as we walked up the street. "Twenty-five hours a week. That's for the privilege of being here, a room with a bed, meals. Above that, we'll actually pay you. Now, there are some things going on here, and others we're planning: businesses, where a given crew gets to share in the profits if we make any. Come, I'll show you."

We crossed the strip of village green and the street to the old white church and then around the back. Some distance behind it was a newly-built, garage-size shack with a silvery tin smoke-stack coming out of it. Songbird took a key ring out of his pocket and unlocked the door. Inside the shack had an immaculate new concrete floor so clean you could eat off it and some industrial-strength cooking vats and some kind of pressure-tank that looked like an iron-lung connected to a bunch of pipes. None of it had been used yet from what I could tell. The brand labels were still pasted on everything.

"This is going to be our tofu operation," he said. "Soybeans are cheap. It doesn't take much to convert them into a very profitable product. There are natural foods stores opening all over the place, especially in the college towns."

"Yeah," I said. "Tofu's great."

"It's going to be big. A lot of people are going veggie. Are you veggie?"

"No."

"Me neither," he said. "But tofu's going to be big."

Next he took me to one of the old barns behind the church. Inside it was a woodworking shop, with all kinds of new power tools set up: a band saw, table saw, drill press. One wall was pegboard with hand tools and clamps hanging up, all impeccably organized. Nobody was around because it was Sunday. They were making out-door furniture there, mainly those big clunky chairs you see on the lawn at resort hotels and country clubs with a flat arm-rest where you can rest your gin-and-tonic. He said they would eventually use wood grown on the property, when it had time to season. They were also turning out rope hammocks and had sold a fair num-ber of them in country stores all over southern Vermont and the Berkshires the previous summer season, a real money-maker. They were going forward with a commercial operation to make a line of herbal teas, and grow the herbs on the premises, he said. Still in the planning stages was a line of candles and maybe cosmetics made of beeswax and herbs. The Village construction crew, five guys and two women, did work outside the Village: so far, house additions and renovations for some professors over at Bennington College. Village members were permitted to take outside jobs, like Robin the waitress, if they had their own car and could get back and forth, and it had to be above and beyond their twenty-five weekly hours of assigned work at the Village. That seemed fair.

"You want to see something cool?" he said when we were leaving the furniture shop.

"Sure."

"I followed him a little way down a switchback dirt road to the river, just beside which was the main building of Simon Alvord's old Catamount Marble Works, a brick behemoth a hundred yards long with a ridge of clerestory windows on the peak of the roof. Some rusty old railroad tracks with rotting crossties ran along the building's long side. We walked inside through a big steel loading door that hung askew off its track, open to the weather. Inside the cavernous place lay blocks and slabs of cut marble, and also a row of cemetery headstones awaiting inscription that had been carved in various motifs of angels and lambs. They apparently never got sent out before the place shut down. The meager November light poured in all purple through giant industrial windows. You could hear the Marble River whoosh and burble just outside because quite a few of the window panes were missing. It was like being in a ruined cathedral dedicated to the religion of industry. Overhead up in the high ceiling loomed a network of steel beams with mechanical hoists and chains hanging down. He pointed up at them.

"That's how they wrangled all this stone around," he said. "Very intelligent. None of it works anymore. We haven't figured out exactly what to do with this big old place yet. We'd like to at least get some hydroelectric going so we don't have to keep paying Southern

Vermont Power and Light. There's a mill-race on the river just beside the building."

"What's a mill race?"

"It's a way of concentrating the flow of river to turn a wheel. You can power an electric turbine with that."

"Sounds promising," I remarked. "Isn't it sad how we just let things go in this country?"

"It's going to get a lot worse," he said. "Those other countries we beat in World War Two, they're back on their feet. The Japs and the Germans are making cars again. Pretty soon they'll make good ones. Things have weird consequences, you know. We bombed the shit out of their factories in the war. Yet they couldn't bomb ours."

"Why?"

"The oceans. We had air bases close to them in England and in the Pacific Islands. They didn't have anything like that close to us."

"I see—"

"But now, twenty-odd years later, look: they have brand-spanking new factories and ours are all beat-to-shit old ones from eighteen eighty-three. And I don't think we're going to replace them. This Vietnam War is just the beginning of a long trip down the drain for America. History is a bitch."

I guess I didn't know much about how the war was actually fought. To me, it was one big John Wayne movie. Songbird had an appealing teacherly manner that I liked.

"So what happens, then? Do the Russians take over the world?"

"Forget the Russians," he said. "Their system is doomed, too. It's just gangster government with a veneer of ideology to make it look respectable."

"Then the Japs and the Germans overtake us."

"Only temporarily. They might even end up fighting each other, who knows? The big secret is: nobody takes over the world. We're fucking up the planet so badly that nature forces us to stop.

Over-population, pollution, bad farming practices, this stupid war in Vietnam. You can see, it's really affecting us."

"So what happens to all those unneeded new humans that keep being born?"

"The usual suspects pay the earth a call."

"And who are these usual suspects?"

"Starvation, disease, war. Vietnam is just the start."

"Do we end up using atom bombs?"

"You can't rule that out, but it's not necessary to put the kibosh on the way we're living. Let's just put it this way: the human race has to retrench, maybe all the way back to the Middle Ages way of life. We'll be forced to, one way or another."

"So that's how come we're here, in the village?"

"Yeah, we're retrenching."

"Do we end up going medieval?"

"Yeah. Something like that. Probably."

"But obviously you're not against power tools and even cars."

"We use what's available in the meantime. It's a process," he said, and heaved a sigh, as if talking about this stuff exhausted him.

"Hey, we could bring back jousting," I cracked. "Wouldn't that be colorful and romantic?"

"Yeah, that would great. And charge people to watch it."

For a long moment we just listened to the river rush by outside.

"So how'd you get the nickname Songbird? You're not exactly chirpy," I said.

He laughed.

"It's not a nickname. My last name is Sohnberg. S-O-H-N-B-E-R-G," he spelled it out.

"Oh…!"

"You know how people are?"

"Sohnberg," I said. "Sounds Jewish."

"I am, by birth anyway."

"Me too," I said.

"Yeah, well, hey...." he said, and pulled off a glove to offer up the hippie high-five. His hand was surprisingly warm.

"Maybe we can put on a Purim pageant this winter if things get dull," I said and then added, "I was a theater major at NYU, where I just dropped out of, you know."

"I guess I didn't know that."

"Do you ever put on plays here?"

"No. Music, yes, but no plays."

"I could do that for you. You've got a nice stage and all. You could put on Broadway musicals in the summertime and charge the local yokels to come watch. Make a bundle."

"That's an interesting idea," he said, obviously not willing to commit to it yet.

"Anyway," I said, looking to change the subject, "I'm totally un-religious."

"Me too."

"Did you have a bar mitzvah?"

"No. I wasn't sent to Hebrew school. Anyway, that would have been the year my parents passed away, when I turned thirteen."

"Yeah, I heard that you lost them at an early age. Sorry. Must be hard."

I couldn't help noticing that there was a row of unfinished headstones just ten feet away. It gave me a chill.

"Yeah, well.... Anyway, ours was pretty-much a religion-free household," he said. "Art was their religion."

"We lit the candles on Hanukah and went to the temple on Yom Kippur," I said. "My mother insisted. But we had a Christmas tree every year, too. My father insisted. He thought Hanukah was a lame substitute for Christmas. He liked the carols and the glitter and sleigh-bells in the snow and everything."

"Christmas is where it's at, holiday-wise, all right," Songbird said.

"Oh, for sure."

I think we were both getting a chill in the ancient, drafty factory. We could see our breath. The daylight was dimming by the minute. But neither of us wanted to cut the conversation short. A vibe had developed that neither of us were in a position to acknowledge. I liked looking at him. I liked the fact that he didn't present himself as a clichéd hippie. I liked his corny clothing, his smooth face, his goofy hat. I liked his clean smell.

"Is it true that your parents were killed by cannibals?" I couldn't help asking.

"Not exactly."

"I'm sorry — it's none of my business."

"That's okay. It was in the papers. You can look it up on microfilm in *The New York Times.*"

"What happened to them?"

"They were in Western New Guinea, on one of those fabled rivers-of-no-return in the middle of nowhere, tagging along with a gang of ethnologists from the Peabody Museum—"

"Where's that, the Peabody?"

"Harvard."

"Was your dad a professor?"

"No. He and my mom collected native art all around the world. They gave most it away to museums. That was their thing. So, they're out there in the New Guinea jungle a thousand miles from anything. One night, they stay behind in a village on the river, supposedly to dicker with the tribe over some precious objects — some little effigy of a rain god, a shrunken head, a necklace made of boar's teeth, who knows what. They collected all kinds of stuff. They were supposed to paddle up river and rejoin the Harvard guys the next morning. They never showed up. No trace of them was ever found. Not even their aluminum canoe."

"Oh, gosh...."

"It was a long time ago, nineteen fifty-six."

"What was your dad's actual job?"

"He didn't have one. Family money."

"Where did that come from?"

"Boy, you're inquisitive."

"Sorry, I just—"

"No, that's okay. It's all public knowledge. But you're cute about it."

That gave me another chill. I didn't know what to say. Luckily, he went on.

"My great-great-grandfather manufactured artillery for the Union Army. He invented a 12-pound field gun that could destroy fortifications a mile away. They called it the Sohnberg howitzer. It was relatively light and they could move it quickly with horses. Then, in the First World War the company came out with a 155 millimeter gun that matched the up-until-then superior German artillery. They made more stuff for World War Two: cannons for tanks, giant guns for the navy's battleships. The Sohnbergs were war profiteers."

"Are they making stuff for Vietnam?" I asked.

"The family dropped out of the game. My grandfather died a few weeks after V-J day in forty-five. The war pretty much did him in. My dad was not interested in the armaments business, didn't like working in it, wanted out. The war was over. So he sold the company to Griffin-Sturtevant, the aeronautics giant that made the first American jet planes. That left him free to pursue his other interests. He got a master's degree in art history at Columbia and met my mom there. Anyway, there's no actual evidence that they were eaten by cannibals, just speculation in the press because the region where they disappeared was known for having head-hunters. That's pretty much the whole story."

It wasn't, of course, because it wasn't Songbird's story, it was the story of his forebears. His story was still mostly in their shadow. He hadn't spelled it out, but it was apparent that the parents had dropped a fortune on him upon their death, and I could only suppose that it made Sunrise Village possible.

We were both shivering now.

"So, should I call you Songbird or Elliot?" I asked.

"You might as well stick with Songbird for now. Everybody else does." he said. "We better get back before they send out a search party for us."

CHAPTER FIFTEEN

S unday night, our second night together, Danny and I were like an old married couple. Nobody was up for playing music. We went back to his room after dinner, fooled around a little, and then we both ended up reading in bed. I was still exhausted after all that travel and those late nights of the preceding week. He was into a book about the Hell's Angels motorcycle gang by a smart alecky new writer named Hunter S. Thompson. He read me passages that cracked him up so much he could hardly finish the sentence. But, frankly, I didn't find those psychopathic morons so amusing. It was just another thing about the *out there* of America that made me nervous and sad.

Believe it or not, one of the books in the stack next to Danny's mattress was *Been Down So Long It Looks Like Up to Me*. Danny had been an English major at Oberlin and he liked to keep up with contemporary lit. I cracked the first ten pages or so. The main character was one of these exuberant show-off types who constantly has to demonstrate how special and original they are, that nothing like them has ever been seen before in history. How tiresome. Anyway, it was clever enough, but juvenile, probably something that adolescent boys would like rather than young women. But when Danny tore himself away from the Hell's Angels for a moment and noticed me reading that book, he informed me that the author, Richard Farina, had died in a motorcycle crash the day after his book came out. Incredible tragic bummer. Also, he was married to Joan Baez's sister. So, now I understood why every Tom, Dick, and Harry was reading the damn thing. I felt ashamed of myself for disparaging it, even though none of that actually made me like it more.

The next day I joined up with the housekeeping crew after breakfast. The woman in charge was a southerner named Lucy Salmon, twenty-one, from Savannah, Georgia. She had dropped out of Bennington College to be in the Village. I would learn that her father was Teeter Salmon, the famous songwriter who penned the Bing Crosby hit "Low Country Moon" and other wartime favorites. Her father was one-quarter Cherokee Indian and so Lucy had jet-black hair with bangs, cut in a kind of flapper bob. Teeter drank himself to death in Hollywood when Lucy was a small child so her mother moved back east and married the President of the Oglethorpe National Bank, a stable, prudent, boring teetotaler. I learned all this later on while running linens through the wash with her. Lucy was relentlessly cheerful. It turned out she was a really good piano player, too, but she could only play from sheet music. By ear, she could barely manage "Michael Row the Boat Ashore." Some people are like that.

I spent my first day on the job vacuuming the hallways and cleaning bathrooms. Even the people who lived in the Zodiac cottages got basic maid service. It felt like the Village was as much a resort as a commune. The work was not hard and I was done at two o'clock in the afternoon with no more obligations for the day, which is when I finally called Larry, my dad.

I scraped together three dollars in change in preparation and made the call from the pay phone off the breakfast bar at the inn.

There was no one else around at that time of day. I got an operator to connect me to the *Newsday* darkroom direct line, where my dad was likely to be at that hour on a Monday. She made me drop in five quarters. His colleague, Buster Cooney, the sports photographer answered, but Larry was there all right and then he picked up.

"Where the hell are you?" he asked, in a rare flash of anger.

"I'm in Vermont."

"What the hell—"

"You have to call me back at this number. I'm on a pay phone and I don't have a lot of change left."

"Christ, Pooh! Okay, give me the number."

I did. It was right there on the dial. He rang back a few seconds later.

"This is on the company dime, by the way," he said. "They take a dim view of us making long distance calls. What's going on?"

"I've moved up here."

"What's 'up here,' exactly?"

"It's a commune. It's very nice."

"Great. You mean, like, one of those hippie communes?"

"They're just people, Larry—"

"Don't call me Larry. I'm your father, not one of your pals."

"Okay, okay. Calm down."

"Your mother's hysterical. She's going to call the police. Maybe she already has."

"I'm sorry. I'm perfectly all right. I'm fine. I'm actually happy for a change. Tell her to cool it."

"Cool it? What are you, living out some Jack Kerouac bongo drum fantasy? Children don't just disappear on Thanksgiving."

"I'm not exactly a child. And I left a note."

"Yeah, that you went to Connecticut. Only it turns out you're in Vermont. So that was a lie. And you are a child, technically. We're still responsible for you."

"I'm nineteen, for Chrissake!"

"We're still your parents."

"Can we not argue about technicalities?" I said.

There was a pause on the line.

"Where is this place you're at?" he said more calmly.

"Outside of Bennington. It's very well-run. You'd like it."

"You think I should join up? Do they need a photographer on staff to record their orgies and freak-outs?"

"Nobody's freaking out."

"How long are you going stay there, Pooh?"

"I don't know. Indefinitely. I'm, like, here."

"And how are you paying for it?"

"It's not camp, Dad. You have to work to stay here."

"Doing what?"

"I made a whole Thanksgiving dinner for more than sixty people. The cook fell down and broke her collarbone and I had to step in for her. It came out really great. You would have been amazed."

"So you're the cook there all of a sudden?"

"No, she's back again. I'm on the cleaning crew now."

"You're, like, a maid?"

"Every new person has to start there."

"Tell me: do you have another boyfriend? Did you follow some guy up to Vermont?"

"No!"

"What about NYU?"

"Well, obviously I'm not there."

"Yeah, I get that. But the semester's not over."

"It's over in three weeks."

"But you're not going to be there to finish it, are you? What about your finals, your papers, all that crap?"

He had me there. I struggled to find a gentle way to put it, but there really was no way to soft-pedal it.

"I'm afraid I dropped out."

"Oh great. A semester of tuition, room and board down the drain. Over a thousand bucks. You just walked away?"

"I'm really sorry, dad. It was making me mentally ill."

"I'm sure getting knocked-up didn't help."

"No. It didn't help. And I know it was my fault. I'm sorry."

"Tell me, honestly: you didn't sneak off somewhere to have a baby in secret, did you?"

"No! I'm not pregnant anymore. I had the procedure we talked about. I'll pay you back someday. I swear."

He sighed at the other end of the line, and I thought I heard a sniffle or two.

"Look, I can't stay on this phone much longer," he said. "Call me at home tonight."

"No. I don't want to talk to Marilyn. She might pick up."

"It would make my life a whole lot easier if you would."

"I'll think about it."

"No, do it!" he said. "And give me your address up there in Vermont. They have US mail service there, right?"

"Of course they do. I'll have to send it. Offhand I don't know it."

"Do you need any money? For stamps or anything?"

"No, I'm okay. They pay us for any work over twenty-five hours a week. I'll be okay."

"I wish you'd stayed in school, Pooh."

"I know. But I just couldn't."

"Call home tonight so your mother doesn't go insane and take it out on me."

"I will."

So that was that call. I felt like a complete shit-heel about the wasted tuition and all on top of the abortion. Then, after dinner that evening, I managed to get on the pay phone again after waiting around for three other people to finish using it, and I called home. Marilyn picked it up on the first ring.

"It's me," I said.

"You goddamn irresponsible little bitch," my mother fulminated. "We send you to that expensive college and you just drop out like some... moron! What's the big idea, taking off like that? Do you know I was *this* close to calling the state police when your father informed me that you're on some goddamn hippie commune?"

"Well, I'm here and I'm staying here."

"No you're not."

"Yes I am."

"I'm going to make sure you don't."

"What do you mean by that, Marilyn?"

"Don't Marilyn me, Erica."

"Don't Erica me, Marilyn. Why'd you stick me with that god-damn name? I hate it."

"You're named after my brother, who gave his life for this coun-try, you ungrateful little wretch—"

The operator butted in and said, "Please deposit another twen-ty-five cents for the next minute."

"I don't have anymore quarters," I said.

"Where are you, Erica?" Marilyn shouted.

"I'll never tell you."

"I won't rest until I—"

There were a series of complicated clicks and the line went dead. That was my call to Marilyn. It actually went a bit worse than I'd expected. It left me shuddering with rage and shame. After I managed to calm down, I scrounged up some stationary from Alison Bartosz and borrowed a stamp and wrote a letter to my dad telling him the village mailing address and I begged him not to reveal it to Marilyn — after apologizing in about sixteen different ways for being such a disappointment to everybody.

The rest of that week, my first normal one at the Village, was one of adjustments. The work routine gave some basic structure to my life. But, after spending three straight nights in Danny Musser's room at the Leo House, he said he *needed some space* for himself and I should try staying in my own room a little more — whatever that meant, like from now on, or just now and again? It was very unclear. My feelings were so unsettled, so all-over-the-place, that I could hardly tell how I felt about it. Even though we'd had quite a bit of sex, I couldn't say I had fallen in love with him. I was really comfortable with him, maybe too much so, because that old married couple routine got firmly established by the second night when we'd have sex and then read. I think the truth was we had our greatest rapport playing music together with the others.

One somewhat disturbing thing happened that week after Thanksgiving: Maya sort of accosted me one evening when everyone was gathering for dinner at the inn. She was holding that crocheted wooly hat that Songbird had given me the day of our interview when we went down to the old marble works.

"Guess where I found this?" she asked.

"The free clothing room," I said.

"That's right," she said. "How did it get there?"

"I put it there," I admitted.

"Why didn't you bring it back to the Aquarius House?"

I decided to tell her the truth.

"I was embarrassed that Songbird lent me something that obviously belonged to you, and I was afraid you'd be angry if I brought it back."

"Well, your instincts were correct."

"I'm sorry."

"Noted," she said and bustled away. I figured I was now on her shit-list and I was determined to steer clear of her, just like since Thanksgiving I'd managed to avoid any encounters with Sophie the cook.

Two other things happened that week. Larry sent me a letter with three twenty-dollar bills in it. The letter was short but forgiving:

Dearest Pooh,

I know this is a tumultuous time in your young life. It's a strange time in America, too, but I probably don't have to tell you that. Just know that I love you very much no matter what. Don't spend all this in one place and please don't buy any dope with it.

Love,
Dad ("Larry" Ha!)

I loved my dad so much. No matter what, he never ever let me down. I suppose he was aware of exactly how bad my relationship with Marilyn was, and he did all he could to compensate for it, poor man. But no one was helping to carry his load, and as far as I knew nobody was giving him any compensatory affection. The money really helped me out because I had completely run out by then. Robin Gratz, the waitress at the diner, was kind enough to bring back two cartons of cigarettes for me from town — I'd been bumming smokes from everybody and it was embarrassing. Padget even referred to me one evening of band practice — we were turning into an actual band — as "Minnie the Moocher."

Since you couldn't lock the door to your room unless you were inside it to work a hook-and-eye, I began to worry about how to protect my valuables, which amounted to my cash, my smokes, one turquoise bead necklace, a Timex watch, and a few silver rings. I wasn't paranoid, but I wondered what might happen if I actually managed to accumulate some savings. Weezil informed me that a lot of Village members had a secret "hidey hole" somewhere outside their rooms, like between some rocks in an old stone wall, or in some hollow of a tree.

So, one day after my clean up duties, I took a hike a little way up the trail to Owl's Head and oddly enough the first spot I tried, in a cleft between two big glacial erratic boulders off the trail, a plastic pencil box was hidden, the kind you used to bring to grade school. I looked inside and there was a bunch of cash, maybe a hundred bucks in tens and fives, and a gold college ring (Bucknell). Of course I put it back right away. Then I realized if I went farther afield, I'd almost surely lose track of where my hidey hole was, so I retraced and found an old fallen log closer to where the woods met the big meadow behind the inn, and actually carved a little chamber for my stuff in the punky wood with a sharp stick, and placed a rock in front of it so you could hardly tell it was there. I noticed that somebody had scratched a heart and two initials into the thin bark of a beech tree that stood on the trail nearby so I would know where to go back and look. That was my stash.

Another good thing that happened was that two weeks before Christmas Weezil told me that she had a "special assignment" from Songbird and had requested me to assist her. It involved a horse. She knew that I'd gone to horse camp as a child, and she'd been around them all her life. Songbird had found an old horse-drawn wagon for sale. And he knew a woman in town who had a big draft horse, and the idea was that we would give rides at Christmas time around the part of town called Old Bennington where the most beautiful old houses were, and make some money, and spread some good will among the locals about Sunrise Village. Maya had made arrangements with the grade schools in and around the county to bring their kids in groups of ten for wagon rides, and she had them all scheduled hour-by-hour after school up until the Saturday before Christmas Eve.

We had to go tack up the horse at one o'clock in order to be ready to go up to the circular drive around the Bennington Battle Monument at two. I arranged to work a slightly different morning schedule on clean-up from seven to noon so I would still get in my twenty-five hours. Weezil said we would get paid two-fifty an hour for giving wagon rides. The horse belonged to a Mrs. Marklin who lived on a twenty-acre estate just west of the monument out the Waloomsac Road. Weezil said she was a former model, forty-something, divorced from a CBS executive and this had been their summer place, which she now lived at full-time. It was a gorgeous white mansion with a big fan-light window in the front gable. She had a really posh barn with two other horses: her own brown and white paint saddle horse, and a pretty little gray Welsh pony for her nine-year-old daughter, Muffy.

The draft horse was a Percheron named Tony who had been dumped on the local humane society for being lame by the Splain Brothers Circus, one of the remnant number of small family out-fits that still worked the New England circuit into the 1960s. Mrs. Marklin said that Tony had once pulled the wagon that contained the Splain Brothers' only big cat, a moth-eaten tiger. She nursed Tony back to health and now she was eager to give him a little work to do besides being an ornament on her estate. "A horse needs a job," she told us when she took us to his stall.

Weezil had grown up on a farm near Lake Champlain with her grandfather, who liked to show off his antique phaeton coach in the various parades that were staged in Vergennes, Vermont, on Memorial Day, the Fourth of July, and the first night of the Addison County fair. She knew how to put on the wagon harness with all its complicated running gear. She also was the one who drove the wagon — held the reins, that is — since my only experi-ence was with saddle horses. Basically, I was there to keep Weezil company while we waited for the school kids and to help manage them, since they were likely to be in a frenzy at the prospect of a horse-drawn wagon ride.

The construction crew at the Village had spruced up the old market wagon and painted the name Sunrise Village on both sides with a sun emblem radiating the rainbow colors of hippie-dom. They'd put in new bench seats with cushions along each side of the wagon box that could hold five kids on a side. We brought a bunch of blankets and quilts for them to bundle up in. Weezil and I also strategically picked up a bag of Tootsie Pops at the store, which kept the screaming down somewhat. Thanks to Maya, we were costumed in "Victorian" greatcoats — which were actually military surplus from some European country that made more stylish army garb than America. Also, wool mufflers. And she scared up a couple of antique top hats for us to wear — very Charles Dickensy.

We had so much fun. Old Bennington, with its beautiful antique houses and ornate white fences, was exactly the kind of fantasy that a child growing up in the ridiculous Long Island suburbs would have conjured up about the perfect setting for Christmas. (Of course we got all our ideas about Christmas from 1940s movies on TV.) The season's latest snowfalls had stuck to the ground and the rooftops. We quickly got our routine down to four circuits each afternoon, past the grand mansions on Monument Drive, through some side streets, and back up to the battle monument, about a mile each trip. There was very little car traffic up there, and they all slowed down to gawk and wave. We started around two o'clock. It took forty-five minutes per trip, including loading and unloading the kids. By the last circuit of the day, we were clip-clopping behind Tony in winter solstice twilight with all the Christmas decorations aglow on the big white houses, and Christmas trees twinkling through the windows, and wreaths on the doors, and the sleigh bells jingling on Tony's rump. It was like a Hallmark card. I started bringing my banjo along and led the kids in Christmas carols. People came out on their porches and waved to us. One lady brought out a big thermos of hot cocoa and paper cups.

CHAPTER SIXTEEN

At the end of our last day, after we put Tony to bed, Mrs. Marklin invited us into the house for "a holiday nip." Her house was very posh. Beautiful antiques, oriental rugs, real paintings on the walls. She had a big "country kitchen," she called it, which was funny to me, as if you had to be reminded that this was the country. It had a broad brick hearth with the fire crackling and cushy chairs beside it and all kinds of polished copper cookware hanging off a wrought iron rack. A tree stood in a far corner but it had not been decorated yet and I wondered if it ever would be. She made us her "special hot toddies," some kind of sweet, spicy apple concoction with a lot of rum in it, and served us little cocktail weenies baked in dough, and put Nat King Cole's Christmas album on the stereo. It was quite lovely, actually, being in someone's nice home. But I detected that she had a head-start on us with the cocktails. You could sense her sadness, apparently because, she told us, by court decree her daughter was down in Manhattan for the holiday with the ex-husband that year. "Call me Carol," she said.

She was a fun, if you didn't mind watching someone unravel before your eyes, a compelling but perturbed specimen of our parents' generation. Though she came out of uptight Boston WASPdom, she swore like a longshoreman, the only daughter in a family with three older brothers who fought in the war, and survived it. The vestige of a modeling career was still visible in her slim figure, and the way her expensive casual clothes hung on her. She talked and talked. She was the kind of person who would ask you something about yourself and use that as a springboard to talk about herself.

"How long had we been in Vermont?" she asked. We hardly answered when Carol said, "This'll be my second fucking winter here — only there hasn't been a whole lot of fucking. I've got to get out. There are no single men in this state. Except up where you are, and they're not in my age bracket, you know," she said with a grin and a sparkle in her eye. "It must be fucking heaven there, huh? — no pun intended. And now there's the pill. I wish we'd had the pill back when. My daddy had to send me to Mexico twice before I was twenty. He almost disowned me. There must be a lot of sex up in your village. All those young bodies full of raging hormones and no adult supervision. Am I right? I've never been there but I've heard a thing or two from Elliot. They used to call it free love. I've got news for you ladies. Love is never free. You pay and pay and fucking pay. Do you swap boyfriends up there? I hear this and that. Elliot tells me all sorts of things."

"How did you two become acquainted?" Weezil asked.

"Oh, Gawd. I knew Arthur and Leila, his parents. We were all in the same summer crowd in Southwest Harbor."

"Where's that?" I asked.

"Oh," Carol said, as if she couldn't imagine anyone not knowing of the place. "Mount Desert, up in Maine. Want another nip?"

"Sure," Weezil said, though I'd had enough.

"My ex's family goes back to the stone age there," Carol said, retrieving the saucepan with the toddy mix from the stove. "I've known Elliot since he was crawling in the grass. You can imagine how his parents' death affected him, poor thing."

"Is it true that they were eaten by cannibals?" Weezil asked.

"Total bullshit," I said, getting into the old cursing spirit.

"How do you know?" Weezil said.

"He told me," I said.

"When did he tell you?"

"When I met with him. All new people have to meet with him," I explained to Carol. "He said headhunters lived in the area where they disappeared and the newspapers played that angle up. But no evidence was ever found. Not even their canoe."

"Something bad must have happened to them, though," Weezil said. "I wonder what."

We silently stared into our drinks while Nat King Cole sang about chestnuts roasting on an open fire. An antique clock ticked on the mantel. It was completely dark outside the windows.

"Anyway, up at the village, everyone calls him Songbird, not Elliot," I said.

"Yes, he told me," Carol said. "You hippies are cute."

"He's a serious person. He thinks about a lot of heavy things. The future and all."

"Are you fucking him?" Carol asked squinting at me, playfully I thought.

"No!" I said. "Definitely not!"

"Are *you* fucking him?" Weezil asked Carol, also playfully. She was half-crocked.

Carol made a coy face as though she wanted us to wonder.

"He's grown up to be a very attractive young man," was all she said.

"There's a rule against fucking him," I said. "His girlfriend warned me about it. She pretty much runs the day-to-day operations of Sunrise Village."

"Oh, Maya…." Carol said, rolling her eyes. "There's a first-class cunt."

Even half crocked, that took us aback. You could sense that Carol suspected that she'd gone too far. She went to the fridge and unwrapped a cheese and nut log and fished some crackers out of the cabinet. Weezil and I had demolished the cocktail weenies.

"Anyway," she said, bringing the food back to the fireside, "Sunrise Village is a very brave experiment. I think Arthur and Leila would be proud of him."

After that, Carol retreated back to the safer ground of talking about herself and her lousy marriage to Gerald, the TV network executive, and what a miserable philandering skunk he was, and how moving here to their summer place full-time after the divorce maybe wasn't such a hot idea, and how much she missed New York, and after another half hour, she was slurring her words and spilling things. Weezil had been keeping up with her on the toddies and was pretty far gone, too, but I'd quit after the Nat King Cole album was over because somebody had to drive Weezil's old Rambler back home. You could tell that Carol really didn't want us to leave and she mentioned that she didn't have anyone to spend Christmas Eve with, and she got all teary. Weezil invited her to come up to the Village where there would be lots of holiday festivity and plenty of company, and told Carol that she was still a great-looking woman and might even "get lucky." That was my cue to put on my coat and help Weezil with hers. From the driveway, you could hear sobbing from inside the house.

I made Weezil give me the car keys. She was way more plastered than me but I was far from sober. As we drove out of town, she kept repeating, "Of course he's fucking her," before she conked out. I drove the Rambler up the mountain roads like a ninety-year-old Hadassah lady the whole way back, worrying about whether the sheriffs were laying out there in the dark just waiting for two Sunrise Village chickies to stop and and arrest for a DWI.

CHAPTER SEVENTEEN

Carol didn't materialize on Christmas Eve after all and I worried about her drinking herself into oblivion down there in town. But it was very festive up in the village, all right. Though there was no special banquet like on Thanksgiving — we got lasagna for dinner — Sophie turned out trays of holiday cakes and cookies, and they made gallons of hot mulled wine, and virtually the whole commune gathered in the fireplace lounge of the inn to sing carols. The grounds crew had put up a big tree and people made ornaments out of pine cones, cardboard, old hood ornaments, glue, sparkles, and odd bits of this and that. There was plenty weed going around. Danny Musser clung close to me when we weren't playing our instruments and dragged me (willingly) back to his room where we did what two healthy, young, adult mammals will do, which only thrust me back into my globe of confusion and uncertainty twenty-four hours later on Christmas night when he claimed to be worn out and asked to be alone — like, was I supposed to be his sex toy when he felt like it and otherwise be a good little girl and get lost? I resolved that we were going to have a straight-up adult discussion about what this relationship meant at the earliest opportunity, but then something else happened.

That Thursday, three days after Christmas, the Village was back to the regular routine. I hadn't seen Danny for days either, not at meals or anywhere. I was worried that maybe he'd split the Village altogether for some reason I didn't know about. Before dinner that night, when darkness has already fallen, I went to the Leo House and knocked on his door. No answer. I tried the knob. The hook-and-eye was engaged inside.

"Hey, Danny, it's me, Pooh. I know you're in there."

"I was asleep," he said, actually kind of a groan.

"Open up."

"I can't. I don't feel well."

"Have you got something?"

"Yeah. I'm sick."

"Let me in. I'll rub your temples and make it better."

"No. You might catch it."

"Are you gonna get up and go to dinner?"

"No, I don't feel like it."

"Want me to bring you a plate? Maybe there's some nice hot soup tonight. Soup might help."

"Thanks but no. I just have to ride it out."

That's when it struck me: I could smell patchouli fragrance wafting through the slight crack in the door. That stuff is pungent. The crack was too narrow to actually see anything inside, but the alarm bell had gone off in my brain.

"Sure you don't want any food?"

"Yeah. Thanks, Pooh. I'll be okay. Don't worry about me."

"Okay, then...."

Only I didn't go back to the inn. I went next door to the Sagittarius house, which was vacant and under reconstruction, and I stole inside and sat on a paint can next to the window where

I could observe the porch of the Leo house, chain-smoking to keep myself occupied. It seemed like forever because it was so cold in there, but my watch said that only thirty minutes had gone by when I saw a female figure step outside. When she turned to make sure the door had closed properly, the porch light revealed Maya, all bundled up in expensive shearling, her kitty-cat face unmistakable, with that familiar, knitted wool cap on her head. I just sat there wishing I'd had a rifle so I could put a few rounds in her skull — a cold, vengeful, morbid feeling that shocked me in its raw aggression.

I waited until she walked up the street toward the inn. Then I went back to Danny's room on the second floor. I didn't bother to knock and the room wasn't locked anymore so I just barged in. Danny was standing up pulling on his bell-bottoms.

"You piece of shit," I said. "You're not sick and I know exactly what's going on."

He had only one leg in his pants and I tried to push him over onto the mattress, but he was agile and managed to stay upright. He grabbed my wrist really hard.

"What's wrong with you?" he said.

"Me? What's wrong with you! Fucking that bitch!"

He kicked the pants off his one leg and dragged me down to the mattress, which was the only furniture in the room, if you could even call it that, and pinned me down.

"You're hurting me," I hollered.

"Lower your voice!"

"Why'd you do this to me?" I said and started bawling.

"I'm not doing anything to you. I'm just living my life. We're not married, Pooh."

"Didn't I mean anything to you?"

"Of course you did... you do! Ah, for Chrissake...."

He let out this snorty exhalation of frustration and neither of us said anything for a while. He relaxed his grip and slid off of me, kneeling beside me on the mattress. I propped myself up against the wall with the pillow.

"I thought we were… together," I said.

"We were together when we were together."

"I wasn't fucking other people," I said.

"I can't believe I have to explain this to you."

"Don't patronize me."

"This is not the regular outside world. There are different rules here—"

"Yeah, and I know one of them is you're not supposed to fuck Songbird's woman," I whispered fiercely, "because that slut was as clear as can be with me that we women have to keep our mitts off of him."

"Okay then, she's a hypocrite."

"Did she put the moves on you?"

"Yeah, if you must know. I wouldn't have put them on her."

"When did this start?"

"Not yesterday," he said.

"You must have liked it, then."

"It is what it is."

"What's that supposed to mean?"

"It means don't look for more reasons to make yourself feel bad," he said.

Was I doing that? Or was Danny just messing with my head? I couldn't untangle it. But he was right about one thing: I felt even worse than before I barged in.

Finally, I just said, "You'd better cut it out. If Songbird finds out he'll kick your ass out of here. And I sure won't follow you in sympathy."

He shrugged his shoulders and lit a butt.

"Don't you want to stay here?" I said.

"I might have to get my ass back in college to keep from getting drafted anyway."

Danny got off his knees and flipped around so he was sitting next to me, up against the wall. He tried to caress my head, pull my hair away from my eyes, but I smacked his hand.

"You're a wonderful girl, Pooh," He said.

"Aren't I enough?"

"Look where we are," he said ruefully. "Look what this is."

CHAPTER EIGHTEEN

We all had pigeonhole mailboxes at the inn. One of the guys drove to Bennington every other day to pick up the village mail at the PO, and then distributed it back home. Friday was payday for people who racked up those extra hours of work at Sunrise Village. They received cash because hardly anybody had a bank account in town, or could even get to the bank to cash a check. After four o'clock, the people who had some extra-time pay coming could find a little brown envelope in their box. I know that they had come in that day because several other people had brown envelopes in theirs. I had only letters from Larry and Ricky Spillman in mine, but no pay. My dad's letter was terse as usual but loving, and it enclosed another twenty dollar bill. He said he was going ahead to purchase that old house down in Oyster Bay village, and that Marilyn was "on the warpath" because of it, and he loved me very much, blah blah. I saved Ricky's for later, since his epistolary method was to over-dramatize a dozen trivial things going on in his own life.

Even though Larry sent me some money, I was concerned about not getting paid for the wagon rides — actually, rather annoyed about it, since at that time I needed quite a few basic things such as decent gloves, winter socks, new underwear, tampons, razor blades (yeah, I still shaved my legs and underarms despite the fashion for going natural) and, of course, a supply of smokes. Anyway, Weezil was busy in the kitchen at that hour, working for Sophie to make dinner for the troops, so I went up by myself to Maya's office in the Odd Fellows hall.

She was still there at four-fifteen, jabbering on the phone, as usual. The door was open. Of course the place reeked of patchouli with overtones of weed. She had one of those curved metal shoulder rests for the telephone and she was giving herself a manicure while she talked. When I appeared, she acted all irritated, told the person on the line to hold on a minute, and said to me brusquely, "What do you want?"

"Just a minute of your time," I said.

"Oh, man...." She said, obviously irked. The person at the other end must have been a friend or something because Maya just said, "I'll call you back," and tossed the receiver back in its cradle. "What?" she said to me.

"Can I come in."

"Hey, you're here. Might as well come in."

I sat down in the funky old swivel chair opposite her with the big desk between us. She ostentatiously blinked both of her eyes at me and twanged her head, as if trying to find yet another obnoxious way to communicate that I was already wasting her time.

"I was expecting to get paid this week," I said.

"What for?"

"Those rides we gave to the school kids down in Bennington," I said, and then, because she seemed slow to comprehend, or maybe was only pretending, or maybe she was stoned, I added, "the horse and wagon rides you arranged with the schools. Remember?"

"Oh," she said, as if snapping out of a trance. "Of course. You and Louise."

"Right."

"You keep track of the hours?"

"Yes. Sure. It was thirty hours in all."

"How do you figure thirty?"

"It was two o'clock to five for ten school days over two weeks. Actually that doesn't include the time harnessing Carol Marklin's horse and then bringing him back and putting him away in the stable and all."

"But obviously you didn't count that time."

"Well, I guess I didn't, but—"

"So we'll call it thirty hours," she said.

"All right." I gave in on that point, a tactical error on my part. I should have included it from the start.

Maya took a cash box out of a lower drawer. She made some calculations on a legal pad and handed me thirty-seven fifty.

"I assume you got in your basic twenty-five hours those two weeks," she said.

"Yes, sure, on the cleaning crew," I said, trying to count the money. "You can ask Lucy. Hey, I think this is short."

"How do you figure that?"

"Weezil said we were supposed to get two-fifty an hour. That would come to seventy-five."

"That was two-fifty and hour for both of you," Maya said.

"Huh? You're kidding."

"No, I'm not kidding. Louise must have misunderstood."

"Honestly, Maya, when someone says a job pays such-and-such an hour, it always refers to one person."

"Who says?"

"You've had jobs out there in the real world, haven't you?" I said, showing a little pique myself now.

"Yeah...?"

"When did two-fifty an hour not refer to one person doing one job?"

"Well, yeah, but you were two people doing one job."

"No we weren't."

"You were only put on that job because Louise asked for you."

"It's not like I was just along for the ride. Someone had to keep their eye on the kids while she was occupied with the horse. You should have been there. Some of these kids were popping out of their seats and standing up and clowning around. Someone could have got hurt. You needed another person to control them. Not to mention unhitching the wagon, and getting the harness off, and grooming, and feeding and watering, and all."

"How did this become a sob story?" Maya said. "Giving wagon rides in a pretty New England town at Christmas time? Please! Look, we've got a lot of expenses running the village and taking care of all you wayward children—"

"Oh, thanks. Like now this is an orphanage?"

"Don't get smart with me, Pookie—"

"Pooh, like Winnie the. And anyway, I know for a fact that the schools were paying the Village twenty-five bucks each day, times ten days, equals two hundred and fifty bucks, so you were making money on this deal."

"Who told you that?"

"One of the teachers who brought her kids over."

Maya finally put her manicure stick down.

"Look, we have various of ways of generating income. Ideas for products we can make, businesses, services. The whole purpose of Sunrise Village is to become a self-sustaining enterprise. Don't you grok that?"

"Of course I grok that—"

"So we're just at the beginning of this… project… and you worker bees—"

"Wait, are we worker bees or wayward children—"

"—should not expect," Maya's voice rose dramatically, "to get rich while we figure out how this develops. We're trying to find a way outside this disgusting capitalist system. If it was up to me, we wouldn't even use money here with you people, but it's a little early in this revolution that's underway. In the meantime, we have to go with what works."

"Well, personally, I don't think we're ever going to have a system where people don't expect fair pay—"

I thought steam was going to start coming out of her nostrils.

"Oh, are you an economist?" she asked.

"Of course not, but I've read *The New York Times* practically every day since I was fourteen. Really until I came here."

"Good for you. I happen to have a degree in political science with a minor in economics. I was in North Vietnam in sixty-five. People there do what's good for the collective. They're not hung up on individual money-grubbing and self-aggrandizement. That's why they're kicking our ass in this stupid war. If money is what you want, why don't you just hitch-hike to Hollywood and sit at a soda fountain on the Sunset Strip and wait for some agent to buy you a chocolate malt? I don't even know why you want to be here. All you do is complain and give me a hard time—"

"At least I'm not fucking your boyfriend."

"If you were, you'd be out of here faster than you could say Lyndon Baines Johnson."

"Then how about you stop fucking mine?" I said.

She did another one of her bug-eyed blinks with the head twang thing again.

'What are you talking about?"

"Danny Musser."

"Oh? He's your boyfriend is he?"

"I was working on it."

"That's funny right there. And you imagine that there's something going on between him and me?"

"I don't imagine anything. I know it for a fact."

"For your information, Danny's been balling everything and everyone he could point his cock at since he arrived here. Don't you know that?"

"Including you," I said.

"Please," she said. "That's utterly… ridiculous."

"I know you were in his room the other day with the door locked. And I know that you know that I know."

Maya narrowed her eyes now and drilled them into mine, as if this was a technique she'd used before successfully to intimidate other females daring to challenge her dominance.

"Why would anyone believe you?" she eventually said in a growly voice down in its lower register so as to sound menacing. "Who are you around here? Just another piece of meat with a hole in the middle in bell bottom jeans."

"Is that what you think of the other women here?"

Quite suddenly, Maya unlocked her gaze from me, bent down to the lower desk drawer, took out the cash box, and plopped it on the table. She extracted a wad of bills and two quarters and slapped it all down on my side of the desk.

"Maybe you're right," she said. "What we had here was a failure to communicate. Go on. Take the money. And get out of my office."

She must have seen *Cool Hand Luke*, too, when it played down in Bennington back in November. I took the additional thirty-seven-fifty and went over to supper (moussaka with salad and brownies).

CHAPTER NINETEEN

The next few days I was walking on eggshells, expecting at any hour to find a note in my pigeon-hole telling me to pack my stuff and get out. But no such thing happened. I went through all my regular routines. These included practicing with the string band, which was starting to go by the official name Happy Anarchy — Alan Kaplan's idea — even though Danny was there and kept attempting to make up and, very obviously, to inveigle me back onto his mattress at the Leo House. There was very strong chemistry between us and it was hard to say no, but I managed to not cave in. All that tension between attraction and resistance came out in our music. We were getting good, developing a deeper song-list with complicated harmonies and interesting arrangements. After Christmas was over I spent a lot of my spare time practicing the banjo and I improved dramatically, especially my finger-picking and learning tunings besides the open G. Alan suggested that we were ready to play out, to find gigs outside the village or maybe even beyond the immediate area. There was a bar in Bennington, the Catamount Room, popular with the college crowd, that Alan said he could book us into. The owner brought in acts from the New York-Cambridge folkie circuit. Supposedly, Bob Dylan played there in 1962 when his debut album came out. Nobody knew who he was yet then and hardly anyone came to see him and the album didn't sell. Ha! Tom Rush, Dave Von Ronk, Tom Paxton, Spider John Koerner, Eric Von Schmidt, Judy Collins, all the big names of folk music, they had all played the Catamount Room. But most weeks they had to make do with less celebrated talent.

Quite a few of the guys of Sunrise Village were regularly coming onto me while I tried to figure out what I was supposed to do about my sex life, post-Danny. But I didn't want to get my heart bruised again right away and I didn't encourage any of it. I often wondered if Songbird and Maya selected people on the basis of their looks. Besides Sophie the cook, who was rather homely but had special skills, you couldn't help noticing that so many Sunrise Villagers were fine specimens of *Homo sapiens*.

Some of the chicks came on to me too, but I was just not into that. I was aware of what was going on around me: that just about everybody was having a lot of sex with everybody else. Oswald Strangefield was said to have an orgy room with a whole floor of mattresses where he lived, in the Capricorn House, though I hadn't been invited to see it. There were so many hormones in the air at Sunrise Village that you were sexually alert at all times to some degree, if perhaps only sub-consciously. I just lay low and took refuge in the banjo and waited for Maya to take her revenge, which didn't happen. Possibly Maya was a little nervous about me knowing about her dalliance. I hoped so, but just kept it to myself. Anyway, we shortly got a lesson in how the real world of the ever-grinding American doomsday machine could come in and shove your little personal melodramas aside.

On Thursday night between Christmas and New Years there was literally something weird in the air. A freakish warm weather front blew in. The temperature rose above fifty during the day and after dark the wind banged around fiercely outside. I was up in my room around midnight getting ready to turn in alone, feeling a little sorry for myself, the old loose panes in my bay window rattling, when I saw streaky blue light shooting around outside. Then I heard a commotion of voices, and footsteps, and doors slamming, and barking orders, and I groked that a bust was underway. About five seconds later a pot-bellied sheriff's deputy kicked open my hook-and-eye lock on the door. He shined a flashlight right in my eyes. I was wearing just a plain cotton camisole and my underpants to sleep in.

"Where's your stash, sister?" he asked. I had to shade my eyes to see him from the flashlight on down.

"Stash of what?"

"You know what."

"No I don't."

"I'm gonna go through all your stuff." he said.

"Do you have to shine that thing right in my face?"

It might have sounded like I was bravely resisting, but I was literally quaking in terror.

"Okay, have it your way," the officer said. He went over to the chest of drawers I'd scrounged up and started rooting through it, tossing underpants, T-shirts, and socks over his shoulder. "What'd you burn all your bras?"

"I don't own any bras," I said.

"You should consider it. Girl built like you. Twenty years from now they'll be hanging so low you can toss them over your shoulder. Get off the bed — or should I say mattress?"

"I only have underpants on."

"What'd I just say? Hint: it wasn't a suggestion."

I grabbed the blanket and wrapped it around my waist like a sarong as I got up.

"Go stand over there." He pointed his flashlight in the corner, then proceeded to flip my mattress over. There was nothing under it, of course. In the process, he managed to knock over the reading lamp on the floor just next to it so I heard the bulb explode with a little pop, and he also flipped over an ashtray fully loaded with butts. By now, he apparently realized I didn't have what he was looking for, at least not where he was looking. If he had looked in my banjo case, he would have found a plastic baggie with maybe an eighth of an ounce of weed in the little compartment where I kept my fingerpicks, but he didn't look there, the dumb bunny.

He didn't say anything else, or even apologize for messing up my room. He just split. I stood in the corner clutching my blanket until there was no more commotion on that floor of the inn. When I ventured into the hallway, I saw light coming out of an open door and hurried down to Jan Heathcoate's room. She was wearing a plaid bathrobe watching the scene outside her window, which faced the front of the inn. Scotty Provost and Tanzy also drifted in. Outside, three sheriff cars were lined up along the snow-covered village green with their blue gumball lights rotating. Deputies were still pulling people out of the inn and some of the other buildings, dragging them to the cruisers, and stuffing them in the back seats, treating them quite roughly. They were only taking guys, none of the women — Strangefield, Hog (Bob Haugstead, who was actually quite handsome despite his nickname), Gary Chan, Jodie Palko, Mickey O'Neill, among others, nine in all. Then the cars peeled out.

Many of us gathered downstairs in the fireplace room. It was after one o'clock in the morning. Everybody had a similar story about being treated rudely and had their stuff messed with. Maya came in and told us they were dealing with it and there was no reason to freak out. She said it was actually a good sign that the revolution had already begun and a sign of weakness that the "pigs" — as the cops were being called all across the nation — had resorted to Gestapo tactics, because it meant they were getting desperate. And then she ordered us to go back to bed, like she was the house mother in a dorm. It was interesting to see how everyone meekly complied with her commands.

Those arrested returned in time for breakfast. We learned that the sheriff's office had used a defective warrant because the document was mis-dated by the Shaftsbury township justice of the peace, who also happened to be the cousin of Bennington County sheriff George Grout, that is, not a disinterested party in the eyes of the law. The incident even got into the local paper, *The Bennington Banner.* "Sloppy Paperwork Foils Drug Bust," the headline said. All the charges were dropped and such a mood of jubilation prevailed in Sunrise Village that it was decided to open our planned New Years Eve party to the public in order to further enhance our standing with the community at large.

CHAPTER TWENTY

Welcome 1968, a momentous year. We were closing in on 1970, which seemed to me like the threshold to a dubious science-fiction future, when all the Hollywood fantasies of space-age America would explode into reality. We'd become *The Jetsons* traveling around in flying cars and taking our food in pills. How depressing. The Vietnam War dragged on, of course, and America only sank deeper and deeper in the Big Muddy. LBJ flew to Cam Ranh Bay in Vietnam and told the troops we had the enemy on the run (total bullshit). Back at the Village, we put on our New Year's extravaganza at the Oddfellows hall.

We posted flyers down in Bennington, and on the college campus, inviting the public to come. About a hundred townies and undergrads showed up, everyone from town greasers to flower children to the hip professors. We charged two bucks to get in and fifty cents for a can of beer or a paper cup of Dago red wine. Maya actually got the *festival permit* from the Vermont Liquor Control Board. The state drinking age was eighteen and we were extra-special careful to check ID at the bar. Maya told everybody about five times that there would be no pot-smoking in the hall that night. Anybody caught would get bounced out of the village. By eight o'clock, cars were parked all down the road for a quarter mile. If we were daring the county sheriffs to come up and hassle us, they proved to decline the invitation, still licking their wounds.

The village rock and roll band, now called Avatar, with Maya starring as chick singer, was the featured attraction, with a trippy light show designed by Billy Herman. Our folkie band, Happy Anarchy, opened for them, our first gig in front of strangers. I was so nervous. It was much worse than acting in a play at NYU. I was afraid of screwing up on my banjo parts. It went a lot better than I'd feared, though. We did five numbers, the close-out being a raucous arrangement of "The Lily of the West" with a long, wild, instrumental break featuring Danny's fiddle that went on for maybe ten minutes, because we were electrified for the first time and our sound came out in such a new thrilling and powerful way that we didn't want it to end. The audience yelled, "More, more, more!" I could see that Maya, standing just offstage, was galled and she sent the crew, Teck and Oz, out right away to rearrange the mic stands and the amps for her band so we couldn't play an encore. While that was happening, Songbird came up to me and said he really liked us, and me especially. I was flustered and just said something vapid like, "Thanks, that means a lot." By then, Maya was onstage and I was pretty sure she saw us together.

That made me want to be invisible, so I managed to slip into the crowd, and soothe my nerves with some of that red wine. Before too long I was able to calm down. Maya was really hamming it up onstage, wearing one of those filmy, drapey outfits that allowed her to flutter around the stage like a butterfly. Despite the fact that we seemed to loathe each other, I had to admit that she had great pipes. That girl could sing. She did a cover of Janis Joplin's (originally Big Mama Thornton's) "Ball and Chain" that was more soulful and less show-boaty than Janis's version, and unlike Janis's band, Big Brother and the Holding Company, Avatar managed to play in tune. Several guys in the crowd who were not villagers hit on me, all starting with some version of the line, "Hey, you were great up there," but I didn't encourage any of them. I just said I couldn't hear what they were saying because the band was so loud, and they gave up. Then, as soon as the band took a break, I heard this mellow voice behind me say, "Hey little schoolgirl."

I wheeled around. It was the black guy they called Mule. He was a kind of phantom presence around the Village, rarely at group meals or other events. He actually wasn't that dark-skinned but rather a cream-in-your-coffee color. I always noticed when guys were taller than me because I was pretty tall myself, and I liked it when I had to look up instead of down. He was probably six-two. His hair was only semi-kinky and he had green eyes. The overall impression that you got from his long face was of intelligence mixed with sadness. He had on a burnt orange, form-fitting V-neck sweater under an open black leather jacket so you could see his muscular torso.

"School's out for me," I said.

"What's your name, baby."

"Pooh," I said, "like in Winnie the." By now you realize I had to say that to everybody. Of course, I assumed he wouldn't know what the hell I was referring to.

"Call me Eeyore," he surprised me by saying. I didn't consider myself prejudiced, since the civil rights times were only just yesterday, and we were all behind it, but I somehow assumed that a black child would never be exposed to old A.A. Milne. "Hey, you want to find a quiet, cozy corner somewhere and get acquainted?" he asked.

It made me smile, but I didn't want to just rush over to his bedroom and make it with him.

"I don't see any cozy corners in this place, Eeyore," I said.

"I'm thinkin' back over there, by the fireplace." He jacked his thumb toward the entrance.

"You mean the Inn?"

"That's right."

"I dunno. There's a party going on here."

"Dat so?"

"Well, look around."

"Hmmm. There's somethin' going down for sure. Lot of white people rubbing elbows, pretending they can dance. Whaddaya say?"

"I'm not going to ball you?" I said.

"Did I ask you for that? I don't think so."

"You'd probably get around to it."

"I would have to like you first."

"Why do you want to be with someone you don't like?"

"I wouldn't. But we don't know that yet, do we? All I know is you ain't bad on the banjo and you can sing. Yeah. And I like your look, too: tall drink of water."

The band had come back from their break and were picking up their instruments. Maya flitted out on stage in a different outfit than she had in the first set: black leather pants and a puffy white blouse open and tied up at her naval so you could glimpse her bosom joggling around inside, and a little face-mask like the one *Zorro* wore on TV. Guys were hooting and whistling at the stage. The loathing I felt for Maya returned.

"Okay, I'll go sit by the fire over at the inn," I said, "But I have to get my banjo."

"Yeah? Okay. Meet you outside on the front steps."

So, we went over. It had turned cold again and snow flurries fluttered down. We were the only people over at the inn, apparently. He dragged two padded chairs up near the hearth and re-kindled the embers that had been burning there since dinner. I settled in. It was a relief to be away from all that noise, actually. He got a couple of juice glasses from the kitchen and proceeded to pour us two drinks from a pint bottle of Johnny Walker Black that he had stashed in his jacket pocket.

"I know you don't really go by Eeyore," I said with the whiskey warming me. "It's Mule, right?"

"Well," he said, lighting two Kool cigarettes at once and handing me one, "Eeyore's a donkey, right. That's like a mule's cousin."

"Come on. Why do they call you that?"

"I don't want to talk about it," he said. "Let's talk about you Winnie-the-Pooh."

"How do you know about Winnie the Pooh anyway?"

"You think Negroes don't give their kids books?"

"Hey, a lot of white people never heard of it. I have to explain it to practically everybody."

"My mama liked books. She gave me a lot of them. *Gerald McBoingBoing*, Dr. Seuss, *Millions of Cats, Madeline*. I read all that shit."

"Where are you from?"

"I don't want to talk about that now, either."

"Sorry," I said.

"We'll get to it some other time."

We sipped our drinks.

"They called me Piglet when I was real little," I said, "but then my dad changed it to Pooh."

"At least nobody called me Tigger. Sounds too much like nigger, know what I mean? They shoulda called him Mahatma or something."

"You're a strange bird," I said.

"Flattery won't get me to like you quicker. Let's talk about you?"

I was already pretty buzzed so I told him my boring life story about the Bollinger family, and how I couldn't stand Marilyn — who I couldn't even refer to in casual conversation as my mother. And eventually we got around to the abortion.

"That's some sad shit: having to kill a life growing within you," he said, pouring me another three fingers of scotch. "I'll tell you something worse: shooting a pregnant woman in the belly."

"Christ," I said. "Who would do that?"

"I did," he said.

I bobbled my whiskey glass, but managed not to spill it.

"Where?"

"A tiny village called Thu Bồn near Da Nang."

"You were in the army?"

"I wasn't a tourist."

"What happened?"

"She died. The baby died too."

"Why'd you shoot her?"

"She was running at us. We thought she was rigged to blow. It happened a lot like that over there."

"Was she?"

"It turned out, no. But my boys were shouting, 'She's a red-hot mama!' Rockets and all kinds of shit pouring in from their side, our side. It was chaos."

"That's terrible."

"Yeah, Vietnam: there's nothing like it."

He retreated into himself. I didn't know what to say after that. My instinct was to reach out to him, but I didn't want to give him the wrong idea. Frankly, I wondered if he might have invented the whole thing just to win my sympathy and get me into the sack. But then I thought, nobody would admit to something so awful if it wasn't true. He seemed smart enough to come up with a better pick-up tale. Anyway, my mind was churning with all this when he suddenly got up from his seat and said, "I'm not in such a party mood, I guess. It's been nice getting acquainted with you. We got a few things in common. Maybe we'll be friends." He placed his empty whiskey glass on the hearth and headed toward the front door of the Inn. I didn't go back to the party myself.

CHAPTER TWENTY-ONE

So finally the holidays were over. We now settled into the grip of a Vermont Winter. I remained celibate. I did my job every day and practiced with Happy Anarchy at least four nights a week, and fended off unwanted attention. Maya left me alone. She wasn't even around for the better part of a week. Her band, Avatar, played a gig at a club up in Burlington where the Vermont state university was, and then another one for a fraternity at Dartmouth, just over in New Hampshire.

I acquired some winter clothes, including a nice pair of Red Wing work boots and went on exploratory hikes along the old logging roads that threaded and criss-crossed the National Forest adjacent to the Village property, sometimes with Weezil. It could be dark and daunting back there in the woods during those short days, not so difficult to get lost. Weezil and I took it upon ourselves to mark the trails, using the lids of tin cans spray-painted various colors, nailed onto trees. Then we got hit by a twenty-six inch blizzard that prevented us from going back in there. We didn't have snowshoes. It took three days for the county highway department to plow out the road to Timlinton and nobody could get into town for anything.

I'd been searching for some way to be useful besides cleaning bathrooms, and I finally hit on something. I took advantage of Maya being away to bring the idea directly to Songbird. After the blizzard, the various parts of the village were linked by this network of deep footpaths carved out of the snow by the grounds crew. I caught up with him one afternoon when I was finished with work. He had just left the tofu hut, which was finally starting up production — they'd been testing the stuff on us: tofu breakfast scramble, tofu egg salad sandwiches, tofu chop-suey. I still wasn't crazy about it, but they were sure it was going to be a big hit in Hippiedom.

"Hey, remember me?" I said.

He seemed genuinely happy to see me.

"Pooh. Yeah, sure, what's up?"

"I've got an idea for something we could do here."

"Walk with me," he said. We tramped along together. The construction crew was building a maple sugar shack at the edge of the old field behind the inn, where a big glade of maples grew. They called it the sugarbush. The sap would start running in February. The Village could make money and have some great maple syrup left over for itself. He was going over there to check on its progress.

"Okay, here's the idea," I said. "You know what a pain in the ass it is for us to get stuff from town. Drugstore stuff. Especially cigarettes, we're constantly running out—"

"Hey, I'm out," Songbird said. He laughed. "Can I bum one from you?"

"Yeah, sure." I lit up two Winstons like I saw Mule do and handed him one. "See what I mean?"

"I do."

"So where are you going to get some, huh?" I said. "Drive all the way into town, right? Just for a carton of smokes?"

"Yeah, maybe when everyone stops letting me bum off of them."

"Did you ever go to camp?"

"Yeah, a couple of summers."

"Remember how they had the canteen? At least they did at my camp. It was this kind of half-assed store where you could get candy bars and batteries and shoe-laces and other little necessities."

"Okay. You want to start a canteen here?"

"You see, only about eight of us here have a car and it's at the point where they feel put-upon to fetch stuff for everybody when they go into town."

"I get it, Pooh. Sure it's a good idea. I should have thought of it myself."

"Really? You like it?"

"Yeah. There are three empty store-fronts up from the inn. Pick the one you like. You can set it up in there."

"And, you know, there's a little bit of regular traffic going through the Village. They might stop here in the middle of no-where and buy stuff — the products we're making, hammocks, lawn chairs, maybe maple syrup. I don't know about tofu—"

"Don't worry, we've got a bunch of health food stores lined up."

"But Sophie could make some of her brownies or chocolate chip cookies to sell."

"Sure."

"I don't know if it would make any money."

"Breaking even would be good enough," Songbird said. "I think you're right. The people here need it."

"Gee, you're easy."

"What's not to like about it?"

"I'm afraid Maya's going to disapprove, and she runs all the day-to-day operations."

"Why wouldn't she do it?"

"She hates my guts."

He actually stopped tramping and faced me. "What'd you do to her?"

"Not a damn thing." I said. "It's not like I came onto you or anything,"

"No, it's not," he said, and there was something in his look that unsettled me, his eyes searching my face, as though he was touching my cheeks, my lips with them. It was a fraught moment. I'm sure we both sensed it. Then he turned away and resumed crunching up the snowy path. "You're an enterprising girl," he said. "I like that."

I followed behind him.

"Uh, thanks. The thing is, we need some, like, seed money to stock the merchandise."

"All right. I'll give you some start-up dough. Let's say three hundred dollars. Don't get too much stuff. We'll see how it goes. And I want you to keep an account book, a record of what's coming in and going out. You can do that, right?"

"I guess," I said. "What about when Maya finds out?"

"This is between you and me. Just use whatever profits you get to buy more stuff so that the thing can sustain itself. And don't worry about Maya."

"Okay."

"I'll tell Bob Haugstead you can use the village van to make runs into town. You must have a driver's license, coming from Long Island."

I was surprised that he remembered that.

"You couldn't exist there without one," I said.

"There's a little wholesale operation in town that sells candy, cigarettes, and bar supplies. I'll get the address. Drugstore articles you'll probably have to get retail for now and just flip them. I assume you mean toothpaste and shampoo and stuff."

"Tampons especially," I said. "Not a good thing to run out of. The chicks here are constantly mooching off each other. It's worse than the cigarettes."

He stopped again. We were just short of the sugar shack construction site. So far, they'd put up the floor platform on a foundation of fieldstones. He put his hand on my shoulder.

"I'm all for this project," he said. "Go forth and make it happen, Pooh. Manifest it!"

I was so happy. Then, the next day I got abducted.

CHAPTER TWENTY-TWO

I was eating lunch (bean soup, whole wheat bread) with Jan Heathcoate, when I saw these two guys make their way into the dining room of the inn out of the corner of my eye. We were all instantly suspicious because you never saw guys with suits and ties around the village. A hush fell over the big room. One guy was middle-aged with a steel-gray brush-cut, very large and powerful. The other was half his age and two-thirds his size, with a narrow ferret face and a bowl-shaped mop-top haircut like the Beatles used have back in 1964, which looked dumb and out-of-date now. The smaller guy bent down and said something to little Poppy, the cute young blonde, who pointed at my table.

They came over. Other people started to get up and leave the room. The vibe was poisonous.

"Erica Bollinger?" the big guy said, looming over me. I put down my fork.

"Who are you?" I said.

"Are you Erica Bollinger?"

"Maybe."

"Oh, sometimes you are and sometimes you're not?" the little guy said.

I was already shuddering. My brain was getting overwhelmed with anxiety.

"It's her," he said to his partner. "Would you mind coming with us?"

"Yeah, I'd mind. You still didn't say who the hell you are."

"Vermont State Police. Detectives Rathko and Dougherty," the little one said.

"I didn't do anything."

"We're not judging you," the big guy said, "but we'd like you to come with us."

"What for?" Jan said. "This isn't Russia. You can't arrest people for no reason."

"This doesn't concern you," the shorter one said.

"Yeah it concerns me. She's my friend."

"You're a good friend," the big guy said. "We should all have good friends. But it's beside the point. Come on ma'am, don't turn this into a struggle."

Just then, Scotty Provost, of all people, came over to the table. His body language was obviously truculent, chest all puffed up under his flannel shirt, nostrils flaring.

"Do you have some kind of ID, man?" he said. "Badges or something?"

"Yeah, we have badges," the little guy said. "Of course, we don't need no *steenkin'* badges," he added with a ferrety laugh, "But here they are."

The two guys both took out these leather wallet-like cases and flipped them open."

"Can we see them?"

"You're seeing them."

"Close up."

The big guy let me inspect his and Scotty examined the little guy's. It was a pretty official looking gold badge. It didn't say anything about Vermont on it. But there were engraved scrolls both top and bottom with what looked like Latin words inscribed.

"These guys are a couple of jive turkeys—" Scotty said and almost instantaneously, the little guy dropped him on the floor with some kind of judo chop to the Adam's apple.

"Someone go get Hog," Jan yelled.

Meanwhile, Scotty was writhing on the floor, holding his throat, making horrible choking sounds.

"Please come along," the big guy reiterated.

I was petrified and I didn't want anybody else getting hurt.

"Okay. Okay."

I got up. The little guy tried to take me by the arm. I shook him off.

"I said, I'm coming."

I walked toward the front door of the inn between them.

"Don't go," Jan and some of the others said, but they were obviously intimidated.

They ushered me outside to a big black Buick waiting at the curb. The engine was still running. The little guy got in behind the wheel. The big guy opened the back door, put his hand on the top of my head, and sort of stuffed me in the back seat and slid in beside me. Imagine my surprise to see Marilyn sitting in the front passenger seat in her camel hair coat. She turned.

"Hello, dear," she said.

People had come onto the front porch of the inn. They were hollering pointing at us, at the car really. Then I understood what they were saying through the closed windows.

"It's got New York plates! New York plates!"

The little guy hit the gas and did a dramatic turn around the village green, screeching the wheels. We headed down the road toward Bennington. The big guy next to me clamped his hand over my face. He was holding a rag with some smelly chemical on it right up against my mouth and nose. A few seconds later, I blacked out.

CHAPTER TWENTY-THREE

I came to I don't know how long after I was abducted. We were in some kind of a motel room, fairly large, with two double beds, but rather crummy. The beds had those cheap cotton tufted bedspreads in a particularly vomitous baby blue. The TV was an old one from the fifties, teardrop-shaped. I could hear the toilet tank running. At first I was coming in and out of consciousness, but eventually I was more awake than asleep. That chemical smell still lingered in my sinuses.

"Where the hell am I?" I said.

The two so-called detectives sat on the edge of each bed. Marilyn loomed in the foreground. She came over to me carrying a cardboard plate covered with tin foil. They'd stuck me in one of those naugahyde lounge chairs, the crappy kind that you only saw in college dorm lounges and cheap motels.

"Sorry we had to interrupt your lunch, dear," Marilyn said. "Here, I picked something up beforehand. Your favorite, veal parm."

She took the foil off the cardboard plate, put it on my lap, and handed me a plastic knife and fork. I picked it up and threw it directly at her yellow cashmere sweater where a big piece of gunk with red sauce stuck briefly, before sliding off onto the floor.

"You little bitch," Marilyn said. "Is that how they taught you up there to behave around normal people."

"You're not normal," I said.

"Obviously, you've been brainwashed."

"Ma'am," the large detective said. "Let us take it from here."

Marilyn screwed her face into a mask of contempt, shook the rest of the gunk off her sweater, and exited the room.

The little guy got up from the end of his bed and ambled over to me.

"Some way to treat your Mom," he said.

"I hate her."

"You could have just said no thank you."

"Where the hell are we?"

"A safe place."

"You're not any official Vermont state police. If you were, we'd be in a police station. You'd be pressing charges."

"For some delicate situations, we have a different approach that requires a different setting, a place more quiet and peaceful."

"Yeah? What if I start screaming my head off?"

"I'll put duct tape around your head."

"Oh yeah...?"

I started yelling my head off. The little guy hurriedly took a fat roll of silvery tape out of a canvas bag. The big guy got up and held my arms from behind the chair. In a minute my mouth was all taped over, wrapped round and round over the back of my head, my hair and ears. Then they taped my arms down, running the tape roll all the way under the bottom of the chair and back over the arm-rests so I was immobilized. I just went limp and started crying.

"That's enough, Norm," the big guy said. He dragged the flimsy desk chair over and set it real close on my right side and sat

163

down. He had on the same aftershave that my dad used. It freaked me out. He waited quite a while for me to stop bawling.

"Let's calm down and try to go about this rationally," he said.

I tried screaming again, but with all that tape on me only a pathetic muffled squealing noise came out.

"I'll just wait until you can act like a lady," the big guy said.

He flipped on the TV and went to one of the beds, watching *The Price is Right.* His compadre cleaned up the veal parm off the crummy carpet, then went to lounge on the other bed, propped up against the pillows reading a newspaper. It was a good thing I didn't have a cold or an allergy because I could only breathe through my nose, and I was in a state of semi-panic the whole time. I just sat there through the stupid program and half of the next, *Truth or Consequences,* before I decided I had to switch tactics. Instead of screaming, I made like I was trying to communicate in words through the duct tape. The little guy had actually rolled over to take a snooze by then. The big guy was engrossed in the TV show but I managed to get his attention. He got up, switched off the boob tube, and came over to me.

"Had enough of being a bad little girl?" he said.

I nodded and said, "Uh huh."

"Promise?"

I nodded. He went and got a pair of heavy-duty scissors out of the canvas bag and cut the tape off the side of my head. I could feel quite a bit of hair get pulled out in the process.

"Ow!"

"Sorry about that."

By now, the little guy had woken up and was pouring coffee out of giant thermos bottle into a drinking glass from the desk.

"I have to pee," I said.

"Fair enough."

The big guy cut the tape holding my arms down and made a *help yourself* gesture with his open hand to the bathroom door. I was kind of wobbly but got in there under my own power. Guess what? Someone had nailed plywood over the window on the outside. I tried pushing on it since banging on it would only get their attention. It was fixed on there good and tight so I couldn't slip out. There was no lock on the bathroom door, either, so I couldn't barricade myself in there. I guess the idea was if you were the only one in the room, or with a loved one, there was no point in having a lock on the bathroom door. I couldn't escape. I did have to pee, though, so I took care of that. I came back out and the big guy made the same open hand gesture back at the chair. I sat down.

"I'm hungry," I said.

"You should have eaten that nice veal parm," the little guy said.

"I've got a little something you can have," the big guy said. He took a pack of Oreo cookies out of the canvas bag.

"Hey, those are ours," the little guy said.

"Be nice, for Chrissake. The little lady's hungry."

"You should make her earn them."

"Be quiet, Norm."

He scissored open the cellophane and handed me the pack.

"Have as many as you want. We can always get more."

I started devouring them."

"Can I have some of that coffee."

"If you promise not to throw it at me."

"I promise."

He filled up the other drinking glass with coffee and brought it over. It was light with a lot of sugar.

"What do you say?"

"Thank you…"

He handed it over.

"…asshole," I couldn't help adding.

He made a disapproving face.

"Let me introduce ourselves. My name is Doc. It's not my Christian name, of course, but that's what my friends call me."

"I'm not your friend."

"Well, all right. But that's what I go by. And my young partner there, you've probably gathered by now that he's Norm—"

"As in normal," he said from across the room.

"You're not police, are you?"

Doc hesitated a moment and swapped glances with Norm.

"Actually, no, were not. We're private."

"Private what? Detectives? You need a license for that I think, and anyway you'd be out-of-state. Your car has New York plates."

"You're a very observant girl."

"Then what are you, exactly?"

"We're professionals who help people with this sort of problem."

"What sort of problem do you think I have, besides a hateful mother who can't mind her own business."

"Your mother's very concerned about you, Erica."

"Didn't she tell you, Doc? I don't answer to Erica."

"What do your friends call you?"

"You're not my friend, Doc."

"All right, what do you go by?"

"Pooh, as in Winnie the."

"Winnie the what…?"

"Oh fuck you. Go ahead and call me Erica."

"Uh-uh-uh-uh-uh," Norm said, waggling his finger at me. "I'll take those Oreos away."

"I wish you would," I said, chucking the bag across the room at his bed. It landed on the floor, of course, and the cookies scattered all over.

"Tsk tsk," Norm said, not the mere sound but the actual words: "Tsk tsk."

"Knock it off, you two," Doc said. "Erica, the problem is you've joined a cult."

"Oh? Is that what she thinks? She doesn't know what she's talking about. It's just a village of people who happen to be around the same age and have things in common."

"Your generation is something else."

"Except for me," Norm said, holding his newspaper aside. "I'm normal."

"We're normal too, I assure you," I said. "Probably more than you."

"Can you tell me something about the beliefs of this place?" Doc continued.

"We don't have any beliefs."

"You said you have things in common, right? To have all gathered in this special, uh, community, out in the middle of nowhere. Some creed must be holding it together."

"There are lots of places like it all over America now. They're called communes. Don't you read *Time Magazine*? They can't shut up about it. What do we believe? That the war is illegal and idiotic. That American middle-class life is insane. That the city is a horrible place to live. That we can make it on our own without all that crap."

"That's ridiculous," Norm interjected. "The guy in charge of this outfit is a rich kid who's subsidizing the whole operation. Did you know that?"

"Yes, as a matter of fact I do."

"Really?"

"Yeah, really. His family made a fortune selling weapons of war. I know all about it. His father sold the company more than twenty years ago. Is it against the law now to inherit money and do something positive with it?"

"Anyway, you're not making it on your own," Doc said. "You're all in his service, so to say."

"That's absurd," I said. "You don't know what you're talking about that either."

"I need a break, Erica," Doc said. "You're wearing me out."

"Am I a hard case?"

"You're very argumentative," he said. "I'm going to let Norm take over. He's closer to your age. You'll probably *relate* to him better."

167

Norm handed off the newspaper to Doc and approached me as if he relished the chance to work me over. Doc took to his bed. At least he didn't turn the TV back on.

"Do you ever hear people voicing subversive thoughts up there in fantasyland?" he said, turning the chair next to mine backwards as if this was a super casual chitchat in your high school home room. He was dandling the roll of duct tape the whole time.

"Subversive thoughts? What do you mean by that?"

"Like, against the United States."

"Oh sure. Like I said, we think the country has lost its mind. We talk about it all the livelong day."

"How about the government?"

"What about the government?"

"Do they talk about subverting it?"

"No, we talk about changing it, fixing it."

"Oh, okay. Like how?"

"Like getting rid of President Johnson."

"How are going to do that?" Norm pantomimed holding a pistol and made *kshh kshh* noises with his mouth. "Like this?"

That gave me a chill.

"You think we're plotting to assassinate the president? Is that what you think, too, Doc?" He put down the paper, shrugged, and went back to reading. "You guys are two sick bastards. We support Senator Gene McCarthy. He's going to run against Johnson in the primaries and he's going to beat LBJ, just watch. People are sick and tired of this stupid war."

Norm suddenly slapped me. I couldn't believe it.

"You shut up your dirty little mouth," he said. "My brother Vincent is serving our country over there. Hundred and First Airborne. The Screaming Eagles. We're very proud of Vincent."

"Is he killing babies over there?"

Norm slapped me again.

"You tell him to stop hitting me," I appealed to Doc.

"Stop hitting her," Doc said, without even peeking out from behind the paper.

"She's very fresh. She hates America."

"I don't hate America. I hate the goddam government."

"Same thing," Norm said.

"No it's not," I hollered at him.

He held up the roll of tape. I got the message.

"I guess we just see things very differently," I said.

"Sheesh, do we ever."

Little Norm hectored me for an hour, asking in six dozen different ways about the supposedly subversive activities of Sunrise Village. It wasn't like I was trying to cover up anything, because I hadn't seen or heard anything of the kind in the weeks since I first got there. I quit trying to be a smart-ass, though, because he kept smacking me when I did, and Doc didn't actually do anything to make him stop. For the last half hour I just stopped answering altogether. Then Marilyn came back in the room. She carried a big shopping bag. I could smell some kind of cooked food.

She asked Doc and Norm how it was going. They said they were making progress.

"No they're not," I said.

"She's a bit of a hard case, ma'am," Norm said.

"A lovely girl, though," Doc said. "When we get her out of that rats' nest, I think she'll do really well in life. Maybe find a nice boy like Norm here to settle down with."

Marilyn just made a face. She didn't like being patronized.

"I have supper for everyone," she said beginning to take articles out of the shopping bag and put them on the desk. "There's another veal parm — don't give it to her! — and a hamburger plate with fries and cole slaw, and a club sandwich with fries, neither of which will do much damage if she gets violent again. I got you boys a six-pack of beer, too, but don't give her any."

"Why, thank you Mrs. Bollinger," Doc said.

"Here's a No-Cal soda she can have. She's gotten chubby up there."

That was bullshit, of course. Just another one of Marilyn's neurotic obsessions, really a projection of her own weight anxiety.

"I'll have the veal parm," Doc said.

"Wait a minute," Norm said. "I want that."

"Who's in charge here?" Doc said.

"Okay, but you don't get to decide *that*."

"Why don't you two flip a coin?" Marilyn suggested earnestly.

"You eat too much too," Norm said to Doc. Then to the rest of us: "He eats too much."

"Assholes...." I said.

"Don't you talk to them that way," Marilyn got all revved up again.

"Dad's gonna divorce you when he hears about this, you fucking witch," I said. "And, believe me, he's going to hear about it."

"I'm going to take my meal back in my room," Marilyn said with a weary sigh, ignoring me, and just as she turned to go, the door flew open. It was already dark outside and cold air rushed into the room. In the doorway was Bob Haugstead, "Hog," a six-foot-two sinewy panther of a man, one of the few people besides Mule from the Village who had actually served in the Army in Vietnam. There were other people behind him and they filed into the room: Oswald Strangefield, "Teck" Hesslewhite, Songbird, and finally Mule, who was dressed in a charcoal gray suit with a red paisley tie. To me, they looked like the good guys from The Legion of Superheros.

"Thank Gawd," I said.

Marilyn went straight for the phone.

"I'm going to call the police," she said. But she didn't dial the operator, obviously bluffing.

"I thought these guys were the police," Mule said. "Go ahead and call them."

"And just who the hell are you?" Norm said.

"My name is Arden Blanchard," Mule said. "I'm the attorney for Sunrise Village."

That blew my mind, all right. Gone completely was his jive ghetto accent, his hipster manner. He was transformed. He took a card out of his inside jacket pocket and handed it to Doc.

"I don't know exactly who you two clowns are," Mule said, "but I know you're not legit and you can go ahead and call the police because when they get here you're going to be arrested under Vermont statute title seven, chapter fifty-five, kidnapping, and section two-four-oh-six, unlawful restraint, punishable by imprisonment for not more than five years or a fine of not more than twenty-five thousand dollars, or both—"

"That little fucker has been smacking me all day too?" I said.

"Oh, is that so, " Mule said. He went up to Norm. "Then we can throw in battery, sections ten-twenty-one and ten-twenty-three — we'll let the DA sort that out."

Just then, Norm tried that karate chop move he'd used on Scotty Provost back at the inn. Mule did a Cassius Clay head-snap move, caught Norm's hand in mid-flight, and twisted it in such a way that Norm dropped to his knees at the foot of the bed squealing in pain.

"We don't want any trouble," Doc said.

"You've already got trouble, mister," Mule said. "And shame on you Mrs. Bollinger for hooking up with these shady morons."

"They're de-programmers," she said, clearly shaken. "You've brainwashed my daughter."

"That's idiotic, Mrs. Bollinger," Mule said. "She's legally an emancipated adult and she's there of her own free will. Try this again and they'll throw the book at you, too, along with these cretins."

I'd remained in my chair the whole time, wanting to stay clear in case any physical scuffling broke out. But then I saw Songbird gesture at me to come, and I shot out of my seat to him.

"By the way," Mule said. "We've got your license plate. If we see or hear anymore of you around here, you're going to regret it."

"Let's go," Songbird said.

We piled out of that crummy room. Never had the air of a cold winter night felt so good.

CHAPTER TWENTY-FOUR

We all crammed into the Sunrise Village van with Hog behind the wheel. It turned out I was being held at a dump called the Windigo Lodge outside of Manchester, about twenty miles north of Bennington. Sunrise Village had one previous experience with this sort of thing, the past summer when Karen Kolblenz's father — Karen who worked in the kitchen — sent a couple of ex-army PSYOPS clowns to browbeat her into coming home. The guys in the village found her right down at the Vermonter Motel in Bennington. So they had an idea how it worked, and this time they even had the New York license plate number and make of Doc and Norm's Buick to look for. There were maybe only twenty motels in the local orbit to search at, and they found me about three quarters of the way down the list.

This new breed of hustlers like Doc and Norm styled themselves as de-programmers, Songbird explained to me. They rescued the supposedly captive children of concerned parents out of communes and claimed to be able to reverse whatever brainwashing the kid was under, especially whacko religious ideas. Except there was no program and no brainwashing in Sunrise Village and it was certainly not a religious outfit. It was political, perhaps, in ways that I would come to understand later on, but I certainly hadn't been indoctrinated into any set of beliefs.

Everybody was in high spirits, though we didn't smoke anything because we didn't want to get stopped with pot in the van by the sheriffs. I mentioned that I was starving and we stopped at the diner where Robin was working her shift and Songbird bought us all dinner. I ate two whole cheeseburgers with onion rings and banana cream pie for dessert. There were quite a few people waiting around the big common room at the inn when we got back, and they cheered when the boys brought me in.

Of course the first thing I did when I got back was call my dad and tell him what Marilyn had done. There was an unnaturally long pause on the line.

"I'm going to divorce her," he finally said.

"What? Because of this?"

"No," he said. "I've been thinking about it for quite a while. More than thinking, really. Planning. I actually decided to go ahead with it a few weeks ago. I'm sorry to have to tell you this."

He was right. Despite how much I hated Marilyn, it hurt to think about the whole family breaking up after all these years. It made me teary again, though I wasn't bawling.

"What about Bobby?"

"He'll be all right. He's got one more year of school before college."

"Did you tell him?"

"No. I haven't told anybody, most especially your mother. Only you."

"I don't know what to say."

"You don't have to say anything. It'll be fine. I'll be free to come up and see you sometime without getting an earful."

"That'd be nice," I said, sniffling. "Maybe you'll want to join up, become the village photographer after all."

"Ha Ha." he said. "There's something else you don't know."

"Oh God, what now?"

"Nothing terrible."

"What?"

"I'm going to work for *The Times*."

"*The New York Times*! Really! God, that's fantastic."

"Yeah, yeah. They like my stuff. They contacted me back in November. I sealed the deal just the other day. It's manna from heaven, I guess, under the circumstances. A real nice raise and great fringe benefits."

"Marilyn should have to go out and find a job. She's only forty-four, for Godsake. She should go back to teaching math. She's perfect for it."

"Frankly, I'd be much happier if she marries some other guy who would take her off my hands. The sooner the better."

"Aw, don't say that. You're not even divorced yet."

"You don't know what it's been like."

He was right. Being Marilyn's daughter was bad enough but I wasn't married to her."

Someone had put a big tumbler of red wine in my hand just before I made the call and I was finally relaxing. I regaled Larry with the whole story of Norm and Doc and he just kept muttering "Jesus Christ" through the whole recitation. Finally, I told him I loved him and that was all.

All kinds of people wanted to console me that night, most especially Danny Musser, in his patented fashion, but I declined and eventually just drifted back to my room with my own familiar things. I had a half a roach in my banjo case and lit it up and tuned in the Bennington College FM station on my big Zenith portable, and they were playing a song by someone I never heard of before, "Different Drum," by one Linda Ronstadt, and I was stoned, I admit, but I couldn't help thinking, I could do that, I could sing like that, I could get on the radio, but it would have to be a song nobody ever heard before. A good one.

The notion excited me so much that I got my banjo out and started writing a song about the *failure to communicate* between the generations, based on the abduction.

Baby girl in the cradle
Welcome to the light of day
Wait until the moon comes out
Then I'll tell you what life's about.
You're too little to have any say
Leave it to me to show you the way.

That was the first stanza of the first song I ever wrote, in fact, and I had no idea where it would take me but I worked on it for hours, building it into something fresh-sounding with a modal shift in the chorus:

Be like you?
Never in a million years
Be like me
First I've got to wipe away the tears
And tell you I'm on my own... now

Obviously the song was about Marilyn and me and the fact that it was over between us, mother and daughter. I was divorcing her as much as Larry was, and of course it made me terribly sad to grok the full impact of that, which really only hit me in the act of writing that song. I felt as sad for her as I did for myself.

The radiator was clanking and my room was actually too hot. I didn't feel sleepy at all. I was all agitated, though it was one-thirty in the morning and I'd had a pretty long and harrowing day. I could see through the window that a nice three-quarter moon was gleaming over the snowy Vermont woods so I put on some warm clothes and my boots and I went outside to walk off my agitation.

It was so cold you could feel your nostrils frost up. But after being held captive all day in that crummy motel it was glorious just to be outside in the moonlight, free. The snow had thawed and re-frozen so it was crusty and rather hard to walk on. Most of the lights were out in the inn and the other buildings on the little main street, and almost all the zodiac cottages where people lived except one. That was the Libra House, which was a peculiar little brick structure with a stepped roof, a sawed off tower at the near end and a chimney at the other. Yellow light glowed softly in the two front windows. There was a red Volvo parked beside it. I knew that it was where Mule lived. I could faintly hear the strains of some be-bopish jazz from out there. Since he was up, I thought it would be a good idea to thank him for saving me from those morons. Plus, of course, I was extremely curious about who he actually was.

I knocked on the door and it took him so long to answer that I almost turned to leave. When he opened it, he was dressed only in a pair of green army fatigue pants and a silk kimono open so you could see his bare chest.

"Oh, I'm sorry if you're with somebody," I said.

"I ain't with nobody."

"Oh...."

"What's going on with you now?" he asked rather harshly.

"Now? Nothing," I said.

"You just come by to see me?"

"I came to say thank you."

"Oh?" He cocked his head quizzically. "You want to come in?"

"I dunno...."

He pulled the kimono sides together to cover his bare skin.

"We can't talk like this letting the cold air in," he said.

"All right."

I stepped inside. He shut the door. It was all one big room.

"What was this place?" I asked.

"It was a chapel. Made by them weird people way back when."

"The Edenists?"

"Yeah, them."

"Who's that?" I pointed to a poster on the wall. It was of a very handsome young Negro man in a leather coat and a beret, sitting in a wicker chair with a fan-shaped backrest. He was holding a rifle in one hand and a spear in the other.

"You don't know who that is?"

"No."

"That's Huey P. Newton, Minister of Defense of the Black Panther Party. You never heard of him?"

"Well, I've heard of the Black Panthers."

He looked amused, shook his head.

"Why you still up — all you been through today?"

"I couldn't sleep. I've got to get a guitar."

"Huh? A guitar? What's that got to do with anything? I don't have no guitars on hand."

"Of course. Sorry. Just thinking out loud."

"What you want a guitar for all of a sudden?"

"I want to write songs. The banjo just doesn't cut it."

"Yeah, well. Banjos. They's a slavery instrument."

"It's just limiting."

"Yeah, slavery was limiting, too."

There was a sheet of plywood set up on two saw horses as a makeshift table with some bottles, cracker boxes, and some kitchen stuff on it. A few plates, glasses. He went over there and poured a glass of that good scotch he liked.

"You want a little taste? Might make you sleepy."

"Okay,"

"Cold as shit out tonight."

Then he went to the woodstove that fed into the chimney in the rear and stuffed a couple of split logs in. There was a ratty sofa down there, a low table piled with books, and a wine bottle with a drippy candle in it, all of that across from a double bed with a knobby brass headboard. I went and sat down on the sofa close to the fire. He sat down next to me. A pack of Kools lay invitingly on the table. I shook out two, lighted them, and handed him one.

"I guess you're learning something," he said.

"Thank you for rescuing me."

"Line of duty," he said.

"My mother's a crazy person."

"Maybe she learned something too today. Light that candle."

I did. In defiance of Maya's rule, he had a film can of weed right out on the table and some Zig-zag rolling papers, and he rolled a joint faster than you might open a can of tuna. He lit it off the candle.

"Want some?"

"Sure.

We passed the J back and forth a few times and just sat there quietly sipping our whiskey. The music was mesmerizing and relaxing.

"What's that on the hi-fi?"

"Miles with Wayne Shorter and Herbie Hancock."

"I'm a jazz ignoramus," I eventually said.

"Don't sweat it."

"What was that name you gave to those morons tonight when you crashed in on us?"

"Name of what?"

"You. Your name?"

"Arden Blanchard."

"That's a lovely name. Very musical. Why don't you go by it?"

"I do when I feel like it."

"Nobody calls you that around here."

"Not too many of 'em know me."

"You're very difficult to get to know."

"How do I mystify you, Miss Winnie the Pooh?" he said, and he cracked a smile for the first time. I guess the weed and the whiskey had relaxed him a little.

"The way you speak, for one thing. One moment you come on like some jive-talking ghetto spade and then you turn around and sound like you walked out of the Harvard Law school."

"I work both sides of the street," he said.

"Are you really a lawyer."

"Yeah."

"Where'd you go to law school?"

"Harvard."

"You're kidding. I was only saying that."

"It's a fact, Jack."

"You really went there?"

"Veritas."

"What?"

"Latin. Truth. It's on the school crest."

"I'll be dipped in shit."

"No you won't," he said. "That's reserved for my people."

"Aw, don't say that."

"See, talk just confuses things. Maybe we don't have to speak at all," he said.

Our gazes locked. The way his green eyes drilled into mine didn't intimidate me anymore. Instead, it turned me on. I suppose the weed and the whiskey amplified my feelings. His kimono had fallen open again. Without even thinking about it, just going on pure emotion, my hand reached inside to his warm body. I could feel the heat there reflecting off the fire in the nearby wood stove. Our faces came together and our mouths found each other. We were kissing desperately and both of us struggled to free me from my jacket, which I still had on. Without another word, we moved to the bed. He took my hiking boots off and then my jeans and underpants. His fatigue pants dropped on the floor. I pulled my sweater off and the T-shirt underneath went with it. Then we just feasted on each other in a revolving set of positions that had me coming repeatedly until it all melded into one big orgasm. And finally he came, too, with a pained and elongated groan.

"I guess that's one way of saying thank you," I said, after we lay on our backs inertly for quite a while afterward.

"You're welcome then," he said. He swung off the bed, got the pack of Kools and the candle from across the room, and returned. I had wiggled under the sheets and blankets. He came in there with me.

"You feel wonderful," I said. "So warm."

"I guess I like you after all," he said, balancing an ashtray on his stomach.

"I want to know about you," I said. "You're very complicated."

"Not really," he said. "Just the natural product of certain forces and things."

"Like what? Where do you come from?"

"Let's talk about you."

"You already know all there is to know about me. What forces? What things?"

"Christ. I dunno. American history and all."

"Tell me your history," I insisted.

He sighed, releasing a big cloud of mentholated smoke in the dim light.

"I dunno where to start."

"Your parents, of course."

He sighed. "Okay. You asked for it. My daddy was the bandleader Roland Blanchard. His daddy, the Arden I'm named after, was principal of the Roper Normal School, a teacher's college in Swainsboro, Georgia, real country, about a million miles from Atlanta. Grandma was a teacher there, too. They were well-off enough to have a piano in the house and Gran' locked my daddy in a room two hours a day to force him to practice. He got good and when he was seventeen, he bought a train ticket out of there and landed in New York City. He worked on the docks during the First

World War. Then he enrolled at Columbia University thinking he might become an engineer, but the pull of music was too great. He dropped out. He was waiting tables at the Twenty-one Club back when it was a speakeasy and was allowed to play piano there late at night. He caught the ear of Dillard Hastings who led a jazz band called the Dixie Rhythm Dukes. They played the Oriole Club, the Cotton Club, Club Alabam, the Roseland Ballroom. Roland went with them. He wrote a number of jazz band instrumental standards: "The Sandtown Crawl," "The Santee Shuffle," and some songs with lyrics like "The After Hours Blues," and "For Myself Alone," which was recorded by his first wife, Minnie Norman, a vocalist that the Dukes acquired. She was a piece of work. They became known as the Battling Blanchards and he divorced her."

"So that wasn't your mother."

"No, no. He got shed of her before the stock market crashed in twenty-nine. She was stabbed to death by a boyfriend a few years later."

"Yikes!"

"Yeah, she was a femme fatale. It's a real type. Roland was a good arranger and around the time he ditched Minnie, he started his own band, the Roland Blanchard Orchestra. Up until then, he'd stayed in New York, but as the depression wore on, he had to rely on touring more, riding a bus all over, staying in the colored hotels, playing a lot of one-night stands in places like Dayton and Louisville. His abilities for managing the business of a band were not equal to his musical attainments. He started drinking too much. The band fell apart in thirty-seven. He went back to New York, dried out, and got a job playing piano in the CBS Radio Orchestra, a nice, safe, dependable, regular gig, with hard times still on in America. That was where he met my mother."

"How old are you, anyway?"

"I'll be twenty-six soon."

"So you were born in, what, forty-two?"

"That's right."

"How come he wasn't in the war."

"Too old. He was born in the nineteenth century, fifty-three when Pearl Harbor happened. My Mom was a white girl from Roanoke, Virginia. She was a flautist, flute player, in the CBS orchestra, quite a bit younger than Roland."

"What was her name?"

"Miriam Scales. Her daddy, who I never met, was a union organizer on the railroad. Her mother was stay-at-home. Roland used to take her to Schrafft's for hot fudge sundaes. He didn't drink anymore. It got more serious. So many other men off to war and all. She got pregnant and he married her. I was born on Easter Sunday. A mixed marriage like that was unusual in those days, but not unheard of in New York, and they lived in Greenwich Village where anything went. My mother volunteered at the NAACP, which was still very much a black-white thing in those days and she got Roland involved. That was how they met Leila Sohnberg, who was on the national board. The Sohnbergs were bohemians, very arty, and they lived in a big town house on Washington Square full of primitive shit from around the world — African masks and South Seas fertility statues and Eskimo carvings. My mother quit working after I was born and Leila had a baby the next year, and they became pretty tight, taking the kids to Washington Square every day and then me and Elliot playing together at their house or our apartment."

"You've known Songbird your whole life?"

"Yeah. Like brothers."

"Is it true about his parents?"

"Yeah, they got killed in New Guinea. Very little else known abot it. But that was later. See, Roland had a stroke in 1951. I hadn't turned nine yet. He was gone a month later. My mother was very fragile psychologically after that. There wasn't any life insurance. She hadn't been working since I came along, you know, out of practice, which is tough for professional musicians. Roland had left her without any means. Leila and Arthur Sohnberg took us in. A white woman with a black child. That was a tough situation. So, we moved into that big house filled with spooky art. A year later, my mom got hit by a truck in Sheridan Square—"

"Oh Gawd, did it kill her?"

"Oh, yeah. After a week in St. Vincent's Hospital, anyway. All my grandparents were gone by then. The Sohnbergs adopted me. They even got their lawyers to sue the trucking company on my behalf. And that's the story of my origins. Maybe not quite as colorful as you imagined."

"It's quite a story. But then they got killed, the Sohnbergs. What happened to you two kids?"

"We were sent to Elliot's grandmother in Brookline, Mass, just outside of Boston. But we were hardly ever there. She was all right, the little I saw of her, just a little uptight in that Boston way. She put us in prep school in New Hampshire, Ponsonby Hall, a very severe place. Cold showers and shit. I was the only Negro in the whole joint and I guess I rebelled. I joined the army to get out of there when I was seventeen. You know what happened with that. As it happened, I got out short."

"Short? What's that?"

"They mustered me out early, before the end of my tour. I was in a Jeep wreck in Saigon. Broke some bones, including my skull."

"Are you all right?"

"Yeah. It was a lucky. What they call a million dollar injury. A lot of guys wish they'd gotten out like that. But Vietnam made me a serious person. I grew up fast. By then, Elliot was a sophomore at Harvard. The family lawyers got me in despite me dropping out of Ponsonby. I only just finished law school last June."

"Don't you have to take some kind of test after that to be a lawyer?"

"Yeah, the bar exam. I'm licensed in Vermont."

"But you don't go to an office every day."

"I have one client: Sunrise Village."

For a while, neither of us said anything. He shifted toward me and ran his fingertip around one of my nipples.

"So, you were basically raised in the world of white people," I said.

"Yeah, I guess I was."

"So what's with acting like a ghetto Negro."

"The one-drop rule."

"What's that?"

"If you've got one drop of black blood, you're black. That's how it works in America."

"But that doesn't mean you have to act a particular way."

"It's late, and I'm tired of talking about myself, and there's something else I'd rather do with you, as long as you're here."

He kissed me and we made love again, slowly and tenderly this time, and then we both conked out.

CHAPTER TWENTY-FIVE

Perhaps I flattered myself to think that I was learning something about men, but when Arden turned up in the dining room the following evening and asked if I wanted to come over to his place, I declined. He looked insulted. I told him maybe later in the week. But he didn't hassle me. I'd decided that the reason I was getting taken advantage of by guys like Danny Musser and even Dreamboat back at NYU was that I was too compliant, too easy, and I should make myself less available, harder to get. Obviously I had feelings for Arden, who was such an interesting, complicated person, and wonderful to sleep with. But I didn't want to get tossed aside by him like a banana skin.

Anyway, after the interruption of getting abducted, my life in Sunrise Village was returning to normal, including the practice routine for our band, Happy Anarchy, which had changed its name to Don't Look Back, in honor of the documentary movie about Dylan's tour of England that came out the previous year. I didn't think it was such a great idea, since we'd probably be pegged as Dylan coat-tail riders, but I was overruled by the Big Three: Danny,

Padget, and Alan Kaplan. I also asked Alan if he would teach me how to play the guitar and he said sure.

Meanwhile, I turned my energies during the daytime to setting up the canteen for the Village that Songbird and I had talked about. Mark Tanzio, Tanzy, was less busy during the winter months, since he ran the gardening squad, and he volunteered to help me. First we had to clean up the dusty old shop-front and paint it. Tanzy rousted out all sorts of colorful antique junk from the barns to put up as décor on the one wall that didn't have built-in shelves — old signs for Red Man Tobacco and Quaker State Motor Oil, broken pitchforks and hay rakes, some old sepia photographs of when the village was a gambling resort in the twenties, a ratty old stuffed deer head. Songbird came in to see how we were doing and handed over an envelope with three hundred dollars in twenties. Curiously, Maya did not come around at all and I wondered if something was going on behind the scenes, like if she was plotting against me — which, I admit, sounded paranoid.

When the shop-front was ready, we drove the village van to Bennington and loaded up on cartons of Winston, Lucky Strike, and Kool cigarettes, boxes of Milky Way bars, Almond Joys, Necco Wafers, Aspirin, Chapsticks, Tampax, skin cream, shampoo, toothpaste and brushes, dental floss, Zig-Zag rolling papers, tube socks, bandanas, envelopes, and pads of writing paper. We stopped at the PO and bought rolls of stamps. That was the stock we started with.

I'd saved money of my own over the weeks, including some that Larry had sent to me. There was a music store on Main Street that sold records, hi-fis, and a small selection of instruments. The few decent guitars they had — Gibsons and Martins — were out of my price-range brand-new, but the nice man who ran the place, about thirty I thought, who was letting his hair and sideburns grow out to look hip, directed me to a shop on North Street that sold old stuff on consignment and I found a flat-top Epiphone guitar there for sixty bucks. The strings were shot, of course, so we swung back to the music store for new ones. When we got back to the Village I gave the guitar to Alan to check out. He volunteered to set it up — change the strings, adjust the neck, clean up the wood, oil the tuning machines — and when he gave it back the next day, he declared it was "a pretty damn good axe for the money."

We put our sparse merchandise on display in the canteen and we had our grand opening the next afternoon. I still worked my morning job on the cleaning crew, and I opened the canteen between three and five weekdays and ten to noon on Saturdays, so I earned twelve extra hours of pay a week. Plus, during the spells when I sat in the canteen with nobody around, I got to practice the guitar. Alan lent me books with the chords and showed me licks and turn-arounds. I was at somewhat of an advantage knowing the banjo, and was already a decent fingerpicker, but the chord shapes on guitar were completely different and the neck was so much fatter it was hard to get used to. Alan was also well-versed in music theory and he helped me understand the architecture of the musical keys in the diatonic scale and chord relationships as well as the mechanics of playing the instrument. I was suddenly in heaven, running my little store, practicing every day. I got pretty good on the guitar fast and started writing more songs as I acquired more technique.

Two days after I rebuffed him, I took the initiative to be with Arden again. I hadn't seen him around much, and he made no attempt to communicate, so I slipped a note into his mailbox — which was labeled "Mule," by the way — and he responded later with a terse note that said: *Okay. 11pm my place.* So I went over that night. He seemed nervous, agitated. When I came in, I attempted to kiss him and he said, "Don't do that," and held me at bay.

"You're mad at me."

"I ain't mad," he said.

Uh-oh, I thought. He's back to his ghetto spade self.

"You did ask me to come over," I said.

"I didn't ask, I told you."

"Oh? I don't think I like the sound of that."

"Don't take it personally."

"What? It's pretty personal, ordering somebody around."

"Take your clothes off."

"I'm not taking my clothes off. Not until you tell me what's going on with you all of a sudden."

"You don't know me."

"I probably know you more than most of the people around here."

He went and got his whiskey bottle — a fresh one I noticed — and retreated to the sitting area near the wood stove. He conspicuously didn't invite me to join him, but I groked that he was putting up some kind of psychological defense to placate his pride since his ego trip wasn't working on me. I got a jelly glass off the makeshift table and went down and sat next to him and helped myself to a shot.

"You're sulking," I said.

"No I'm not."

"Is it because I turned you down you the other day?"

"Naw. There's plenty others around here."

"Oh, so you're balling other chicks?"

"I could if I wanted to."

"What the hell's going on with you, Arden?"

I thought he was going to cry. His mouth got twitchy and he turned his face away.

"I'm ashamed," he said.

I reached out and stroked his cheek with the back of my fingers.

"Don't do that," he said. "I'm not your pet."

"Okay."

I quit touching him. It happened that I had a pack of Kools on me — he'd turned me on to menthol smokes — so I lit two and gave him one. He turned his head back around, even shifted his body a bit more openly toward me.

"I don't think I can be here much longer," he said.

"Here at the village?"

"Yeah."

"But you're needed here."

"I'm needed elsewhere," he said. "My brothers and sisters need me. I think I have to go out to California."

"What's out there."

"The Panthers."

"You're not that kind of street radical."

"They're going to need lawyers. Huey's going to trial this summer out in Oakland. The police tried to set him up last fall. There was shoot-out and a cop died. I think I can help."

I couldn't argue with that. We smoked and sipped our whiskey listening to his perpetual jazz playing low in the background.

"What's on the stereo?" I asked. It was all honking saxophone and tickety-tickety drums.

"Trane. A Love Supreme."

I listened strenuously for a minute. The virtuosity was obvious, but it was just not my thing.

"Don't you like it here?" I blurted out, realizing at the same moment how fatuous it sounded.

"This is as unreal as it gets, baby."

"We're working on making it real."

"Yeah, well good luck with that."

"It's safe here, at least. The system out there is spinning out of control like some infernal machine. If you join the Panthers, you'll be jumping right into the gears where everything gets ground up like hamburger."

"Don't worry about me. Look, I wanted to help Elliot get this thing started. The family lawyers, they think he's out of his skull. They put a lot of obstacles in his way. I've been as close to him as anyone in my life. I admire his idealism. But this ain't real. There's a war going on far away outside the country and there's a war going on in-country and there's a call I've got to answer."

"When do you think you might go?"

"Soon."

"Does Songbird know?"

"I haven't told him yet."

"Don't you think you ought to?"

"Certainly I do." He poured us two more drinks. I was getting to like whiskey. "That's what's going on with me, Pooh. That's the straight-up shit."

Of course, we ended up making love. It was sad and beautiful. I wanted to be needed and Arden was in need, at least in need of saying goodbye to part of the world he was letting go of.

CHAPTER TWENTY-SIX

He must have left the very next morning. His red Volvo was gone. We'd had our goodbye, I guess, but I still felt cheated. There was no announcement made to the villagers, but it got around before the day was out that "Mule" was gone and the collective mood was blue. Even though he operated mainly behind-the-scenes, he was a reassuring presence. Then the days went by and life went on at Sunrise Village. There was always something happening, some project, some celebration, new people coming around, the mighty flux of romances starting, romances ending, music-making, skit nights, feasts, and all the routine hard work to keep the place going. After Mule split, Songbird had to go back to Boston, I assumed to hassle with the lawyers and bankers.

The canteen was an immediate success. People who had had to depend on the few others with cars to fetch their bare necessities for them were very relieved to be able to just buy a pack of smokes and a Chapstick up in the village. I got some additional items in stock: guitar strings (duh), a few art supplies, batteries, bobby pins, sewing needles and thread. I was making a marginal profit on the business, enough to keep buying more stuff. On one of my resupply runs to town, I acquired a set of snowshoes at the second-hand shop. They enabled me to get out into the woods again on the deep March snow and rediscover the joy of solitude. Living cheek-by-jowl with a big tribe of people was very stimulating, but I had forgotten the blessings of being truly alone, especially alone in nature.

There was a book of animal tracks in the inn library, and if we had a few days without any snowfall, the traces of the animals going about their daily and nightly business remained visible on the old snowpack until it looked like there was a whole city of wild animals moving around out there: fox, rabbit, raccoon, squirrel, opossum, mink, deer, of course, and even bear. There was a veritable highway network of deer trails deep in the woods where they made their habitual rounds from the thickets where they browsed to the sheltered places under ancient pine trees where they "yarded up" for protection against the elements. I rarely saw the animals themselves during the daytime. The utter stillness of the winter woods amazed me, a delicious silence. The days were getting noticeably longer, too. It was still light out now when they rang the dinner bell.

I especially grew to appreciate the structured existence I'd created for myself: breakfast with friends, a few hours of physical work. I started skipping lunch. (Even though I knew it was sheer neurosis, it bothered me when Marilyn insinuated that I was putting on weight. Uccchhh!) Time alone out in the woods in mid-afternoon, back to the Village to open up the canteen and practice guitar, dinner with friends, band practice most nights. I'd never been an especially disciplined person before, but I could see how beneficial it was to know what you were doing most of the time, and I never experienced boredom. I also managed to steer clear of romantic entanglements for a while. Staying real busy helped with that. Then the worst thing in the world happened.

I was eating dinner — red beans and rice — with Jan, Alan, and Lucy Salmon one night when Billy Herman came over to tell me there was a phone call for me. I was excited expecting to speak to my dad, but it was Marilyn.

"What do *you* want?" I said.

"Your father's dead," she said without expression.

"What did you say?"

"Larry… is… dead," she said emphasizing all three words equally.

"You're kidding," I said reflexively. I couldn't comprehend it.

"Would I call you up to kid about something like that?" she said angrily.

I started bawling uncontrollably.

"What happened?"

"I can't understand you."

"Tell me what happened, goddam you!"

"A car crash on the expressway…."

I just completely broke down when she said that, ditched the phone, ran shrieking upstairs to my room in the old back wing of the inn, and lay sobbing in the dark with my face in a pillow to shut out the world. I'd never experienced anything like that depth of mental anguish before, ever. I really don't know how much time went by before people came into my room: Padget, Danny, Alan, Jan, Alison, Weezil, Tanzy, Karen Koblenz, but also Walter Hesslewhite and Strangefield, two of the most senior guys in the Village who happened to be around eating dinner when that happened. They were very kind. They lit candles and sat on the floor patiently with me all around my mattress. At some point, I rolled over and dragged myself up on one elbow and looked around at them. Some of them were chanting something and it took me a while before I realized it was the Hebrew Kaddish, the prayer for the dead. Oddly, it was Strangefield who finally spoke — because, I learned, he was the one who heard Marilyn yelling on the dangling handset of the pay phone, and picked it up, and talked to her. In his supernaturally calm way he said, "Your mother told me the funeral is on Thursday. She said, come home."

Weezil slept in my bed with me that night. She had some powerful sleeping pills, Tuinals, "rainbows," and they just pounded the consciousness clean out of my brain. The absolute worst thing was waking up in the morning and realizing that it was not a bad dream. It would turn out that the accident happened on my father's way home after his last day working for *Newsday* in Garden City. He'd been so looking forward to taking the train into Manhattan to his new job at *The Times*. It made me sick to think about it.

So, I had to go back to Long Island suddenly. Songbird was away when all this happened and somehow Strangefield got the assignment of driving me home. The village took care of its own. He had an old Jeep with a heater that hardly worked, so you had to bundle up inside, but we were getting the first taste of a spring thaw, the temperature went up to nearly fifty, and the roads were good. We didn't talk much the first hour or so, or rather I was so paralyzed with sadness that couldn't speak, or even think about anything except imagine the crash scene: the revolving police car lights, their radios crackling, my poor father strapped to a gurney with his face covered up....

When we got to Stockbridge, Strange stopped at a donut shop and bought a big bag of jelly donuts and two coffees for us. That was kind, I thought. The nourishment brought me out of myself. Once we were back on the road. I told him I couldn't possibly stay at my parents' house once we got to Oyster Bay.

"We can go to a motel," he said, adding immediately, "I'll get you your own room."

"I'd really appreciate that."

Strangefield, with his long beard and bony frame, looked like a flinty old New England farmer, though he was just twenty-seven. He was also wearing an interesting costume: an old vintage suit from the thirties with big notched lapels, from a second-hand store, a wide tie with a red-and-green hummingbird painted on it, and a snappy brown old-time gangster hat — his "good suit for important occasions," he said, bought at the same Bennington thrift shop where I found my guitar. He had a very interesting smell, too, a combination of tobacco with overtones of hay and earth. It wasn't unpleasant. It made him seem elemental.

"Why'd they send me down with you?" I asked "They could have put me on the bus."

"We wouldn't do that under the circumstances," he said. "Remember, I've seen your mother in action." His voice was deep and resonant, like his words came from a limestone cave in the earth where cosmic secrets were hidden.

"You're here to protect me?"

"Yes I am."

"I like that," I said. "I appreciate it."

That brought me a little more out of myself. I asked him about himself. His father was majority leader of the New Hampshire state senate. His mother ran the newspaper in Keene. They were both fascists, he said. Growing up, he spent as much time as he could in the woods just to keep away from his parents. They'd finally sent him to the same prep school as Songbird and Arden Blanchard, Ponsonby Hall, though he didn't go on to Harvard like they did. Instead of college, he worked as a guide for the Appalachian Mountain Club for a couple of years and then studied boat-building in Maine, where he got to be an expert carpenter. He got out of the draft by fasting before his physical until he looked like "a walking skeleton," and then drinking a gallon of coffee the morning of, so he seemed to be a complete wreck, emaciated and trembling. It worked.

I told him about my adventures on snowshoes, following animal tracks. He'd had many adventures in the woods. He offered to repair those snowshoes I found at the junk store in Bennington. At the village, he ran the furniture shop. But his main interest these days was politics, especially working on "the revolution" that he was convinced was imminent. He was forming a "study group" this spring and said I was welcome to come and learn about making revolution. I said I had to get past this funeral first, and that made me all weepy again. He bought me a cheeseburger in Danbury, Connecticut. We got to Oyster Bay around four in the afternoon. I guided him to the house. Driving on the Long Expressway freaked me out again. I kept wondering exactly where Larry got killed.

There were several cars parked in the driveway at the house and along the street in front. I held onto Strange's arm as he accompanied me up the walk to the front door and he came in with me. Everybody was sitting in the living room drinking coffee: Uncle Morris, Marilyn's brother, Aunt Judy and Aunt Evelyn, Larry's sisters, and Grandma Bayla, my only surviving grandparent, Marilyn's mother. Also, my brother Bobby of course. They all turned around at once when we came in and stared. Grandma Bayla, who was a little weak in the head said, "What, people don't ring the doorbell anymore?"

"It's Pooh," Bobby said and he immediately came over and threw his arms around me. He had actually grown another inch since I'd left home and I could feel beard stubble against my cheek when we embraced. "Oh, Pooh, it's so terrible."

"I know," I said, and started weeping again.

By then, Marilyn had gotten up and marched into the foyer. You could read the consternation in her body language.

"Who's he?" she said in a loud whisper, as if Strange were not standing right in front of her.

"Oswald Strangefield, ma'am," he ventured to introduce himself with a rather courtly demi-bow. He held his hand out she ignored it.

"Oswald?" she said, looking him up and down disdainfully, "like the *meshugener* who shot Kennedy?"

Strange seemed amused by her.

"I suppose, ma'am. But I was named long before that happened."

"You ever think of changing it?"

"You can just call me Mr. Strangefield, ma'am."

"Is this your new boyfriend," she asked, jerking her thumb at him.

"He's just a friend," I said. "Tell me where the funeral is going to be. I'm not going to stay here tonight."

"You're not going to stay here?" she said indignantly.

"What did I just say?"

"But this is your home."

"No it's not."

"Where do think you're going to stay?"

"A motel."

"A motel! With him?"

"We'll have separate rooms, ma'am," Strange said.

She glared at us.

"Just tell me where the funeral is," I repeated, "and we'll be there tomorrow."

"What! You're not even going to say hello to your family?"

"Okay, sure,"

So, we both came into the living room and I kissed the aunts and Uncle Morris and Grandma Bayla. You could tell they regarded Strange as if he was a Martian.

"Would you like some coffee?" Marilyn asked.

"I'd like a drink," I said.

"A drink! In the middle of the day?"

"It's the end of the day," I said. I went over to the bar on top of the stereo console and helped myself to a straight scotch.

"Want one?" I asked Strange.

"Uh, sure," he said.

"She's drinking whiskey now?" I heard Grandma whisper to the two aunts.

"It was a six hour drive," I said. "My brain is fried."

We just stood there sipping our drinks. All the seats in the living room were actually taken.

"So you're up in the country somewhere now, I hear?" Uncle Morris said.

"In Vermont," I said. "Outside of Bennington."

"A hippie commune," Aunt Judy explained.

"Is that so?" Uncle Morris said.

"Yes, we're naked most of the time and high on drugs, except on Sundays when we sacrifice animals and pray to our favorite demons."

"What craziness is this?" Grandma said. "This country has lost its mind."

"I'll drink to that," I said.

The awkwardness was like a poisonous miasma in that room. The older generation seemed more out of it and absurd than ever. I couldn't stand being around them.

"What do you do there?" Uncle Morris followed up.

"We live."

He nodded, pretending to understand. The aunts just stared into their coffee.

"Are you hungry?" Marilyn asked. "Uncle Morris was going out to get Chinese."

"No, we'll be all right."

"You have to eat."

"We'll eat," I said. "But not here."

I knocked back the rest of my drink.

"We have to go now," I said. "Where's the service tomorrow and what time?"

"Eleven o'clock. The temple, of course," Marilyn said. "Where else would it be?"

"I don't know. My father was not religious."

"Your father. My husband, Larry!"

"Yes, that's who we're talking about. He didn't believe in all that."

"Maybe not. But he was of the people nonetheless and he will have a proper service."

The others grumbled among themselves.

"And he'll be buried in the Hebrew cemetery," Marilyn added.

"All right. See you tomorrow, everybody," I said, and started to the door along with Strange. Marilyn followed us.

"Maybe you can explain this rude behavior of yours," she said.

"Sure: I haven't forgiven you for hiring those two goons to kidnap me."

Marilyn recoiled as if she was surprised I remembered that.

"We're sitting shiva after the burial," she said, deflecting the issue. "You should sit with the family for a day at least. Show your respect."

"I'll find other ways to show my respect."

"Oh? How's that?"

"I'll keep him lovingly in my heart."

"You're going to humiliate me if you don't sit shiva."

"You'll get over it."

"Tell me: how did I raise such a hateful daughter?"

"That's a very good question for you to mull over. Did you know Larry was going to divorce you?"

"What! Now you're really talking like a crazy person. You're certifiable you know. You're going to end up in a mental hospital."

"No, he told me he was going to," I said.

Her mouth became a thin line of antipathy for a moment.

"For Chrissake what does it matter?" she whispered. "It's moot now, isn't it? Are you high on drugs, by any chance?"

"Oh, please. I'll see you at the temple tomorrow."

We left just like that and headed out to the Jeep. A second later, Bobby bounded down the path to us. He had tears in his eyes, such a contrast to his suddenly grown up appearance.

"Hey, Pooh," he said. "Can I come up to where you are after the funeral."

"Oh. Bobby," I said and took him in my arms. "You have to get into college. They're drafting everyone now. I don't want you to die in Vietnam. Just put up with her for one more year. I know she's a monster, but you can do it. Be brave and stick around one more year and get into some college, please."

He cried on my shoulder for a while.

"He was the only thing that made living here okay," he said quaking and sobbing in my arms. "Please take me with you. I can finish school up there."

"It's not possible. You're under eighteen. She'd just call the police and forcibly drag you home."

"Can I at least have dinner with you tonight."

I swapped a glance with Strange.

"Sure," I said. "But go in and make nice and tell them we'll drop you off later. And get your coat!"

CHAPTER TWENTY-SEVEN

We had dinner at what was actually my father's favorite restaurant: the San Soucie overlooking Long Island Sound up at Bayville, where we always went for birthdays and special occasions. It was quite expensive and fancy. The maître d' gave us a snooty look — my blue jeans, Strange's long beard and zoot suit, no doubt — but seated us grudgingly. The place was not busy. Strange said we could order whatever we liked, it was on the village. I got stuffed clams and shrimp scampi. Bobby ordered a shrimp cocktail and ribeye steak and Strange got lobster fra diavolo with spaghetti. He ordered a bottle of white wine and snuck Bobby some in his water glass. It was a strangely jolly interlude amidst all that grief. Strange held forth for Bobby on the subject of radical Marxist anarchism, his preferred political brand, and Bobby seemed enthralled. We dropped him back home around eight and then went to the Mid Island Motel on the Jericho Turnpike.

Strange got us two rooms as promised. But the wine wore off quickly and I found myself growing extremely nervous to the point of feeling panicky alone in my room, like I was going to start climbing the walls, and I realized I just couldn't stand being alone under the circumstances, so I got dressed and went to Strange's room.

"What's up," he answered the door in just his antique suit pants with the suspenders up on his bare shoulders.

"Can't sleep. Can I come in."

"Sure," he said. The TV was on. He was watching *The Beverly Hillbillies*, of all things.

I sat down in the crummy armchair and Strange returned to the bed, where apparently he'd been reclining when I knocked.

"This is very illuminating," he remarked.

I was still semi-freaked out, my mind racing and my stomach churning.

"Huh? What is?"

"How amazingly dumb the public must be to watch this garbage," he said. "Fascinating."

There wasn't any TV at Sunrise Village, of course.

I pretended to watch the show, too, for a couple of minutes. The one clear thought I had was that all of Long Island and the human life in it seemed to be in black-and-white, like the stupid TV show, whereas at Sunrise Village everything was in color.

"Do you mind if we turn that off?" I eventually asked.

"No. Sure," Strange said. "Go ahead, shut it off. I've seen enough."

I did.

"I suppose it freaked you out to be around your mother," he said.

"Completely," I admitted. "Everything she does, everything about her, drives me up a wall."

"It's possible she's even worse than mine," Strange said. "And that's saying a lot."

"Don't take this the wrong way, but would you mind if I come lie down next to you."

He actually held his arms out as in an invitation. It was so sweet, I thought. I went to the bed and tucked myself up to him. His arms were so lean and strong, like the branches of a great old oak tree.

"Thank you so much," I said, and started crying again.

"You'll be okay," he said, rubbing my incredibly tight neck muscles.

It was so reassuring to be next to him. That smell of tobacco and the earth was so perfectly masculine and fatherly, his sonorous voice so peaceful. We lay like that quietly for a long time. At some point, he kissed my forehead and I just sort of lost it. I sought out his mouth and began kissing him desperately, and pulled off my sweater and then everything under it, and my jeans, and then pulled his trousers off and then I climbed on top of him. Being a man he was instantly ready, kissing my breasts, pushing and pulling my hips. I put him into the wet and slippery, and we made it. We did it again and again, as young people can, until we finally fell off to each side in exhaustion. I can't say I felt wonderful afterward, exactly, but I sure felt different: still very sad but mentally clear, like that poisonous fog had cleared away, and I knew exactly where things stood, and there were no more family mysteries to agonize over. I also felt a great surge of gratitude to Strange for sheltering me, for being my protector and companion on the journey to this dismal place.

We made it again in the morning, too, waking up to our mutual warmth. His disposition was sweetly accommodating rather than romantic, as though it was all part of taking care of me properly, and I didn't mind being cared for. We had plenty of time to get ready for the service. We took a shower together and he washed me. I liked that. He took me out for a lumberjack breakfast at a diner on the Turnpike, eggs, hash, pancakes, and we got to Temple Beth Shalom right on time. I sat between Bobby and Uncle Morris in the front, with Marilyn on Bobby's other side. There were perhaps fifty people in all there, including six of his buddies from

Newsday, and their social friends from Oyster Bay, and five surviving guys who had been in the war in Larry's air squadron. Strange sat way in the back. It was all over in an hour. Then we joined the motor procession to the cemetery in Huntington. Larry was in a simple pine box, kept closed throughout the proceedings according to Jewish custom. The rabbi chanted the verses committing him to the earth. They lowered him down into the grave on a motorized contraption. Marilyn, Bobby, and I all threw a handful of earth onto Larry's coffin, and then the crowd, except for us, began to slowly disperse.

"I expect you to come back to the house now," Marilyn said as we lingered at the grave-side. "Show the family some respect,".

"I'm afraid not," I said. "Daddy's buried. It's over and done."

"What? You're not going to come back now?"

"What did I just say?"

"You're disgusting Erica, you know that—"

"No, I don't know that—"

"And you're despicable for bringing that, that *stranger* to your father's funeral."

"He's a good man and he's taking care of me."

"Is that so? You stink of sex!"

Something inside of me clicked into place, like a precision mechanism in a clock or a gun.

"This is the last thing I'm ever going to say to you, Marilyn: with all my heart I wish it was you lying there in the cold cold ground and not him."

I took Strange by the arm and steered him back to the line of cars where the Jeep was parked.

"Let's get out of here as fast as possible," I said.

CHAPTER TWENTY-EIGHT

I just felt like a completely empty vessel on the drive back. Strange talked and talked about his vision of revolution, and the alienation of the proletariat, and the materialist conception of history, and the internal contradictions of industrial capitalism, etc. He had a patient, professorial manner and it was soothing to just let him yak until he got bored and then we just watched the scenery as the landscape of New York's suburban outlands, with all its punishing clutter and visual incoherence, gave way to more pleasing vistas of New England farms and quaint little towns.

We got back to the Village around eight o'clock that night to learn that while we were away federal marshals had come and arrested Danny Musser for dodging the draft. He'd lost his student deferment after dropping out of Oberlin, was called in for the induction physical and sent back the draft board's letter marked "not interested in your organization... take me off your mailing list," and sent the second notice back marked "deceased... return to sender." I'm sure they appreciated the humor. So, the marshals just drove right in and snatched him. Songbird had returned from

Boston by then, and did what he could to try to mediate the situation, but it quickly became obvious that these marshals were for real with authentic badges, ID, and guns — not like the two clowns Marilyn brought to snatch me — and there were four of them, so Danny just surrendered. They said they were going to take him to a federal detention center near Saranac Lake over in the Adirondack region of upstate New York, until some kind of hearing took place. Songbird drove over to Saranac a few days later and Danny was no longer there. And then nothing. Three weeks went by and we got a postcard from Danny, addressed to all of us villagers, depicting the main drag of *Chinatown in beautiful Toronto, Canada.* It turned out he was released on a five thousand dollar bond and skipped out across the border. I knew that Danny's dad had the biggest Chevy dealership in Bucks County, Pennsylvania, and he could probably take the financial hit, apart from however the family felt about Danny evading military service and having to leave the country. Danny's sudden departure was hard on the band especially. And, of course, not a few chicks in the village were broken-hearted over it.

Some new people came in as winter swung into spring: Charlie Meeker, another dreamboat type physically, catnip to women, six-two, blonde angelic curls like the lead singer for The Who, no dummy though, a quoter of T.S. Elliot and William Butler Yeats and also a very capable livestock manager from one of the great dairy-farming families of Windham County, Vermont. Brad Kimmel, stocky, dark, broody, and muscular in a Kerouac kind of way, was an architecture student who dropped out of Rensselaer Polytechnic over in nearby Troy, New York. He immediately designed a handsome post-and-beam shed with curvy brackets and a cupola for the new front-end loader that Songbird purchased. Drew Kleiber was a yoga instructor from Cambridge, Mass., who Maya recruited after her rock and roll band, Avatar, played gigs at the big new club called the Boston Tea Party, where they opened for The Velvet Underground. He called his special brand of yoga Dynamic Tension. A lot of us goofed on it. He was obviously pretentious, but quite handsome and physically fit. It was generally suspected that Drew was Maya's new lover. Songbird seemed oblivious, as usual — emphasis on seemed. That arrangement was short lived as I'll get to presently.

In April, Kris Wingo arrived with her cello. She was a classical musician drop-out from the New England Conservatory and had never played traditional or folk music before, but I persuaded her to try, and soon she occupied Danny's place in the band with a wonderful new instrumental voice, the cello, possessing a beautiful lower register that could move between bass to contralto. She was reluctant to sing, having never done it as a performer, but we got her into it and she was an instinctive harmonist. Jackie Mayo came on-board with her potter's wheel and set about building a raku kiln, pottery being another potential source of income for the Village. And the notorious Kitty Lapudis came along out of U-Mass in Amherst, styling herself very consciously as a vamp, black hair, Gypsy head-rags, big hoop earrings, showy boobs and all. I came to wonder if Maya planted her there as a sort of time-bomb.

I spent that first night back from Larry's funeral by myself in my room at the inn, emotionally exhausted. People were still bummed over Danny Musser, too, so the whole village was in a down mood. But I was hugely relieved to be back in this safe and happy corner of New England among friends after revisiting the horrible Long Island suburbs. I caught up on sleep and the next night I went and called on Strange at his place, the Capricorn House. He had just finished one of his political meetings, of which he had a core group numbering twelve Villagers who identified with radical Marxist anarchism. He was getting high in the first floor parlor with one of his acolytes, Stacy Reihm, petite and muscular like a gymnast, who worked on the grounds crew. I started to back off and apologize for interrupting but they said, no, come join them, sit down and smoke with us. They had some red wine too and I guess I wanted to get high to tamp down my ruminations about Larry and Marilyn and all the family crap. And one thing led to another until pretty soon we were all in Strange's big bed together, the three of us. I'd never done anything like that before, never been physically sexual with another chick. I guess I got into the spirit, being stoned and pretty drunk, and both of them were sweet and loving, but I knew it was not my thing, and when I woke up in the morning I felt bad about it — as well as being painfully hung-over — and snuck out leaving the two of them sleeping there.

Strange came into the canteen the next day ostensibly to buy some smokes. There was nobody else around, just the two of us. He was wearing a different hat than the nice one he went to Long Island with. This was his work hat, beat up and all sweat-stained where the crown met the brim. He also had overalls on. He looked like an Okie out of *The Grapes of Wrath*.

"Can we talk?" he asked, lingering awkwardly at the counter after I gave him his four packs of Lucky Strikes.

"Sure," I said. I had a glass bottleneck on my pinky finger, learning how to run it up and down the guitar neck in what would become my favorite style of playing. *Baahwong*.

"All right," he said. "Quit playing a minute and pay attention."

"Okay...." I put the instrument down.

"I like you a lot," he began tentatively.

"Yeah? I hear a *but* coming."

He sighed. "But if you're looking for a boyfriend, you're probably going to be disappointed."

"I'm not looking for a boyfriend," I said, a lie, of course.

"There's an ethos here. Total sexual freedom."

"Sure."

"Try getting into the spirit."

"I guess I'm pretty conventional."

"Shake off those conventions. You've got nothing to lose but your inhibitions."

"Okay."

"This is a glorious experiment. You ought to take full advantage of it."

"Okay."

"Someday you'll be old and this will all seem like a wonderful dream."

"It seems like that already, sometimes."

"Aw, Pooh: I like you very much, how you look and how you are. But it ain't me babe."

"I've been dumped before, but never this way," I remarked.

"I'm not dumping you. We can ball again. But not exclusively."

"Gee, thanks."

"What happened in that motel down there. It was real."

"Sure it was."

"I'm just not boyfriend material."

"It's okay. I don't really understand politics anyway."

He took his hat off and mopped his brow with his sleeve. He seemed finally to be at a loss for words.

"Okay, I guess I'll see you, then," he said and turned on his heels to split.

"Not if I see you first," I cracked, and picked up my guitar again: *Baahwong.*

He stopped and turned back at the door, a pained look on his face.

"That was a joke," I said.

Aside from sort of getting dumped, and my sense of humor being unappreciated, I did grok what he was saying. He was right about the *ethos of the village*. The place was like a giant rabbit hutch. I'd blundered into people making it in odd places around the Village a few times — Sophie the cook going at it in the pantry with Oz, Albert Ozmer, little Tanzy with Krista the Valkyrie in the woods — a startling sight. It was constant and everywhere. Even the few couples who more or less had a steady thing going, like Padget and Alison, wouldn't find much sympathy if their lover happened to stray and they got upset about it. And this was true for the women as much as the men. At Sunrise Village, you couldn't complain about a lack of sexual fidelity. That's just how it was.

So I took Strange's message to heart. Maybe a little too much. Because for the next several weeks I balled eight different guys, just to see if I could *get into the spirit* of it, as Strange had said. Getting men's attention was easy. They respond to the slightest signals. I began to feel a little sorry for them, knowing what pushovers they could be. I had three basic rules: don't ball anyone in the band, no more group gropes, and no lesbian scenes. But I did have sex in all kinds of places besides a bed: the sauna, the tool-shed, the tofu lab, the old marble factory, the back of the village van, the laundry room. I balled Hog, Teck, Hans Bierbauer, Jody Palko, Brad Kimmel, Mickey O'Neill, and Scottie Provost — who, apparently was not a hundred percent queer — just to see if I could. I even had an encounter with an outsider on one of my supply runs into town, that nice man with the sideburns in the music store down in Bennington, in one of the closet-like rooms they had for listening to a record that you thought about buying. (afterward, he sent me a painfully earnest letter afterward asking for a "date," and I had to write back explaining that it was just a one-time fling —another demerit against the hippies in our battle with regular uptight America, I guess.)

Was it satisfying? Physically, I came to climax many times, not always, but often enough. It's just how I am. Emotionally it was another story, of course. I felt the resulting emptiness, since the main purpose of sex, besides producing children, is to create a bond between two people, and bonding was effectively frowned upon by this so-called *ethos of the village.* You could see how it went against people's natural inclinations to just like a certain person more than others, and how that is the basis for real love. It was like sex was totally allowed and true love not so much. I don't think this ethos was established in any formal way by Songbird or Maya or any of the original core villagers. It just evolved, with a lot of help from places in the culture such as *Time Magazine* and the movies, and it seemed like a good idea at the time, like a lot of things in history that don't always turn out so well. The sexual revolution was going on all over the country, and among us so-called hippies it probably seemed mandatory. I'm certain it had everything to do with the novelty of the birth control pill coming on the scene, which so easily canceled out the main constraint to sexual freedom: pregnancy. All the chicks in the village were on the pill. Nobody had gotten pregnant that year.

There were consequences though. The first week of really nice spring weather, the village broke out in an epidemic of the crabs: crab lice, the repulsive little bugs that live in your pubic hair. The major sex diseases, syph and the clap, could be cured with antibiotics, and nobody brought those into the village while I was there, but the crabs were a terrible nuisance. First, people noticed that they had an itch going in their pubic region, and then they noticed other people scratching their jeans, and finally the first person looks, and there they are: the revolting little gray bugs and the tiny blood trails where they feed on your skin, and the weird little teardrop-shaped nits glued to your hair that are actually their egg cases, waiting to hatch out thousands more of their kind. Uccchhh.

It had apparently happened once before, the previous spring, and the original Villagers knew the drill for dealing with it. Songbird drove around to all the drug stores in southern Vermont and bought every bottle of RiddO he could get his mitts on. (That must have been embarrassing.) It took him all day and people were so grossed out they started shaving their public hair and underarms just to get a head start on the problem. We lugged one of the big stainless steel vats from the tofu lab, which ran on propane gas, and set it up in the village green across from the inn to boil every garment on the premises and all of the bedding and towels, too, quite a job! The grounds crew strung up what looked like a mile of clothesline between the various buildings and the trees and the tech boys set up an outdoor shower operation.

When Songbird got back with the lice shampoo, we ran a de-contamination line for showering, making sure that absolutely everyone went through the treatment, even the few people who, for one reason or another, hadn't had sex for a while and didn't have the little buggers. It looked like a scene from a Nazi concentration camp — all these naked adults outdoors with different-sized bodies shuffling through the steaming showers. We were so lucky it was sixty degrees out. All the towels in the whole village were still hanging out to dry, so after your shower you were allowed to go inside, but only to the main room of the inn where they had a roaring fire going. The sauna was off-limits because it stunk of Clorox from the attempt to sanitize it and you would have choked to death in there. Meanwhile they got a system going for providing everyone with at least one outfit of boiled, decontaminated clothing to put on, using the multiple clothes dryers at the inn to get it done. It was a tedious process and you just had to wait your turn by the fire, naked, to get some clothes back on. Everyone was joking about turning the village into a nudist colony.

"In the winter I'm a Buddhist, in the summer I'm a nudist," Weezil cracked.

I had the crabs, too, of course, since I was balling so many guys, but I was also still on the cleaning crew, and after getting decon-taminated we had to go around and mop down all the bathrooms and hallways with bleach. Maya also ordered all the stuff from the "free clothes" closet to be burned in a fifty-gallon trash barrel. Everybody had to take all the rest of their clothes and stuff them into plastic garbage bags with their name on it in Magic Marker on masking tape, and put their bag outside for their stuff to be boiled the next day. The first part of the awful ordeal was complete by eight-thirty that night. It was then that we learned over the radio that Martin Luther King had been shot to death in Memphis, a blow to the gut after the ridiculous doings of the day. There wasn't even any dinner that night, just granola for those who had any appetite. Most of us felt like it was a necessary penance to go to bed hungry.

CHAPTER TWENTY-NINE

April of 1968 was a tumultuous time. The day before King got shot, Senator Eugene McCarthy won the Wisconsin Democratic party. McCarthy was the first major politician to challenge President Johnson directly over the Vietnam War, and he got such a large percentage of the vote in the earlier New Hampshire primary that Johnson dropped out of the race. It surprised everybody. That left an opening for Bobby Kennedy to jump in four days after New Hampshire. At the village, the general sentiment favored McCarthy. Despite the deep yearning to recover the Kennedys' lost Camelot, many of us felt that Bobby was being opportunistic, waiting for Johnson to bail out before stepping up to the plate, and now trying to trample over our hero, "Clean Gene."

After Martin Luther King got shot, Washington exploded in violence that lasted five days and there were riots in the black ghettos of scores of other US cities. But we were pretty detached from the events of the day at Sunrise Village. There was no television there. Most of us were too busy working, pursuing our interests, and balling each other to listen to the radio — except for the kitchen crew who had it on all day long, and we often learned about what was going on from them at mealtime. There was always a two-day-old copy of *The Boston Globe* or *The New York Times* around, *The Bennington Banner* was strictly local news about house fires, cow auctions, and VFW dinners. So, we were mostly in our own world, especially as the days got warmer and brighter and we were able to spend much more time outdoors.

After Danny Musser got busted by the federal marshals, Songbird instituted a new procedure for any of the guys who received draft notices. He arranged for a sympathetic anti-war psychiatrist at Putnam Hospital in Bennington to write letters saying that so-and-so was psychologically unfit for the military and was liable to be a danger to others if inducted. We resorted to it twice: when Jody Palko (Maya's drummer in Avatar) and Andy Nathanson (tofu gang) got their notices. Both reported to their respective induction centers (Hartford, Providence) and got grilled by the Army doctors, and presented their letters, and eventually got let off the hook: 4-F — *registrant not acceptable for military service.* We had banquets when they got their official reclassification letters. Dave Padget was called in for the physical (Augusta, Maine) and got rejected for service organically — he was missing his right pinky finger and the tip of his ring finger from a fireworks accident when he was eleven years old. It didn't prevent from playing the mandolin masterfully with a flat-pick.

Apart from the depressing condition of our nation, there was great excitement as we began to undertake the new projects of the year. When the ground thawed, Tanzy laid out extensive new gardens with stakes and mason's twine. There was cordwood to split and stack for seasoning, old stone walls to rebuild, brush to cut on overgrown pastures to reestablish grazing for the village's two new cows, a new goat dairy (designed by Brad Kimmel) populated with young female Alpines for making extra-creamy yogurt, a hundred baby chicks delivered by US mail (yes, they do that!) to get egg production going, beehives to build, the hydroelectric project on-going, a drying kiln to build for the lumber operation, and a pottery production line under Jackie Mayo, as well as the many other activities already established.

I found a refuge from the old family angst in my routine: morning cleanup crew, running the canteen, practicing guitar, playing with the band, which had once again changed its name to Buttermilk Falls, suggested by Padget (after a scenic spot near us on the Marble River), a cornball name, in my opinion — which I didn't get worked up about it because I knew they'd get sick of it and change it again. Jan Heathcoate left us to travel in Europe for the summer, a shocking surprise. That gave me extra incentive to improve on guitar, and Kris Wingo took over Jan's vocal harmony parts. The cello gave us a sound like no other band and also a sense of a fresh attack on older material that had gotten a little stale for us. Alan Kaplan hustled up gigs for us at Williams College, Smith, Wesleyan, and Middlebury, small appreciative audiences in "coffee-house" venues on campus, for people like us with long hair and colorful costumes, except they were still going to classes and playing the establishment game. We got paid a little more than gas money for these shows, but we were getting *out there*, at least. I had sex with a Lacrosse-playing Latin major in a back room of Carr Hall at Middlebury between sets. When he was done, he slapped me on the ass and said, "*vidi, vici veni*," clever fellow. On the way home in the van, with paper towels stuffed in my panties, I had to reevaluate my experiment in sexual dissipation. The truth is, I was accomplishing nothing with it but making myself more depressed, despite my comfortable routine and the satisfactions of music.

In early May, I got a letter from Larry's attorney, Ed Eckmann, informing me that I was the beneficiary of a life insurance policy for the sum of seventy-five thousand dollars which they were holding in an escrow account for me. I didn't understand exactly what it meant so I took the letter to Songbird that evening after supper. It was twilight, a beautiful mild spring evening with the leaves fledging out on the trees and the first crickets of the year starting to sing. He came to the door looking rather disheveled in khaki pants, a plain white T-shirt, no shoes, his eyes red-rimmed, sort of bleary-looking.

"Am I interrupting anything?" I asked.

"No," he said. "What's going on?"

"I need some advice about money."

"Uccchhh," he said. "I'm so sick of money."

"If this isn't a good time—"

"No, it's all right. Come in."

You could see where he'd been lying on the sofa, reading *The Confessions of Nat Turner*. There was a half-finished joint in a surgical hemostat that he used as a roach clip, and three empty green Ballantine Ale bottles on the floor. We sat down together. I showed him the letter. He scanned it and grunted to himself a few times. He knew, of course, that my father had been killed in a traffic accident.

"This is a payout from a life insurance policy your father took out," he stated plainly.

"Yes, that part I understand."

"You and... I guess this is your brother, Robert—?"

"Yes. Bobby."

"—each get seventy-five thousand dollars. It's pretty straightforward."

"My mother's not mentioned."

"She's apparently not a beneficiary. Maybe he had a separate policy for her."

"I don't know."

"You can find out. Call her."

"We're not speaking," I said. Songbird nodded. I think he understood why.

"Call this lawyer then: Eckmann."

I just sat there and gnawed at the inside of my cheek as I do when I'm troubled, wondering what would be the consequences if Larry left Marilyn high and dry. She'd probably find a way to glom onto Bobby's share, knowing her, and him being a minor. But then, how else would she get by? She wasn't looking for a job as far as I knew.

"I hate her guts," I mumbled.

"Maybe after a while you'll find a way to make up."

"I don't want to."

"Okay," he said, puffing out his cheeks and handing back the letter. I suppose my family crap made him uncomfortable.

"What's escrow mean?" I asked.

He explained about fiduciaries and all that. At least it got us off the subject of Marilyn.

"Did you ever have this kind of money before?" he asked.

"God, no."

"I suppose you don't know what to do with it."

"I really don't."

"I don't know off-hand whether you have to pay taxes on it. I was way younger than you when my parents died and other people took care of everything, including their life insurance. You should ask. You don't want the IRS coming after you for penalties and shit. They could end up taking most of it. Apart from that, I'd advise you put it in some safe investments, and maybe keep five thousand in a regular bank account, assuming you might want to have access to some of this money."

"For what? I'm making enough for what I need here."

"You might want to buy a car, or a really nice guitar. Go back to school. Travel. Who knows?"

"It hadn't even occurred to me, frankly."

"You're wonderfully uncomplicated," he said. I couldn't tell if he was being sardonic.

"I don't know. I mean, the money's from a terrible thing that happened. I feel bad about it."

"If you like, I can ask my bank people in Boston to set up a basic investment account for you, safe stuff: treasury bonds, some blue chip stocks. You could open a checking account in town here at the local bank for ready cash."

"You said before that you were sick of money. I hope you don't mind me asking: is this place draining your… uh, inheritance?"

He hesitated before he answered and sighed.

"The winter was pretty tough," he said. "We haven't really got most of our money-making ventures going yet, except for the chairs and hammocks and the tofu. There are a lot of mouths to feed here and regular ongoing expenses. I think it'll balance out a lot better in the months ahead once we get things going."

"Maybe I should donate some of this to the Village? Ten thousand—"

"No-o-o-o!" he said as if the idea horrified him.

"Why not. I've gotten so much out of being here. Just think of all the food I've been eating since November."

"Look, I'm not taking money from the people who come here," he said resolutely. "Other communes get into a lot of trouble with that."

"How?"

"Relationships go bad. People get vengeful. Accusations get flung around. Lawsuits get filed. The state attorney general comes sniffing around and all of a sudden you've got criminal charges. I'm not going down that road. The North Star commune up in Weston fell apart because they looted the bank accounts of two wealthy sisters who joined them. The Fisher twins. Mahoning Steel. We're not going to do that here. There's no need to. Do you want a beer?"

"What if Maya comes in?"

"And what? Sees me drinking a beer with you? Anyway, she's not around."

"Okay, then, I guess."

He got up and brought back two more Ballantine Ales from the kitchen.

"Are they playing away somewhere?"

"Yeah, New York. It's a big deal."

"Where at?"

"The Bitter End."

"That *is* a big deal. You know, I went to NYU."

"Yes, I remember."

"I went to the Bitter End all the time. I saw Mississippi John Hurt there, Sun Ra, the Byrds."

"I love the Byrds," he said. He reached for the roach in the hemostat and fired it up. "*Turn, Turn Turn.* I wore out the grooves in that record."

"Yeah, it was a great album."

We sat silently for a while. His pot was high test. It took only a little to get a buzz on. Oddly, though, just sitting there looking at the letter in my lap, I started to get a little weepy. He noticed.

"Feeling blue?" he asked.

I nodded.

"Me too," he said.

That startled me for some reason.

"Why are you blue?" I asked.

"You know. Just shit happening."

"Oh, that's such a guy's way of saying nothing at all."

"Hey, I'm a guy."

"I'm aware of that. What is it? All the responsibility? Running this place?"

"I don't run this place."

"Of course you do."

"Maya runs this place. At least she used to."

"Is she neglecting her duties?"

He turned to look at me.

"Yes, she is," he said.

"Well, her band is getting hot."

"Yes, it is."

"Seems like they're away a lot."

"Yes it does."

"Are you afraid she's going to split?"

"I can't blame her if people like the band. She's talented."

"She's a good performer," I said. "Is this place going to fall apart if she's not looking after stuff?"

"It's a little more complicated than that."

"Do you want to talk about it?"

He just shook his head and hoisted his beer bottle.

I figured he was also upset because Maya had brought that yoga teacher, Mr. Dynamic Tension, Drew Kleiber, to the farm. Everybody knew him and Maya were getting it on. But, of course, before him Maya had been making it with other guys, like Danny Musser. Maybe she still was, for all I knew. It made me feel sorry for Songbird, like he was being a chump.

"Maya hates my guts," I said. "Why, I have no idea."

"Jealous, I think."

"Jealous of me? That's rich."

"No, she's like that. Especially of chicks who are attractive."

Okay, so it didn't escape me that he said I was attractive, but I didn't comment on that.

"So you've got the blues," I said.

"Yeah," he said and chugged half his beer. "Maya's getting into some dark shit."

"What dark shit?"

"You ever hear of Aleister Crowley?"

"No."

"He was this English cat. Styled himself as a magus, a practitioner of the black arts."

"What, like devil worship?"

"Yeah, Satan and demons and occult shit. He wrote some books about it. She's into him."

"Uccchhh."

"Yeah."

"Bummer."

"You have no idea. She's a powerful person. She can get to people. Look, she got to you."

"Yeah, she's got a definitely witchy way."

"She thinks it's helping her music, courting demons and darkness, with the country all fucked up politically. She thinks it's helping propel her to fame and success. She's feeding on it."

"Yeah, that's pretty depressing."

"There's something else," Songbird said and then hesitated another moment. "She's been embezzling."

"Embezzling? Like, money?"

"That's what embezzling is, Pooh."

"Like, out of the Village?"

"Yeah. A lot of money."

"And you found out?"

"Yeah, I found out"

"Does she know you found out?

"Yeah."

"Oh, shit."

"Yeah."

"What are you going to do about it?"

"Well, I'm not going to call the police. I don't want them poking around here."

"Did Arden know this?"

"Yeah. He was totally against getting involved with the authorities. He said I should just take the hit, avoid opening up Pandora's box... you know, cut my losses and let it go."

"What's in Pandora's box?"

He chugged the rest of his beer.

"I'm telling you this because I really like you and I believe I can trust you. At times, we've moved some pretty large amounts of weed through here and Maya was at the center of these deals. She arranged them."

"Why'd you do that? You didn't need to sell dope for the money."

"Oh, we had this grand rationale: a service to the people. People like us, that is. Providing for them. Like we were heroes of the Age of Aquarius."

"I see.

"Big mistake."

"What are you going to do about her?"

"I just hope she gets a record deal and splits."

I didn't want to ask him: why not just throw her out? It seemed pushy.

"Do you think she'll get a record deal?"

"She's trying like hell. Yeah. Why not. Everybody and his sister is getting a record deal these days. And she's got real talent. Why Janis and not her?"

We just sat quietly for a while again.

"By the way, I know she's balling other guys," he eventually said. "What can I say? Everybody else here is, too. It's the times we live in… the way things are… and who we are."

"Were you fooling around, too?"

"Yeah," he said. "But I was extremely prudent about it. Just two others. And not much."

I was curious who it was, of course. But I didn't dare ask. Instead, I confessed my own recent sexual excesses, and how I had stupidly expected to be treated like I was special by Danny Musser, and Arden, and then Strange, and how they all basically dumped me, and how I just surrendered to the so-called ethos, and balled a lot of the guys in the Village, and finally got disgusted with myself with that boy up at Middlebury. I got all weepy yet again.

"I knew you were getting it on with Arden," he said. "He told me before he split. He liked you a lot."

"I liked him a lot, but then he just up and left."

"He was sorry to leave you like that. He's got a lot to work out. Who he really is. What he's really going to be. It's been hard for him."

Songbird lit the roach and we finished the last of it.

"Guess I better go," I said when I realized we'd been staring at each other for quite a while.

"Yeah, I guess," he agreed.

The next moment, we were kissing. He didn't make the move. It was me. I more or less threw myself on him. It was so thrilling that I actually shocked myself and pulled away. Being stoned only amplified my confusion. Songbird seemed stunned too.

"Okay, I'm going now," I said. "Really."

"Okay," he said, reaching for my hands. He pulled me toward him this time and kissed me again. I melted into him briefly, but then felt these waves of confusion and panic and pulled away a second time.

"We have to think about this," I said, hauling myself upright off the sofa and then hurrying to the door.

"Yeah, of course," he said breathlessly as I was leaving the house. "We better think about this."

CHAPTER THIRTY

I thought about it a lot. For days it was all I thought about. Songbird might have been on the outs with Maya, but her stuff was still in his house, and she would eventually be back there, too, so I took the passive course and waited to see what would happen. Days went by and I didn't see or hear from him. I just let it ride, thinking he had to work some things out. I know he was gone for two of those days in Montpelier, the state capital, applying for a commercial license to sell the tofu we were making.

That week, I took a chance calling Bobby back home. I called around seven-thirty in the morning, a time when he would be getting ready to leave for school, probably scarfing his cereal in the kitchen, and Marilyn would still be asleep, as usual. I was so relieved when he picked up, but he just barely finished saying, "Hey, Pooh," when Marilyn got on the line in her bedroom.

"Who the hell's calling here at this hour?" she said.

"Nobody," Bobby said.

"Nobody! Jesus Christ. Hey, Nobody, do you hear me? It's indecent to call this early in the morning. If I find out who you are, I will make your life sheer hell," she said, and slammed the handset down.

"You still there, Pooh?" Bobby asked.

"Yeah, Marilyn's in good form, I see."

"She's on the warpath."

"Did you get a letter from Mister Eckmann, Dad's lawyer, about the insurance company money?"

"Yeah," Bobby said. "She's pissed off that we got money and she didn't."

"Do you happen to know if there was a separate policy for her?"

"The way she's acting, all mad at the world, I'm pretty sure there wasn't."

"Did you speak to Eckmann?"

"No."

"Why not?"

"Mom said she has to handle it for me 'cause I'm a minor."

"Do yourself a favor, Bobby, and call Mister Eckmann. Don't let her arrange things so she can have access to your dough. It's yours, understand?"

"She said she needs it to pay the bills. She said we'll get kicked out of the house and have to move to Queens with Grandma Bayla."

"That's bullshit. Larry bought that old house in the village, you know. She can sell that, at least get the down payment money back."

"I guess...."

"Is she trying to get a job?"

"I don't know," Bobby said. "She seems to be living just like before. Shopping. Going to the city on Thursdays."

"Call that Mister Eckmann and tell him you need to put that money in some kind of account that she can't get her mitts on. With that money, you could go to any college you want, and have plenty left over to travel afterwards, or go to medical school, or whatever you want to do with your life."

"All right."

"Have you signed anything yet? Any documents?"

"No."

"Well don't before checking with me. Understand?"

"Yeah."

"I mean it. I want you to write to me here and tell me exactly what you're doing. And I'm going to check up on you with Eckmann to make sure you talk to him."

"All right! Don't yell at me. You're sounding like Mom."

That sure hurt. I apologized profusely.

"That's the last thing I want to be like," I said. "But please, communicate with me here by mail. I'll reply with some made-up return address so Marilyn doesn't open it."

"Okay. Hey, can I come up and see you when school's over?"

"I don't know. We'll have to see."

"See what?"

"If Marilyn doesn't give you permission, the police could come in and drag you home and all, and then make trouble for this place. So don't even think about running away."

"Man, being a minor sucks out loud," he said.

"I know. I'm sorry. Get that job you had last year cleaning the boats at the Harbor Club. You liked that job."

"I want to get out of here. I fucking hate Long Island."

"Lookit, you have one more measly year left before college. Concentrate on that, on finding some college you really want to go to. And focus on school so you can get into that college. Remember, there's a war on. Do you know there were over two hundred GI's killed in action just last week?"

"No."

"It was in *The Times*. That's just one week. You have got to get your ass into college or you'll get drafted and sent to Vietnam and you'll come home in a box."

"I know, Pooh. We talk about it, me and my friends. We know it's fucked up. Uh-oh. I gotta get off. I think she's coming down."

We hung up.

Later that day I called up Eckmann. He said Marilyn had already been in to see him. It figured.

"I know my father was making plans to divorce her," I said.

"That's true," he said.

"Then he'd discussed it with you?"

"Yes he did, frankly."

"So wouldn't it be improper if you let Marilyn get involved in this insurance money thing with Bobby?"

"She came in and I met with her, but I'm not going to do what she requested," he said.

"Which was what?"

"She asked for power of attorney in this matter, but your father set it up so it's in trust until Robert's eighteenth birthday."

"Well, thank God for that," I said.

"As for your share, we await instructions in writing to send your check out and you can do with it what you please."

"It's a lot of money," I said. "I've gotten some good advice and I'm going to be careful with it."

"That would be a good thing," he said.

CHAPTER THIRTY-ONE

Maya and the guys in Avatar returned from New York the following Thursday on a cloud of triumph. The news crackled all over Sunrise Village that they were offered a contract by Verve Records, a jazz label until recently when they signed some of the more far-out rock bands including Frank Zappa's Mothers of Invention and, what do you know, The Velvet Underground. Maya had acquired a manager, too, an operator named Art Mandrill, who wore bolo ties and cowboy boots (though born and raised in Rochester, New York), and who'd started in the business back in the fifties with the Hi-Lows, The Mighty Mercurys, and Maurice "the Marquis of Melody" DeShane. Mandrill drove all the way up from the city in a Lincoln Continental when the Village threw a good luck party in the Odd Fellows hall for Maya and the band, who were moving to New York to record their album and then going out on the road all over the country to publicize it. The band had brought some supposedly great blotter acid back from the city, so a lot of people were tripping, though I wasn't one of them. Considering what I knew about Maya now, I wasn't in a merry mood for celebrating her good fortune, though I went over to witness the spectacle of the big farewell party. And, of course, I was thrilled that she was leaving.

The band played, allowing Maya to bask in adulation and ham it up. At one point in the set she made a little speech promising to return to her "beloved village" when the tour was over. I was standing way back on the side of the hall just under the empty balcony watching the spectacle when I felt somebody touch my elbow: Songbird.

"Hey," he said.

The music was so loud that we had to talk directly into each other's ears.

"Hey," I replied. "That's bullshit, right? She's not coming back."

"Not unless she shows up with a certified check for sixty-three thousand bucks," he said. I goggled at him.

"Is that what she stole?"

"Roughly."

"Jeez."

We watched her carry on. Avatar had quit playing covers and were now doing songs they wrote themselves, mostly Maya's compositions. This particular number, with its carnivalesque synthesizer and scrubby guitar riffs in the dark, Dorian mode was called "Slipknot." The refrain went: *I hate it when we're apart / but nothing ever satisfies the hunger of my heart.* I could see how it might become a hit on the radio. It was like The Doors Meets The Jefferson Airplane. Spooky and trippy.

"Would you like to get out of here?" Songbird asked, pulling me close.

"Okay, sure."

I followed him into the cool spring night. We headed up to his cottage, which made me a little uneasy, but when we got there he opened the door of his Range Rover for me.

"Where are we going?" I asked.

"Grab a little dinner in town, okay?"

He took me to an Italian restaurant in North Bennington, near the college, old fashioned and semi-fancy. It had white tablecloths and real napkins, pretty nice for the boondocks, except our table was teetery and he had to stick a matchbook under the pedestal to stabilize it. There were some college professor types in there, people over thirty with long hair who looked half-intelligent. It had been a while since I was even around other human beings out of my age group. The weirdness of it struck me. I ordered veal Milanese and he got the Parmagiana. We got Chianti with the basket around bottle. Despite Maya being around again, Songbird didn't seem to be in a blue mood, rather he seemed downright chipper. He talked about the various Village projects. Eventually, he got around to what was apparently the purpose of the dinner.

"I've been thinking you might take over Maya's job."

"What? Like, running things? The whole operation?"

"It's not that complicated. You keep books, you pay bills, you order stuff, you manage some of the people problems, check out the drop-ins. Believe me, she wasn't working her fingers to the bone."

"I don't know that much about money."

"You've been running the canteen. You seem to be doing a good job with it."

"The canteen is simple. Run out of cigarettes and candy bars, get more cigarettes and candy bars."

"I believe you're an honest person. You're smart. I trust you. You'll learn how to do this. I'll pay you a hundred dollars a week."

"Well... okay. I'll give it a try."

We clinked wine glasses and then the food came. He seemed so much more relaxed in this setting, away from the village, like a normal person, not a figurehead. He went into more detail about the particular problems with our projects, like how to get our hammocks into stores throughout New England, finding a decent used refrigerated truck to move the tofu, and getting a commercial dehydrator for the herbal tea operation. I realized I could figure those things out and I got excited about taking over the job. He said I would have to find a competent replacement to run the canteen. I was pretty sure Weezil could handle that, if she wanted to. It gave me a lot to think about. I also thought about where things might go between Songbird and me personally. I was certainly attracted to him, but I was uncomfortable about taking Maya's place in his bed, and in his heart, like you'd swap players on a football field. It also seemed kind of strange that he would be swapping a rock singer for a folk singer.

These were some of the things that troubled me when we finally drove back to the Village. I was relieved when he pulled up near the front of the inn to let me out, rather than at his cottage. The party seemed to be still going on at the Odd Fellow's hall. The lights were on in there and "Dance to the Music" by Sly Stone was playing on the PA system so loud you could hear it from the car.

"Can I kiss you goodnight," he asked.

I didn't even answer in words. I just grabbed the back of his head and pushed it toward me. I was wearing these goofy loose overalls and his hand went foraging inside the bib and into the turtleneck underneath, where they found my breasts. Of course I had no bra on.

"You're making me very bothered," I said.

"Good," he said.

"She's probably back at your place now."

"Unless she's banging Dynamic Drew."

"I'm sorry about that."

"Yeah, well."

"You taste like garlic."

"So do you."

"I like garlic."

"I like you."

"We better stop," I said.

"Why?"

"Because she's still around."

"Don't you think it's funny that I started a commune and I'm the only person in it now who can't get laid."

"Yeah, it's funny, but it's not true."

"What do I have to do?"

"Be a little more patient."

He pulled away from me and sighed.

"You're something, Pooh."

"You're something else, Songbird."

"Please call me Elliot. Songbird's a cartoon character."

"All right. Elliot. Thanks for a very nice dinner. And goodnight."

CHAPTER THIRTY-TWO

As it happened, Saturday after my last shift working on the cleaning crew, I went up into the woods behind the big meadow to get some cash out of my hidey hole. We hadn't been paid in ten days because Maya had been away with the band and she had apparently given up all her regular duties, and I hadn't even gone into her office yet to pick up where she left off. I had a few hundred dollars there, a roll of bills in an old peanut butter jar stashed in that hollow log, and all that was left was the empty jar. I wasn't the only one, either. Three other people came into the canteen that afternoon and asked to run a tab because their stashes were robbed, too. Then, before I closed up for the day, who should come in for cigarettes but Maya. She was wearing very fancy jeans embroidered in satin with hummingbirds and flowers and a virtually transparent silk blouse that you could see her boobs clear through. Also, about a half a ton of silver bangles on each arm. She was already acting the role of rock diva.

"Having fun playing store?" she said, when I handed her the two packs of Kools she asked for.

"Yeah, actually," I said. "I guess you're going to be the female Jim Morrison now."

"Hmmm. I hadn't thought of it like that. Not a bad way to look at it though. How about you? Are you going to be the new female Pete Seeger?"

"No, I'm actually going to be me, someone you haven't seen before."

She put on a kind of scowly smile.

"Good luck with that," she said. "I hear you're all set to take my place," she said.

"I'm going to do your office job, if that's what you mean."

"Think you can?"

"With my hands tied behind my back and a paper bag over my head."

"Yuk yuk. Want to come sing back-up for me in Avatar instead?"

"You're not serious?"

"Yeah, I'm just fucking with you. You don't have the pipes. Elliot seems to like you, though."

"No comment."

"Just a little warning," she said, leaning on the counter toward me with that awful patchouli wafting my way. "He's weak. A weak, weak man."

"Like you said, you're fucking with me."

"No, I'm serious about that. Why do you think I had to stray?"

"Because you're a faithless bitch."

"Ooooh, so hostile. I just want you to know: I put a curse on you."

"Oh? How'd you do that? Bury a dead cat in the moonlight?"

"That would be crude. I'm much more subtle. You'll see, though. When it happens, it'll be a big surprise. And you'll never get over it."

"I don't believe in black magic."

"You don't have to believe. You're just the victim."

"I think you've got a few screws loose in your head."

"Peace, baby," she said with a big smile and flashed the V-for-Victory sign before sashaying out.

"Go get fucked," I said as the screen door slapped.

I wished I'd thought of a better comeback.

CHAPTER THIRTY-THREE

Maya was gone for good on Monday. She left the Village in the sporty orange Karmann-Ghia convertible that Songbird had bought for her back when their relationship was fresh, new, and exciting. I didn't see her go. I was up in the office at the Odd Fellows hall painting the walls to drive the lingering scent of her patchouli cologne out of the room. Around the same time that morning, apparently, Elliot walked into Drew Kleiber's yoga class in the big main room over at the inn and began thrashing him with a plastic wiffle ball bat, yelling at him to get out of the Village. Kleiber was not a big guy, but he was pretty strong and agile from being Mr. Dynamic Tension and he managed to get the bat away from Elliot and then proceeded to beat him up, culminating in some kind of knee drop with Elliot on the floor that broke two of his ribs. The class was all chicks except for Tanzy, who was quite small, and who heroically attempted to intervene but got his nose broken in the process. Kleiber packed up his VW Beetle and was gone, too, inside half an hour. I didn't find out about it until lunchtime, when I emerged from up in the Odd Fellows hall and learned that Albert Ozmer drove Elliot and Tanzy to the hospital in Bennington. They made up some cockamamie story about rolling over on a tractor so as not to give anyone the wrong impression about how things were at the village.

Later that afternoon, when I learned he was back, I went to see Elliot in his cottage. He was creeping around the kitchen in a lot of pain.

"Hurts to breathe," he said.

I couldn't help but laugh, the way he said it, leaning on the counter with this little-boyish look of helplessness on his face. He also had a fat lip where he got punched. When I laughed, he started laughing too, but it obviously hurt him and he kind of slipped down against the lower cabinets until he was sitting on the floor, laughing, wheezing, and crying at the same time.

I joined him there on the tile floor, kissed his cheeks and his forehead and took his hand in mine. Eventually, he quieted down.

"You're funny," I said.

"What I get... I guess... for defending... my honor," he croaked.

There wasn't much the doctors could do for him, no cast or anything. They just gave him some pain pills and some sleeping pills and told him to take it easy. Tanzy, on the other hand, had a big white dressing over his nose, but nobody dared make fun of him because he'd bravely come to Elliot's defense.

I stayed with Elliot in the cottage that night, our first time together. The place was a mess from Maya dumping drawers upside down and rifling the closet. She left a lot of her clothing behind, mostly on the floor, expecting, I suppose, to buy herself a new diva wardrobe in the city. I stuffed it all in a couple of garbage bags to take to the Salvation Army in town — I didn't want to see any of these garments on the other chicks in the village. I changed the sheets, which Maya had not been doing for a while, and around six o'clock I went over to the inn and got a bunch of food from the regular dinner spread they put out — shepherd's pie and carrot salad — and brought some back to the cottage for us. I helped him into a chair at the kitchen table.

"Thanks for taking care of me," Elliot said.

"I like taking care of somebody," I said. Actually, it was quite a new thing for me. I barely even took care of my brother over the years, except babysitting him occasionally when he was really young, and that didn't amount to much more than watching TV with him. To this point in my life I hadn't known what it was like to take care of another person. Now I had my first taste of it, and I liked it.

He had taken a pain pill and then drank some beers and he began to open up to me about his private worries and fears. No doubt breaking up with Maya and her leaving bummed him out. Apart from whether she was a good or bad person, they'd been together three years. He was discouraged about the village, he said, whether it could ever be a truly self-sustaining thing. He was demoralized by what he called "incorrigible human perversity," the fact that even the best ideas grudge up opposition, that people almost always misunderstand one another, and will usually do just about anything to prove they are in the right.

"The first two, I'm not so sure about," I said. "But needing to be right all the time? Yeah, that's a pretty deadly hang-up."

Mostly he was questioning his assumptions about what was happening in the country, which were the main reasons behind starting Sunrise Village.

"I really thought there was going to be a revolution because of the war and everything," he said. "We traveled a lot the fall and winter before we found this place. We went out west, Maya and me. You could feel the bad vibe all around the country. She was crazy about California. I wouldn't be surprised if she ends up living there. To me, it was still like *The Day of the Locust*," he said, referring to Nathanael West's apocalyptic novel about Hollywood lowlifes in the nineteen thirties. "I hated LA. She loved it and wanted to stay, and she held that against me ever since. She never really wanted to be here in the Vermont woods."

"If it's any consolation, I think the whole country's gone nuts and this is just the right place to be now. I don't know about the revolution, but regular politics are getting crazy enough. I'm really worried about George Wallace," I said, referring to the former Alabama governor who was running for president on a third party ticket, the American Independent Party. Wallace was the guy who had defiantly stood in the schoolhouse door a few years earlier when JFK tried to enforce school desegregation down south. Wallace had said, "*Segregation now, segregation tomorrow, segregation forever!*" Naturally, he was real popular among the bigots, the lowbrow hard-hat types who came out to heckle antiwar demonstrators, men who worked on the auto assembly lines, gun freaks. He liked to brag in his campaign speeches that if any hippies lay down to protest in front of his limousine, he'd be glad to run them over.

"Here's the thing," Elliot said. "If Bobby Kennedy wins the California primary, he's going to get the nomination—"

"I thought we were for Gene," I said, meaning Senator McCarthy who had just won the Oregon primary.

"Gene's a good man," he said, "but it's like the original sin of these times was the JFK assassination and if we could only sort of un-do that this country might get its shit together again. And Bobby getting into the White House could make that happen."

"Bring back Camelot?"

"I know it sounds corny and sentimental," Elliot said, "but there's an historical inevitability about it. And if he does get elected, well, that would pretty much postpone the revolution. I've come to admire Bobby a lot these last few months. There's something about him, some glow of real purpose, of gravitas. He even seems like a deeper person than his brother was, more committed to justice. I think we could become a good country again if he got elected."

"I'm not so sure we were that great a country even under JFK," I said. "Maybe we just romanticize it because he died so young and was so handsome and witty, and had a beautiful wife."

"There was more to him than that. JFK wasn't a lightweight. I don't think he would have jumped into the quagmire of Vietnam feet first the way Johnson did."

"You have to give Johnson a lot of credit on civil rights, though. That was brave for a southerner."

"Sure, but Vietnam has just totally eclipsed all that. The history books will remember the war, not just the waste of lives and money, but the imperial stupidity of it, the hubris of it. People are sick of this national disgrace. I'm pretty sure Bobby Kennedy will end the war."

"But we'll still be the America of Pepsi Cola and Disneyland and the suburbs and stupid TV shows," I said. "And all that stupid shit is sure to get worse, even if Bobby is president. I don't see any end to that, no matter who gets elected."

He sighed and grimaced as he tried to shift his weight and get more comfortable.

"Yeah, Pooh, You're probably right about that."

"I don't see Bobby stopping all the crap that's destroying the land itself," I said. "All these shopping centers and ugly, boring housing developments and new highways everywhere. That's what killed my father: having to drive on that fucking Long Island Expressway all the time. He knew it was a death-trap. He talked about it all the time. He shot photos of accident scenes for *Newsday* every week. And then it killed him."

"I'm sorry about your Dad."

"Yeah, I know. Anyway, I don't hear Bobby Kennedy or anybody else talking about how all that is dragging the country down as much as the war is. That's why it's important to keep this village going, to prove you can still live outside all that accelerating stupidity, to stay real."

"Yeah," he said. "It's true. That's why we came here."

He reached across and took my hand. I came around and helped him up and led him up to the bedroom, helped him take his clothes off and get into bed. His chest was furry. I liked that. The springtime night air was still quite cool. He got under the covers.

"Ah, fresh, clean sheets," he said. "How nice."

Then I took off all my clothes, watching him watch me with a rapt look on his face.

"You're beautiful," he said.

I was already wet. We made love very very carefully, me on top. That was the moment in my life when I first began to feel like an actual adult, lying there with Elliot in the cool spring air, two people who understood each other, who had shared a way of seeing the world, and had a real interest in it, and could talk about it, and do something together. The very next night, Bobby Kennedy won the California primary, and sometime after midnight, some little shit shot him in the head in the kitchen of the Ambassador Hotel in Los Angeles. It changed everything in a split second.

CHAPTER THIRTY-FOUR

B obby Kennedy lingered for a day in the twilight zone of intensive care, and it was just agony for us. Everything stopped in the village. People sat around the old bar in the inn all day and night with the kitchen radio set up there, sometimes praying in groups, burning incense, chanting for Bobby to pull through. But even if he'd lived, there was little chance that he would be the same person mentally after that bullet to the head. And he certainly would not have been able to continue running for election that year, so the whole episode was just an elongated, gruesome tragic ordeal. And then in the wee hours the following day, they announced he was dead.

The people in the village were just devastated over the RFK assassination. Like Elliot, a lot of them, it turned out, had been swayed by Bobby, too, over the evolving spring primary election season, and the thought of a second Kennedy brother getting cut down at such a crucial time just about killed them emotionally, along with the recognition that the Democratic Party establishment would now probably end up nominating that ridiculous sellout, LBJ's vice-president, Hubert Horatio Humphrey, with his piping little voice, pushed-in pig-face, and pasted-on fake smile. We just couldn't believe that God, or fate, or the universe would allow this to happen. We took it very personally.

That was probably the moment when Strangefield started making his grievous plans for jump-starting the revolution around the Democratic Convention a couple of months down the line, though he kept it all completely secret from us villagers except for his little coterie of Marxist anarchists. Senator Kennedy's death re-focused Elliot Sohnberg in his conviction that the country was heading into some kind of revolutionary convulsion and re-dedicated him to what we were doing in this little rural corner of Vermont: setting up a kind of lifeboat to continue civilized existence once the *Titanic* ship of America started sinking.

In the days following the assassination, the political mood only grew darker and darker. The compound effect of two Kennedys plus Martin Luther King getting bumped off — seemingly by an evil zeitgeist — really pushed the collective consciousness over the edge in America generally and at Sunrise Village in particular. And for me, it rubbed salt into the wound of my father's senseless death. Days after the shooting, people would spontaneously burst into tears over their breakfast oatmeal. The crew leaders were on edge, barking orders at their workers. Billy Herman put two speakers facing out the window of his room in the front of the inn and blasted The Doors song "The End" over and over across the heart of the village — and the weird part was, nobody asked him to stop. It seemed appropriate to the moment. We felt as if we had to immerse ourselves in that dread-saturated revelation of the country's darkening drift. We never really got over it emotionally. It left a lasting scar. But after a week, the outward workaday routines of regular village life did return to apparent normality.

Paradoxically, the period that followed RFK's death shifted to a happy time for me. I pretty much moved in with Elliot. I didn't care that the time between Maya and me was as brief as the space between songs on a record. I was rapidly falling in love, and it was so easy (as Buddy Holly said) because we fit together so well. Elliot was clear and direct. There were no mind games with him. He allowed me to love him. He gave me love and acceptance back. And he was uncomplicated about sex in the same way as me. It seemed miraculous, maybe even too good to be true. But I allowed it to be.

I certainly did sense a change in the way the other people in the Village regarded me. Except for Weezil, my girlfriends were noticeably more guarded. They didn't gossip around me anymore, didn't share their crushes and heartbreaks. The men, of course, absolutely quit coming onto me, both the ones I had had sexual relationships with before, and the ones I hadn't gotten around to in my months of experimental promiscuity. It was understood that I had been elevated to a higher station in the village: Songbird's Old Lady, to be treated with deference. I didn't like the way that felt, but one thing you learned from life in the village was that the human race is deeply hierarchical, no matter how much people pay lip service to equality, even in a so-called commune. You can't change essential human nature, so I just decided to go with the flow.

I got up to speed working in Maya's old office and started new accounting books to clear up the financial picture for Elliot so he finally got an accurate notion of how much was coming in and how much was going out. Weezil took over the canteen for me. It was a smooth-running operation. We knew how much candy and cigarettes and tampons to buy every week, and it was all paying for itself.

Now that the weather was nice, tourists stopped by and we were able to sell some hammocks and chairs at retail price, plus bakery items, and hippie craft geegaws — soap, candles, our biggest seller being the God's Eye, a little *totschke* made by wrapping a few cents worth of colored yarn around two (free) twigs, which took about three minutes to make, and which we charged a buck for. People were crazy about them, we sold scores.

We were spending around six hundred dollars a week to pay the people who exceeded their mandatory 25 hours, and that was mainly the major work crews: grounds, construction, tofu, hydro, and gardening. It cost three hundred a week to feed everybody, though I got it down by half quickly, ordering stuff like flour, sugar, rice, beans, and oatmeal in bulk from wholesalers instead of buying everything from the Bennington IGA like Maya did. The first two weeks of June we spent three hundred sixty dollars on parts to repair washing machines, the village van, plumbing supplies, garden seeds, and tractor tires. The electric bill for May was a hundred and fifty. We laid out a hundred and ten to buy a commercial grade chainsaw. We were spending about fifty bucks a month on gasoline for the various vehicles and machines, and as much on propane for the tofu works. At least the heating season was over so we were done buying furnace oil until October. The office phone was about twenty bucks a month.

The village (that is, Elliot) had been spending a hundred bucks a month on free wine for everybody — something I put an end to by shifting it to the canteen operation so that people could buy their own if they wanted it. We laid in cases of cheap Gallo Hearty Burgundy (red) and Chablis (white) and marked it up slightly to account for the gasoline we burned to get it up the mountain, but it was still quite cheap. Nobody complained. If someone wanted harder stuff, they could buy it themselves down in Bennington. Same with beer, which was just too bulky to bother with. Finally there was the one-time expenditure of a thousand bucks for a used 1959 Ford refrigerated box truck to haul our tofu around in.

Our sales revenue in that period was nine hundred fifty from hammocks, seven hundred from lawn chairs, four hundred from our first batches of tofu, three hundred fifty from the canteen, and a hundred for two gigs played by Buttermilk Falls (our folk band) at the Catamount Club in town. Maya's band, Avatar, had been bringing in quite a bit more money for their gigs, playing in much bigger and more important venues, but there was no record of how much they actually had been paid or whether any of it ended up in the village coffers. In any case, that dough was no longer coming in. Altogether, we were spending about twelve hundred dollars more than we took in every month. Elliot appreciated knowing what the score was for supporting the whole outfit. I asked him how long he could expect to underwrite the operation the way it was going. He said, "quite a while." I never wanted to ask him how much money he had in the family fortune as a whole, like, I didn't want to know, it seemed gauche. I assumed it was a lot. There was always enough in the village bank account. He arranged with his Boston bank to give me permission to sign village checks so that I could pay the various bills that came in. I couldn't help asking if he was worried I might embezzle the account like Maya did and he answered, "Absolutely not."

I was optimistic that the village finances would balance out better once we got our additional money-making endeavors going. The herbal tea venture looked promising. Tanzy had prepared three new acres of gardens and planted rose hip rugosas, lavender, bee balm, angelica, lemon balm, chamomile, coriander, echinacea, calendula, verbena, and different kinds of mint. Alison Bartosz, who'd dropped out of art school, designed beautiful packaging for the various kinds of tea, and I was specking out commercial printers for it. We still had the egg, goat dairy products, and maple syrup businesses to figure out, and the construction crew had started a number of outside projects for the local rich summer folks — additions, kitchen renovations, and a whole house for one Bennington College professor. So, I had reasonable expectations that soon we'd cut the losses way down, maybe even get to break-even.

I liked doing all this stuff, organizing things, researching where to get what we needed, working the phone with suppliers and vendors. The book-keeping was straightforward and fairly simple for someone who considered herself a math moron, little more than addition and subtraction. Actually, the most tedious routine task was putting together the Friday pay packages in little envelopes for all the worker bees and distributing them to the mailboxes. It was Maya's system and I kept it up. Issuing checks would have forced everybody to make a trip to the bank in Bennington, which would have been a huge pain in the ass, since most didn't have their own car. We also wanted to keep them out of the payroll tax system of the evil government.

I decided to start a village newsletter so that everybody would be properly informed about projects and events and even gossip. It was the most fun part of my duties, just a couple of pages run off on the Rex-o-graph machine every Wednesday. Other than song lyrics, it was my first experience in writing for the sheer pleasure of it. I'd run off about twenty-five two-page copies stapled together and they'd circulate around. Copies always ended up in each bathroom and in the sauna.

Then, to my great surprise, Marilyn gave Bobby permission to visit for two weeks in late June. He came up on the bus and I went to get him in town. It looked like he'd grown another inch since Larry's funeral, and his chestnut hair billowed down to his shoulders. He looked quite handsome and grown up stepping off the bus in his bell-bottom jeans and psychedelic satin shirt, like the one Dylan wore on the cover of *Highway 61 Revisited*, with a string of tiny turquoise beads around his throat and Ray-ban sunglasses on. I thought: *this kid is cool!* I actually worried whether he would be debauched by the chicks up in the Village. In fact, I had to resign myself to the idea that he would be, knowing the *ethos* of the place.

Mr. Eckmann, the lawyer, had arranged Bobby's share of the insurance money so that it was in a trust account that Marilyn couldn't get her hands on. I'd had several conversations with him over the weeks — one of the benefits of having a regular phone in the privacy of my office. What I didn't know until some time later was that Marilyn — the miserable twat — had used those two weeks Bobby was visiting me in Vermont to go to Fire Island with one of Larry's old friends, Morrie Saperstein, the *Newsday* sports editor, recently divorced, who lived a few miles west over in Glen Head. Like, only three months after her husband died.

But that news was yet to come. I put Bobby in Danny Musser's old room in the Leo House where Dave Padget might keep an eye on him, and I assigned Bobby to work in the gardens so he could exert himself in the sunshine and fresh air. I saw him virtually every day for meals, but I was extremely busy myself and didn't exactly hang out with him. He was apparently very busy, too, having a good time, because he didn't even bother to come along to hear Buttermilk Falls play when I told him we'd be gigging at the Catamount Club in Bennington the first Saturday he was there. Weezil, who knew everything that went on in the village, said that the ever-ready Icelandic bombshell, Krista Ragnarsdóttir, was giving him a crash course in the ways of the world. The following week, she said that little Poppy Flagler, Krista's physical opposite, was working him over. And I assumed others in between.

One thing that made the early summer so magical was that we could swim in the old abandoned marble quarry, which I'd barely even been aware of that long fall and winter. It was the hidden gem of Sunrise Village. The water was the most astounding turquoise, the color of a tropical sea, and so clear that you could see fish hanging twenty feet below the surface like they were encased in a glass paperweight. The quarry was spring fed. The marble company had continually pumped the water out when they worked it decades ago, but after they shut it down, the big hole in the ground slowly filled up. It was about four acres, with steep, blocky, buff-colored marble cliffs on one side that the more dare-devil guys liked to dive off. Teck Hesslewaite, had been a platform diver on the University of Arizona aquatics team, and he could do amazing twisty-turny somersault dives from thirty feet up, entering the water at the final, critical moment like a knife blade. Billy Herman just ran off the edge at full speed with his legs furiously pumping, like Wile E. Coyote in the old Warner Brothers' *Roadrunner* cartoons. On sunny days in late June, we'd all assemble there at the end of the work day, before dinner — seventy-odd naked people, young, mostly with very fit bodies, skinny-dipping. It was surreal. Nobody hassled us. It was a private paradise. We drank wine and smoked some weed, and it was just the perfect way to transition into night-time, with all its lovely pleasures. We were in heaven.

Word was getting out across the hippie universe about the allure of Sunrise Village and a lot more young people were showing up, hoping to be let in. We discussed it — not just me and Elliot — but a committee of the crew chiefs and Sophie the cook, and we set a limit on eighty people, which was the number of regular beds we actually had in June, 1968. We ruled that we could only replace people who left. So, in my new position, I personally had to turn a lot of people away. However, having visitors did present an opportunity to get some more money coming in. We decided to make one of the old barns we weren't using into a hostel, a kind of bunkhouse for visitors, who would pay ten bucks a night to stay for a maximum of three nights — so they didn't get too used to the place. The construction crew framed in a big room inside the barn with nice clean plank siding. It was rustic but charming. We furnished it with five double bunk-beds, and a common table in the middle with chairs, so we could take ten visitors at a time, co-ed of course. We built it cheap and fast. It didn't have any electricity or running water. Visitors could buy candles and flashlight batteries at the canteen. They had to either use a nearby outhouse or the bathrooms back at the inn. We charged extra for sheets and blankets. Some came with sleeping bags. They also had to pay extra for meals. Why not?

Often hippies would show up with tents. But we forbade camping elsewhere on the property, and it was a large property, hundreds of acres, with the Green Mountain National Forest behind it. The grounds crew would go into the woods — about as far as you would want to hike from a parked car — searching at dusk and easily locate campers by seeing their flashlights or lanterns, and try to diplomatically kick them out. Some of the campers were surly about it, but Hog could be an intimidating guy, and his crew guys were muscle-bound gorillas, so there was never any question of who would win an argument. It became a joke in the village to utter the phrase, "Hey, man…" in a whiney voice, because that's what these poor schnooks always said when they were told they couldn't camp there — Hey, man… like, how can you do this to us…? We're all one….

This new position running the Village combined with my new home life with Elliot to produce a most beautiful, gratifying time of my life. I felt that something had definitely changed inside me. I was growing up. I had a job that required me to be responsible for a broad range of different activities. I had become a respected person in a real community. I was living in a beautiful corner of the country. I was learning how to play the guitar quite well and making pretty good music with friends. I had financial security from the insurance payout backing me up. I didn't have to depend on Marilyn for anything, or even communicate with the bitch. I had a relationship with a man that was really working. It couldn't have been better, really. And then I over-reached and got into trouble.

CHAPTER THIRTY-FIVE

Ever since I arrived at Sunrise Village I'd enjoyed this fantasy about putting on plays there, being a former theater major. I found myself thinking more and more about it as I got comfortable with my new duties and summer approached. Elliot and I talked about it, and he encouraged me, even said he would underwrite the cost of a production — though I doubt he knew exactly what he was getting into. We could use the Odd Fellows hall now that Avatar was gone and didn't leave their equipment onstage there all the time anymore. I thought we might make some money, selling tickets to the summer people around the area. It had also gotten to the point where the folk band, Buttermilk Falls, was on automatic pilot. We had our established playlist and were well-practiced, and played around enough at the local colleges and some clubs, and I thought it would be okay to step back from that for a few weeks to do some theater, perhaps get something going on a regular basis.

I picked a project that was extremely ambitious: Peter Weiss's political extravaganza, *The Persecution and Assassination of Jean-Paul Marat as Performed by the Inmates of the Asylum of Charenton Under the*

Direction of the Marquis de Sade, usually called in shorthand, *Marat/ Sade*. The playwright was German, but an English translation of it had been staged by the Royal Shakespeare Company in London to stellar reviews, and then they brought the whole production to Broadway where it was a smash sensation. I saw it my freshman year at NYU and it just knocked me out.

It was a play within a play, basically the story of the French Revolution set just as the title says, in an insane asylum, in the year 1808, the height of Napoleon's glory, a decade after the revolution had fizzled out. Napoleon's stand-in is the warden of the asylum, Monsieur Coulmier, seated comfortably at the edge of the stage with his family. He periodically has to interrupt the proceedings to restore order when the inmates get too worked up by the bloody story they're telling. The Marquis de Sade, who in real life was confined at Charenton, is onstage throughout the play as the "director," also interrupting the "actors" — his fellow inmates — with philosophical speeches about the indifference of the universe to human suffering and the need to give meaning to our pain by imbuing it with passion. He often "debates" the other central character, Jean Paul Marat, the idealistic revolutionary firebrand, who sits at center stage, confined in an old-fashioned tin bathtub to sooth his skin disease — acquired, it was said, from his days and nights hiding in the sewers of Paris. Marat, ironically, is played by a paranoiac. The play had a very large cast including all the various inmates and guards, and it was originally staged as if the audience itself were an 1808 claque of Napoleonic era rich Parisians coming out to the asylum to be entertained by the antics of the lunatics — which was a true historical fact.

I was inspired to put on that play because it seemed like a perfect vehicle to convey the angst that we were living through in America, with all our political tribulations, and the whiff of revolution in the air —much of which emanated, of course, from us hippies and war protesters, so the *mise-en-scène* of the play had an extra layer of irony. The French Revolution, unlike the American one, did not have such a happy ending, and the play is largely focused on that gruesome phase of it called the Reign of Terror, when the revolutionary government was chopping off heads by the thousands, with the guillotine running day and night like an infernal machine foretelling the coming industrial age. As performed on Broadway, the play also notoriously contained nude scenes, which both scandalized and titillated audiences — and were becoming an increasingly common feature onstage in other shows like *Hair*, and The Living Theater's Off-Broadway spectacle, *Paradise Now*. We'd been immersed in this stuff at NYU while I was there.

I wrote up a notice in the village newsletter that we would be putting on the play, and explained a little what it was about, and announced auditions for a Monday night in late June. People came up to me at mealtime and at the quarry to talk about it and were enthusiastic. Quite a few had acted in high school plays. Two besides me had actually seen *Marat/Sade* on Broadway. I needed a capable stage manager to assist me, keep notes, and later on to manage some rehearsals when I couldn't be there, to record blocking (the movement of the actors on stage), and finally run the lighting and sound crews in performance. Billy Herman volunteered. He was organized and intelligent, and had enough respect in the village so that others would do what he said, which you need in a stage manager, whose job is like a drill sergeant.

We held the audition at the Odd Fellows hall. I'd ordered twenty copies of the paperback play script from the bookshop in town. It felt great to be back "on the boards." And unlike that demoralizing experience with Professor Arnie Dremling back in the fall semester — which seemed like a million years ago — this time I was in charge. I was, perhaps, over-optimistic about being able to fill the major roles from the ranks of the villagers. I managed to cast all the principal characters except the two title roles, Jean Paul Marat and the Marquis de Sade, which were very demanding, with long speeches, and required a certain maturity. I wasn't sure what to do. Elliot suggested I try an audition down at Bennington College, but I couldn't feature people having to drive all that distance to the village every evening for the month of rehearsal I had planned. Instead, I came up with a really wild idea.

I had five thousand bucks in the bank and I decided to put some of it to good use. I booked two hours of time in a rehearsal studio in the New York City theater district for sixty dollars. Then I took out an ad in the casting call section of *Daily Variety*, the trade publication of show biz. The ad said:

> Seeking two actors, male, 35-50yrs, for leads in summer stock production of *Marat/Sade*. Two weeks, $100/week + rm/bd + bus fare. Beautiful Vermont setting. Give yourself a summer break, make a little cash, and have some fun. Auditions: Essex Studio Building 331 West 52nd St. 1:00pm June 28.

The idea was to bring them up only for the final two weeks of rehearsals and a week of performances. I could use stand-ins and work around them for the initial two weeks of blocking. I also had to pay two hundred dollars to the theatrical licensing company for the performance rights. If you put up posters and advertised a play, and didn't pay the fee, you could get sued, even a bunch of amateurs. I learned at NYU that you had to be careful about that.

I took the bus down to New York alone the night before and stayed at the Drake Hotel, which Elliot recommended, quite fancy, something I'd never done before, but it was worth it. I ordered a scotch from room service and enjoyed it in the bathtub. For inspiration, and since I was living it up, I got a ticket to see the Broadway play *A Cry of Players*, about young William Shakespeare's life back home in Stratford-Upon-Avon before he went to London and his career at the Globe Theater. I stopped at Bonwits on my way to the Drake to buy myself a little black A-line dress for the audition and the play that evening. Young "Will" Shakespeare was played by Frank Langella, who I'd developed a mad crush on my last year in high school when first I saw him in an adaptation of Herman Melville's sea story, *Benito Cereno*, about a slave revolt on a Spanish ship. To truly marinate myself in the Broadway milieu, I took myself out to Sardi's for supper before the curtain and had their famous steak tartare, along with two glasses of red wine that was a couple of notches above Gallo Hearty Burgundy, the staple in Sunrise Village. I saw the actor George C. Scott across the room eating a Caesar salad. He was appearing in Neil Simon's *Plaza Suite*. It was a fantastic night. I was so happy.

The next day my mind was blown when thirty-two professional actors showed up at my audition. I had my A-line dress on, playing a role I thought of as *a young professional lady* — as opposed to *a hippie chick*. But you could tell they were a bit taken aback by me. Quite a few of them asked how old I was. I lied about my age, saying I was twenty-five. Many of them read adequately for these two parts, but two in particular stood out because they were physically right. Reading all who showed up, I took their phone numbers, made notes, and told them I would notify the ones selected for the roles. My Jean Paul Marat, Jerome Brooks, 41, had just come off a run of Chekhov's *The Cherry Orchard* that closed literally a few before days before. He'd played, Lopakhin, the wealthy merchant who buys up the estate where the cherry orchard is. He was dark-haired, slender, and very intense, a perfect paranoiac.

You'd think an actor coming off such a plum role would be set in his career. But actors are pathetically insecure, both in their psychology and in the practical ups and downs of daily life. They always think they'll never get another acting job. When I asked Jerome flat-out how come he was willing to work for peanuts up in the Vermont boondocks, he said he was desperate to get out of the city during the middle of the summer, and it was a challenging role, and he already had a small part in an upcoming movie called *The Wild Bunch*, a western that would begin location shooting in Mexico that fall. Plus, he said, he'd never been to a commune before and was curious. I should have been a little more suspicious about that.

My Marquis de Sade was Paul Gabler, 54, who, when I called to give him the part, confessed tearfully to me that he hadn't had an acting job since he understudied Hume Cronyn in Edward Albee's *A Delicate Balance* back in 1966, and said he was hugely grateful for the opportunity to do this great role. Paul was very sweet and endearing but Jerome seemed more self-possessed. Neither of them had a car, of course, living in Manhattan. I told them I'd mail them a check for bus fare to Bennington and specify the exact date we'd need them to arrive. I had no idea how these two aces-in-the-hole would turn out to be such pains-in-the-ass.

CHAPTER THIRTY-SIX

We began rehearsals on Sunday, the last day of June. Everything went pretty well the first week. I could get my regular office duties all done in four hours, so we rehearsed afternoons. The set was going to be minimal, except I asked the construction boys to build a twenty-foot thrust platform extension out from the proscenium to bring the action right out into the audience, so they would remain consciously aware of themselves watching the lunatics. We also raked it, slanted it, which allowed actors upstage to loom up higher when necessary. While the guys built that, we taped out the dimensions of the stage on the auditorium floor and I started to chart the movement of the actors in their scenes — the blocking. Unlike the loosey-goosey Arnie Dremling method of letting actors just wander around when and where they felt like it, I wanted this play to be tightly choreographed, and I expected the actors' movements to be the same every rehearsal, once it was set. I showed Billy Herman how to record it in his stage manager's loose-leaf book.

The play was such a zoo of complicated action that I bought a football coach's whistle so I could stop whatever was going on up there without hollering. There were several big musical numbers, with lots of movement. Alan Kaplan, who could read music and arrange musical parts, put together a pocket orchestra, with himself on harmonium, a little lap organ that gave an eerie carnival sound to the songs. Donald Kaiser, one of the tofu crew, had a trombone, which added a creepy Brechtian dash. Kris Wingo's cello elevated the sound in the sad, quiet interludes. Alison played rhythm guitar. And we had Hans Bierbauer on percussion, with bongo drums, a snare, a tambourine, a ratchet, a bunch of tin cans on a rope, and various bells for sound effects. Good old Dave Padget was the stand-in for the Marquis de Sade and Dean Shays of the garden squad stood-in for Marat. Mark Tanzio played the Herald, an inmate who narrates much of the action, Josie Sale from the kitchen crew played Simonne, Marat's nurse and mistress, Charlie Meeker played the sex maniac, Duperret, Lucy Salmon played Rossignol, the main singer in the four-person chorus, and most problematically, I gave the big role of Charlotte Corday, Marat's assassin, to the fairly new arrival, Kitty Lapudis, because she radiated sexuality. She played games with me right from the start.

The first point of conflict was when we were blocking the big set-piece about Charlotte Corday's arrival in Paris, which included a musical number and then a long speech about the horrors Corday encounters in the streets of the city amidst the revolution. Kitty started arguing with me when I told her where to take her soliloquy. She had a better idea, she said.

"Okay," I said. "Let's see."

She went upstage, that is, to the rear, and played the scene as though she was flirting with the asylum guards, shaking her bosom, grinding her hips.

"That's not right," I said when she was done. "I want you downstage and rather still. It's a quiet, intense speech."

"But wouldn't it be funny if she's talking about all these horrible sights while she's messing with the guards?"

"This isn't a comedy," I said.

"Yeah, but it has funny parts. It's ironic, right, that she's trying to tempt them?"

"To what end?" I said. "Like, they're going to ball her right there in front of everybody? I don't think so."

"It's a goof," she said. "She's goofing on them."

"This isn't a goofy moment in the play," I said. "Besides, the inmate playing Charlotte is described by the Herald as a catatonic. She's out of it. You're acting way too frisky for a catatonic."

"What about if she goes over to him," she said, pointing at Coulmier, the head of the asylum, sitting at stage left, "and speaks the lines to him, like Juliet to Romeo?"

"This is not *Romeo and Juliet*, this is *Marat/Sade*, and Coulmier doesn't have any lines in this scene."

"He could react, though. It would be interesting."

"I don't want you to interact with the other characters in this scene. Corday's lost in a world of her own. She's a very injured person, shaky, frightened. She's describing crazy stuff, murder, blood in the streets, hacked bodies. Play the psychosis."

"But she's supposed to be sexual, too. It's obvious."

"Yeah, but her sexuality is all latent, innocent. That's why it's so dramatic when she whips Sade with her long hair."

"But that's later. Don't we have to communicate some sense of arousal?"

"You're playing against her violent emotion, not into it."

"I don't understand—"

"Apparently not. But just try it my way."

She did, but obviously going through the motions which, oddly, made her come off more believably as the detached, sleepy Corday, so I let it slide. That was only the beginning of my struggle with Kitty Lapudis. Into the second week of rehearsal, she was fighting me at practically every opportunity, even in scenes she wasn't in, kibitzing just loud enough for me to hear. By now we were working on the completed thrust stage itself. I generally sat halfway back in the big room next to Billy Herman, giving him notes. We were running through the difficult scene where Marat harangues the national assembly about the enemies of the people. Kitty was off-stage, sitting next to her new sidekick, Terry Givins of the clean-up crew, astrology buff, and notorious village sex maniac, who was playing Coulmier's daughter, a minor non-speaking role. As Marat was ticking off the politicians he denounced, she mimicked him saying, "I denounce Kaplan, Padget, Bollinger...."

"Shut up, Kitty," I said across the room.

Kitty and Terry cracked up in a conspicuous way. I blew my whistle. The people onstage stopped the scene. I told them to take ten and went over to where Kitty and Terry sat. They reeked of weed.

"What'd I say at the start about getting high for rehearsals?" I said.

"I forgot," Kitty said and they both cracked up again.

"I want to talk to you outside."

"Now?"

"Yeah, now," I said, my voice rising. "Let's go."

She shrugged at Terry as if to show her innocence, but she followed me out the side door. I led her around the Odd Fellows hall to a little grove of birch trees between it and the tofu shack.

"Why are you fighting me at every step along the way?" I asked, shaking a Kool out of the pack.

"Can I have one of those?" she said.

"They sell them at the canteen, you know."

"I'm tapped out just now."

I gave her a cigarette as a gesture of good will, I guess.

"Thanks," she said, accepting a light and kind of looking me up and down. "How old are you, by the way?"

"I'm going to be twenty in October," I said.

"Oh? You're still a teenager, huh?"

"Technically, I suppose."

"I'm going to be twenty-three in August. Honestly, I feel a little weird taking crap from someone who's practically still a kid."

"It's not crap, it's stage direction."

"You're a control freak."

"I'm the director of this play. It's as simple as that."

"You stifle other people's creativity."

"It's up to me to pull this together, to make it coherent."

"That's funny. It's supposed to be an insane asylum, right?"

"Yeah, but not pandemonium."

"I don't even get this fucking play. It's hard for me to take it seriously."

"You tried out for the role and you got it. So even if it doesn't make sense to you now, I expect you to do what I tell you. Frankly, you're better when you're just going through the motions than when you try to act. Too often you're just mugging up there."

"What's mugging?"

"Exaggerating your stage business to a ridiculous degree, drawing attention to yourself."

"How did you get in this position, anyway? Oh, wait, I know."

"Can you stop being snotty for just one minute?"

"I'll try," she said and squinched her eyes up as though she were making a great effort.

"Don't come to rehearsal stoned again or I'll have to kick you out of the cast. And if I have to fire you, I'll also kick you out of Sunrise Village."

"You can't do that."

"Oh, yes I can. And I will."

Kitty seemed to fall in line for a while after that. At least she stopped hassling me all the time and she at least appeared to take her role seriously, or pretended. The play was shaping up and I began to think that we might actually pull it off. Weezil got a crew of four chicks working on costumes: simple, raggedy, muslin inmate outfits, wild winged starched hats for the two "nuns," breeches and a nice linen shirt with jabot for Monsieur de Sade, and a military tunic for Coulmier. Marat got his 18th century style tin bathtub shaped like a giant shoe, made out of sheet metal by Hog's guys. The props came together. Then we got to the third week of rehearsal and my two ringers came up from New York.

I think the village cast members were impressed by the professionalism that Paul and Jerome displayed the first couple of days they were onstage. The two had their lines down, they picked up the blocking easily, and fell easily into the rhythm I had tried to establish. Paul in particular was very nice to me, very complimentary about the stage movement I'd devised. He'd seen the Royal Shakespeare Company production when it played on Broadway, too, so he knew the play at its best. The rest of the cast's performances sharpened in response to the two pros. Even Kitty behaved herself. Jerome and Paul seemed dazzled by the Sunrise Village scene, especially when we broke every afternoon around five and went over to the quarry for the daily pre-dinner skinny-dipping frolic. Jerome was like a kid in a cupcake bakery, chatting up all the chickies, putting on the older man charm. It also happened that he was rather well-endowed, and proud of it, posing himself actorishly in an at least semi-tumescent state with all the naked ladies cavorting around him.

Paul availed himself of the supplies in the canteen and brought a bottle of wine with him to the quarry each day, and finished it himself before supper, and polished off another one with supper, and was noticeably more sluggish for the two hours of evening rehearsal that we were doing in the final two weeks. It started to get real hot in the middle of July, with the temperature near ninety, scorchers for Vermont. And later on in those stifling evenings Paul liked to hang out on the porch of the inn in the cool night air with a bunch of the other actors and put away more wine, sometimes passing out there so the guys had to carry him up to bed. By the beginning of the final week of rehearsal, he showed up half-plastered in the middle of the afternoon, and I began to really worry about him.

Only a few days after he arrived, I noticed that Kitty and Jerome were touching each other a lot during rehearsals and it dawned on me that they were balling up a storm — which I didn't have any objection to, until Kitty started to let it impinge on her scenes. In the play, as in actual history, Charlotte Corday comes to the door of Marat's lodgings three times, and is refused entry twice. Finally, she worms her way past Marat's keeper, Simonne. She stands behind Marat seated in his bathtub. He can't see or hear her well and says, "come closer." Corday says, "I'm *coming* Marat...." So, Kitty played the line as if she was in the throes of an orgasm before she pantomimed plunging her dagger down. I blew one sharp blast on my whistle.

"Hold it," I said. "That's not how you've been playing the scene."

"I know," Kitty said. "I added a little touch."

"It's not so little."

"But it makes sense, right? She's all worked up into a sexual state, right?"

"No, we've been playing against the obvious. She's still an inmate acting Corday, not Corday herself."

"Yeah, sure. But she's all repressed being stuck in the asylum, right? Finally, it comes out in the heat of the moment."

"She's still a fearful catatonic, so afraid of the emotion inside her that she falls asleep when she senses it. She's not overtly expressive. That's why all these scenes of the sex maniac Duperret chasing after her are in the play. To show that she's put upon."

"Put upon what?" Kitty said. "Maybe it makes her horny."

Several cast members laughed at that.

"The way you were playing it before was better," I said.

"This gives the scene a nice *frisson*, I think," Jerome butted in. "Don't be a little prude."

I squelched my impulse to sass him back, considering that he was a pro, and a lot older than me.

"The audience is going to be worked up enough at this point," I said. "I don't want to whack them over the head as if we're saying, hey, did you not get the point of how the Marquis de Sade is mixing up lust, passion, and revolutionary politics?"

"I can tone it down a little?" Kitty said.

"No, it's mugging. Go back to what you were doing before."

"How is it mugging?"

"You're hamming it up."

"Well, I don't see it that way."

"Persevere," I said.

"What—?"

"Quit the acting and get on with the play."

"Quit acting…?"

"Run the speech again without all the moaning and gasping."

Later on, with everyone milling at the inn just before dinner, Jerome came over and steered me to a quiet corner near the fireplace.

"You don't have to be so mean to Kitty," he said.

"She's been trying real hard to antagonize me since way before you got here. I just want her to follow directions."

"You're hardly Eva Le Gallienne," he said, referring to the grand lady of the stage who directed the recent production of *The Cherry Orchard* that Jerome was just in on Broadway. "You're just a kid."

"Maybe, but I'm responsible for making this work."

"Would you like some pointers from an old pro?" he said, squiggling his index finger into the vicinity of my bellybutton.

"Cut that out."

He did, but he said, "You know, you're very attractive Miss Bollinger. We should get to know each other better."

"It's my impression that you and Kitty are screwing up a storm," I whispered.

He made a peevish face. "Well, I'm not married to her," he said. "Say, how about we skip dinner, you and me, and steal up to my lodgings and have a nice romantic interlude."

"Absolutely not."

"I assure you, you'll be very pleased."

"Don't you know I've got a boyfriend?"

"Aw come on. Nobody's really got a boyfriend around here. It's a free-for-all."

"Not for me. Look, I'm flattered, but no."

"I can tell, you're wavering."

"I'm not wavering. The answer is no."

"What if you never have this chance again?"

"Mea culpa...."

"If you change you're mind, just whistle," he said, pantomiming it with his lips pursed. I was turning to leave when he touched my arm. "She's actually quite a good little actress, Kitty," he said. "Not so good between the sheets, though, as it happens."

"Look, if you have any influence, please ask her not to stick anymore new impromptu business into her scenes. It's driving me crazy."

Even later that night at home at the cottage with Elliot, I asked him if he'd back me up if I decided that Kitty had to go. He knew she'd been giving me trouble.

"Oz tells me he suspects she's the one who robbed the peoples' stashes," he said, meaning the various hidey holes where they kept their money.

"Why didn't you tell me that?"

"Because you're stuck with her in your play and I didn't want to complicate things. But we probably better ask her to leave as soon as it's over."

CHAPTER THIRTY-SEVEN

The night of our technical rehearsals was especially hot with a nasty red moon rising over the Vermont hills through the big open windows of the Odd Fellows hall. The tech rehearsal is a drawn-out ordeal where you have to set all the lighting levels and sound cues, and it always goes on hours longer than a normal run-through of the full play. The actors have to stand around in costume so you can see how the lights hit them and it's aggravating for them, I know. But I expected my two ringers, at least to be more patient and respectful. As it turned out, Jerome was busy literally trying to screw his way through the female half of the cast that night, making up for lost time, I guess. I had to send Billy Herman out to look for him three times, and each time he was making it with someone else (though not Kitty) in a different location: the dressing room, the prop room, the birch grove outside. Meanwhile, Kitty sulked in a cloud of cigarette smoke inside. When it came time to set the lights for the climactic assassination scene, she jammed her wooden prop dagger so hard against the soft hollow above Jerome's collarbone, that he shrieked and batted it out of her hand.

"What's going on up there?" I asked from out in the audience, distracted from my back-and-forth with Teck Hesslewhite, who was running the rather limited small dimmer box we'd bought second-hand from Bennington high school.

"She's trying to kill me," Jerome said.

"He's being a little faggot," Kitty said.

"Watch your mouth," Jerome said.

"Can we please just get through this," I said. "I know it's tedious and annoying."

"He's tedious," Kitty said, looking right at Jerome. "A tedious piece of shit."

"And you're beyond annoying, you vicious little strumpet," Jerome said.

"Take ten everybody."

I didn't announce out loud that I wanted to talk to Kitty, but as the actors left the stage on break I went and found her backstage and managed to steer her into the stairwell there. She had been crying.

"What do *you* want?" she said.

"Just to see what's going on with you."

"Oh, like you actually give a shit."

"I give a shit about this play."

"I fucking hate this play."

"I know. It's a good credit, though, the role of Corday. If you ever audition for anything else."

"From this little rumdum theater nobody ever heard of? Or ever will? What does it matter?"

"You never know," I said. "For what it's worth, Jerome said you're a good actress."

"I fucking hate him. He's just a giant prick with a tiny, deformed man attached."

"If you can keep it together, and get yourself through the performances, we'd all really appreciate it, especially your fellow cast members who are working hard."

"Like I said, I don't give a shit anymore."

We stood quietly for a few moments. Kitty dabbed her eyes and sniffled.

"Okay, lookit," I said. "I'll pay you two hundred bucks if you get through all the performances this week, and you do the part the way we rehearsed it, with no mugging, no funny stuff, no surprise improvisations, and no fighting onstage with Paul."

Kitty finally looked me in the eye, apparently weighing the deal.

"Two hundred bucks?" she asked disdainfully.

"Yeah."

"You're trying to buy me off."

"Yeah, that's exactly right. Think of it as a job you're getting paid to do."

"Three hundred," she said.

"Two fifty," I said, and that's final. "I'll do the part myself if I have to."

"Oh, you'd be great," she said with a nickering, snorty little laugh.

"You have no idea."

We had a ten second stare-down.

"Okay," she said. "I'll do it. Half in advance, though."

"No. You only get the money at the end, if you don't fuck up."

She gave me a sharp look.

"Okay, Whatever," she said.

"Is that yes or no?"

"Yeah, I'll do it."

We returned to the main hall and got through the tech rehearsal at one o'clock in the morning.

CHAPTER THIRTY-EIGHT

The next evening, Tuesday was going to be our dress rehearsal, with the opening performance on Wednesday night for a four-night run. We'd printed up posters and put them up all over southern Vermont, now at the height of the summer tourist season. It had a little map on it, showing how to find us. I figured if we got fifty outsiders in the audience, that would be a triumph. I'd sent letters out to the arts editors of every newspaper from Albany to Montpelier, inviting reviewers to the opening. Many of them put us in their weekly listings of events. I had arranged things so that Wednesday during the day we could just take it easy and relax, but, of course, the universe wouldn't allow that. I found a note in my mailbox at the inn after breakfast. It said.

> Come to my room (no. 17) at the inn at 11 a.m. I have something very important to discuss with you. I'm serious. J. Brooks.

That was Jerome, of course. I dreaded to imagine what he was up to, but I knew I had to comply. So, at eleven a.m. I knocked on his door. He opened it wearing a Japanese kimono.

"Ah, there you are," he said. "Punctual as all get out."

"What do you want?" I tried to sound pleasant.

"Why, for you to come in."

"Said the spider to the fly...."

"I'm not a spider. I'm a very nice fellow. Now, quit the acting and come in."

I did. He shut the door behind me.

"I've been observing you for the past couple of weeks, Miss Bollinger."

"You can call me Pooh."

"Oh, we'll get to that. I must say, you're quite capable, considering."

"Thank you."

"No, I admire what you've managed to make of this. Such a big cast. All this kinetic movement. Big ideas. And you, so young. It's quite extraordinary."

"Thanks again."

"It would be a pity if it didn't come off."

"Why wouldn't it come off?"

"If, for instance, one of the principals wasn't here."

"Are you skipping out?"

"We're getting a little ahead of ourselves. The thing is, Miss Bollinger... Pooh, I find you irresistibly desirable."

I lowered my eyes and stared into the floor, gray-painted boards with a small oval rag rug in front of the bed, which was an actual bed with box springs and all. We'd tried to make the accommodations nice for the professional actors.

"I can't," I shook my head.

He came closer and put his hand on my shoulder and lifted my chin with his other index finger. He had a lot of cologne on.

"You can," he said gently.

"Don't make me do this," I said, getting all weepy.

"You do want the show to go on, don't you?"

I nodded.

"Come, sit down."

I let him lead me to the edge of the bed and I sat down there.

"Behold," he said and opened up his kimono.

"I've seen you naked before," I said. I had, of course, onstage and up at the quarry.

"Yes," he said. "But never quite like this, hmmm?"

His thing was inches away, bobbing before me like some ghastly, pale, blind snake creature from the depths of a limestone cavern where sunlight never entered.

"Come on now," he said. "Take that shirt off. I want to see your breasts."

"You've seen them before at the quarry."

"I know. I admired them a lot at a remove. But I want to touch them now."

This was the point where I should have run from the room shrieking but I was too unnerved.

"Jerome, please. Is this really necessary? Aren't there ten other chicks out there who would gladly ball you? Really?"

"I suppose," he said, "but I really want you."

"It's so unfair."

"I know. I'm coercing you. It's true. But I don't think I can perform in this wonderful production of yours without some encouragement and affection. The part is so demanding, you know, and we actors are fragile creatures. We have these pathetic little egos. We need consolation, reassurance. Indulge me once and I promise I'll be a good boy."

I shook my head and inhaled all my weepy snot.

"Just be a good sport. It's not asking much," he said and sat down next to me.

"Poor Pooh. So... put upon."

I wanted to smash his face, but instead I reached down and pulled my T-shirt off.

"Wow," he said. "You're really something. Lie down."

I lay on the bed and allowed him to take off my sneakers, my jeans and my underpants.

He slid down beside me and fondled me, kissed my shoulder and neck and sought my lips.

"No kissing," I said.

"Aw, come on."

"This is not love."

"It's like love, though."

"Just do what you have to do."

"Okay," he said with a sigh. "I'll have to moisten you up, though. Bear with me."

He slid down and worked on me below with his tongue. He was gentle and I'm ashamed to say that after a while I felt something like arousal. It went on for a while. Eventually I opened up and allowed him to enter me. He was very large indeed and at first it hurt. Then, not so much. There was a window a few feet from the bed. It looked out on the rooftops of Sunrise Village and Tanzy's magnificent gardens, and the forest beyond and Owl's Head beyond that, all perfectly still except for a red-tailed hawk wheeling distantly on the warm summer updrafts. Then I began to feel the sheer animal carnality of him and my mouth formed an "O," and I couldn't help myself as he seized my jaw and turned my head forward.

"Look at me," he moaned. "Look at me you beautiful creature. Oh, God, look at me...."

"You're not there...." I said.

His back arched and his head jerked with each of several spasms.

Then he rolled off to the side, trying to recover his breath. I lay next to him not more than a few seconds before I climbed over him and got on my feet.

"Aw don't go," he said. "Stay and have a smoke."

"Curtain's at eight o'clock. Be there."

"I'll never forget this."

"I hope I do," I said. I picked up my clothes and walked naked down the hall to the bathroom, where I washed what I could of him off of me and out of me.

CHAPTER THIRTY-NINE

Wouldn't you know it, Paul Gabler, my de Sade, was still in his room fifteen minutes before curtain. I sent Padget and Hans Bierbauer over to roust him out and we hosed him down with coffee so he could at least blunder through the dress rehearsal, a wide-awake drunk. Elliot, who had been down at the hydroelectric site all day, came and sat next to me during the performance. Feeling the heat radiate off his body in the seat next to mine kept me so achingly aware of what had happened earlier in the day that I could barely pay attention to the play. Through the whole first act, I kept rationalizing that I had gone through my slut phase, balling all these guys, in the weeks before Elliot and I came together, and he apparently didn't hold that against me, so maybe I didn't need to feel so guilty about what Jerome had forced me to do. But I couldn't really convince myself not to feel bad about it. It made me hate what I was seeing on the stage. Somehow, I pulled myself together enough during the second act to scribble some notes for the actors. At least Jerome and Kitty performed their roles as rehearsed, with no monkey business. They had a genuine work ethic.

When it was over, I let the actors and techies go after a few notes. The dress rehearsal had been good enough, at least as far as I had been able to pay attention to it. It had been an exhausting week for everybody. I wanted them to preserve their energy for the opening and feel confident about it. After the others all left, Elliot and I remained in the empty theater.

"We've got to do something about the guy playing Sade, " I said.

"Yeah, he seemed kind of toasted."

"It's really serious. His boozing is out of control. We have to keep him off the hooch tomorrow, and for the three days after that."

We sat silently for a minute while Elliot mulled it over.

"I can put Tiny on his case." he said. Tiny, a.k.a. Steve Shagan, was one of Albert Ozmer's grounds crew guys, a six-foot-three former linebacker on the Syracuse University football team. "I'll tell him to stick to the bastard like a shadow."

"He'd better sleep outside his door. Maybe even follow him into the bathroom."

"I'll tell him to do that," he said. "Are you okay, Pooh? You seem... kind of remote."

"This thing has beat the shit out of me," I said, and just started weeping. He torqued around in his seat, a look of surprise on his face, and let me cry against him for quite a while. "I'm all strung out."

"Aw, Pooh. You did it though. You made it happen. You did great," he said, stroking my head. "Don't worry. It'll all be downhill from here."

He meant it differently, but he was more right about that than he realized. I couldn't make love with him that night back at the cottage. I was still sore from what Jerome did to me, and full of disgust with myself, and after going to bed, despite being utterly exhausted mentally, I lay awake in the darkness for hours worrying about everything and nothing.

CHAPTER FORTY

The day of opening night, with no more rehearsal, I dropped all my other duties and took myself for a long walk in the woods. It was such a relief to get out there by myself after being stuck inside the stifling theater for weeks, I almost started to feel normal again. I knew my way around in there pretty well, I thought. I had blazed some trails with colored trail markers in the National Forest land back in the winter. But I was so engrossed in my thoughts that I found myself in a completely unrecognizable part of the woods, which went on for miles and miles behind the Sunrise Village property. It was a very undeveloped corner of New England. I knew for sure that I was lost when I came into a kind of garden of boulders, a place full of large glacial erratics the size of bungalows, which I had never been to before.

For a while, I tried an old trick my father taught me years ago: the principle of sinistrality, he called it. Derived from the ancient French, sinistrality pertains to something coming from the left side. The idea is that right-handed people, when lost, tend to move in right-handed circles. So to compensate for that, you try to consciously turn left when faced with a choice. The boulder garden was in some kind of a valley of mature old growth forest without much understory, so I could move around okay, but I couldn't see any distant landmarks, like Owl's Head, and I had lost any clearly marked trail. My father had showed me another trick: in the northern hemisphere, the sun follows an arc along the south side of the dome of the sky. It's never straight overhead, though this tendency is much more pronounced in wintertime when the earth is rotated at a greater angle and the sun rides lower on the horizon all day. So, at noontime shadows on the ground will generally point north. I tried to use the north-pointing shadows from the trees to move in an westerly direction, thinking that sooner or later, I'd hit the highway that ran north-south to the Village. But, two hours later, I was still lost.

I was getting a little frantic by then, when I heard voices and saw two figures up ahead coming toward me. They were women, it turned out, young women, a couple of hikers like me, and I was so relieved to see them. I didn't have any water with me and I hadn't crossed any brooks or rills since much earlier. They both had canteens and were glad to share some water with me. Dehydration and the mid-day heat had probably affected my brain. As the water got back into my system, my head seemed to clear and I calmed down. It was then that I noticed how strangely the two girls were dressed. They had really new blue jeans on, with the legs rolled about one-third up, like pedal-pusher length. One had a tan cotton shirt on with a big floppy collar and the other a kind of striped, boat-neck pull-over. One had long brown hair under a beret. The other had an oddly frumpy hairdo, like the woman on the Betty Crocker cake mix box. Both had lipstick on, which struck me as bizarre. And both had those pointy Keds sneakers with white ankle sox. Their canteens were like the ones in the western movies, with blanket fabric on the sides. At first I thought maybe they were from Europe, but they said they were from Bennington College, attending summer school. They introduced themselves as Dot and Peg and stuck their hands straight out to shake, like men would. I'd heard that there was a lot of Lesbian action over at the college, but neither of them seemed butch and their voice mannerisms were downright little girlish. They asked where I was from.

"Sunrise Village," I said, thinking they'd heard of it. But they just copped a mystified glance at each other.

"What's that," Dot asked. "A camp?"

"No, it's a commune," I said.

Peg made a face as if sensing an unappetizing odor.

"A commune?" she said. "Are they communists?"

They both shared a laugh.

"No, like hippies," I said, using the word that was becoming increasingly annoying, since *Time* and *Newsweek* started grafting it to everything they wrote about. I was embarrassed to even hear myself say it.

"Oh?" Peg said. "Well, I'm glad you're not reds."

We seemed to be on completely different wave lengths, like maybe they came from some isolated part of New England that was socially backward. It was only now that I informed them I was lost. They laughed.

"Oh, the road's right over there," Dot said, pointing with her hiking stick through the sunny glade they had just emerged through. "A few hundred yards that a 'way. We just came from there. You can't miss it."

I was hugely relieved, of course.

"I better get a move on then," I said, and told them we were putting on a play that night. I gave them the full title of the piece and they turned to each other looking mock-horrified and laughed again.

"That's a mouthful," Peg said.

"Well, it starts at eight o'clock, in case you want to see it. Where are you two going?"

"Up to Eagle Rock," Dot said. "Have you been there?"

"No."

"Oh it's swell. You can see for a hundred miles up there. Well, toodle-loo."

They struck off in one direction and I headed through the sunny glade to the road. It was right there, just as they said, but I didn't see their car anywhere, if they had one. Maybe someone dropped them off, I thought.

CHAPTER FORTY-ONE

The Odd Fellows Hall looked great at seven o'clock, the chairs all lined up, floor swept, stage curtain down with the pre-set lighting on it. I was feeling quite a bit better. Sophie had put out my favorite Sunrise Village supper: chicken pie. I'd just brought down a box of Rex-o-graphed playbills to give to the ushers when Alan Kaplan came out from backstage and told me that Paul Gabler was in bad shape. I hurried to the dressing room, which was crammed with cast members, some of them still putting on their inmate make-up. Paul was in the back corner, seated in his Sade costume, with Tiny standing right next to him. He was staring fiercely at the floor and his hands were shaking really badly. I knelt down.

"What's going on, Paul?" I said.

"Oh, for godsake, please get me drink," he said in a shaky voice.

I looked up at Tiny.

"He's been off the sauce all day," he said.

"Go up to Songbird's house," I said. "There's a bottle of vodka on the kitchen counter. Bring it down here."

"But he's not supposed—"

"Just get it. Hurry."

He split.

"Do you think you can do this if you have a nip?" I asked.

"I don't know," he said. "Maybe."

I kept an eye on him while I checked out the other actors' costumes and make-up, trying to keep myself busy and not panic. Tiny was remarkably fast, a legacy of his days scrambling around the gridiron, I guess. I found a glass and poured Paul a good stiff three fingers of Smirnoff. It was seven-thirty now. As the booze got into his blood and his brain, Paul visibly began to straighten out. His hands stopped shaking, he sat up.

"How do you feel now?" I said.

"Better," he said, and started to cry. "I'm so sorry. I'm such a bum. Please forgive me...."

"You're a wonderful actor," I said, taking both his hands in mine. "You're so good in this play. Think you can go out there and do it for me now?"

"I can, I guess," he said wiping away his tears.

"Steve here—" Tiny "—will hold onto your, uh, medicine—"

"My liquor, you mean," he said, letting out one big sob. "I'm a bum... oh God...."

I poured him another stiff shot. He knocked it back.

Another minute went by and he lifted his head up, so leonine and magnificent with his halo of white curls. He really did look like an 18th century French aristocrat.

"Okay," he said. "I'm okay now."

I kissed him on the cheek.

"Break a leg," I said, then whispered in Tiny's ear: "Don't give him any more until I come backstage. He's got to stay on a fine line without getting too loaded."

"Yeah, I dig," Tiny said.

I went back out front. To my amazement, people, outsiders, were streaming into the hall, the ushers handing them their playbills, excited murmurs filling up the big room. Then I went outside. Hog's guys were directing cars to park around the village green. The last rays of the evening sun slanted through the treetops and the Village looked adorable. At ten minutes to eight I went backstage again. Paul was now on his feet in the dressing room, which had emptied out considerably. He was doing vocal warm-up exercises watching himself in the mirror, standing in his wonderfully graceful aristocratic pose, waving a prop handkerchief stuffed into one puffy sleeve. The musicians were tuning up onstage.

Eighty-nine people from outside Sunrise Village managed to find their way up the back road to see our play at five bucks a head. I was amazed that anyone showed up. Perhaps half of them were youngish hippie types, college students, junior faculty types. The rest looked like older summer city folk in blazers and summer dresses. Counting the Sunrise Villagers who were not in the play, we filled a hundred and forty seats — we had set up two hundred chairs on the main floor. Billy Herman was up in the balcony throwing light cues with Teck on the dimmer board. We didn't seat anyone else up there.

The curtain went up at five after eight and the goshdarn thing actually came off very well. There were gasps of astonishment along with nervous laughter during the climactic scene of *Marat's Nightmare,* when Jerome leaves his bathtub completely naked, but nobody walked out. Kitty behaved herself, no doubt mindful of the cash payment at stake. I made two more visits backstage to dole out liquor rations to Paul — more visits than Charlotte Corday made to Marat's door. He was magnificent onstage. You wouldn't have known he was a trembling wreck an hour before. I didn't know anything about the psychology of alcoholism, but he seemed to function quite well on moderate doses. Perhaps if he had a full-time minder like Tiny with him in his regular life, he might have been a more successful actor. When the curtain finally came down, the applause was shocking to me. They actually liked it. A few people even yelled *bravo*. I went backstage afterward and knocked back a shot of that vodka myself. The bottle was almost drained. I had to send Weezil to the canteen to get a case of wine for the cast, plus a personal bottle for Paul, to make sure he got a decent night's sleep.

CHAPTER FORTY-TWO

I drove down to Bennington with Weezil the next morning to get some more hard liquor for Paul, to see him through the rest of the run, and to find some local newspapers to see if anyone had come to review our play. On the way down, I told her about my meeting with those two strange chicks in the woods.

"They were so old fashioned-looking," I said. "And the way they acted was...weird."

Weezil was ominously silent for a minute.

"That's funny," she finally said, not looking very amused.

"You don't mean ha ha funny."

"No. Creepy. There were two Bennington college girls who vanished back in those woods years ago, when I was a kid."

"Yeah. Billy Herman mentioned that on Thanksgiving morning when we hiked up to Owl's Head. He gave me the whole condensed history of Timlinton."

"How were these two old fashioned looking?"

"Remember the bobby-soxer look?"

"Sure. I was one in the sixth grade."

"That was their look. Brand new jeans with the cuffs rolled up. Nobody does that anymore. They also talked strangely. Not quite like us. One said, 'swell' when I told her the play was opening. Who says that?"

"My mom."

"And 'toodle-loo' when we split."

"That is weird as shit," Weezil said. She retreated back into herself for a moment, then said, "I actually remember the incident. I was eleven. It was in the papers. They searched all over hell for them for weeks."

"Do you remember what year it was exactly?"

"Well, I was eleven, so it was fifty-seven. The summer of."

"These girls I met, they were alive as you or me," I said. "I shook their hands,"

"Yeah, well… it's weird as shit, though."

We got into town. Weezil had to stock up on candy bars, cigarettes, and other canteen stuff. She let me off in the center of town and we agreed to meet back up in front of the bank at noon. I set off immediately for the town library. My curiosity was burning up. They had an archive of the local paper, *The Bennington Banner,* on microfilm, and I got a roll that went from July 1 to October14, 1957. I set it up in one of those projector machines that's like a booth on a tabletop that you stick your head into. I was going on nine years old the summer of 1957 and those papers evoked such a different era: Khrushchev, *I Love Lucy* on TV, the Dodgers and the Giants get permission to move to California (bummer), Elvis puts out "Let Me Be Your Teddy Bear." In the scroll of pages, it was all just normal day-to-day 1957 crap, until I came to July 26. A two-column headline on the upper left said: "Hikers' Fate Remains a Mystery."

Two Bennington College summer students who went for a hike in the woods are still missing forty-eight hours after signing out of their residence house Wednesday morning. Dorothy Weldon of Lexington, Mass., and Margaret Brookheiser of Pound Ridge, New York, told friends they intended to scale Mt. Aiken in the Marble River region of Green Mountain National Forest near the village of Timlinton. The two said they would return for bed-check. Yesterday, State Police found Miss Weldon's 1951 Packard 250 convertible parked at a Long Trail trailhead lot along State Route 100. The two girls, both juniors, are members of the Bennington Outing Club and have climbed several of the state's notable peaks....

That was when it hit me: Dorothy and Margaret. Dot and Peg. My stomach sank like an elevator with a broken cable. I scrolled through all the front pages the week after and the week after that. There were school photos of the two in one of the stories but the quality was so grainy I really couldn't say I recognized their faces. The story crescendoed after ten days as it became apparent the two could not be found, and then it dribbled out of the news altogether later in August when the official search was declared suspended. I put the microfilm roll back in the file cabinet and went up to the librarian, a white-haired lady whose desk nameplate said "Mrs. Garbark." We exchanged pleasantries — though I could see she noticed I wasn't wearing a bra and didn't approve. I told her I was researching the 1957 disappearance of the two college girls and asked if she remembered it.

"A-yuh," she said and left it hanging in that Vermont way. "You a family member?"

"No. Just interested. Did anything ever turn up afterwards? Years later maybe?"

"Nope. They scoured the woods for 'em for quite a while. Never found a trace. Called it off finally. Sad."

"Well, thanks," I said. It didn't soothe my nerves to hear that. Only then I remembered to look at the daily papers for a review of the play. They had them hanging in a wooden rack. There was nothing in *The Bennington Banner*. But there was a story on the bottom of the front page of *The Albany Times-Union*: "Vermont Play Features Revolution, Nudity." It was an incredibly dumb story. They even got the title of the play wrong, calling it, "*The Assassination of Marat de Sade*." It mentioned that it was put on by "a hippie commune," and gave our name, and had a florid paragraph about how Jerome Brooks "flouted [sic] his sexuality for a full two minutes while spouting revolutionary rhetoric." It didn't say whether the play was good or bad, or really what it was about. But it did say near the bottom that the Bennington County sheriff's office was "aware of the escapade." I made a Xerox copy of the story, but I was not inclined to show it to anybody. I figured the sheriff's quote would just make everybody paranoid.

After that, I stopped at the bank to get some cash so I could pay off Kitty Lapidus, and picked up three bottles of vodka for Paul Gabler, and eventually Weezil swung by in the van and picked me up. I was torn about whether or not to tell her what I learned in the library about the vanished girls. I definitely wasn't going to tell her about the dumb-ass *Times-Union* review of the play. On the way back up the mountain out of town, I was all inwardly-focused, nibbling on the inside of my cheek.

"You're awfully quiet," Weezil commented.

I really had to unload what was on my mind.

"I went to the library and looked up the old newspapers from 1957 about the two chicks," I said.

"Yeah…?"

"Their names were Dorothy and Margaret."

Weezil didn't say anything.

"Don't you get it?" I said.

"You don't meet many Dorothys and Margarets these days."

"No, stupid. Dot and Peg. The two chicks I met in the woods."

"Yeah, so…?

"You don't get it: those are the short nickname versions for Dorothy or Margaret."

"Oh… I see what you mean."

"Yeah, see how weird that is."

"It's more than weird, man. It's fucking trippy."

CHAPTER FORTY-THREE

W e had an overflowing house for the Thursday performance, beyond sold-out. We literally ran out of chairs to
put people in. We allowed some to stand along the sides, but we
actually had to turn some people away. Elliot, among many others,
was astonished. Me, not so much. The Villagers were still unaware
of the story in *The Albany Times-Union*. Elliot and Strangefield sub-
scribed to *The New York Times* by mail — it generally came two days
late — but nobody at the Village read the Albany paper. And they
didn't deliver out where we were. I didn't show anybody the Xerox
copy I made at the library, either. Of course, I was uneasy about the
reference in it to the county sheriff, and I just hoped that nothing
would happen, since we hadn't heard anything from them during
that day.

In fact, they did turn up for the performance and, rather stupidly it seemed, stood right in plain sight before the show. Two
uniformed deputies and a third, older gentleman in a khaki suit
wearing a brown campaign hat — the County Sheriff himself —
bought tickets and took places standing near the back of the Odd

Fellows hall. Gail Glaviano, who was running the box office — a table at the entrance — gave me a heads up. Two sheriff's department cruisers sat idling outside the Odd Fellows hall with more deputies at their wheels. Obviously, they were setting us up for a bust.

I hurried backstage to the dressing room, found Weezil, who was in charge of costumes, and Jerome, who was running his lines with one of the nuns, a *zaftig* village chick named Isabel Comfrey, who I had caught him balling in the stairway a week before. He happened to be sitting there naked. Backstage had become his own personal nudist colony.

"The cops are out front," I told him. "And we have to take out your nude scene tonight."

"That's absurd," Jerome said. "Marat's dream is the climax of the play."

"No, I mean, do the scene but not naked."

"*Hair* has been running on Broadway for months with nudity," he said. "Nobody's tried to interfere with them."

"That's Broadway. This is small town America. And the sheriffs are out there tonight waiting to bust us, I'm quite sure."

"Oh, let's do it and see what happens," he said. "Stand up for freedom of expression and the first amendment and all that."

"I don't want to make martyrs out of us. I just want to get through the run of the play."

"It would be great publicity, though."

"Maybe for you, personally, but we've only got two more performances. We don't need extra publicity. And we sure don't need the hassle of getting busted."

"I guess you people don't have that old revolutionary spirit after all."

"I don't want trouble for village. We're putting you in a loincloth for the show."

Weezil held up a strip of white bed sheet and some safety pins.

"What?" Jerome squawked.

"Stand up, please, and let me pin this onto you," Weezil said.

"I'm not going to wear a diaper out there!" he said.

"It's not a diaper."

"It sure looks like one to me."

I glanced at my watch. It was already a couple of minutes after eight.

"Jerome," I said, "the curtain's about to go up and you are going to get covered up for the performance, and we can't argue about it anymore. So please stand up and cooperate."

He did, but with a kind of surly hesitation. Weezil went to work. I noticed that Jerome was kind of checking the rig for tightness with his fingers.

"This looks idiotic," he said. "I'll look like a New Years Eve baby out there."

"It's dashing," I said, and then leaned close to whisper in his ear. "Don't even think of wriggling out of it in your bathtub. I'm sure you've noticed that big guy over there hanging around with Paul the past two days. If you come out of that tub naked tonight, or do anything else but act your part correctly with dick covered up, I'm going to tell him to beat the living shit out of you after the final curtain."

He turned around so that our faces were about an inch apart. We were exactly the same height. His eyes bugged out with hostility, but I detected a glimmer of fear mixed in.

"You realize there are laws against that sort of thing, too," he said.

"You could take your chances with that," I said. "And maybe show up on that movie set in Mexico with a cast on your leg."

He turned away and I was fairly confident he got the message.

I left it there, went back out to the audience, and took a place standing in the rear with Elliot. He'd noticed the sheriff's delegation, too, of course.

"Are we about to get busted?" he asked.

"I took out Jerome's nude scene, "I said. "But I think you ought to go backstage at intermission and tell the cast and crew to refrain from lighting up any doobies when the show's over. They'll listen to you."

"Good thinking," he said.

The show went as we had set it, with no untoward surprises. Jerome played the nightmare scene with his loincloth on, a huge relief. Once we were past that I relaxed. It was fun seeing the play with a really full house. There's always a lot of electricity in an audience when that happens. They signal each other in little ways that it's okay to laugh or shriek or applaud. It energizes the actors, too.

The lawmen did not stop the show. We gave them no excuse to. When the final curtain came down and the audience headed for the exit, the officers lingered out among the empty seats. Meanwhile, I went up to the balcony to tell Teck and Billy not to light up any weed. Below, a stagehand swept the forestage. The ushers were lining the chairs back up. The older lawman in the khaki suit and the mountie hat went over to Elliot. He glanced up at me in the balcony and then followed the sheriffs underneath and out the door. I hurried back down to make sure they weren't dragging my old man off to the hoosegow. They were all out on the village square, by one of the cruisers. The deputies had turned on the revolving blue light on the roof of one of the cars to show off and make us nervous, I think. The head guy was writing something out on a pad. I drifted over and stood by Elliot's side. The head guy ripped the sheet off his pad and gave the carbon copy to Elliot.

"See you in court," he said.

Then the lawmen all saddled up in their cruisers and drove away.

"What was that about?" I asked as the blue lights disappeared down the road out of town.

"A summons."

"What for?"

"Exceeding the legal occupancy of the hall."

"What?"

"It's Mickey Mouse bullshit," Elliot said. He didn't seem very concerned.

"I don't even think there is any established occupancy for that building," I said. "There's no sign anywhere in there."

"That's exactly right."

"You're going to fight it then?"

"Of course I'm going to fight it."

"I'll pay the fine, if there is one," I said.

"No you won't. There won't be any fine," he said, grinning. "Come on, let's go home and get horizontal."

CHAPTER FORTY-FOUR

Later, I was still all wound up about the attempted bust, still feeling the emotional after-effects of Jerome forcing me to make it with him, and in the background of my jagged thoughts the still-disturbing mystery of Dot and Peg, whoever or whatever they were, twanged on my imagination. It felt like anxiety was eating me up inside. Back at the cottage we smoked a little hashish, drank some beers, and I managed to get over myself temporarily. We had a session in bed — I made an extra effort to be pleasing, though I could not get to orgasm — and we ate a whole pint of chocolate ice cream afterward.

I figured the worst was behind me with this play — though, considering all the stress, I was not quite sure if there was a best part to it, other than making it happen. I began to ruminate on the experience more coldly. I wondered about the ego-tripping that drove me to do it. What was I trying to prove? What was it about being *the director*? Did I actually like controlling other people, telling them what to do, pushing them around? And now that this play was over, was I supposed to do another one, or wait until the next summer (assuming I would even still be there), or pass the baton to some other person? Or, if I was serious about working in the theater, would I eventually have to move back to New York? (A sickening prospect.) I didn't want to be an actor, going to cattle-call auditions like the one I held. Uccchhh. What a life! And how did one go about becoming a professional director? I didn't even finish my sophomore year as a theater major. Or maybe I was just fated to be Elliot Sohnberg's old lady, push out some babies and… I don't know what, because I couldn't imagine us leading a straight life outside the cocoon of Sunrise Village, even though in a matter of a few weeks I had gone from being a hippie commune slut to acting like a settled down old married lady in a regular home. It was very perplexing and it kept me awake for hours after Elliot nodded off.

Luckily, Friday was a near-normal day, much of it spent up in the office happily by myself, back to mundane duties, paying bills, switching a few people around on the job crews, inquiring on the phone about a used Hobart mixer for Sophie's kitchen — the old one's motor died. Besides the play, the big thing just then was getting ready to bring in Tansy's first crop of botanicals for the herb tea business. We set up one of the barns with an array of stacked old window screens on saw-horses to use as drying racks, and a crude production line of long tables for sorting and packaging the stuff into the colorful printed boxes that we'd had made.

Friday night we did the second-to-last performance of the play. The audience was still pretty full, but not like the previous night. There were some empty seats and nobody standing in the aisles. No law officers dropped in as far as I could see. If the sheriff sent a spy in plain clothes to check up on us, we didn't hear about it afterward. I'd finally gotten up the nerve to show Elliot the Xerox of the *Times-Union* story. He seemed a little peeved that I'd waited that long. His court date was next Tuesday. With Arden Blanchard gone, one of the family trust lawyers was coming from Boston to appear with him. The performance that night went okay. Paul was functional on his ration of hooch. I made a point to visit both Jerome and Kitty backstage beforehand to remind them of their continuing obligations to behave themselves.

Saturday was closing night. I took Weezil down to Bennington and we bought a case of cheap champagne, and a lot of beer, and all kinds of chips and Cheez Doodle crap for the cast party. You have to have a cast party. That was the last money I was going to shell out for this project, which had cost me an appalling twenty-three hundred dollars, when all was said and done, roughly half my ready cash bank account from Larry's insurance money. You could hve bought a new car for that. For that final show, the seats were about three-quarters filled. The total four nights' ticket sales netted just under two thousand, which I put into the Sunrise Village account. Wouldn't you know, fucking Jerome came out for his final curtain call minus his loincloth. But I figured we were beyond the wrath of the law now with the play closing, and I knew he was catching the Sunday morning bus back to the city, so I just let it go.

I wasn't in a party mood afterward, especially to be around the several people who had been such a pain in the ass to me for a month. In fact, I was feeling unusually down, some sort of post-partum blues, I supposed, on top of the grinding anxiety that wouldn't go away. But I couldn't skip out on it without seeming snooty to the rest of the cast, who had worked so hard on the play. We cleared the chairs off to the sides of the hall and set up some long tables. Sophie's crew brought in a vat of chili and pans of cornbread. They mixed a big galvanized metal tub of punch with the champagne and cranberry juice and other crap. Everybody in the hall was back to smoking weed. Billy Herman had his turntable rigged up to the PA system and the Band's *Music From Big Pink* was reverberating off the walls. Tansy had a light show projector play-ing jiggly blobs of color over the now empty stage set. To counter my grim mood, I pounded down the punch and smoked a bunch of the weed going around.

Then there was the matter of paying off Kitty. I had an envelope stuffed with the two hundred and fifty bucks. It also contained a typed letter from me saying that we were asking her to leave the Village. She was all gypsied up after the show in a ruffly skirt, satin head-rag, off-the-shoulder semi-sheer blouse cut very low with sneaky nipple display, and big hoop earrings. She was entertaining several of the village guys not in the cast when I approached her and asked to speak with her privately. She obliged readily, seeing the envelope in my hand. We ducked out of the hall through the side door. I handed her the envelope. She opened it and first counted the money, of course, which was all in twenties and tens. Then she read the letter.

"I was leaving anyway," she said, handing it back to me. "This place has no magic. I enjoyed your boyfriend, though. Give him a farewell kiss for me."

"What do you mean enjoyed?"

"You know. The man-woman thing. I thought you knew. Everything's so open around here."

I was pretty sure she was messing with my mind, as usual with her.

"You're really a piece of work," was all I said, and turned to leave.

"Better keep that boy on a tight leash..." she managed to get out before I slammed the door returning to the hall.

Of course it upset me, even though the rational part of my brain realized it had to be a lie, just a final zinger to ruin my night. Back inside, I guzzled down more punch and made off with half a joint that Lucy Salmon passed my way and I went around the hall thanking all the people who had acted, or played music, or worked backstage on the play. Elliot was hanging with Hog and his gang, talking power tools and projects. The *Big Pink* album was ending on the Dylan song, "I Shall Be Released." It struck me because when that lyric in the chorus came around — "I see my light come shining" — I actually saw a strange shimmery light from the corner of my eye, like somebody was pointing a flashlight at me, but when I turned my head slightly there was nothing there. It persisted as I made my way across the room to Alan Kaplan, and the light seemed to come from more than one direction, pulsing slightly. I told Alan how grateful I was for him putting together the music for the show, and how I yearned to get back to playing regular music with Buttermilk Falls, our band, and he laughed saying they'd talked about changing the name again to the Weevils.

"Where'd you get that?" I said. "The Weevils?"

"Like the Weavers," he said, referring to the seminal fifties folkie group that Pete Seeger started. "Only with a touch of evil."

"Ha ha," I said. "What's evil about us?"

At that very moment, Billy Herman dropped the phono needle on another album, Iron Butterfly's *In-A-Gadda-Da-Vida*, a huge hit record that came out at the beginning of the summer. It was a new species of ghastly sonic noise, later to be known as heavy metal, that I absolutely loathed, with incoherent lyrics to go with it, and somehow it resounded powerfully in my brain with Alan's gag about us having a touch of evil, and I felt a wrenching emotional jolt go through me as if I had only just noticed that there was a touch of evil in everything going on around me, everything about us. Only I couldn't locate the exact source of it. It was more a generalized feeling than a coherent thought, a sense of revulsion mixed with fear.

"Are you all right, Pooh?" Alan asked. I must have looked out of it.

Of course, when he said that, I realized that I was probably not all right.

"Is that just regular weed going around," I asked, "or is there some other crap mixed in?" Lately, it had become known in counter-culture circles that pot was turning up laced with para-quat, an herbicide that Mexico was spraying on its marijuana fields at the behest of the US government. All kinds of other shit was being added to pot by the dealers: DMT, which makes people hal-lucinate, and sometimes animal tranquilizer.

"Didn't you know?"

"Know what?"

"There's acid in the punch."

I was flabbergasted, and I felt it to an exaggerated degree, a deep resonating emotion of betrayal and rage.

"Who did that?"

Alan shrugged and made a face, which was intended to be com-ical, but which I saw as evil, like a mask concealing some deeper depravity. Meanwhile, I realized that the pulsing light I was seeing had gotten more intense, as was the sensation of being filled with powerful negative emotions that I could barely sort out. I hurried across the room to Elliot and pulled him away from Hog and the guys.

"Somebody spiked the punch with LSD," I informed him.

"Who?"

"I have no idea, but it's coming on and I don't like it. Aren't you feeling anything?"

"We're drinking beer," he said, hoisting a brown bottle of Narragansett.

"I don't know what to do," I said, starting to get teary.

"Try just going with it. It's only acid."

"Only acid!" I yelled, trying to overcome the horrible music. "I never had acid before."

"You haven't?"

"No! Never! I have to get out of here."

I was panicking. Elliot's face was going all melty and my percep-tion of everything around me became fractured, as if the images on my retinas were in shaky layers that didn't quite jibe with how they overlaid each other, like double vision, but shifting, vibrating. Also, everything was getting a kind of aura around it, objects as well as people, like a phosphorescent outline in glowing neon colors.

I was not enjoying it one bit. I ran toward the front entrance of the hall, away from all the people down by the stage, and away from the light show, and the gabble of voices, and the smell of chili, and the terrible music. Instead of being relieved to get out of there, I only got worse. The heat of the summer night outside seemed exaggerated, oppressive, the humid air like Jello that was too thick to breathe. I started gasping. Out in the street, away from the building, I looked up and saw the immensity of the starry sky and felt overwhelmed by it, lost in all that empty space and tortured by the meaninglessness of it. I started running for the cottage across the Village. A quarter moon rose over Owl's Head. The big hill never looked more like the giant head of a fierce predatory bird before. The moon frightened me even more. I began to think that it might come loose from its mooring in the sky and crash into the earth, and that it would be the end of the world.

I tripped on pine root about fifty yards short of the house. I didn't realize that Elliot had been following me. He picked me up, saying, "slow down... it's all right...." But I just hurried spastically the rest of the way. I'd sprained my ankle but didn't really register it. Inside the house, I went straight to the bedroom and got under the covers with my clothes on and pine needles and crap all over me. I had really lost it. There was a light show going off in my head, even with my eyes closed. I couldn't stop it. I couldn't control my thoughts, feelings, or the rush of sensation. I just kept repeating over and over, "I'm scared... I'm scared." Elliot sat with me in the dark for a long time, holding my sweaty hand, telling me I was going to be okay. The awful feelings of cosmic dread came over me in waves. It would subside for a while and then it would return with greater force. I thought my heart was going to explode.

"I'm dying," I said.

"No you're not," he said. "You're tripping. It's just the acid. It'll wear off after a while."

"I'm losing my mind," I said.

"Calm down. Listen: breathe in on a count of four, hold your breath on a count of seven, and exhale on a count of eight."

"I can't count!" I shrieked.

"I'll do it for you. Just breathe."

"You have to take me to the hospital."

"I can't do that, Pooh. Not for drugs."

"I'm going crazy. I'll never be okay again."

"You'll be okay. Breathe! One, two, three, four...."

And that's how it went for I'm not sure how many hours. The breathing exercises helped a little. Eventually, Elliot fell asleep next to me, sort of on top of me, actually, as if he were protecting me from a bomb blast. I was a sweaty mess underneath in the stifling heat, with all my clothes still on and a sheet and blanket on top of that. But it helped to have his body pressing against mine. Birds were tweeting through the window just before I finally fell asleep. Their sound was powerfully beautiful and soothing and sort of floated me out of the zone of terror into the sweetest sleepiness. I was probably asleep for five hours. When I woke up, Elliot was gone. I had a vivid dream about a place that was like Sunrise Village, only in a past century. There were people in old time costumes, women in long dresses and clunky shoes who spoke to me in beautifully-worded sentences, and a young man with a beard who seemed weirdly familiar, though I couldn't figure out how, and who provoked the deepest feelings of attachment in me.

CHAPTER FORTY-FIVE

When I awoke, the lovely dream dissolved and memories of the night's LSD terrors came back to me instantly. I could still see some slight color auras as I glanced at things around the room. I was shaky, but my thoughts had slowed down and seemed orderly again. Mostly, I was desperate to get into the shower and wash the sweaty residue of the experience off of me. My ankle still hurt from tripping on that pine root. When I came out of the shower and went downstairs, toweling off my hair, Elliot was back, puttering around the kitchen.

"How're you feeling, Pooh?"

"I dunno. I think I'm getting over it. It was horrible."

"I brought you some food from the inn."

"Thanks. Did you happen to ask around who put that fucking acid in the punch?"

"Yeah, nobody knows," he said.

"Or says they don't."

"If it comes out, I'll kick their ass out of here," he said.

"Did anyone else have a freak-out?"

"Not that I heard, but some were pissed off about it. Nobody should foist acid on the unwitting," he said. "It's unethical."

I was actually quite hungry. He brought me two of Sophie's wonderful cinnamon buns, full of buttery brown sugar swirls and some strips of bacon, too, which he knew I loved. He'd put the coffee pot on and it was now perking. I poured a myself a steaming mug.

"I wonder if it was that goddamn Kitty Lapidus," I said.

"Oh, she split," Elliot said. "I heard Oz drove her to the train station in Albany."

"That's a long drive. She must have promised to blow him in the parking lot."

"Well, anyway, she's gone now."

"Did you ever make it with her?"

He recoiled slightly.

"Did she tell you that?"

"Yeah."

He puffed out his cheeks. I stirred milk into my coffee, waiting.

"We balled one time, back when Maya was still here, you know, fucking everybody in the village, trying to make me feel bad. It was revenge sex, I guess."

"So you did make it with her."

"Yeah."

"You didn't want her again?"

"Once was enough. And I told her I liked somebody else?"

"Who else were you making it with?"

"Nobody yet. That somebody else was you."

"Oh."

That got me all weepy again. My emotions were still raw, right on the surface, like my skin couldn't protect me. I couldn't help thinking about how low I'd sunk to let Jerome have sex with me just the other day. I was so ashamed and disgusted, but I couldn't tell Elliot. It ate at me inside.

Eventually, he suggested that we just get the hell out of the village for the day and take a break from everything. I was all for it, being Sunday, an excuse to take it easy for a change. The play was over and done with, and it felt kind of weird to have nothing pressing to do all of a sudden for the first time in over a month. By around noontime, I was no longer seeing colored auras and I had reason to hope that the LSD was out of my system. I swore that it was my first and last time with that crap. I never wanted to be that high again.

We got into the Land Rover and drove an hour to Wardsboro where the Barking Dog commune was located. I'd heard about it. People called it "deep" and "heavy." The founder of the outfit, one Doug McReynolds, a self-styled "earth spiritualist" had organized the venture around his druid-like religion, very different from our completely un-religious Sunrise Village. He also had been trying to organize what he called "The Vermont Commune Confederacy," a kind of mutual aid society, and bugging Elliot by mail to come see him, so we did.

I was frankly shocked by the look of the place and the people there. You could quickly understand why they'd be interested in mutual aid. There was only one proper building on their land, their so-called "Earth Spirit Community House," poorly constructed out of scabby materials, plywood here, boards there, mismatched windows, saggy front steps. That was their hang-out lodge and mess hall. Mostly, though, the fifty odd "earth spirits" lived in a collection of more primitive dwellings: several Mongolian yurts, three tepees, and something like an Iroquois long-house made of bent saplings covered with bark. Doug McD, as they called him, was especially proud of the long-house. He took us in to see it. About twenty people lived in there, sleeping on crude bunks made of logs and canvas, but with all kinds of modern plastic crap strewn about inside: buckets, water jugs, patio chairs, transistor radios, bongo drums, clothes hanging everywhere. The only light came from a hole in the center of the roof where they shoved a bark plate askew in good weather to let the sun in. The smell in there was amazing: like an old unwashed gym sock stuffed with tuna fish and Roquefort cheese. It made me a little woozy.

The people at the place, sad to say, looked like the very epitome of the "dirty hippies" you read about in the papers and the news magazines. They had holes in their grimy clothes, had matted hair, and most went barefoot. And their body odor was ferocious. Elliot had told me that the group was forbidden to use birth control and half a dozen young children ran around naked like little aborigines — though they made a lot of happy noises playing, had golden hair and deep tans, and seemed healthy. The adults, on the other hand, all wore the same grim and wary facial expression, as if we were visitors from Mars with hostile intentions.

They had big gardens — Doug McD toured us through them — but unkempt, very weedy with a lot of bug damage, and they kept two cows in a miserable muddy pasture full of frost-heave rocks, with a half-assed run-in shed made of poles and peeled-bark roofing for their only shelter. Chickens ranged all over the place, one struggling with a missing foot. We had lunch with the earth spirit people on the ramshackle front porch of their community center: watery cabbage soup with rock-hard sourdough bread. I noticed that they dunked the bread in their soup to soften it and, anyway, there was nothing to spread on it, no butter or jam or cheese or anything. Watching them eat was like being in a Bruegal painting of fifteenth century peasants. It made me appreciate the civilized amenities of Sunrise Village.

While Elliot had his meeting with Doug McD, I hung out with three of the young mothers and their kids outside one of the yurts. Work was forbidden on Sunday there, but the women seemed bored and restless. They weren't even allowed to work in the gardens, except they could pick stuff, like for lunch and dinner. We didn't really know what to say to each other. I tried politics, but they didn't follow the news, not even the election for president. It was extremely awkward. I couldn't wait to get out of there.

"Wow, that was creepy," I said as we drove away, waving goodbye to the chief earth spirit standing in front of a broken-down school bus painted with swirly, psychedelic colors that they had driven in from Bloomington, Indiana, two years before in search of their earth spirit utopia. It was a relief to be on the road again, but I soon became aware of being uncomfortable moving so rapidly, as if my brain was having trouble visually processing the passing landscape. "Hey, can you slow down a little," I asked Elliot.

"I'm only going fifty miles an hour."

"Seems faster."

I retreated into myself again for a while, still ragged from little sleep. We got off State Highway 100 and drove a bunch of back roads, going slower. My nerves settled down somewhat, but an underlying layer of anxiety was still grinding away inside of me. I wondered if I had some of that acid left in my system.

"We seem pretty *bouzshie* compared to those people, don't we," I remarked, meaning bourgeois. "Look at us: clean clothes, a car that actually works, out on a Sunday drive, like an old married couple."

"Compared to them, we surely are bouszh," Elliot said. "I'm getting a little pessimistic about where this hippie thing is leading. A couple of years ago it was more, I dunno, select. Now it's getting down to the dregs, the ones who seem plain lost, the marginal types. Any idiot can grow his hair long and put on love beads."

"Do you think there will be life after Sunrise Village?" I asked, realizing it was a pretty heavy question. He didn't answer right away, so I added, "I mean, for us."

"You and me?"

"Yeah. Us."

"Sure," was all he said, but he didn't elaborate. It made me jumpy again.

We drove around southern Vermont for a couple of hours, making a long circular route through the ski country and mountains that were taller than the ones over where we lived. We talked, of course, but mostly about things we observed as we passed by: how ugly modern houses were, even the ones on back roads out in the country, like America was incapable of building anything really nice anymore, as my dad had said so long ago, things with grace notes. We talked about getting a cat. Talk about going bouzshie! I always wanted one back home but Marilyn would never allow it. Elliot said he wasn't against it, which I took to mean don't rush out tomorrow and get one. We talked about village stuff, getting our new herb tea out there into the health food stores, the hydroelectric project, which was proving more costly and difficult than they'd originally thought, about Sophie the cook who was apparently making noises about leaving and opening a restaurant somewhere. We couldn't blame her. It was the hardest job in the village and she could probably make a whole lot more money running her own business. Elliot had no idea who might replace her. We stopped for an hour at an antique barn in Winhall where, going bouzshie to the limit, I bought an antique wooden music stand for twenty bucks. On the way home, we stopped at a German restaurant outside of Manchester. It was modeled on an alpine beer hall, apparently aimed at skiers, though at this time of year there was only a scattering of customers for the dinner hour. While we waited for our sauerbraten and schnitzel Elliot cracked jokes about the Nazis, including the popular World War Two ditty that went:

Hitler, he only had one ball
Goering had two but very small
Himmler had something similar
And Goebbels had no balls at all

I think he sensed my nervous mood and was trying to cheer me up, but I just didn't feel good, and drinking two big mugs of beer actually made me feel worse, downright depressed. We got back to the village at twilight, around nine, and went to bed. He wanted to make love. I couldn't have been less in the mood, but I indulged him and this time I went as far as faking orgasm, to my enormous self-disgust. I'd thought that I could retreat into slumber afterward, but I could not get to sleep. My mind was churning, not about anything in particular or important. I began to wonder whether the acid had messed up some part of my brain that regulated sleep. As happened the previous night, I finally went unconscious when daylight started stealing through the window, and I had that same dream again about long ago people in a long ago village and the young man with a beard who I had some special attachment to. It left me feeling unmoored.

CHAPTER FORTY-FIVE

The Tuesday after the play ended its run, Elliot went to court
in town with Albert Hustings, a Boston attorney associated
with the Sohnberg Family Trust. I came along with a contingent
of about twenty villagers to support our cause. The proceeding
was farce. Hustings got his chance to grill County Sheriff George
Grout right away and asked him to produce evidence that there was
any official set occupancy standard for the Timlinton Odd Fellows
hall. Grout claimed it was self-evidently beyond capacity because
people were standing in the aisles. Hustings asked him how many
people were seated in the balcony. Grout said he hadn't counted.
Hustings asked why not. Grout said he wasn't aware that there was
a balcony. It turned out that he'd been standing under it the whole
time and never even looked up there, didn't even know there was
a balcony. Hustings called Billy Herman and asked him if he was
in the balcony of the Odd Fellows hall the night in question. Billy
explained he was up there stage managing the play, and what that
meant, throwing light and sound cues, etc. Was anyone up there
with him? Yes, Billy said, Walter Hesslewhite, who was running the

light board. Anybody else. Nope. Why? It would have distracted play-goers to be around us with our work lights and technical patter. How many empty seats were up in the balcony? All of them, Billy said. One hundred and twelve. They'd counted. By now, there was some tittering laughter in the crowd that had assembled to watch Sheriff Grout hand it to the hippies who were becoming such an obnoxious presence in their midst. Only now the tables had turned and they were watching their bumbling champion get humiliated. Albert Hustings moved for dismissal. The judge banged his gavel and that was it. It was an interesting demonstration in the fickleness of mobs.

On the way out, Sheriff Grout said to Elliot, "We're not done with you yet, sonny. I hope you've got eyes in the back of your head. You're going to need 'em."

"Is that a threat?" Elliot asked him.

"Gosh no," Grout said. "It's a warning."

I heard the exchange. In the car on the way home I apologized to Elliot for causing the trouble in the first place with my play, and getting the law on the village's ass. He told me it was all right, not to worry about it, but I felt responsible and I did worry about them finding some other way to come and harass us.

In the days that followed, my state of mind deteriorated sharply, perhaps because my sleep remained extremely disturbed. On a good night I was getting only a few hours, with long stretches of insomnia between midnight and dawn. A couple of times, I don't think I slept at all. I'd lay still, pretending to sleep so as not to disturb Elliot, but it was torture, and I couldn't even pretend to be interested in sex. It was all turning into a strange kind of agitated depression, like some sinister presence inside of me that wouldn't let me alone, wouldn't let me be still. The restlessness wouldn't allow me to concentrate on all the little office chores that I had formerly taken pleasure in. I couldn't even make myself practice the guitar or the banjo. I felt like I had to get out and walk, but I was afraid of walking in the woods after that episode meeting Dot and Peg, so I just went on long walks down the road to Bennington and then back to the Village, which left me unsatisfied, exhausted but still jumpy. Meanwhile, Padget and Alison pestered me to return to band practice with the Weevils or Buttermilk Falls, or whatever name they were going by now, and the pressure made my agitation worse. I had to leave the first practice session after half an hour. I'm sure they were sincerely baffled about what was going on with me. On top of all these weird feelings, I was having trouble remembering lyrics to songs, even ones I'd memorized when I was fourteen years old and had played hundreds of times. It was alarming.

I kept all this to myself for days. I didn't complain or try to have a heart-to-heart with my girlfriends because none of this was about any particular problem I knew how to talk about, other than the fact that I was falling apart mentally, and it scared the shit out of me to consider the possibility that LSD had actually damaged my brain. I especially didn't reveal all of this to Elliot though I'm sure he knew something was wrong, and he treated me very gently, cleaning up after both of us and changing our sheets, bringing me meals, making me hot milk with honey at night. But the insomnia remained fierce. After nearly a week of it, I began seeing strange visual effects again, like the ones I experienced on acid: retinal flashes, auras, objects seeming to shift shapes in my fields of vision.

One night, lying in bed together, I finally said to Elliot, "I need to see a shrink. I'm having a lot of problems."

"I know," he said.

So he called up the psychiatrist at Putnam Hospital in Bennington, the same guy who had been writing letters to get our guys out of the military draft. The next afternoon he drove me down for a session with Dr. Art Hauser, early thirties, hipsterish, who wore a beatnicky Van Dyke beard-mustache combo, brown corduroy pants, and suede shoes. Everything about him had a soft texture. He gave off a warm vibe, too, with his pleasant smile and calm manner and didn't act overly doctorish, though he had all the proper diplomas and certificates on the wall. He had a nice cushy sofa you could really sink into, like a kangaroo pouch, and his second floor window looked out on the woods behind the hospital, all serene and reassuring. Elliot and I had discussed on the way down whether I should reveal that I'd gotten dosed with LSD and we decided that I couldn't possibly withhold that bit of information. So when Hauser asked, "What's going on with you, Erica," I told him about my acid freak-out and how I was still having weird visual sensations and insomnia and all the rest. He said "Hmmmm" a lot.

It was a relief to unload some of that, but I didn't see where that left me. The rest of the session he asked about my family and I had to tell him about dropping out of NYU and my abortion and my father getting killed just a few months ago and where things stood between me and Marilyn, and that seemed to perk up his interest, all that family sturm and drang. We spent most of the session on that. He didn't have much to say about whether my brain had been affected by LSD. I suppose he had very little knowledge or understanding of psychedelic drugs — but who did then in the straight world? It might have been more edifying to visit with Dr. Timothy Leary, the celebrity acid-tripper-in-chief, but he wasn't available.

Before I knew it, the fifty-minute session was over. Oddly, I felt fairly normal during the time in Hauser's office, but when I came back out back to the real world my state of mind reverted to that state of doomy, anxious, depressed agitation. Plus, I was getting more and more uncomfortable being in motion in a car. I could barely stand the sensation of moving faster than twenty miles an hour anymore. The whole way out of town on Route 9, I had to keep my eyes closed because I felt like an idiot asking Elliot to slow down. He probably thought I was making up for lost sleep, but I just couldn't stand to look through front window and see the world rushing toward me.

I saw Hauser again twice that week. Elliot was paying for it. He told me that he felt responsible for the acid getting dropped on me and not to worry about the cost. Actually I didn't believe that he was responsible. There was a certain respite being cocooned with Hauser in that cushy, tranquil room, but back outside I wasn't getting any better. Then, the thing happened that kind of shoved me over the edge.

I was spending most of my time holed up in Elliot's cottage, hiding out because being around the other people at the village made me feel so anxious. But on Friday morning I made myself go into the office and sift through a pile of mail, attend to bills starting to pile up, and, most importantly, put together the pay packets for our people. I realized that I would have to make a trip to the bank in town and get a bunch of cash. I should have asked Weezil or somebody else to drive the van, but I was paranoid of everybody learning how messed up I had become, so I just gritted my teeth and went on my own.

It was a disastrous trip. I couldn't drive anywhere near the speed limit because my visual perception was so disturbed and it frightened me so much. When I turned onto Route Nine, the main road into Bennington, going maybe twenty miles an hour, I quickly accumulated this parade of angry motorists behind me and it was difficult for them to pass me on the twisty highway, so I had to pull over and let them all go by. When I started up again, I had gone no more than a mile when I saw a police light flashing behind me and he made me pull over. I certainly wasn't speeding. My heart was racing and I thought my head might explode when he came up to my window. It was a county sheriff's deputy. Uccchhh. That made me even more paranoid because the van had the Sunrise Village insignia painted on the door. Luckily I did have my license and the van's registration was in the glove box.

"You from out of state?" the deputy asked, handing back my license.

315

"Yes I am. It's a valid license, though."

"Living here now?"

"I guess."

"I suggest you get the Vermont license."

"Okay," I said.

He didn't speak for what seemed like an excruciatingly long moment. He just peeked though the window around the interior, maybe sniffing for a tell-tale sign that I'd been smoking pot, or something. I worried that he was going to hit on me, ask me for a date, or worse. He was a middle-aged guy, lean, with a hawkish, mean face. It was a lonely stretch of road. My anxiety was going though the roof.

"You know why I stopped you?" he finally said.

"No."

"You're driving very slow."

"I'm sorry," I said. "Is that against the law? It's not like I was speeding."

"You had twelve cars behind you. You're obstructing normal traffic."

"The van's been acting up," I said. "The transmission, I think. I was heading into town to have it checked."

"Oh? Want me to call in for a tow?"

"No. I'll get there okay."

"It would be a pity if you broke down out here."

"Please, just let me drive there. It's only, like, three more miles."

Again, he left it hanging for an uncomfortable interval. I was practically squirming in my seat. But then he just said, "All right. Good luck with the vehicle," and banged on the roof like he was hitting a horse on its ass, and walked back to his patrol car.

I started the engine back up and managed to drive those few miles at about forty, though it made me want to scream. Once in town, I had to stop at the library and just sit in the parking lot there for twenty minutes until my nerves quieted down. The bank was just a block or so away. I walked over there finally and wrote out a Sunrise Village check and, because it was a fairly large sum of money, and they had a new bank teller who never saw me before, she hassled me and called over a bank officer to confirm that I was authorized on the account. My vision was going trippy again as my nerves frazzled standing there. Finally, they gave me the money. I put it in the blue cash bag that I always used and walked back out on the street feeling like I was utterly losing my mind. There were people on Main Street, going about their normal business, just a regular day in small town Vermont, but they seemed sinister and menacing to me. My paranoia was shooting past the red-line. Even worse was that I recognized my own paranoia, which only pushed up my anxiety, making me even more paranoid. It was all I could to do not run back to the library parking lot, and when I did get there, I couldn't quite face being in the car again. So, I dumped the money bag on the front seat and dashed into library for refuge.

There were only a few people in the library at that hour, of course, and despite the fact that it was quiet and peaceful, I couldn't bear being around them. I was so anxious that I thought I was going to scream, or break down, or lose control of myself. I found the ladies room and dashed in and sat in a stall, so bent out of shape that I started crying. I considered making an unscheduled stop up at Doctor Hauser's office but couldn't get myself to move. So I hid in the stall for a while and eventually was able to calm down. Nobody else came in while I was there. It was as peaceful as a tomb. I told myself that all I had left to do was make the half-hour trip back to the village and it would all be over. I'd be safe again. I left the bathroom and went outside to the car. The money bag was gone. I'd forgotten to lock the doors.

I searched desperately all around the van in some vain delusion that the money bag slipped off the seat or somehow eloped under its own power into the big rear compartment. But, of course, it just wasn't there. No doubt somebody passing by just saw it and snatched it. Yes, even in small town USA. I couldn't believe my carelessness. I started hyperventilating and thought I might lose consciousness or puke. Some blind instinct made me run back up the library steps and inside to that same stall in the bathroom. My craziness had just resulted in the loss of over a thousand dollars in cash. It blew my mind. I just sat there weeping. After a while, somebody came in the bathroom door. I could see her shoes under the door of the stall, old lady shoes. A librarian, evidently.

"Are you all right, Miss?" the woman asked.

"Yes, I'm okay," I said, realizing at once that it sounded stupid. "Actually, I'm having a bit of diarrhea today."

"Oh dear.... Is there anything I can do?"

"No, but thank you for asking. I'll be okay."

She left, thank God. I did those breathing exercises Elliot had taught me and managed to calm down again. But the trouble was I just had to bring cash back to the village. Those people had to get their money, and I realized I'd have to replace the stolen cash with money from my own account. What a bummer. Luckily, I did have my bouzshie shoulder bag with me with my personal checkbook in it. I had nineteen hundred bucks left in the account from the original five grand. Soon I'd be broke, except for the rest of the insurance money that Elliot's people had put into investments for me. Anyway, I steeled myself for another trip to the bank.

I was trembling so badly at the teller's cage that she must have thought something odd was up. And, obviously, she had good reason to. She'd look at me and glance down at the check and look back on me. Then, all of a sudden, that same bank officer from before was at my side there at the teller's cage, a short, plump, mild-mannered man with silver hair in a worn suit with shiny elbows: Mr. Purvis. He asked me to come sit at his desk. I guess the teller must have secretly buzzed him.

"Are you all right, young lady?" he asked when I sat down.

"Of course I'm all right," I shot back. I was getting sick of people asking that, even though I knew quite well that I was acting like a crazy person. "Excuse me, sir," I said. "It's been a difficult day."

"Oh?" he said.

So now I felt like I had to explain it.

"I'm having car problems all of a sudden," I said. "You know how that is."

"Ay-uh," he said. "Murphy's Law: what can go wrong will go wrong."

"That's so true."

"The thing is: you've written two checks for large sums of money today."

"Yes, I did," I said

"It's a little irregular."

"They were on two different accounts," I said.

"Yes, that's so. But for nearly identical amounts."

"I know. I have to buy a new car."

"Are you paying twice?"

"The first was the down payment."

"What was the other?"

"That was the rest?"

He just kind of stared at me with an inscrutable little smile. I struggled mightily to appear normal, sweating like crazy. His face seemed to be going all melty.

"Mind if I go now?"

"Don't you want your money?"

"Oh! Silly me...."

"Miss Huphnagel will give it to you. We try to be careful. Due diligence and all."

"Of course. Thank you."

I went back to the teller who counted out the dough and put it in a manila envelope for me. I staggered out of the bank, groggy from all the anxiety, and half-ran back to the van. In the meantime, I'd half-brainwashed myself into believing that there was something wrong with the van, and I was surprised when the engine actually started up and I was able to back out of the parking space okay. Then I had to make the thirteen-mile drive back to the village. I kept the speed up to forty on Route Nine, blubbering all the way to the turn-off. Then I crept the rest of the way to the village. I was a mess when I pulled up to the Odd Fellows hall.

It was all I could do up in the office to assemble the pay packets. My hands were shaking like crazy the whole time. Things were glowing and shifting, going all trippy again. I could barely read the pay sheet. I cried and cried, thinking that my mind was wrecked. I managed to complete the task somehow and put all the little envelopes into the willow basket that I toted stuff back and forth with, and went down to the inn to put them in the mail cubbies. But once down there, Scotty Provost came by and noticed how I was. Of course, he asked, "Are you okay, Pooh?"

"No, I'm not," I said, wiping tears away, shaking like some kind of giant wind-up toy. "Please put these in the mail boxes for me."

I just shoved the willow basket into his stomach and rushed out of there.

I was afraid to go home, to the cottage that is. I didn't want Elliot to see me this messed up if he was there. So, I went out the back door of the inn. I didn't know where I was going, really, or what I was doing anymore. I just desperately wanted to be alone, away from other people, until I could pull myself together. I was afraid of going into the woods, like, if I went in there I'd never come back out. From behind the inn I could distantly see Tanzy and several other people stooped out in the fields harvesting our tea botanicals. Finally, on impulse, I decided to just hide in the sauna, assuming the stove wouldn't be burning at this hour of a midsummer's day and nobody would be in there. I opened the door and stepped into another world.

It wasn't even the sauna inside anymore. It was somebody's room with a bed in it, and then a man stepped out from behind my right side.

"I've been waiting for you," he said.

He was dark-haired, twenty-five maybe. He seemed to be in costume: old-fashioned trousers, gray canvas with a buttoned flap front, a blousy linen shirt, dusty black boots. The strangest sensation came over me of all my anxieties falling away, replaced by the most intense feeling of tenderness, consuming, overflowing, along with the conviction of being placed correctly in the world after a long absence. But it was definitely not my world. He was the same person I had seen in my recurring dream of recent days.

"Come," the man said. He took my hand and led me to the bed. It was an odd size bed, not a single or a full in our sense but something in between. I could see ropes strung in holes along the bed rails. The mattress was hard. I was wearing a long skirt instead of my jeans, but it felt natural, as if I'd always worn clothes like this. And next I was unbuttoning the bodice of this simple dress and pulling it off me along with the skirt. Under it I had on a plain muslin chemise, no bra, my breasts swimming loosely within. The man beside me drew off his shirt and trousers, kissed my neck, my throat, my breastbone. His smell was strong and masculine, but quite natural, appealing, with overtones of wood smoke. I turned to him and held his large head in both my hands. We kissed. The most thrilling commotion of desire rose in me like a rush of blood to the brain. He lay me back on the bed and I allowed him to enter me.

"Ah, you are my Eve," he said as his body pressed against mine. "You are truly my Eve." I lost myself in the sheer pleasurable sensation of his roving lips and hands, surrendering to him completely on waves of euphoria more intense than anything I'd known before, my mouth a perfect O as he labored against me and inside me. And then he subsided, and for a timeless interval we lay together on that bed and I gazed outside the open window across the room at the summer landscape, with Owl's Head in the distance, and a profound quiet interrupted only by the chirr of insects and the clip-clop of a horse somewhere, and the horse snorting, and perfect contentment was in me and all around me.

"Where is this?" I said.

"This is forever," he said.

"Who are you?"

"I am your Adam," he said.

I was in such a transport of happiness that I didn't require anymore enlightenment. By and by, he left the bed and put his clothing on, and I did too, and I was impelled by an inner certainty that I had to go, had to leave him. And when I had put myself back together, he swept me into his arms and kissed me a last time, and said, "Go now." And I did.

I stepped outside the door of that room, or cabin, or whatever it was, and found myself back standing in the grass behind the Sunrise Village inn, just outside the sauna, back in my normal clothes, with Tanzy's garden crew laboring in the distance, and a blackness of roaring despair falling over me like a poisoned cloak. I had no idea what had just happened to me.

I stumbled across the back of the village to the cottage and got into bed with my clothes on and pulled the covers over my head. I must have fallen asleep for a few hours. Then, Elliot was sitting beside me calling my name with his hand pressed tenderly on my shoulder. I opened my eyes. There were auras everywhere around everything in the room, and all of it seemed to flow like a light show.

"I have to go to a hospital," I croaked. "I've lost my mind."

CHAPTER FORTY-SEVEN

E lliot took me down to Putnam Hospital in town right away. It was evening by then and some regular night duty doctor, not a shrink, talked to me for a few minutes and admitted me. Elliot stayed with me in the room. A nurse came around with some syrupy liquid in a plastic shot glass and told me to take it: chloral hydrate, primitive but effective. I was unconscious in two minutes. When I woke up with daylight flooding the room, and realized where I was, my first reaction was to think I'd made a huge mistake. Only a tinge of the weird visuals remained. I looked at my watch. It was nine-thirty. I must have slept for more than twelve hours, and I guess it helped. A breakfast tray sat on a rolling table next to the bed and I nibbled some of the cold toast wondering what on earth I was going to do. Just then, Elliot came into the room accompanied by Dr. Hauser.

Hauser asked how I was feeling, blah blah, and I said okay blah blah, but then they got to the heart of the matter.

"We've been talking," Elliot said, "and the doctor thinks it would be a good idea if you took a bit of a time-out in a good place—"

"A good place?"

"Yeah, where they help people with problems."

"Like, a sanitarium?"

"They don't call them that anymore," Hauser said. "More like a private clinic."

"I wish you'd tell me what my problem is exactly."

"I won't stick a diagnostic label on you. It's not really helpful," Hauser said. "But you're clearly having problems with anxiety and some cognitive disturbance, perhaps as a result of your drug experience."

He was right. At least, it made sense to me."

"How much of a time-out?" I asked.

"A couple of weeks maybe," Elliot said, copping a glance at Dr. Hauser, who half nodded, half shook his head in a non-committal way.

I started getting weepy, but I remembered very clearly now that I'd asked to be taken to the hospital in the first place. So, I didn't protest, but I just made the lame statement, "I don't feel so bad anymore."

"Dr. Hauser thinks you'd benefit from, uh…um—"

"More attentive treatment," Hauser explained.

"I've called MacLaren Park," Elliot said. "It's not that far away, down in Lenox, Mass., an hour or so from here."

"It's a very good place," Hauser said. "First rate."

"What will they do to me there?"

"You'll talk to your doctor. They may put you on a course of meds. You'll be coddled a little. You'll be with other people like yourself."

"People who have flipped out?" I asked. "People who have lost their minds?"

"Other young people," Hauser said, "who are having a hard time."

Nobody said anything for a while.

"When would I go there?"

"Elliot can drive you down this morning," Hauser said.

"It's all set up," Elliot said. "They're expecting you."

And that's exactly what happened. Elliot had even grabbed a bunch of my clothes and packed them in a beautiful leather bag of his. Dr. Hauser gave me a pretty potent tranquilizer for the trip down because he knew I was having trouble riding in cars. Librium, I think it was. It made me feel quite stoned in a mellow way, with no psychedelic fireworks. I hardly minded the journey. We yakked about roadside trivia, as usual: my obsession with the hideous modern architecture popping up on the landscape everywhere, the new shopping strips and drive-in crap at the edge of all the little New England towns. It was more like a Sunday drive than a trip to the loony bin, which was how I was starting to think of my destination. I even ventured to declare to Elliot that I was feeling pretty good, and maybe we should forget about me going to this MacLaren Park and just turn around and go home to Sunrise Village, a place I sincerely loved. But Elliot reminded me that I was on tranquilizers and I should just give it a chance.

MacLaren was a half-mile outside the town of Lenox on a twenty-acre campus of lawns, meadows, and woods. The original building from when it began as, yes, the MacLaren Sanitarium — a euphemistic gloss on the even more archaic term insane asylum — was a gray stone Gothic heap out of a Vincent Price movie. My heart sank at the sight of it. And then, coming around the circular drive, you could see a newer wing in an atrocious steel and glass modern motif, with pink panels under the windows. Ucchh. Inside, a nice lady took us directly into an office of the head guy, Dr. Charles Andrus. It was all dark wood wainscoting with a lot of built-in bookshelves and deep-set Gothic windows of little leaded diamond-shaped panes. The nice welcome lady asked Elliot to wait in the anteroom. Dr. Andrus came out from behind his big desk.

He was shockingly tall, six foot six, like a basketball player, but very handsome in a middle-age way, like he could be senator or a TV sitcom dad. We sat on a little sofa and easy chair grouping across from his desk, me on the sofa.

I began by saying I was embarrassed to be there and wasn't even that sure I was truly crazy, but he assured me that it wasn't about being crazy. He asked what was going on with me and I told him about my acid experience and all the ensuing weirdness, and apparently I passed the entrance exam because next he was explaining the rules to me, what the routine was, how I could have visitors and make phone calls, blah blah. I hardly absorbed any of it. Then Elliot was saying goodbye to me and hugging me, and before I knew it, the nice welcome lady whisked me off to the ward. It was on the second floor of the newer wing and, like Hauser said, was dedicated to people around my age.

A nurse led me into big bathroom and asked me to undress with her standing there watching. She was looking for knives, razors, anything I might be concealing to hurt myself with, and probably drugs, too, though she didn't say that. She watched me take a shower and I was allowed to put my clothes back on. Then I was told they were serving lunch. It was like eating out in a boringly nice restaurant. There were five big circular tables and the flatware was real silver. They had tablecloths and real napkins. We even had silver napkin rings. They had already made out one of those plastic name labels for me and stuck it on a napkin ring for me. Erica B, it said. Lunch was Salisbury Steak with whipped potatoes and corn, and fruit cup for dessert. It depressed the shit out of me. For one thing, it reminded me of high school, which I loathed. I also realized if I ate a lunch like that for two weeks I'd gain ten pounds. But I was starving, having not eaten all day during that madness in town the day before, in and out of the library and the bank, and having only eaten a half a piece of toast that morning at Putnam.

I was also intimidated by the other patients. It was really hard to tell what was wrong with them exactly. Two of them at my table seemed surprisingly normal, Sandy and Linda. Sandy would have been a junior at nearby Mount Holyoke if she hadn't been in MacLaren, short, blonde, a somewhat froggy face, but very vivacious. Linda, slender, less chatty, had long dark hair that look like she ironed it, and a very pretty fox face. One thing I did notice: she had florid pink scars on her wrists. That told a story right there. But neither of them seemed overtly crazy at lunch. A third person at the table, Carol, was older, out of college, from a nice family it seemed from her demeanor and manner of speech, a want-to-be artist living down in New York, twenty-five at least, not very pretty, almost as tall as me, on the heavy side, with short hair that looked like somebody chopped it off at the kitchen table. And her clothing was a very drab frockish *schmata* in yellow and monkeyshit brown, like a house-dress your grandmother would wear. She acted like you expected a depressed person would: glum, inwardly-focused. And finally there was David, a very skinny red-haired boy in loose chinos and button-down oxford shirt, not bad looking, but very youngish, though he would've been going into his senior year at Harvard if he wasn't at MacLaren.

I had no idea what these people's problems really were, and some of them would remain mysterious even though we sat in many group therapy sessions together. Despite listening to each other so much, there was always an inner core of torment and struggle that remained private for all of us, or at least only between us and our shrinks. Sandy and Linda asked me about myself and they were very interested to hear that I'd come from a commune. After that lunch, I had my first meeting with my assigned shrink, Dr. Peter Lascoff. He was not much over thirty and had the most beautiful leonine head of auburn hair and matching dark-frame tortoise-shell glasses. I immediately developed a crush on him, which made me feel like a slut again, of course, because I was very much Elliot's old lady and not supposed to notice other men. We were in a special room for such sessions, no desks, just some comfortable padded chairs.

"Well, Erica," he began, shuffling papers in a folder on his lap. "I see you go by the nickname Pooh."

Uh-oh, I thought. He's going to ask me.

"After Winnie the Pooh?" he quickly added.

I was amazed. "How'd you know? Nobody else does."

"My mother read all the Pooh books to me," he said. "Did your mother?"

"God, no," I said. "She couldn't be bothered. My father did. He gave me my name."

And so we began, with the first hints of what was not quite right in my emotional life. Otherwise, and notwithstanding my immediate attraction to Dr. Lascoff, the session seemed superficial to me, but probably because I was working so hard to appear normal.

Before I knew it, it was over. There was one activity later that afternoon, an art therapy session, which seemed exceedingly stupid to me, like kindergarten, and then dinner — another hefty meal: chicken and dumplings — and nothing formal to do after that. There was a TV lounge on our wing across from this big room that was off-limits to patients called the nursing station, where they sorted out medications and made notes about us, like we were a science project in a terrarium. They had a rotating cast of aides, non-nurses, mostly young guys, whose job seemed to be taking your blood pressure three times a day and being on hand to maintain order if a patient went bananas. I didn't really see them in action until a little later.

Besides the lame sessions like art therapy and recreational therapy, which was apparently limited to volleyball outside in a kind of grassy fenced-in area like a prison yard — except the fence was really nice wood, painted white, with fancy finials on the posts — and group therapy three times a week, and talking to your shrink alone three times a week, the routine at MacLaren was quite boring. There was a lot of time just to sit around. Many of the people had become addicted to the *Star Trek* TV show. Some, like Carol and David, hid in their rooms reading. I called Elliot the next morning after my admission and begged him to bring me my banjo and guitar. He did.

They had a kind of parlor room where you could sit with your visitors. It had a window in the door so you couldn't have sex, or fight with your relatives, or misbehave in some other way without the staff seeing you. I couldn't honestly tell Elliot that I was making much progress, though my visual disturbances were down to nearly nothing, probably because they gave me more chloral hydrate and I was catching up on all that lost sleep. Also, they were trying out some tranquilizer drugs on me. I complained some about whether I really needed to be there and he convinced me it was a little early to decide that. We talked about politics. The Democratic convention was coming up soon in Chicago, and everybody was expecting trouble from hippie protestors flooding into the city because the fix was in for the detested administration stooge Hubert Horatio Humphrey. A crew of about six villagers, led by Hog, was going to drive out there and join our hippie brethren in the streets. I kind of wished I was going with them, though I doubted my nerves could have taken it.

"Can I still have my job when I come back?" I asked Elliot, all weepy.

"Of course you can, Pooh," he said.

"How about my place in your bed?"

"Are you worried about that?"

"I'm worried about everything."

"Well, don't worry about that," he said, "I'm real sure you're going to get over this thing. You already seem a whole lot better."

"You think so? Really? Maybe you should just take me back with you today."

"No, Pooh, you better stick around for at least week. After that, we'll see what they say."

I nodded and pressed my forehead against his shoulder and left a little wet spot there from my tears, and he kissed the top of my head, and then kissed me for a long time on my mouth, so that I was actually getting a bit worked up, despite the drugs I was on, and then we said goodbye. And that was the last time I saw Elliot Sohnberg.

CHAPTER FORTY-EIGHT

Along with the nightly dose of chloral hydrate, they had put me on this little orange pill called thorazine, which was supposed to "clear your thoughts," the head nurse, Mrs. Taggler, told me. It also made you feel like you had ten pounds of lead in your ass, but it did level off my jagged emotions somewhat, so I didn't put up a fight about it. The other patients constantly complained about their medications. It seemed stupid to me, a distraction from their actual problems. There were proportionately more females than males on our ward but two of the males were the most obviously damaged among us. One guy named Randy glided stiffly up and down the halls as if he were rolling on a little cart with wheels on it. He never moved his head and he wore a weird fixed smile on his face. When I learned what his problem was, from Sandy, it really freaked me out: a bad acid trip. He was in much worse shape than me. He never spoke to anyone, at least not us other patients. He was clearly awake and in motion, yet quite out of it. He must have eaten a whole blotter full of hits. The scariest part was that it turned out he'd been in MacLaren for six months — and he was still all fucked up. Like, what good was it doing him? So, I started worrying again that I was permanently damaged, too, and that sent me spiraling back down into that roaring despair. I tried to pump the nurses for more about Randy but they just said that patient information was confidential.

Then there was Charlie, about twenty five. He looked like he was still living in 1958. He had a buzz-cut, and those flesh-colored clear plastic eyeglass frames, and he wore green janitorial trousers and white T-shirts like a kind of uniform, and he could talk but barely did. I learned on the patient grapevine that he had been discharged from the army for mental problems, but not much more. We didn't know if he had actually made it to Vietnam — he didn't talk about it — but apparently something bad happened to him. He watched television incessantly, though he didn't mind if you changed the channel. He'd watch any old thing: soap operas, *The Beverly Hillbillies, The Mod Squad, The Price Is Right.* Often, he would drop down from the sofa and do twenty-five push-ups, and then just go back to sitting and watching TV. When I asked him why he was doing all the push-ups he said, "It relieves anxiety." One thing about Charlie: he was very strong and trim, just socially unreachable. I often wondered what he would be like if he let his hair grow, and put on more interesting clothes, and learned how to have a conversation. Answer: he wouldn't be him.

I found out from Carol what was wrong with David, the young Harvard guy. He'd had a terrible intestinal ailment, colitis, which was so bad they'd had to surgically detach his lower bowel and hook it into a metal port implanted in his abdomen where his bodily wastes emptied into a plastic bag. Imagine that happening to you when you were twenty years old. Uccchhh. He later told me that they had talked him down from a third-floor window ledge in Harvard Yard. He said he was sorry that he hadn't thrown himself into the Charles River instead.

That first week I was in MacLaren, another guy was admitted under rather unsettling circumstances. It was around ten-thirty at night. I was still up watching *The Dean Martin Show*, with Charlie and Sandy. There was a commotion at the end of the hall. They were pushing a gurney down toward us with a man strapped into it, screaming and raving, and rolled right past us. Two of the aides, Tom and Walter, along with a doctor and two nurses, got this luna-tic off the gurney and stuffed him into what they called "the quiet room," which was, in effect, a good old padded cell next to the nursing station. The screaming and raving continued for quite a while after that. I turned in sometime after Johnny Carson came on the air. My room was at the far end of the hall but I woke up a couple of times during the night to episodes of muffled scream-ing and wailing. The mysterious newcomer remained in the qui-et room for another two days. They brought meals in there for him and everything. After all that, plus a shower and a change of clothes, he finally emerged onto the ward. It turned out he was quite a handsome young guy named George, over six feet tall, long, dark, shaggy hair, a student at Franklin Pierce College over in New Hampshire, but from New Jersey, and Jewish, with the old reliable Jewish sense of comedy. He was a sleeping pill addict. Seconal. Reds, as they were called, a downer drug reputed to produce the most vicious withdrawal symptoms of all, even worse than heroin, they said. So that's what he had been doing in the quiet room for three days: kicking a barbiturate addiction cold turkey. Afterward, he was gregarious and full of jokes and you never would've known how messed up he was, or that he'd been through withdrawal twice before already and was liable to get hooked all over again when and if he got out of the MacLaren loony bin. That's what I'd been calling it, trying to to take the scary edge off the fact that I was afraid I actually might not get out for a long time. Carol, the painter from the city, who was on her third month, had an even better name for the place. She called it the laughing academy.

The Democratic Convention came on TV the beginning of my second week at MacLaren. The first days were just procedural bullshit so there was nothing much to watch, but hippies were pouring into Chicago by the thousands and they were beginning to generate friction with the police out on the streets. Also that week, it was on the news that someone had planted a bomb in a trash can behind the federal building in Montpelier, the Vermont capital. It went off at eleven o'clock at night and blew the leg off a janitor. It gave me a very bad feeling, but I was overwhelmed with so many other bad feelings that I didn't fully register the incident. That Monday, Marilyn came up from Long Island to see me. She brought my brother Bobby. I was already in a fragile state because I'd heard nothing from Elliot for two days and I was unable to get him on the phone, and nobody answered the pay phone at the inn or the office phone up in the Odd Fellows hall and I was getting all bent out of shape about that.

I was in art therapy when one of the aides came to tell me I had a visitor. It had been a bad session anyway. As usual, we were asked to make a painting of something with gloppy poster paint and then talk about it. I had painted a kind of savage fantasy of a wolf pack ranging through a pine forest, and the wolves all had blood dripping from their muzzles, and believe it or not Mrs. Langhorne, the art therapist, was scolding me for it, like it was un-cool to reveal such dark emotions, when Walter the aide barged in. They told me at the nursing station that my mother, Mrs. Bollinger, was there to see me with my little brother.

"I don't want to see her," I told the head nurse, Mrs. Taggler.

"Well, you can refuse to see her," she said.

I was amazed. "I can?"

"Yes. You can put her on the list of people you don't want to see."

"There's a list?"

"Didn't they explain it to you at admission?"

"How should I know? I'm all fucked up mentally," I said, in a rather angry tone that elicited a stern look over the cat's eye eyeglass frames from Mrs. Taggler. "Sorry," I added.

"You don't have to see them," Mrs. Taggler patiently reiterated.

"I want to see my brother, though. Can they send him in and not her?"

"Sure, if that's okay with Mrs. Bollinger."

"Can you pass that on? That I want to see him, Bobby Bollinger, but not her?"

"Sure," Mrs. Taggler said, adding, "remember, we're on your side here."

"Okay, thanks," I said.

It took about five minutes, but Walter unlocked the main door to the ward and Bobby walked in. You could tell, the place freaked him out. I was used to it by then, but his mouth was open and he was taking it all in like he had just entered the House of Wax, waiting for old Vincent Price to pop out of a door wringing his hands. I rushed up and hugged him and virtually dragged him into the visitor's parlor, as they called the little room. On the way, he noticed Randy gliding down the hall.

"What's wrong with that guy?" Bobby asked as I shut the door.

"He's fucked up, like the rest of us, only more so," I said.

Bobby sat there nervously jiggling his leg for a while. Neither of us knew what to say, I guess.

"Mom's pissed," he eventually said.

"Well, fuck her," I said. "I don't want to see her."

"She wants you to come home with us."

"Oh? That's rich. That's absolutely the last place I would want to go."

We just sat quietly a while longer. It calmed me down to see how handsome and grown-up Bobby was getting, even more than back in June when he came up to the village. Plus, he had a really good tan that was set off by the white Mexican shirt he had on. You could see chest hairs at the V where he had it buttoned rather low down on his sternum.

"You look fantastic," I said. "Have you been working at the Harbor Club?"

"Yeah," he said. "What the hell's going on, Pooh?"

"I had a bad acid trip," I said. "I've had some after-effects and kind of a hard time getting over it. Listen: whatever you do, don't take that shit. Don't take acid. It can really mess you up—"

"I've already taken it. Like half a dozen times."

"Well quit taking it. You could end up like me."

He tried to suppress a smile, as if he knew better.

"I'm serious. That guy you asked about in the hall, Randy, he took too much acid and look what happened to him."

"All right, already! I'll never take the shit again," he said, and changed the subject. "How long are you going to be in here?"

"I dunno. Until the end of the week, maybe. Something like that."

"Are they curing you?"

"It doesn't work quite like that. How'd you even find out I was here?"

"Some police called Mom."

"Police?" I gasped. The inside of my head seemed to turn blood red. "What police? About what?"

"I don't really know. Something about your boyfriend. You have that boyfriend, right? Up at the village."

"Yeah, I have a boyfriend. What about him?"

"I don't know, Pooh. Mom wouldn't tell me. You could get her in here and ask her."

"I don't want to talk to her. Or even see her. You find out. You pump her on the way home and find out what the hell is going on, and you call me tonight when you get there, understand?"

I didn't know what else to say to him. The news was only making me more frantic and agitated. I started seeing auras again. We sat there a while saying nothing, Bobby just jiggling his leg and me trying not to jump out of my skin or start bawling.

"I better go," Bobby finally said. "She told me not to stay in here long."

"Yeah, okay."

So, we hugged and I walked him back to the door of the wing. I never got even a glimpse of Marilyn.

I called the phone numbers back at the village several more times that afternoon and nobody answered. I was really freaking out. I called Dr. Hauser's office back in Bennington before five o'clock. He was gone for the day, a secretary said, but she took a message from me.

That night, I had a fight with Carol about hogging the ward phone. There was only one phone for our whole floor of the new wing, believe it or not, and she was on it for over two hours after dinner, so I started yelling at her, and the aides came down and tried to intervene, and I yelled at them, and they got a couple of nurses, and I yelled and cursed them and before you knew it, they stuffed me into the quiet room. The chief night shift nurse, Miss Haverstraw, told me to feel free to scream my head off in there. I had called her a "fucking pig." She was rather roly-poly and probably didn't appreciate it.

CHAPTER FORTY-NINE

I never felt so alone and forsaken, and I was so worried about Elliot and how come he wasn't calling, and what the hell was going on back at Sunrise Village with nobody picking up any of the phones. It was like my whole world was collapsing and there was nothing I could do but sit on the padded floor of a padded cell and cry my eyes out. I was only in there a few hours, but when they let me out after midnight it was too late to call Bobby, and anyway I was afraid that if I called the house Marilyn would pick up. I finally turned in at one-fifteen, with a dose of chloral, and woke up after nine the next morning when Bobby would've already left for school. Through breakfast, which I could barely eat, I struggled with the idea of just calling Marilyn to find out what she knew. But it became unnecessary. At ten, I was informed I had another visitor.

He was an FBI agent named DeKamp. He actually showed me his badge. It was back to the visitors parlor again, me trembling as if electricity was running through me. He was a straight-arrow guy, nice gray suit, thirties, tall and fit, slight sideburn action as if trying to show some simpatico with the times, a notch or two more intelligent-looking than the average cop, but nonetheless a representative of the hated establishment. I burrowed deep into the easy chair for self-protection.

"I'll get right to the point, Miss Bollinger. You've been a member of the Sunrise Village commune for how long?"

"Since around last Thanksgiving," I said. "What's that? About ten months?"

"Are you acquainted with Elliot R. Sohnberg?"

"Yes. Of course."

"Would you say that he is the person in charge at Sunrise Village?"

"What is this about? Why are you asking me these questions?"

"For the moment I'd like you to just answer the questions, ma'am."

"Don't I get to have a lawyer present."

"This is not that kind of interview. You're not in custody and I'm not taking you into custody. So, no, ma'am."

Agent DeCamp took out a pack of Winstons.

"Hey, can I have one of those?" I asked. Mine were in my room. He shook one out for me and gave me a light. I was trembling so badly I could barely hold the cigarette to the flame. "You know this is a mental hospital, don't you?" I said.

"I understand what this place is, ma'am."

"I mean, what value is the testimony of a crazy person?"

"This isn't testimony. You're not under oath here. And you don't seem too crazy to be of help to us."

"Where's Elliot?"

"He's in custody, ma'am."

I felt like a hundred pound anvil had just fallen on me.

"Where?" I croaked,

"He's in the Bennington County Jail at the moment. Tell me: is he the person in charge at this Sunrise Village?"

"I guess. As far as that goes. He's not, like, anyone's guru or a dictator. He founded the place. But he doesn't tell people what to do."

"Are you acquainted with the following people? One Oswald P. Strangefield, Scott D. Provost, Michael J. O'Neill, and Tracy L. Reihm?"

"Yes."

"Who are they?"

"People at Sunrise Village."

"These people are in custody, too, in connection with the bombing of the federal building in Montpelier, Vermont. They were apprehended in a car south of Waitsfield the night of."

I started crying, as usual. I thought my head was going to explode. Agent DeKamp was looking all psychedelic to me.

"Can you tell me anything about their activities?" he said.

"I'm sure Elliot had nothing to do with it." I said. "I know him. He's my... boyfriend."

"Yes, frankly, that's why I'm interviewing you. Were you aware of any plans to carry out this bombing?"

"I never heard a thing about it until it was on TV the other night," I said. "He couldn't have been involved. He's not political like that."

"We'll get to the bottom of it, ma'am. Anyway, Mr. Sohnberg's due for a bail hearing. What about the others?"

"What about them?"

"Can you tell me if they subscribe to any violent political beliefs?"

"No."

"Mr. Strangefield proclaims himself to be a radical anarchist," DeKamp said. "Have you ever heard him say that? Make that claim?"

"Yeah, I guess. But everybody and their uncle has a political leaning these days. I thought it was just... posturing."

"How about the others?"

"No."

"No what? You don't know or to your knowledge they don't subscribe to any violent political beliefs?"

"Both, I guess."

"Did you ever hear any of them advocate the violent overthrow of the government?"

"No."

Agent DeKamp just drilled his eyes into me for a long moment.

"We may conduct a more formal interview with you, Miss Bollinger. You'll be notified in advance and if that happens, you will be permitted to have a lawyer present in that event. I suppose it's not easy on you in this situation. Mind if I ask why you're here?"

"Nerves," I said. I sure didn't want to say I flipped out on LSD, like they needed additional reasons to think the worst about Sunrise Village and maybe even come up with more charges against us.

"What about Sunrise Village got on your nerves?"

"Nothing," I said. "It's what's going on in America that got to me."

"For what it's worth, ma'am, you don't seem crazy, and I hope you feel better soon. You're a nice young lady."

Then he got up and excused himself and left me alone in the room. I sat there in stunned terror for about a quarter of an hour. Eventually Mrs. Taggler came in.

"Are you in some kind of trouble with the law, dear?" she asked.

"I don't know," I said and a fresh Niagara of tears flowed out of me. In the midst of all that swirling confusion and angst, I decided that I had to go up to Bennington somehow and go see Elliot in the Bennington jail. "I have to get out of here," I said.

"I'm afraid that's not possible," she said.

"No, I'm serious. I'm checking myself out."

"You can't, dear. You're here on a two physician certificate."

"What? What the hell does that mean?"

"It means that two doctors have said you need to be here for now."

"Against my will?"

"Yes. It's a legal protocol."

"You can't keep me locked up in here!" I shrieked at Mrs. Taggler.

"I'm afraid we can," she said. "And we will."

CHAPTER FIFTY

I t was true. It was a locked ward. It should have seemed obvious
since the aides and nurses used keys to take us around to our
activities off the ward. I hadn't so much as tried to go outside for a
walk by myself until then. I was just being a good girl doing what
people told me to do. But hearing that I was formally committed to
the joint just set me off. I oscillated back and forth between weeping and screaming. I lost count of the times they stuffed me in the
quiet room the next forty-eight hours. I was becoming a genuine
crazy person, surely proving that I deserved to be committed to a
mental hospital. What amazed me was that they were completely
uninterested in the reason I wanted to leave the place, namely to
go see my boyfriend in jail and do what I could to help him. It sim-
ply didn't enter into their thinking that that was a normal, sane,
legitimate desire. I just kept hassling them at the nursing station to
be let out, and each time the scene would escalate to me shrieking
at them, and it was back to the quiet room. One of those intervals
when they let me out, I noticed on the TV that Hubert Horatio
Humphrey had been officially nominated to run for president.
Uccchhh.

My relationship with Dr. Peter Lascoff deteriorated sharply. When I pressed him in our next session, he confessed that he had signed the commitment papers and that set me against him. I went on strike. I'd sit in the therapy room and just sulk or answer his attempts to converse with snotty remarks about his haircut, his corny tie, or some other irrelevant thing. Though at times I saw auras and experienced other distorted perceptions, that stuff was never as bad again as in the days just after my acid trip. What was out of control were my emotions. Consequently, they upped my medications, which flattened things out and put me in a fog, but didn't alleviate the underlying despair I felt. The drugs also had weird side effects, like making your mouth dry all the time, and causing you to put on weight. My jeans were getting tight. Being forced to take the drugs provided more reasons for me to fight with the staff and Dr. Lascoff. Then, at the end of that terrible week I had another visitor, who brought information that just sent me plunging to the bottom.

They fetched me from my room to find Dr. Art Hauser from Bennington waiting in the visitor's parlor. I was extremely glad to see him at first, because I considered him a potential sympathetic ally in my battle to get out of MacLaren. But he looked deeply glum as I settled into the soft chair.

"I have some bad news, Pooh," he began starkly. "Elliot Sohnberg is dead."

Even on all that Thorazine, my heart sank through the floor. I must have just stared blankly at him, not responding, because he began talking again.

"He apparently hanged himself in a cell at the county jail. Personally, I think there's something not completely kosher about the story...."

I don't remember any more about the meeting. I just zoned out when he dropped the news, and in the weeks directly after, I remained deeply out of it, depersonalized, numb, mute. I was becoming like a female version of Randy, gliding stiffly down the hall, going through the motions of daily life, lying around in my room doing nothing, not even reading, whenever I was not compelled to go to some activity, art therapy, rec therapy, group therapy, where I barely participated, and my seemingly useless sessions with Dr. Lascoff. No one from Sunrise Village tried to communicate with me. I didn't know what had happened to the place, though I assumed most if not all of them had fled somewhere after the bombing incident, whether they were involved with Strangefield or not — and I'm pretty sure most of them had nothing to do with it. I had no idea how to get in touch with Arden Blanchard out in Oakland, California. And he surely had no idea I was in the nut house in Lenox, Massachusetts. I could not process the idea that Elliot was dead, and I had no more information about what happened to him in the Bennington jail, though Dr. Hauser's remark about it not being kosher provoked me to imagine some kind of foul play.

So, in that poison globe of seclusion, I barely even noticed that the seasons had started to change. Red and orange color crept into the treetops. The air outside had a new crisp bite to it when they took us to the volleyball court. The nurses taped red maple leaves up on the windows of the nursing station and brought pumpkins in to decorate the TV alcove. Once, they took a bunch of us out to the movies in Pittsfield, a small city with a General Electric plant a few miles up the highway. They sent two aides and a nurse along with us to make sure we didn't misbehave. The movie was *With Six You Get Eggroll*, with Doris Day, the most vapid piece of crap ever put on celluloid, and it agitated me so much that I kept on asking to get up and go to the lobby, and Tom, the aide, had to come with me and make sure that I didn't skip out on the group, and he got mad at me for making him miss half the movie. I wasn't exactly making progress.

One Saturday in early October, Bobby came up to see me alone. It was going to be my birthday on Tuesday, which I had nearly forgotten. I would be twenty years old, no longer a teenager, even technically. He brought me a lovely turquoise necklace. It amazed me that he was at the point in life now where he actually had good taste. He had gotten his full adult driver's license at the end of the summer and used some of his insurance money to buy a sports car, a second-hand MG Midget. He made me look out the window at it in the parking lot and admire it, but it just filled me with dread to think of him driving that little tin can on the Long Island Expressway where our father got killed. I was glad to see him but I could barely utter a coherent sentence. He told me that Marilyn had dumped Morrie Saperstein, Dad's old friend, and was now dating a divorced orthodontist from Roslyn named Barry Resnick. Where did she find these guys, I wondered. Bobby said he had read about the Montpelier bombing and what happened to Elliot and all and I just screamed at him that we didn't know what the hell really happened to Elliot and then all I could do was just cry and cry. I'm afraid it wasn't a very nice visit for him.

As for Marilyn, she didn't even try to reach out. While it is true that I did not call her or write her a single letter from MacLaren, neither did she make any effort to repair, or even explore, what had gone so wrong between us in recent years. It took me a long time to understand that it mattered to me.

It was a very hard time, that fall. I'd slipped down that white rabbit's hole and become convinced that I wasn't coming back. I had suicidal thoughts, thinking that there was an outside chance if I pulled it off, I could get to a place where Elliot was and we could be together again. I missed him so much. I missed those months at the village when everything was good. I missed the cottage we'd lived in and those beautiful summer days swimming in the quarry. I missed Padget and Alison and Kris and Alan and making music, and Weezil and Tanzy and everybody, and I had no idea where they all were or how to get a hold of any of them. The village phones had gone dead over the weeks. I had no sense of any future.

At least I kept those suicidal thoughts to myself or God knows what additional drugs they would have put me on. I even developed the interesting delusion that two of the night nurses were named Dot and Peg. We were supposed call the doctors and nurses Doctor, Miss, or Missus This-and-That — though not the aides — and their name-tags all identified them as such, so we didn't know all their first names. But with these two who worked the eleven-to-seven graveyard shift, and who I actually rarely saw or had dealings with, it somehow got into my head as Dot and Peg. Which freaked me out, of course.

As for my fellow inmates, Carol had become my enemy ever since I screamed at her about hogging the phone. Sandy was discharged in October and went back to school. Linda was forever scheming up foolish battles with the staff over trivialities just to distract herself from her personal problems and she resented my lack of interest in playing that game. George was okay to banter with at mealtime and art therapy, but he was constantly trying to put the make on me in the TV room and, apart from the strict rules they had at MacLaren about sex between patients, I just didn't have the slightest desire to get physical with him. David, the boy who'd been maimed by intestinal surgery, was smart and had a sly, mordant sense of humor, but he was too bottled up to talk about anything that mattered, like his childhood or his illness. He did, however, have a portable phonograph and he was into old time jazz, and we used to listen to the Mississippi Sheiks and Ma Rainy and Big Bill Broonzy in his room for hours without having to talk. He didn't show any sexual interest in me, but that was understandable and okay with me. For weeks, I just existed in that fog of thorazine and despair, and then it all changed.

CHAPTER FIFTY-ONE

By some mysterious alchemy of head-shrinking, a malign paralysis of the will let go inside me and allowed me to climb out of that foggy vale of depression back into feeling alive and engaged in the world around me. You'd be surprised how your mind can work through things without you being entirely conscious of the journey. The sheer passage of time might have had something to do with it. In all those sessions with Dr. Lascoff, when I barely cooperated in my own therapy, something transpired to shift me out of that childish hostility and toward an active interest in things and persons outside myself.

There was one particular hour around Halloween when I stumbled into a startling revelation about myself. I was finally revealing the details about the day I truly went mad, when I fled from my office in the Odd Fellows hall out to the sauna behind the Sunrise Village Inn and stepped into a strange room that seemed to exist out of time, where I met the mysterious young man in old-fashioned clothes and submitted to him sexually and felt the most intense emotion toward him. I'd been afraid to tell Lascoff about it because it seemed so crazy. I realized that the young man looked like my father, Larry Bollinger, in his World War Two photos. I mean, exactly. Lascoff knew Larry had died the previous spring, of course, and I'd explained the family dynamics over the weeks, especially in the early going, before I turned truculent and uncooperative.

"Did your father ever behave sexually with you?" he asked.

"You mean, like, rape me? No."

"Touch you, fondle you?"

"Why are you even asking me these things?"

"This dream you had—"

"It wasn't a dream."

"All right, this… incident, experience, whatever we decide to call it — it suggests the suppression of a deeply troubling memory."

"I never had sex with my father. He never molested me. Nothing of the kind ever happened. I understand you're trained to unravel these dark Freudian conundrums, but this just isn't a gold nugget of neurosis in my psychological mine shaft."

"You called him Larry."

"Yeah, I did."

"Always?"

"After a certain point."

"What point?"

"I dunno. Thirteen. Fourteen."

"And what was going on then?"

"Junior high school."

"What else?"

"I dunno. What do you imagine was going on?"

"Puberty," Lascoff said.

I lit another cigarette, despite the fact that I had one already going in the ashtray. I started trembling uncontrollably.

"Yeah, sure. Puberty," I said.

"You were becoming a woman."

"I'm telling you, there was never any perverted hanky-panky between me and him. Never."

"But you loved him deeply."

"Yes, I loved him very much."

"There didn't need to be any actual sex act between you."

"There wasn't."

"Except in that... incident."

"Yeah, which wasn't real."

We didn't take it further than that, but I actually did understand something fresh about myself, though it was unsettling. Of course, I didn't exactly *snap out of it* that day, just get all better overnight — in fact I was particularly depressed by that session for a day or two afterward — but something shook loose in me that started to send the log-jam of mental crap downstream out of my life in the present, setting me free. The weeks that followed felt more like a readjustment than a recovery, strictly speaking. I was keenly aware of having gone through an ordeal, but I was suddenly catching a glimpse of a plausible future. I began to play the guitar and the banjo again after a long layoff. Songs came to me effortlessly, in a rush. I spent hours arranging them and learning them, working quite hard after weeks of indolence. I began to take better care of myself, watched what I was eating, fixed my hair. After a while, Lascoff took me off thorazine. I developed an intense fascination in what other people were saying, thrilled to be outside the bubble of myself. My sessions with Lascoff turned to the question of what I was going to do now. I sort of fell back half in love with him, and even learned that he was single, but I entertained no fantasies about being with him, having a relationship, taking up with him there in Lenox, Mass. If anything, I was preparing to get on with my life without him around to help me.

In fact, I was brewing a previously unimaginable new plan for myself, which was to go to Los Angeles and see what I could do with my music. A year ago I never would have considered moving to the maw of cultural crapola out in the crapola capital of the world, California. But I was reading voraciously about the music industry in those weeks after Halloween, as I came back to my normal self. They were letting me out of MacLaren on day passes as my behavior became stable and I got off the medication. I'd go to the nearby Lenox Free Library, which was an excellent one because Lenox was a wealthy town — the author Edith Wharton had lived there on a grand estate whose property actually abutted MacLaren Park — and I devoured the music trade papers, *Billboard* and *Cashbox*, and the fairly new (one-year old) counterculture journal called *Rolling Stone*, and anything else I could get my mitts on, and it was obvious that the center of gravity in rock and roll was shifting from New York to LA. And I thought: why not? I wouldn't have to live there forever if I didn't like it, if I flopped, if it didn't work out in some other way, I could come back east again.

Dr. Hauser from Bennington drove down to see me again during that period when I was coming back to myself. I learned a little more from him about the government case against the bombers. There was going to be a trial. But he said there was frustratingly little new information about what happened to Elliot. The sheriff's office was treating it as an open-and-shut suicide. He'd met with the Sohnberg Foundation lawyers and they were extremely frustrated with the process. Elliot had been cremated, he said. It made me bawl, but I did not sink back into that white rabbit hole of despair and confusion. He gave me a big hug when we parted, a sweet man.

Dr. Lascoff had actually set a discharge date for me in the third week of November. Coincidentally, it marked exactly a year after I dropped out of NYU and joined the commune at Sunrise Village. Of course, in those thrilling weeks when I emerged from my personal darkness, Lascoff and I talked about these plans I was cooking up. He didn't try to browbeat me into returning to college. He knew that I had enough insurance money from Larry's death to make a new life for myself out west. I had also made an interesting discovery when I went through my discharge plans with the MacLaren Park business office: my bill was being paid all along by the Sohnberg Foundation. Apparently, Elliot had given his lawyers instructions at some point before he went to jail to see that I was taken care of. Frankly, I hadn't thought about who was paying for MacLaren in all those weeks when I was out of my skull, but it was a huge relief when I found out. And then, by an interesting act of cosmic synchronicity, I had another visitor just three days before I was to be released: Weezil.

She looked great. She had a shorter shaggy haircut and bangs and wore a beautiful fall jacket of patchwork satin over jeans bleached to perfection. I was so glad to see her. We hugged and hugged.

"Hey, you've got to lose a few pounds, sister," she started off all jokey.

"I know," I said. "The food here's so terrible, I couldn't stop eating it."

But after the initial bantering, we both turned more somber.

"When are they going to let you out?" she asked.

"On Wednesday, as a matter of fact."

"Oh? Jeez! Then, you're okay now?"

"Yeah, I'm okay."

"What'd they do to you here?"

"Nothing." I said.

"Nothing?"

"Nothing but talk to my shrink, really. I'm all right. I'll never get over Elliot and what happened. But I'm going to get on with my life now."

We sat quietly a moment.

"You know about the bombing and all?" she asked.

"Yeah," I said. "I had a visit from the FBI."

"Me, too," Weezil said. "What did you tell them?"

"I told them the truth," I said. "I had no idea those guys were going to bomb anything. What about you?"

"Similar. I told them I always thought Strange was just one of those armchair revolutionaries," she said.

"I thought I knew him a little," I said. "He was very decent to me when my dad died."

"Did you ball him?"

"Yeah, a couple of times. He was quite sweet, actually."

"I know. I was balling him for while, too," Weezil said. "And then he tossed me aside like a Snickers wrapper."

We let that lay. Weezil bummed a smoke from me and we lit up.

"Does anyone know what really went down in the county jail with Elliot?" I changed the subject.

"We think they killed him," Weezil said.

"Not the feds?"

"No! The county sheriffs. Those fucking pigs."

"Do you think he knew what Strange was up to?"

Weezil made a face. "Gawd no. Nobody outside of their twisted little circle knew. We were all shocked."

"Where are Strange and Scotty and the others."

"They're in the federal lock-up over in New York. They're going to prison for a long time, it looks like."

"Sad," I said. "What a waste."

"Dumb shits," Weezil said. "They really fucked up a good thing."

"Yeah. It was sweet... the village," I said. I got all weepy again thinking about Elliot. "I can't imagine he would've killed himself over any of this. It just wasn't like him."

"Some kind of foul play went down in there, all right," Weezil agreed. "I wish I could tell you more. He was alone in that cell. After the cops picked up Strange and Scotty and the others, they drove over and busted the village, the federal marshals, the state police plus the sheriffs. They rounded everybody up, but ended up letting us go after two days. The FBI was also in and out looking for shit connected to the bombing. I guess they found a bunch. You know, Strange and them really hurt this poor young guy who was janitor of the building they bombed. One of us."

"One of us?"

"A long-hair, a freak, working his way through the law school in Randolph. They blew his leg off."

"Uccchhh. Yeah, I heard. He'll never be the same."

"Yeah. Horrible."

"Where is everybody now? The rest of the people? Alan and Padget and Alison and Tanzy, Billy Herman and everybody?"

"I really don't know. Scattered. Back home, I suppose. Or somewhere else. There are maybe ten people left up at the village. Hog and the ones who went to the convention in Chicago. A few others. Mr. Heathman is still there, bless his heart."

"Are you still at the village?" I asked.

"No, I'm back on the farm for now," she said, meaning the family farm in Vergennes. "I'm waiting tables at this fancy place in town, the Champlain House. It's great money. I'm saving a shitload. I'll figure out what to do next. Just not sure yet. What about you?"

I told her my plan.

"You're gonna be a star. Huh?"

"I dunno. I'm going to see what I can do with my music."

"Can I come out to LA and hang out with you when you're rich and famous?"

"Sure."

"Don't you miss the Village?"

"Yeah, I do," I said. "But there's no going back to it. It was a special time and place, like JFK and Jackie in Camelot, and now it's over."

Weezil got teary when I said that, and I did, too, of course. We hugged again for a long time as if holding onto the fading dream of Sunrise Village. She invited me to the family farm for

Thanksgiving and it actually worked out great because I had no idea how I was going to get around after leaving MacLaren, and I had a bunch of things I had to take care of before I could go out west, including getting a car. In the preceding weeks, after I started to crawl mentally out of the hole I'd been in, I'd gotten back in touch with Ricky Spillman out at Kenyon College and I had a vague plan to stop and see him on the way when I drove out to California.

CHAPTER FIFTY-TWO

So, a few days later I was released from the laughing academy and enjoying a classic Vermont Thanksgiving on Weezil's farm, with her really great, huge family. Just being back out in the world was such a novelty, everything so fresh and new to me, and the farm turned out to be really quite grand and lovely. Weezil regaled the table with the tale of our exploits in the Sunrise Village kitchen the previous Thanksgiving, and I drank some of her Uncle Ray's hard cider, my first alcohol since going into MacLaren back in the summer, and got a little buzz on, and played folk songs with her brother Albert and cousin Liz around the fireplace after the feast, and slept in the same bed with Weezil for the night because the big farm house was jammed with relatives.

Weezil drove me down to Bennington the next morning. The week before I'd left MacLaren, I'd called the investment account manager in Boston who was in charge of the bulk of my insurance money. On my request they'd sold some stock and sent ten thousand dollars to my checking account in Bennington. Weezil and I went car shopping at the Ford dealership there. I bought a brand-new "Highland Green" Mustang convertible for twenty-five hundred bucks. We talked about her coming out to California when I got settled and had another tearful goodbye. Then she had to drive back to Vergennes to work the Friday night post-Thanksgiving dinner at the Champlain House. The car dealer said they could get the registration and the plates on before the end of the day, since I was buying the car without a bank loan. They let me leave my musical instruments and a suitcase in the sales office. I still had a couple of things to do before I left Vermont.

First I went to the bank. I had to get a certified check to pay for the Mustang plus a thousand bucks in Traveler's Checks for my trip out west and to settle in LA once I got there. To take care of all that I had to sit down and talk to that bank officer, good old Mr. Purvis. They had received my money from Boston, he said, thank God. He gave me an amused, squinty-eyed look when I told him I was buying a car.

"Didn't you come in here last summer to get money for a car?" he said.

"Oh, that was a used car," I said, recalling that fiasco of the day when I was going nuts.

"You sure go through cars at a brisk clip."

"This one's a new car."

"Isn't that nice?" he said with a half-smile.

He made out my certified check with meticulous care, like he might be hoping I'd get bored and tell him to forget it and leave so they could hang onto the money a little longer.

"You were one of those youngsters up in that village on the mountain," he said when he handed it over, a statement that was really a question.

"Yeah, I was."

"They set off that bomb, those people."

"It was a small secret group of political crazies within the village. The rest of us didn't know anything about it."

"Is that so?"

"Yes, it's so."

"They found drugs there," he said. "You moved a lot of money in and out of this bank. Was it from drugs?"

"No, it's from a life insurance policy after my father was killed in a car crash."

That shut him up. I told him my money wouldn't be cluttering up his bank anymore because I was moving to California and I'd call with instructions in a week or so for transferring it to a bank in LA.

"Drive safely," he said when I left.

Then I walked over to the county building.

The county sheriff, George Grout, was actually up in his office at quarter after one. It wasn't a very elaborate operation. Just him and a secretary on the second floor of the musty old building with clanking radiators and grundgy sea-foam colored paint on the walls. The secretary just sent me in without an appointment. He looked up from some paperwork at his desk and watched me slip into a chair off one corner of his desk.

"Have a seat, Miss," he said facetiously.

"Thank you, I will."

He had a jowly bulldog face with furrows that etched his mouth into a permanent frown.

"What can I do for you, young lady?"

"I want to talk to you about Elliot Sohnberg."

He seemed to strain a bit mentally, lines on his forehead scrunching up.

"Oh, yes. Him," he said. "And who are you with?"

"I'm not with anybody."

"You a relative?"

"No, I was his girlfriend."

He nodded slowly half a dozen times as if finally sizing me up.

"Unfortunate thing what happened," he eventually said.

I didn't reply. I just sat there drilling my gaze into him, observing the tiny gestures that telegraphed his discomfort despite his efforts to appear stolid and self-possessed.

"How did he hang himself?" I eventually asked.

"Do you really want to concern yourself with these unappetizing details?"

"Apparently I do."

"Used his own shirt," Grout said. "Tied it 'round the crossbar on the front of his cell wall, t'other end around his throat, then just sat down."

"Strangled himself?"

"Apparently he did," Grout said.

"Do you have photos of it?"

"I suppose. Somewhere around here."

"Could I see them?"

"Well now ma'am—"

"I 'd like to see them."

He paused and bounced the tip of his ballpoint pen on his desk pad a bunch of times.

"I can't do that," he said. "People can't walk in off the street and just ask for evidentiary materials. I have a feeling that you're neither an attorney nor an officer with any other law enforcement agency."

"What was done with the body?"

"We have a morgue."

"Where did it go from there? Did you ship him somewhere?"

"You'd have to ask the coroner. He's down the hall. Name of Philo D. Granby."

"Surely you have some idea what happened to his body."

"Mr. Granby is the one to ask," he said.

We sat in silence again, still sizing each other up.

"I think you killed him."

"That's a reckless accusation, young lady."

"Well, there it is."

"Get out of my office," he said and made a show of returning to the papers on his desk.

"I hope you've got eyes in the back of your head," I said before I vacated my seat. "You're going to need them."

Philo D. Granby was not in his office. I waited there for over an hour and he never came in.

CHAPTER FIFTY-THREE

The Mustang was ready for me at three o'clock, all buffed up with a free tank of gas. That fabled new car smell was intoxicating. For days I'd thought about going up to Sunrise Village one last time to see who and what might be left there. So I did, driving normal speed like a normal person in my new car. When I pulled in, Sumner Heathman, who'd lived as a sort of hermit in Timlinton before Elliot Sohnberg came along and bought the whole kit and caboodle, was sitting on the porch of his little cottage in the sad, waning fall afternoon light, all bundled up in a wool army blanket, clutching a cup of coffee. He'd been something like the community's pet older person. I was never sure how much old Sumner was really there mentally, but he'd been able to take care of himself, at least, before there was any Sunrise Village.

"Where you been, Pooh?" he said when I stepped up to the porch.

"Out of circulation, Mr. Heathman. Is anyone else around?"

"Hog and them, they beat it day before yesterday. Said it was no go here anymore. Goddamn shame after all the work they done."

"What are you going to do?" I asked him.

"Think I'll stick around, like before any of you showed up. It's darn lonely here now, though, tell you the truth. I got used to company. It was a hell of a couple of good years. You know about Songbird, I suppose."

"Yeah."

"He was a splendid young fellow. I don't understand it. God and his ways."

I got teary-eyed again.

"He built all this up," Sumner continued. "It was quite the outfit, wasn't it? Now, phhhhttt. Going, going, gone. I've been selling off some of the equipment to make a buck. I hope it's all right."

"Sure, why not."

"Say, you happen to have some weed on you, by any chance?" he asked. "They cleaned the place out." Sumner had become quite the pot-head in the preceding year or so, living with all of us.

"I'm off weed. Sorry."

"I got some seeds saved up," he said. "I'll plant 'em next spring, if I'm still around. Grow my own."

I made supper for us in the kitchen at the inn with stuff I scrounged out of the pantry: canned beans and canned corn with rice. Canned beets on the side. We drank the last of some Dago-red cooking wine, too. The big old place was plangent with ghosts. Mr. Heathman talked about being born back in 1889 when Benjamin Harrison was president, and laboring in the timber camps over in Saranac when he was a young man, and fighting in France in a place called the Belleau Wood in the First World War, and finally working for years at the ball-bearing plant up in Lebanon, New Hampshire, until he retired. I made chocolate pudding out of a box for dessert and we ate it warm.

I spent the night in our old bed at Elliot's cottage. His stuff was still there. It was hard to understand how someone whose presence you could still scent in the sheets was gone from this world.

I needed to feel the full force of that reality to get it behind me. I collected my remaining things, my big Zenith radio, the antique music stand I bought, and some of Elliot's things, a couple of his flannel shirts, an Irish cable-knit sweater. I had no idea what would happen to the furniture and all. I know he had some cousins, and the foundation would probably get around to it. I left early the next morning, daylight just breaking, and no smoke coming out of the stove pipe over at Mr. Heathman's place yet, so I didn't disturb him. That part of my life was complete.

I took my time driving west through upstate New York Saturday on the back roads, getting the feel of my new Mustang, enjoying my amazing freedom, and having a look at parts of the country you'd never go to. That first day, I got as far as glamorous Erie, Pennsylvania, where I bought a walleye pike dinner and spent the night at the Ellicott Hotel on Perry Square. It was slated to be demolished to make way for a new municipal complex, the desk clerk told me. The next day I dropped down into Ohio and got to Kenyon College right smack in the center of the state only a few hours after Ricky Spillman himself returned from Thanksgiving break on Long Island.

"You need to lose ten pounds," was this first thing out of his mouth when I found him in his dorm. He'd been in a production of *Waiting for Godot* that fall while I was in the loony bin. He was in love with his acting professor, a guy named Gerald. He tried to talk me into coming to school there, but I explained that I had other ideas. We sang together a little. It made me cry, course. He gave me his bed and slept on the floor. The next day, I was off to California for good.

CHAPTER FIFTY-FOUR

You can look at my YouTube videos if you're dying to revisit the music of the 1970s. Or put a Pooh Bollinger channel on your Pandora app. I'll never get the Nobel Prize like old Bob did, but I had a good run in the biz. That's a whole other story, though.

It took a few more years for me to reflect on what was going on with me during the time I was at Sunrise Village, the pressures and tensions I was living under, to understand why I fell apart at the end, and how I managed to get myself pasted back together. I burned out in an accelerated passage from childhood into adulthood. The mind is a resilient organ, but a few parts of the experience remain obdurately mysterious to this day. I have to wonder whether I ever did really meet two girls named Dot and Peg in the Vermont woods, or how I found myself in a cabin making love with that certain young man out of time. There are some things about this strange trip called human life on the planet earth that are just unknowable. I have never been religious, but I maintain an abiding conviction that time is more elastic than we imagine, and it gives me a strange kind of comfort to know that.

I was able to reconnect with Arden Blanchard a few years after I got out west. He came backstage to one of my shows at the Fillmore in San Francisco and we reignited what had started back in the winter of 1968 in that little brick chapel in Vermont. He was disillusioned with the Black Panthers and sick of radical politics by then, and he came on-board as an attorney for Warner Brothers Records, my label, in 1972. Music was in his blood and the law was in his brain. He eventually became chairman and CEO. We produced three children who are now considerably older than I was in the days of Sunrise Village and have children of their own who seem to actually like their grandmother. Imagine that. It's more of an achievement to me than the records and the Grammys.

We also shared a determination to bring Elliot Sohnberg's killers to justice.

Arden and the lawyers from the Sohnberg Foundation — of which he took his rightful place as a board member —worked with a team of private investigators to get to the bottom of the case. It took years. They were finally able to depose that coroner, Philo D. Granby, and two sheriff's deputies with confessions in the lynching of Elliot Sohnberg and its subsequent cover-up. Granby told a jury that he had noted diagnostic forensic evidence of manual strangulation on the body — cutaneous bruising with rupture of the neck muscles, abrasions, fractured hyoid bone — and that Sheriff George Grout had personally arranged for Elliot to be cremated the next day. The ashes remained in storage in a forgotten corner of the Catamount Funeral Home in Bennington until 1987 when the investigators located them. Arden flew back east to retrieve them, drove up to Timlinton — which was now an exclusive spa retreat — and scattered them in a walled garden behind the spa fitness center that had been the Odd Fellows hall. George Grout was convicted of the crime but he was eighty-seven years old and died of congestive heart failure before sentencing.

As accessories, the two deputies got twenty years due to the "aggravating factor" of the victim having been in their custody at the time of the act. They served eleven and thirteen years respectively. Philo D. Granby was granted immunity in exchange for testifying. He died in 1994.

I suppose you're wondering what happened to some of the people from that long ago time I've been telling you about. My little brother Bobby Bollinger was a cardio-thoracic surgeon at the Stanford Medical Center for thirty-four years. He retired to Costa Rica where he raises papayas. His two boys, my nephews, work for Google and Apple. In 1971, my mother, Marilyn Bollinger, married the New Jersey-based developer Marvin Moscowitz, a pioneer of the American shopping mall format for retail commerce. She died in 2013 in Palm Beach, Florida, and left the whole of her considerable fortune to her step-children, Mark and Meg Moscowitz. I never spoke to her again after 1968.

Oswald Strangefield was sentenced to fifteen years in the Atlanta Federal Penitentiary but his fate beyond that is lost to history. Scott Provost served twelve years at Lewisburg and I heard sometime in the early nineties that Scott was teaching in a Waldorf school on Cape Cod. Weezil came out to see me once in 1970 when I was still knocking around before my record deal. We stayed in touch but I only saw her twice more back east on concert tours when we arranged to meet in my hotel for dinner. She went to school and become a phlebotomist at the Fletcher Allen Hospital in Burlington, Vermont, married an orthopedic surgeon from Gujarat, India, and had four children. I was informed of her death in 2015 by a daughter who works at Pixar.

Billy Herman published the definitive history of the 1960s counterculture and became a distinguished professor on the Dartmouth College faculty. Alan Kaplan, landed in LA two years after I did, and became a successful record producer with his own boutique studio in Santa Monica. Mark Tanzio started the hugely successful Zodiac Herbal Tea Company in Brattleboro, Vermont, and served two terms as lieutenant governor in the nineties. We got reacquainted at a TED conference in Monterey forty years after Sunrise Village. Danny Musser came back from Canada after President Jimmy Carter pardoned the Vietnam War draft resisters and turned the auto loan department of his father's car business into the loan brokerage Endwell Oversight, which morphed into Endwell Futures Investments, which finally became Endwell Global, a hedge fund. I saw him at a Democratic Party fundraiser in East Hampton in the 2012. He looked well-fed and distinguished with his white hair and beard and said he could still play the fiddle pretty well. He liked those early albums I made back in the day. I read his obit in *The Times* in 2016.

The rock band Avatar had their one and only hit record the year I went out west. I would run into Maya Blue as she styled herself (the former Georgina Hertzel) here and there around the city in the early 70s. We actually talked, but not about anything meaningful. It made me sad to see her. She was not doing well, drugs I suspect. Then, years later, apparently she cleaned up, and I heard that she became a big wheel in the upper echelons of Scientology. She was always a good organizer. Her drummer, Jodie Palko, toured with everybody in the business at one time or another: Bonnie, Linda, Emmylou, Jackson, Joni, Warren, Carly.

Ricky Spillman had a run of success acting in the *Bloodville* series of slasher movies playing the psychopathic pest control technician, Ronnie Jubel, but he couldn't get any traction in Hollywood after that and went back to the New York stage world. He had a sensational hit off-Broadway in 1990 with his one-man show, *What Do I Care?* He died of AIDS-related illness in 1995.

That's all there is to tell about these long-ago events in the strange country called Youth in an era that is now gone by. The years place a comforting lid over these things so that the past seems like a safe and happy place, whether it really was or not. The truth is, I was never an idealist. I wanted to live in the world as it was, hard as it is. I'd like to do something with these memories, but first I'd have to write it all down, and I don't know if I can do that.

THE END

Made in the USA
Middletown, DE
12 July 2017